The Dartist

The Dartist

John Pascal

jnMedia
BOOKS

The Dartist. For more information about this title, address JNMedia, Inc., PMB 109, 2124 Broadway, New York, NY 10023–1722.

http://www.jnmedia.com

Designed by *Jonathan Nathan*

ISBN 1-930128-23-1

Library of Congress Cataloging-in-Publication Data on file with JNMedia, Inc.

_____
_____
_____
_____
_____

So the struck eagle, stretch'd upon the plain,
No more through rolling clouds to soar again,
View'd his own feather on the fatal dart,
And wing'd the shaft that quiver'd in his heart.

Byron

Dedication

This book is dedicated to Justice which, like its fellow Virtues of Prudence, Fortitude, and Moderation, though it is mentioned occasionally is practiced too seldom today; and to John who, mercifully, did not follow in my footsteps.

Contents

PART THREE *MISSIONARIES*

Prologue

When they pried Wychway out of what was left of his rented Mercedes 560 SL convertible on the tenth eastbound lane of the Autobahn twenty-two kilometers outside Munich he was just barely alive. If the accident had not happened in Germany chances are he would not have survived; the Germans are not unaccustomed to these horrendous auto crashes at speeds sometimes in excess of 150 miles per hour. He was alone in the Mercedes and no other vehicles had been involved in the accident, which occured a little after midnight during a heavy, wet Bavarian snowfall in mid-April.

After he was stabilized and placed in intensive care, arrangements were made to send Wychway to a neurosurgeon in Heidelberg, to a Doctor Sibelius, who specialized in traumatic brain damage cases. Wychway was alive, his vital signs were reasonably good; but he was still unconscious, and he had exhibited some extremely odd responses to the electroencephalograms he had been given in Munich. Meanwhile, the German authorities were trying to locate his next of kin.

In this effort they were unsuccessful. His US passport had been sent to the American Consulate in Munich, where it was checked through their computer and revealed only that the passport had been issued from Philadephia to Charles Parnell Wychway, forty-five years of age, born at Fort Bragg, North Carolina, to a temporary address in Baltimore. The passport contained no visa stamps; and at the address in Baltimore to which it had been mailed when it was issued no one had ever heard of a Charles Wychway. The consulate in Munich forwarded the passport to its embassy in Berlin, and there the matter rested.

As to the cost and eventual payment of Wychway's medical expenses, neither the medical authorities in Munich nor Dr. Sibelius at the University Hospital in Heidelberg were very concerned since the German police had discovered $20,000 in crisp, new, thousand-dollar notes in a money belt (a real belt, hand-made in Brazil of good leather, not one of the cheap nylon pouch varieties) when they inventoried the injured man's personal effects. The money, officially accounted for, was in a safe at the police headquarters in Munich. But that money was never to be applied to Wychway's medical costs; payment was to come from another source.

A complete list of Wychway's possessions as well as a receipt for the $20,000 was sent to the American Consul General in Munich. Like the passport, these were forwarded to the US Embassy. As to the money, as it passed from hand to hand in officialdom, Wychway was fortunate, as in the case of his medical treatment, to have had his accident in Germany rather than in any number of other countries, which of course should and shall remain nameless. Nonetheless, if he could have known what the consequences of having survived this crash would be, and could he have made the conscious choice, Charles Parnell Wychway might have preferred to have died there, on the Autobahn, on that snowy night in April.

PART ONE

THE SEMINARIANS

Chapter One

The Cricket Match

It was on a rainy autumn day, between Oxford, where he had been browsing through the Bodleian library, and Ipswich that Wychway, now almost fully recovered from his nearly fatal Autobahn smash, stopped at the Bells and Motley, a pub in Bury St. Edmunds, to refresh himself. It had rained all the way from Cambridge, and it was raining still as he went in.

As he got out of his trench coat and ordered a pint of mild a young man entered the pub, shaking the rain from his mackintosh as he came up to the bar. While his beer was being drawn Wychway searched his pockets for the small box of aspirin he carried to allay the occasional headaches he'd suffered since he'd been released after months of convalescence and tests from the hospital at Heidelberg two months earlier. There also had been dizzy spells for the first couple of weeks after he was discharged. Once, when he was walking along the *Hauptstrasse* in Heidelberg and had winked at a pretty girl, he had become so disoriented that he had gone reeling into an elderly German couple, no doubt confirming their suspicions that there was nothing unusual about an American—as he so obviously was, judging from his clothing—being dead drunk in public view at midday. Even the natural blinking of both eyes, which everyone does more or less unconsciously about a dozen times every minute, had produced a slight lightheadedness for a few weeks. Now, though those manifestations had disappeared (and he had studiously avoided winking at anyone), there were just these occasional headaches, seemingly brought on by such stresses as driving in bad weather, as was the case today, but which were, thank God, becoming steadily less severe.

When the young man standing next to him at the bar asked if he would "care to peg a few 'arrows'," Wychway had been wondering if it had been a good idea to agree to visit that attractive young Hungarian girl who had invited him to her place in Ipswich. After all, she'd just been a chance acquaintance....

As they took their drinks to the dartboard Wychway thought it might be fun to see if he could spend the next hour drinking beer at the expense of his young challenger. He had learned the game from his father, who'd told him his paternal grandmother had been the female British dart champion at the age of fifteen. He knew that although he hadn't thrown a dart in at least five years it was, as he'd often said, like riding a bicycle: you never lost the knack; you only needed a few practice throws to regain the same proficiency. And then with a shock he remembered the incident in the *Hauptstrasse*, and coupled that memory with the fact that he always closed one eye when throwing darts. At this point he could not back down gracefully, so he decided he'd just have to play with both eyes open, the way he aimed and fired a shotgun.

They decided to warm up with a game or two of "Cricket." Despite his resolve and not surprisingly Wychway reflexively closed his left eye before he threw his first dart (to see who would go first). Who can describe his sensation when, fixing his right eye at the dartboard, a little less than eight feet[1] away, the bullseye seemed to detach itself from the board and rush towards his face? Suddenly the red and green bullseye, a mere inch and a quarter in diameter, seemed as large as the entire board! Still holding his dart at arm's length he shifted his gaze to the green double-twenty ring at the top of the board: it seemed an arc half a foot thick and two feet wide! Glancing back down at the "cork" he threw the dart almost casually. Center bull! Now with both eyes open he checked the result: so close to the center as to make no difference!

With a wary glance at his opponent, his young adversary took his place at the line, cocked his arm, and threw—slightly out of the bull.

---

[1] Actually, seven feet, nine and one-quarter inches.

Chapter Two

Catharsis

Admittedly it would be difficult, most would say impossible, when one is engaged in vigorous mutual oral sex with a beautiful young woman, to concentrate on more abstract matters. And although in the position in which Wychway found himself his other four senses were to a greater or lesser degree forcefully in play, it was almost impossible for him to see much if anything even with his eyes wide open, and at least part of his mind (if it could be said to be functioning at all) fought to keep both eyes either fully open or fully closed. Nonetheless, as fervently as he strove to match his companion's sexual ardour, he intermittently was subjected to fleeting flashbacks of his phenomenal experience at the dart board earlier in the day.

He certainly had been able to "see" clearly enough when, after beating his young and incredulous dart opponent quickly and mercilessly in all the five games they had played, he drove the remainder of the distance to Ipswich. He had had to be careful when reading the road signs and once, when he'd closed an eye at the dashboard, he'd suffered a veritable seizure of vertigo which might have ended this story then and there were it not for his skillful driving and a good deal of luck. With all this he discovered that his incredible visual power was limited to his right eye; no amount of experimentation with closing his right eye produced the same effect in the left. And of course with both eyes open he had normal vision. Fortunately the unconscious blinking for the purpose of lubrication, spoken about earlier, had produced no unusual effects.

Later that evening, as Wychway and his newly found paramour were eating a late supper of goulash and red wine, she looked at him intently and quizzically, then shook her beautiful head, and gave him a dazzling but still thoughtful smile.

He had met her while he'd been browsing at the Bodleian Library at Oxford where she'd helped him find a rare edition of one of Congreve's plays. They had had lunch together at the White Hart, and over the second bottle of wine she had invited him to visit her at her weekend "retreat" at Ipswich. It had been clear to Wychway that eventually, after a few pro forma encounters such as this luncheon they would go to bed together. He just didn't think it would happen this quickly.

Now she wiped her lips, took a sip of wine as she stared at him over her glass, and asked:

"How do you spell your family name?"

"W-y-c-h-w-a-y—pronounced as in, 'which shall it be,' for example," he replied casually, going on with the excellent goulash.

"Has it always been spelt that way?" she pursued.

He looked across at her. "Actually, no. I changed it a few years ago when— but why do you ask?"

She was leaning back in her chair, her lovely green eyes alight, staring at him with a smile that an earlier writer would have described as "arch." Then she looked down and shook her head so that her thick titian hair swung back and forth (he recalled that she'd piled it high and pinned it up just before they'd begun their amorous ministrations). She glanced at him and smiled a gentler smile.

"May I ask how old you are, Charles?"

"Why not?— I'll be forty-five next May."

"It was with a *Hexe* (she used the German word), witch,

you say—W-i-t-c-h, was it not, your name?" Now the smile had become ironic.

Wychway put down his fork and knife and said levelly, "How could you possibly have known that?"

"I knew it! Somehow I think I knew it from the first moment, there in the Bodleian. "Because I think I knew— No. I'm *sure* I knew your father. There is too close a resemblance for you to have been anyone else's son. And you have his name, his Christian name...."

"Yes, but good Lord! when did you run into *him*?"

She looked down at her wine glass again, and twirled it slowly by the stem.

"It was at a place called Bumfries, or maybe it was Bumphries with a 'ph'—I still have trouble with these English names. It was during the Christmas holiday several years ago. Anyway, I was a house guest there and so was he, for a few days at least. He was with an old friend, a retired soldier also, a Major Somerville or something like that, I think. The Major's niece and I were school chums at Oxford, and she took me home with her at Christmas. —And so, how is your handsome father, Charles? He is keeping well, I hope?" she added with another brilliant smile.

"I couldn't say how well he's 'keeping.' My handsome father died two years ago," Wychway replied drily as he looked for her reaction to this news.

Magda merely looked down at the table again and said softly in her precise and beautifully intoned English, "I am sorry. I think he must have been a wonderful man."

"He was a lot of things," Charles replied ambiguously.— "By the way, what's your full name, Magda?"

"Magda Karolyi Tisza," the girl answered with a wry expression. "Perhaps I should change my name, too." She looked thoughtful a moment. "Did he ever mention me to you?"

Wychway scratched his chin. There was a mischievous look in his eye. "No, I can't say he did...."

"Of course not. What am I saying? I was no more than a

child when we met. Why should he have remembered little me?"

"Why indeed?" Wychway asked musingly as he recalled that it had taken two glasses of wine and several mouthfuls of goulash to get the wonderful taste of her out of his mouth. He recalled also his father's reputation, at least in his earlier years, as a "lady killer," to use an expression which would have been in keeping with those earlier times. But she was speaking again....

"But why, if I may ask, *did* you change your name?"

"Well, maybe it's silly, but I checked it out once at the Johns Hopkins library, when I was staying with a friend of mine who was studying there, at Hopkins in Baltimore, and it's almost certain that that was the original spelling, with a 'y.' The first time I came to England I verified it. I even found a village named Wychwood. I don't think it would have mattered to my father in any case, but I didn't make the change until after he died. By the way, I know that Major Somerville you spoke of. In fact, a few days after we planted—er, ah, after my father's funeral, we had dinner together. More to the point," Wychway glanced at his watch, not really knowing why he did so, "I'm supposed to meet him in London in a day or two. I have a standing invitation to dine with him at his club whenever I'm in London. I also have one to visit that Bumfries Hall place too, whenever I'm on this side of the pond. They all thought a lot of the Old Boy. He and Somerville must have been thick as thieves. They were in special ops together in a couple of small wars."

Wychway usually was not this voluble, and abruptly he stopped speaking when he realized how he was rattling on. He reasoned that it was the wine and the girl's nearness that made him so loquacious, but upon later reflection he admitted that Magda's possible relationship with his late father probably was a factor also. Magda interrupted these thoughts with:

"When are you going to London? When must you leave?"

"Well, today's Saturday. I suppose tomorrow you're going back to Oxford? —I guess I'll go tomorrow. I'd like to try to call Somerville first, if I may."

"Will you come back?"

"Yeah, well... I think I'm going to have to go back to Germany—that's where I was before I met you—back to Germany for a while, and then... I don't know how long I'll be there. I, uh, have to see someone in Heidelberg."

There was silence until she asked abruptly, "Why did you go reeling across the room on your way to the bathroom this evening?"

"This evening? —Uh, I got something in my eye and I guess it kind of disoriented me, I—"

"That is bullshit, as they say in your country," she commented equably and, clasping her long slim fingers and assuming a patient attitude, she waited.

And that was when Wychway decided to tell her, if not the entire truth, at least as much of it as began on that cold snowy night on the Autobahn outside Munich.

Having expressed her astonishment at Wychway's narrative Magda asked:

"Have you told anyone else about this, this strange experience at the pub?"

"No." Hell, it just happened this afternoon.

"So you are going back to see that doctor in Heidelberg?"

"Well, yeah. Don't you think I should?"

"Yes, definitely; perhaps you will need to see more than one doctor. How can you even think of visiting Major Somerville? I should think that instead—"

"Oh, Christ, I'm here now, and I've got to go to London anyway to get to Heidelberg. Besides, maybe he, Somerville, should know about it. I mean maybe—I don't know what'll happen—maybe somebody... Oh, I know I've told *you* about it now, but I mean, he's a pretty solid guy... I'm getting this all screwed up, but I think you know what I mean, I—"

"You mean, since I'm just a young woman, and a foreign one at that—"

"No! Yes. Oh, bear's ass!—Excuse me. It's not that, but—"

"I know how you feel," she took his hand in both of hers,

"and you're right. I would do it, too, if I were you. But still, I'm glad you told me. Will you tell the Major that I know, also, and tell him where I am to be reached?"

Wychway grinned mock-ruefully.

"Do you think I can trust him to know you?" He almost added, "Any more than I could have trusted my father?"

"Please, Charles, that doesn't amuse me." She thought for a moment, then asked, "Have you ever had a head injury before—a serious one, I mean?"

"Well, yes. In Vietnam I—"

"You also were there?—I heard your father had served in the war there, and—"

"Oh, yeah. I enlisted when I was in my freshman year in college. I volunteered for Special Forces and went to MAC-SOG. That was the outfit he was in. Except that when he joined them it was more or less honestly called the Military Assistance Command Special Operations Group. By the time I got there the authorities, in their infinite wisdom, had changed it to "Studies and Observations Group." Jeesus! I ask you—"

"Yes, but what about that first injury? What were the results?"

"Clean bill of health, eventually. Oh, for a while I'd get these blackout spells—for a time they thought I had become an epileptic; you know, the Julius Caesar-Napoleon-genius disorder. Anyone who's never endured epileptic seizures doesn't know what he's missed; it's a little like dying and then coming back to life. But that's another story. —Anyway, they put me on Dilantin, and I had to go to these neuropsychiatric sessions with an army witch doctor who'd ask me all these odd questions. For a while I did have a series of strange experiences: I'd go to bed and try to sleep—I usually sleep on my side—and I'd lie, let's say, on my left side for a while and try to sleep, and I'd have all these thoughts rushing through my mind. Nothing bad maybe—although sometimes I did—just thoughts. And then I'd roll over on my other side, and as I did my mind would go blank, and then suddenly I'd have other thoughts, totally different thoughts, and what the shrink found mighty interesting (and I gotta admit, I did too) but couldn't explain was that I couldn't remember anything that had been going through my mind a moment before, as I lay on my opposite side, before I rolled over. Weird, yeah?"

Magda muttered something about "left and right hemispheres" and "emotional-artistic, practical..."

"Yeah, well, this went on for years," Wychway continued, disregarding Magda's half-spoken apostrophe, "a few years anyway. And then everything went back to normal, if I can say I've ever been normal," he chuckled. "No more blackouts, no more "split-screen," now you see it, now you don't episodes—believe me, try as hard as I might I could never recall what had been going on in my feeble military mind just seconds before, before I turned over—no more Dilantin, and best of all, no more visits to Doctor Strangelove who, incidentally, had turned out to be a flamer and had started hitting on me. But I think the medics were glad to see the last of me, since none of them could figure out what the hell was going on. So I got discharged and went back to school. Anyway, I lived a fairly normal life after that—at least until that goddam Autobahn crash, and then of course the dart game this P.M. while on my way to your loving arms." Wychway was on his second postprandial cognac by this time. He glanced at Magda's intent face. "I'm talking too much."

"No, you're not. This is all very interesting, fascinating. Once I read about a case where—"

The word "fascinating" recalled to Wychway something from their conversation in the Bodleian a few days earlier. He interrupted her.

"Didn't you tell me you'd changed your course of study after doing an essay about the psychology of poetry, or something like that?" As he said this he got up and went and stood by the fireplace. He pretended to be interested in the small objects he found on the mantlepiece.

"Yes. I became so interested in certain aspects of psychology in itself that I broadened my reading, with my tutor's blessing of course."

"Uh-huh. And so now you're beginning to take a clinical interest in my case, right?" he said as he turned to face her.

"Charles," she looked him over appraisingly as he stood there holding his glass loosely in one large, brown hand—from his hand-sewn Craxwell Wellingtons, to his old-good-looking tweeds, and his neatly knotted rep tie over a pale blue oxford-cloth shirt with soft buttoned-down collar; her gaze finally rested on his clean-shaven, regular features and dark brown hair which was just beginning to go gray at the temples.

"Charles, I think that in the very short time we have known each other I've made it pretty obvious that I've taken more than just a clinical interest in you." She smiled her dazzling smile at him again. I must admit though, your experience would interest, even fascinate, if you prefer that word, even the casual observer. It is so, so *outré*...."

"I know," he grinned a wry, crooked grin: "'Meet Charley Wychway, *Phenomene Extraordinaire!*' If all else fails I could always get a job in a circus or a carnival as a trick shot artist. As a matter of fact I think I'd be better off doing that than what I'm doing now."

Which gave Magda the opportunity she had been waiting for.

"What *do* you do, Charles, if you don't mind my asking?"

Wychway hesitated, stared at his drink for a moment, then answered:

"Stock answers like 'as little as possible,' 'stay alive,' 'survive,' 'live by my wits,' and so on won't do in this case, I think. Those are the things I say when I'm talking to people I usually can't stand, at cocktail parties, in restaurants, and like that." He gave her a gentler look and smiled, "Somehow I don't feel like doing that with you."

"I'm glad," she smiled back. But if you *are* going to tell me I would like hear it as a bedtime story. Can we do that?"

She looked like a little girl asking her father to read her a bedtime story; and he thought that once they got into a bed together it might take him all night to tell her what she wanted to know (or at least what he wanted her to know), but that was perfectly all right with him.

Chapter Three

Communion

Happily ensconced back in Magda's bedroom Wychway told his story "between takes," so to speak. At his suggestion they had taken the Remy Martin along and Magda gladly had accepted another drink as they watched each other undress. This, his third brandy, gave Wychway the courage to ask:

"How was my father?"

"No better than you," she replied unhesitatingly.

"That's not saying a hell of a lot."

"I'm not sure how you mean that; I thought I was complimenting you; but all right then, if you must know, he was absolutely—marvelous to me."

He chuckled. "It's funny.—Now you're about four years older, and you're with me, and when you were just a kid you were with *him*."

"I don't think I ever was 'just a kid.'"

"Lucky Daddy."

Magda, who was lying in bed naked making little circles around the nipple of her left breast, changed the subject.

"Do you think it's a good idea to drink so much, so soon after such a serious head injury, I mean, and especially after you have had such a strange experience with your sight?" She didn't look at him as she said this. Instead of answering her he got into bed next to her, and though for the next twenty minutes there were occasional murmured words, phrases and exclamations there was no conversation.

Their ardor spent, at least for the moment, they were lying side by side when Magda reopened the subject of Wychway's accident.

"The medical payments must have been much. Do you have medical insurance? One hears how difficult it is in the United States to afford proper medical insurance."

"I've got some coverage; and then, I get paid pretty well.—Well, not *that* well, but if I don't make more than seventy or eighty thousand a year, I've forgotten which, the Infernal Revenue Service won't tax me when I'm working in a foreign country," he smiled, "so I can say with certitude that I'll never have to pay taxes while I'm working abroad.—Oh, yeah," he added, "I also have a sort of expense account, but I have to be pretty careful about itemizing..." he finished a little lamely as he recalled ruefully and not for the first time since his accident the $20,000 he'd had on him.

When he had been discharged from the hospital in Heidelberg he'd been given a receipt for the money which as far as he knew still was being held by the Munich police. No one had asked him to pay for his medical expenses, either for the emergency treatment he'd received in Munich or for his subsequent surgery and convalescence at Heidelberg. Dr. Sibelius had told him that because of his delicate postoperative condition the matter of payment would be deferred for a time and then arranged by the authorities in the American Embassy at Berlin, who would effect coordination between the Germans and Wychway's insurance people. Wychway wasn't worried about that. His medical and dental expenses always were paid by the Agency somehow; all he'd had to do in the past was submit the bill or a voucher of some kind. What was on his mind was that $20,000 in confidential funds he'd wheedled out of his sometime friend, Al Jennings, the deputy Chief of Station at the Embassy.

With that money he had intended to pay an Iraqi expatriate he knew, a "hot source" as Wychway had described him,

who claimed to have information vital to US interests in the
Persian Gulf and who, according to Wychway, would not talk
to any American except Wychway. Since Wychway was not a
field agent (and therefore not authorized access to the fund)
and wasn't particularly liked by the station chief, the Deputy
had decided to act on his own, hoping that when Wychway,
whom he trusted, "brought home the bacon" all would be
well. In retrospect Wychway could see that both he and Jennings had committed a rash and stupid act; he didn't know
what Jennings's motives had been, but Wychway knew that
for his own part he'd talked himself into the harebrained
scheme mainly out of boredom. The trouble was that now the
fat was in the fire, to use a very tired metaphor, and, Wychway winced as he reflected, that fire undoubtedly was burning his friend's ass pretty severely. The Germans, goddam
their honesty and efficiency, would certainly have notified
their US counterparts about the existence of that much
money. And now that he was on his feet (well, not at the
moment) only he could retrieve the money. With a feeling of
combined apprehension and self-loathing he saw himself
creeping sheepishly back into the Embassy to return the misbegotten boodle....

Magda, who had been lying next to him sipping cognac
and smoking, interrupted these troublesome thoughts.

"Which brings us back to my bedtime story. What *do* you
do, Charles?"

Wychway cleared his throat. "I read newspapers."

"You read *newspapers*? Charles, we all read newspapers."

"Yes, but I read them for money. —Oh, and I have to do a
lot of writing, too" He decided to give her what the Agency
would call a "sanitized" version of his position. Actually it
was an abbreviation of his cover story.

"I work for USIS, the US Information Service—that's the
form the USIA, the Information *Agency* takes overseas. Anyway,
I studied Arabic at the Army Language School at Monterey—
that's in California—years ago, and then when I got out on a

medical discharge and went back to school I studied it some more—in fact I got pretty good at it. I've also got some German, French, and Italian, and those help me get along in Europe.

"You know—I was considering staying in the service," he went on after a moment, "but the goddam head wound… Well, I would have had a 'profile'; that means I would have been on limited duty. I didn't want that, so I got out and went back to school. There's something called 'vocational rehabilitation'— like, if you're a violinist and you get a hand blown off they pay for your education in another field, maybe you could become a one-handed harmonica player or something. I can't bitch as far as that goes, they paid for everything: tuition, books, fees, and they sent me a stipend for living expenses each month. Of course, if it hadn't been for Vietnam… But you can't look at it that way. So I translate stuff from the Arabic language press here in Europe—which, ironically enough, is like being on limited duty status anyway." He shook his head and smiled sourly. "It's like our FBIS—the Foreign Broadcast Intercept Service—only with me it's printed journalism. Then the articles I cull out and translate into English are sent back to the States, and copies go to the US embassies and consulates here in Europe. Damned dull, I admit, but it's a living."

"That is intelligence work, is it not?"

Wychway laughed and said, "Well, if you really stretch a point I guess you could say that, in a very benign sense."

Magda was thoughtful as she said, "I think you should be grateful you don't have to do anything dangerous anymore." Undoubtedly she was thinking about the period of epileptic seizures he had endured and those strange "thought-changing" experiences, so like switching a computer from one program or "menu" to another, which he had described to her earlier in the evening.

Frowning, Wychway got up and went to find his cigarettes.

"Have you ever seen someone having a seizure?" he asked from across the room.

"Once, years ago, in Budapest. It—it was terrible. One

feels so helpless...."

"Have you ever known anyone who had epilepsy?"

"No—well, I mean, now you; but you don't have this problem anymore, isn't that what you said?"

"Right. I'm all right now, and I've been told by the medics that it'll probably never happen again. but I'll never forget what it was like. And there's a bit of a curse that goes along with it: that word, 'probably,' hangs over you for the rest of your life, and it's a two-edged sword. Years go by, so you tell yourself, 'that's good'—when nothing happens, I mean—but at the same time you know as time passes that if it *is* going to happen again the more time that *does* pass the closer you're getting to it, and the more likely it becomes with each passing day that *this* could be the day. I don't know if I'm making this clear. It's a little like being in combat for a long time: you know that sooner or later the law of averages is going to catch up with you. I mean, they've taken me off the medication—I don't have to go in for checkups, electroencephalograms and all that anymore—but still, that word, 'probably,' is there. And this is to say nothing about what it's like when it *does* happen.

"Obviously my situation is nothing compared to someone who is a fully-fledged epileptic. He *knows* it's going to happen, but he doesn't know when, or perhaps more important, where. How about when he's making a free fall parachute jump, and hasn't opened his 'chute yet? So he doesn't parachute, or fly an airplane, or go scuba diving, or stand near the edge of a high place, or in some cases doesn't even dare to drive a car, especially if someone else is in it, more especially if that person is someone he cherishes, like his wife or one or more of his kids. Or how about if you're making out with your favorite girl, and suddenly... And speaking of favorite girls, what if the poor bastard wants kids? He'll be cursed with the flawed gene bit—if not *his* kids then maybe *their* kids will show the curse. The sins of the father and so on, so to speak. That was one thing I didn't have to worry about at least: if it comes from an injury it just stops there, with the victim; otherwise if it's *in* a person it's *there*, always. There are all kinds of hidden agonies and devils that most people don't even know or care about.

"And think about the stigma that was attached to the disease for centuries—the demonic associations and superstitions. Today's society is supposed to have shed all that, but there's still an attitude towards people who are afflicted. Some people, when they discover it wasn't a heart attack you suffered ('Nothing serious, he just had another fit') they treat it humorously ('Have you heard? Wychway fell down on the job again!'). Wasn't it our good old Bonaparte who said, 'You can always turn tragedy into comedy just by sitting down'? Maybe he should have said 'falling down'; after all, he was a victim, too. And still, here am I: grateful that I can tell you my experience was due to injury and not to a 'natural,' congenital cause. I'm not sure, if I were a congenital, chronic sufferer, that I would have admitted it to you. You feel like you're saying, 'There was insanity in my family.' Well, of course I think if you went back far enough in almost every family you'd be bound to find damn near every 'loathsome' disease and crime imaginable and maybe—"

Magda interrupted this monologue.

"Is there not a warning the victim experiences—a strange smell or sound or something—before the, before it happens?"

"Not always. Sometimes you get a few moments 'notice,' I think it's called an 'aura,' a warning that you're going down, but it ain't a long advisory, I can tell you that." He thought a moment. "Chronic epileptics should only be recluses who are content to sit in comfortable chairs and read books."

"You mean like Julius Caesar and your comic Napoleon?" she smiled.

He looked at her as he said, "Yeah.... I've really wondered about that apparent paradox from time to time. Maybe their having those brainstorms was seen as part of their greatness somehow. Maybe it *drove* them to greatness. I've never gotten around to reading up on that. I guess for one thing I didn't want to be reminded about the subject." He stubbed out his cigarette, poured himself another cognac after offering Magda one, which she refused, and lit another cigarette. "Then there's the 'waking up' phase. Jesus H. Christ! You don't know what happened, or where you are; sometimes you don't even know *who* you are. And usually there are all these people standing around looking down at you and you don't know who they are, or what the hell they're doing there. And one or more of them is telling you not to worry, everything's going to be all right, and so on, which is more terrifying than having a blank mind because, having a blank mind, you don't know what you're doing down there in the first place, or why. The thing is, you don't know what the hell's *wrong* with you. It's a lot like being wounded and losing consciousness over and over again. You don't know if you're going to die, or if maybe you're already dead. It's incredibly hard to explain the feeling....

"Then you're taken away somewhere where you can sleep, because after one these episodes you're exhausted, completely drained. So you sleep, and when you wake up you might remember that you had some sort of 'spell,' but you don't remember anything else; maybe you don't remember what you've done over the last week, or even longer, and sometimes it takes days to get your memory back. Meanwhile you try and try and try again to remember....

"I can't bitch. Hell, I only had three attacks. They told me these were due to the damage caused by getting dinged in the head. My brain damage heals, so no more attacks. Q.E.D. But still...

"But now there's this *other* freak show. — 'Hey, Charley, eyeball that blonde across the street!' and I say, 'Naw, that's no blonde; look at those black roots under the blond hair.' Christ! What next?" He looked directly at Magda who except for her question and her comment about Caeser and Bonaparte hadn't uttered a word during this last lengthy disquisition. She was looking straight into his eyes but he couldn't interpret her expression. Then she held out her arms:

"Come," she said.

When, after they had made love again and then slept for a couple of hours, Wychway came back from the bathroom and found Magda sitting up in bed with her arms around her knees.

"Women are physically superior to men," he said. "I've heard their bladders hold at least fifty cc's more than ours do. And besides, they usually don't drink as much as men do," he said as he stretched out next to her.

"Are you apologizing because you had to go to the toilet?" she laughed. (An American woman would never say, toilet, Wychway reflected, they had at least a half-dozen euphemisms for the word.)

"If it makes you feel better, I'll go too." She started to get out of bed but he restrained her.

"Only if you really have to."

She put her arms around him and gave him a great hug.

"I don't really have to." She pushed him back onto the pillows and looked into his eyes. "Are there things you want to do and aren't doing? No, no, not here in bed with me," she laughed. "I mean this job you have, do you really hate it?" she asked seriously.

"I don't know. I mean, here am I, on the wrong side of forty, cutting out maybe not paper dolls, but newspaper articles. On the other hand, it's steady, it pays pretty well, and it's safe. I live comfortably, I get to travel at someone else's expense—all that. Like I said, I can't bitch."

"But would you be doing it if you hadn't had those medical problems? You said you wanted to be an officer, like, well, like your father. He must have had some influence on you. When one thinks of what *he* must have done—"

"Somehow I knew he was going to come back into it," Wychway interposed with asperity. "Look, he was, if not great, at least very good at what he did. You could almost say he was a legend, although perhaps not in his own time. I've never known whether he enjoyed what he did or maybe just got trapped by it and kept doing it because he was good at it and never learned to do anything else."

"But he became a teacher, a professor, after he left the government, did he not?"

"Yes, there *is* that," he answered a little lamely. "But whatever he was or did I know one thing: I don't want to compete with him—well, he can't do much competing now, can he? I meant, with his record... you know what I mean! But I'd like to think that if I really wanted to, I could." Then he added with a chuckle, "After all, look at Alexander of Macedonia; ultimately he made his father, Philip II, look like a bum by comparison."

"That is the best way to look at it, I think," said Magda evenly.

"You mean the safest, don't you?" he replied looking up at her.

"Not at all; not if you really meant what you said. I remember my father saying that an honest man who has confidence in himself has no reason or desire to prove himself, either to others or perhaps what is more important, to himself. Besides, we are all of us different; there is no reason why anyone should follow in his father's footsteps. —By the way, Charles, do you have children? I hope you do not mind that I ask."

Wychway decided this was a good time to change the subject; she had given him a good cue.

"No, no children. I was married just once—so you see in at least that respect I wasn't trying to emulate the old dad—but it didn't 'take.' My absence while I was in Indochina, plus the injury, hospitalization, and the weird consequences were all more than she could bear. Hell, why am I giving you all this bullshit? —Actually, she left me for another guy."

"I'm sorry."

"Don't be. —You know, Magda, you *are* a great listener. Here I've damn' near told you the story of my life and I still don't know anything about you—well, about your life anyway," he laughed.

She smiled and kissed him.

"Tonight we will concentrate on you; I will have my turn later." And suiting action to her double entendre gently and expertly began bringing him back to life.

Chapter Four

A Good Samaritan

As he drank coffee in Magda's kitchenette Wychway chuckled as he thought of the conversation they'd had in the bathroom earlier when she'd showered and he'd shaved.

"What is so funny?" she called from the stove area.

"You; and dead hair, toenails, and fingernails."

When Wychway had noticed in the mirror while shaving that Magda was washing her thick, luxuriant hair with a bar of soap, he'd said:

"Christ, I thought women used all these exotic shampoos and conditioners...."

"Bullshit," Magda shouted between scrubbings, "as I told you already, hair is dead—like fingernails and toe-nails. Can you imagine—what it would be like—to go to a barber—if your hair were alive?—or to cut your nails?—It's the scalp that matters, the roots. Would you wash your dishes—with shampoo and conditioners?"

"You know," Wychway shouted back, "I remember now; my father used soap on his hair, and he died with a full head, of hair I mean. He washed *his* about once a month, when he was home anyway, but he brushed it a lot. I don't know if it was true, but I remember him telling me that for the first ten years he was in the service he used to shower with Ajax, not soap."

"What do you use to wash *your* hair?"

"Shampoo, and conditioner."

Though they hadn't gotten out of bed until eleven he'd still gotten too little sleep, but he felt—not surprisingly, considering everything else he'd gotten— extremely fit. And for some reason he wondered about but didn't examine he wasn't as reluctant as he usually was to talk about his father.

Wychway put his coffee cup down and looked at his watch.

"Well, it's after twelve; I'd better call Somerville.—Can I use your phone?" he asked. As he rose Magda arrived back at the table with fresh coffee.

"Of course." She poured herself some coffee, then said, "Charles, I *will* see you again, won't I? You *will* come back won't you?"

He caressed her cheek gently with the backs of his fingers as he smiled down at her.

"You know I will, as soon as I can," then he went to the phone in the sitting room.

Magda followed him to the rental agency, where he turned in his car, then drove him to the train station. Wychway had reasoned that having arranged to have Somerville meet him at Paddington Station, which was near the Major's flat and club, he'd have no need for the car. The train ride from Ipswich to London would take about an hour, and he wanted that time to himself so he could think, without having to concentrate on driving, especially without having to be concerned about the new and bizarre quality of his right eye. If Somerville didn't offer him a ride to Hearthrow next day he'd take the train or a taxi.

He and Magda stood on the platform waiting the few minutes before his train's arrival. His feelings were complex. He was extremely pleased that he'd met this wonderful girl, but he fervently would have preferred to have met her under more favorable circumstances. It was difficult to concentrate on her while he had this other thing on his mind, to savor the joy she'd given him wholeheartedly and selflessly during the last twenty-four hours. Twenty-four hours? He felt as if he'd known her much longer than that. And it wasn't simply because they had enjoyed each other's bodies so intimately and so intensely, he was sure of that. What would the visit to Sibelius reveal? Despite his insouciance when she'd asked why, under the circumstances of his astonishing self-discovery, he would even consider stopping in London to see J.D.F. Somerville, he now found himself wishing he hadn't arranged for the visit. At this moment standing there on the station platform in the chill October air, without the promise of another merry evening with Magda, without the warmth and comfort of Magda's lovely body near him—he wished he were walking into Sibelius's clinic in Heidelberg right now.

Magda hated lingering farewells as much as he, and his departure from her though poignant was brief.

As he sat in his first class compartment (he was paid enough to be able to afford these small luxuries) Wychway noticed idly that the only other occupant was the old woman who'd been sitting on a bench reading *The Times* as he was standing there hand in hand with Magda on the otherwise deserted platform. He had not been able to resist closing his left eye and scanning the news on the back page of the woman's newspaper—ten yards away—which had contained nothing of interest to him.

During the entire journey to London the woman didn't look at him once. He was grateful he didn't have to endure a talkative gossip, as had happened to him only too often. He had enough to think about at the moment.

J.D.F. Somerville—retired Guards Major and one-time officer in the British S.A.S.—waited dutifully on the Paddington Station platform as Wychway's train pulled in. Dressed punctiliously, he was tall and still trim and active for his seventy years. He stood ramrod straight, hands over his highly polished walking stick, in his beautifully cut Savile Row suit, regimental tie, gray suede gloves, and black bowler. His ginger moustache and ruddy complexion completed the picture of the well-to-do retired British officer. Wychway recognized him immediately.

Like most sensible people in this age of self-help Wychway was a light traveler, and they lost no time in throwing his valpac and suit bag into a waiting taxi, piling in after it, and heading for Somerville's Bayswater lodgings.

Half an hour later, after Wychway had changed into clothing more appropriate for dinner at Somerville's club, they relaxed over a drink. Somerville threw one long leg over his chair arm and leveled a smile at Wychway.

"I noticed by your letter that you'd changed the spelling of your name."

Wychway wondered how many more times he'd have to explain. During and after his recruitment by the Agency he'd been asked endlessly by people who had known his father slightly or only by reputation if he could have been a distant relation of a fellow named Witchway. Those few who knew he was Charley Witchway's son either asked rudely why he'd changed his name, or at least commented on the fact, as Somerville just had. He groaned inwardly as he realized not for the first time that since his father had been all over the world, resoundingly, any number of times and since he, "Witchway the Younger," did resemble the old man rather closely this presumably would go on forever. He gave Somerville the same answer he'd given Magda, which was the truth, about discovering that the spelling he now used was the original or close to it, and added that he'd always thought the other spelling, the one he'd lived with for so many years, was rather silly. What if he'd been a girl and his parents had named him Hazel? Of course, he reflected, it could have been worse, it could have been Whichway.

Somerville went on.

"I suppose you've been told, but you do resemble the old squire to a remarkable extent, you know."

"Yes, I've been told. I've never been sure whether it's a curse or a blessing."

"More to the good, my boy, would be my opinion, if you're anything like him. Too bad he's gone. I mean to say, here am I, at seventy, in the pink more or less, and he's gone. I knew him many years and had ample opportunity to see what he was, what he could do. There's no doubt, in my mind at least (and after all, what else matters?), that he was the better man. And believe me when I say that this isn't what my old Latin master would have referred to as *de mortuis nihil nisi bonum*, if I've got it right, and so on. I do mean it."

"That's high praise, coming from you, I'd say."

Somerville drained his malt whiskey and said, "If I may borrow from your namesake, old boy— 'bear's ass'! " with which he put his empty glass down, rubbed his hands together briskly, and suggested, "Now, I don't know about you, but I'm growing rather peckish; what say we toddle over to The Scribes and tuck in to something edible?" Wychway smiled and nodded assent. He was glad for a break in the conversational topic.

They decided to walk to the club, Somerville saying that at his age anything that would stimulate his appetite even more was worth doing. And the weather was pleasant: good, brisk autumn was in the air. There was a faint smell of woodsmoke and Somerville, noticing Wychway sniffing in its pungent fragrance, commented, "The gentry round here still like their wood fires, despite all the modern conveniences...." He was looking about him as if searching for something or some place as he said this.

"It was right around here that we ran into the arms of a Peeler one night about Christmastime a few years ago, me and old Charley. —We were being pursued by several low characters—you would call them 'the bad guys'—at pistol point, I shudder to remember. We weren't armed, ourselves, so we ran—right into the arms, literally, of one of London's best, if not brightest, constables. I never thought I'd be so happy to be 'in the arms of the law,' so to say, but there it was." He shook his head wonderingly and chuckled.

"That was in his book—I remember it."

"Oh yes!" Somerville nodded.

Wychway hunched his shoulders as he walked beside the briskly-striding major and tried to picture the scene. He felt he should say something more:

"The first time you went to the States was for my father's funeral, wasn't it?"

"Yes, well, barring one trip to Fort Bragg's Special Warfare Center, in the sixties, when I was still on loan to the S.A.S., that's true. (Wychway speculated correctly that Somerville's wording indicated he'd been a regular with a venerable and honored Guards' regiment.) After the funeral I spent six months or so looking the place over— 'walk about,' you know, as the Aussies say. Even visited this cove I'd met here in London, at his place in Hawaii for a time. Quite a town that Honolulu—right out of Somerset Maugham. Remind me to tell you a story about a chap I met at a club called the Outrigger some time.[1] All rather interesting."

By this time they had arrived at The Scribes, and as they headed for the main stairs they encountered Palmer, the Club Secretary. When Somerville introduced Wychway the man brightened visibly and said he remembered Colonel Witchway very well, cheerfully welcomed Wychway to the Club, and then with suitable sobriety added that he was sorry to have heard of his father's 'passing.' Wychway was grateful that this oral exchange obviated spelling his name.

Upstairs in the bar they found a number of Somerville's fellow Scribes gossiping over their preprandial drinks. Introductions were made in an informal way and again much was made of recollections of Colonel Witchway, who apparently had visited the Club with his friend Somerville on a number of occasions. Again, condolences were graciously offered. Wychway was beginning to wish he'd changed the pronunciation of his name as well as its spelling.

---

[1] See "The Outrigger" in *Antipodes 10* by John Pascal; American Literary Press, Baltimore, 1995.

After two drinks they excused themselves, amid much
bonhomie, and headed for the dining room. On their way they
passed a room with a brass plate alongside its entrance which
proclaimed: **SILENCE is OBSERVED**. How characteristically English, thought Wychway, as much as was Puccini's
famous exclamation, "Silence is forbidden!" characteristically
Italian. He guessed this was the club library—he'd noticed several superannuated gentlemen in comfortable leather chairs,
one of them sound asleep, open-mouthed, as he and Somerville
went by, and he couldn't resist a chuckle as he recalled an old
Dorothy Sayers mystery novel he'd read years ago.

"May I share in your humor?" his companion asked pleasantly.

Hoping he wasn't being guilty of a social gaff Wychway
replied, "Oh, I just noticed those old boys in that room we
passed and I couldn't help thinking of a book I read—*The
Unpleasantness at the Bellona Club*, I think it was called—by
Dorothy L. Sayers...."

Somerville stopped, and turning with an appreciative smile
gripped his younger companion by the upper arm.

"Yes. Yes! The dead nonagenarian in the chair and everyone thinking he was just asleep. And when they discovered his
true condition his hysterical nephew shouts, 'Take General
Fentiman away; he's been dead these two days, and no one
knew it!' or something like that. Oh, I've read all her books.
That was one of her best, I think. —And you're right, you
know: I've always thought someone, the club secretary or his
rep, should go round from time to time and check pulses, so to
speak." He laughed heartily at his own joke, put his arm
around Wychway's shoulder and guided him to the dining
room, "Come along, dear chap."

Wychway was beginning to take a strong liking to this old
but still vigorous and engaging gentleman, despite all his
archaic Colonel Blimp mannerisms.

Over a dinner of excellent pepper steak and even better
claret they chatted amiably and desultorily for a while, and

then the conversation reverted, as Wychway knew it must eventually, to his father.

Wychway had answered, in a general way, Somerville's inquiry about what he'd done in his adult life: his going to Vietnam as a young man, being wounded, and its consequences; his short-lived marriage and subsequent return to school when he realized any military career was out of the question; he even told him about his recruitment by the CIA when he was in graduate school. He explained how he'd worked at Langley for six years—he'd been there when Somerville and his father had had their great adventure in Europe during those Christmas holidays (that Christmas his father had met Magda, he mused), which had been the basis of his father's best-selling book, *The Twelve Days of Christmas*—and finally how a year after his father's death he'd been transferred to Europe and had lived and worked there, barring an occasional visit to the States to see Katja Witchway, his stepmother, ever since. He explained his current work as he had explained it to Magda, with the difference that he admitted to Somerville that he still was with the Agency. But he didn't reveal anything about his most recent and dramatic experiences. Somerville had listened to all this in sympathetic silence. Now he poured more wine for both of them and asked:

"How did your father feel about your working for 'The Company'?"

"Do you mean, did he wish I'd gotten an assignment in operations, like he did?" Wychway asked with the merest hint of asperity in his tone, "Did he ever talk to you about that?"

"No indeed, my dear fellow, he never did. On the contrary, on those rare occasions when he confided in me about his family he seemed mightily pleased that you had managed to avoid the nasty, joyless, and mainly thankless part of the organization in which he, to his misfortune, had been forced to participate—Man's Rotten Fate, he used to call it. What he did he did extremely well—I speak with authority—but I think that all the same, at bottom he hated it."

Wychway blinked. "Are you serious?"

"Perfectly. My dear chap, do you think I'd lie about something like that? I'm surprised he never told you himself."

"I wish he had." Wychway raised his eyebrows and shook his head. He felt he'd just been relieved of a great burden. Before he spoke he looked down at the table for a few moments.

"You know, I had this job during the time I worked for the Agency in the States, and it was, it was—did you ever see a movie called *The Three Days of the Condor*?"

"No.... I seldom attend the cinema; you see, I prefer reading."

"Well if you get the chance, go see it and it'll tell you pretty much what I was doing. It's about a guy who works for the Agency and all he does is read novels. I was a sort of archivist, spent most of my life in libraries, reading Arabic texts—thank God I didn't have to read Arabic novels—and I always thought the old man despised me for it. I mean, he knew I had this disability, but I always thought he wished I hadn't, that he was cursed with a son who couldn't perform—like he could. See what I mean?"

"Oh, I see what you mean all right, but you're dead wrong. What a pity!" the Major added, half to himself; then, seeing Wychway smile and finish his wine in one draught, he signaled the waiter and called for another bottle.

"I guess I don't have to tell you, but he was quite a character, Major," Wychway said quietly as the waiter opened the new bottle.

"Call me, J.D., please."

Wychway grinned. He was getting a little tight, happily. "Okay. That's what my old man used to call you, if I remember right."

"Yes, among a number of other things," Somerville smiled, "but please go on."

"Well, he told me once—when I was just a kid—he told me that before inspections, when he was a young paratrooper, he'd take his brass belt buckle apart with a screwdriver and pliers and polish the inside! And he kept his spit-shined jump boots in a refrigerator. —And then there was 'the elephant': he had this little, stuffed, calico elephant my sister gave him one Christmas when she was about two years old. He took it everywhere with him."

"Oh, yes! I know about the elephant, as did anyone who knew him more than just casually. I seem to recall a small rubber fish or a whale or something, also."

"My other sister. —Then there was a guy who knew him in the early days who told me the standing joke about him was that he was so 'G.I.' he'd go to sleep at the position of attention and wake up at exactly two A.M. and give himself 'At Ease!'"

"I wouldn't be surprised," J.D. laughed. But then there's also the fact that he went back to school after his retirement and acquired three more degrees, including a doctorate!

"But to get back to the point," he went on more seriously, "whatever you did after you left the service your father would have no cause to be ashamed of you. You've been in action, and your father was proud of your fine record. You were awarded the Silver Star, if I'm not mistaken—"

"They gave decorations away in Crackerjack boxes over there," Wychway answered with a snort, "as 'morale builders'."

"Crackerjack...? Oh, yes, I see. Caramelized, popped corn, isn't it? And there's a little prize inside? I see what you mean—a metaphor."

"Right." Wychway hid his amusement. "Well, if you were a company grade officer, for example, and you were in reasonably good odor with your C.O. and you made contact with a hostile force—got into a firefight in other words—you could pretty well count on getting your—what would you call it— your gong? We hadn't had a real war since Korea, and a peacetime army gets very hungry for medals, so you've gotta get 'em while the getting's good." He laughed cynically.

"The day I went to our headquarters in Saigon to get decorated a buddy of mine came along for the ride. They put us, the ones to be decorated, in one rank; my friend was standing just behind me. There was this general, and his flunky followed him around with a cigar box full of medals. When they'd get in front of somebody the flunky would read out the order and then the general would hang the medal on, and so forth. Well, the general gets to me and he pins my medal on and shakes my hand, and so on. Then he sees this pal of mine hovering behind me, and he turns to his flunky and whispers, 'What's he supposed to get?' or something like that, and the flunky, kind of flustered, whispers back, 'I don't know, Sir!' and the general says, 'Give me a Bronze Star,' and hangs it on my friend, who's already got five or six of them (we used to get one every time we came back from a long-range patrol) and shakes his hand; and then we went back to our unit laughing our asses off. Later, my friend told me he was going to issue all his other medals out to his relatives, if he lived, but he was never going to give *that* one up....

"And then there was 'Super-L.R.R.P.,'[2] a young buck sergeant I knew in one of the line divisions. He already had nine Bronze Stars and was going for more. Every time he came back from an R.O.N. patrol the division C.G. would hang another medal on him. Christ, even *I* can remember when patrols were considered a routine duty for an infantryman."

When he stopped for breath and to beg pardon for talking too much, J.D., in a paroxysm of laughter, merely waved off his apology. By this time Wychway, his personal concerns temporarily forgotten, was thoroughly enjoying himself, and he didn't mind at all when J.D., in a slightly more sober mood, returned to the subject of *his* old friend, Charley Witchway.

They had one or two more drinks in the library, which at this hour they had to themselves and where Somerville happily went on talking about his dear, late friend, Colonel Charles Witchway.

---

[2] See the Glossary for this and other abbreviations or acronyms.

Chapter Five

A Playful Pilgrim

"No doubt you've heard a great deal about your father's professional exploits, the more obvious and publicized ones, I mean," J.D. said quietly as they sat by the dwindling fire in the library. "But there's a side of him that perhaps you don't know as much about.—Would you like to hear what he did to me once, years ago?" he added with a genial chuckle.

Wychway could hardly refuse; and he realized that now, after their recent conversation, he wanted to hear more about his father.

"It was back in '78 or so as I recall," J.D. continued. "We both were retired. I was living here in London, in the same flat as a matter of fact. Your father had come over for a visit; he was divorced from your mother by that time and hadn't got his university job yet. He stayed with me for a few days and then pushed off to the Continent.

"He had been gone for several weeks before I received a postcard from him, stamped Palermo, saying he was feeling fit, enjoying himself, and was making for Catania, planning to visit several towns along the way. A postscript said he would write more fully soon. I heard no more until I received his letter.

"The letter, the text of which was startling enough, was of interest also in a physical sense in that it was written on *butcher's* paper, torn or crudely cut to fit its envelope. But even more interesting was the fact that the envelope was addressed in a strange hand, while on the letter itself your father had himself written my address out in full. I could only deduce that as he had had no envelope at the time he wrote an envelope was addressed later and the letter posted by someone else. What was as arresting was the character of the handwriting itself. Your father, who normally wrote in a clear, strong hand, must have written in great haste, or was greatly agitated, or both, when he produced this sinister account (of which more later). In places his script was barely legible; if I had not had the occasional experience of reading his letters I doubt I could have deciphered the damned thing. Considering all these facts—the paper, envelope, hasty scrawl, and most important, the dire content of his message—I found it extremely odd that his narrative was so detailed and exacting an account of his movements and experiences.

"He left Palermo by bus, his letter said, bound for Catania, with planned stops at Agrigento, Vittoria, Nota, and Syracuse. This information I already had received in the postcard of which I spoke earlier. The letter apparently was written in Vittoria, from which it also was posted.

"He reached Vittoria late on a blazing July afternoon. After checking into a small *pensione* for the night, he strolled through the main *piazza*, on the far side of which he found an air-conditioned *trattoria* with a name he found irresistible: Texass Restaurante. Here, he thought, there might be a story.

"He entered an atmosphere of cool spiciness, and liked the place immediately. A lone young waiter nodded a greeting, and with a sweeping gesture indicated any available table.

From his corner table Charley could see most of the room and its few diners. The young waiter brought a menu, and in his flawless Italian Charley ordered a half-carafe of the house *vino rosso*. As you know, your father was an imposing figure, to say the least of it—at the time he was on the right side of fifty, in good condition, and stood a lean six-foot-two—and undoubtedly it was that combined with his command of the language which brought the owner-operator of the restaurant, carrying a bottle of damned good local wine—Cerasuolo di Vittoria, I think it was—to his table.

"This proprietor, a Signor Scolapasta it was (I couldn't forget a name like that!), was a large man also, but decidedly was not lean; of average height, he must have weighed at least 250 pounds. Genial and cheerful, he insisted upon replacing Charley's wine with the Cerasuolo at no extra charge; but when your father invited him to join him in a glass, Scolapasta politely refused. He was busy, he said, but would return later when, he added, he would expound on Vittoria's places of interest.

"The young waiter retrieved the wine carafe, and as Charley chatted easily and commented on Scolapasta's generosity the boy's reserve softened, and alluding to his employer's size he said that among their regular patrons Scolapasta was known as "King Kong," adding, not unkindly, that though he might look like a gorilla his boss in fact was a lamb.

"But as he waited for his food Charley reflected that somehow Scolapasta, despite his cheerfulness, lacked genuineness. There was another quality, expressed in and around the man's prominent eyes, and Charley decided that that quality was fear. The truth of this astute judgement soon would be borne out.

"Charley was ordering coffee when King Kong returned. The fat man settled himself ponderously in a chair and there began a desultory conversation, during which your Governor confirmed his earlier appraisal of the other's masked apprehension. The man did not glance up or down occasionally as most self-assured people do, but continually cast his eyes left and right, and more often than not in the direction of three men who were seated at a nearby table.

"Well, when Charley asked if the restaurant were the man's sole occupation, his companion's lips twisted cynically as he replied that he had hoped to open another restaurant on some land in the Gela area, left him by a late uncle, but that the enterprise had proven *inutile*, hopeless. The last word was a virtual snort. When asked about particulars, King Kong abruptly changed the subject, and asked what Charley thought of the *trattoria's* name. Charley replied—I can see that famous grin of his now— that that was what had brought him in and in turn asked if the fat man had ever been to Texas. No, he was told; he had used the name in the hope of attracting rich tourists, *Americanos*, for choice. Nothing was said about the quaint spelling.

"From this point matters moved quickly. The three men sitting nearby, who obviously were taking a great interest in your father's conversation with the proprietor, now took a hurried consultation, casting frequent glances at Charley's table; then one of them got up and came over, smiling and greeting King Kong, who rose and with his nervous smile welcomed the newcomer with, '*Salve*, Salvatore!'—or some such name—and introduced your father.

"Well, Salvatore seated himself before King Kong had regained his seat, then turned and beckoned to his companions to join him. Introductions again were made and a bottle of *Stock* called for. A convivial gathering of friends, thought Charley as he resigned himself, not unhappily, to a longer evening than he had anticipated. He always sought encounters with new acquaintances who might relate stories about what he referred to as "the human condition." In this case he was not to be disappointed.

"In a town of some 30,000 souls, which is the size of Vittoria, strangers cannot remain anonymous for long and your father, for all his linguistic accomplishment, decidely was a stranger. But more than that, he was a 'loner,' traveling on his own, not part of one of those benighted 'tours' one encounters all over the Continent. And in the area of Sicily where he found himself there is a tendency on the part of the inhabitants to make inquiries of so personal a nature as would in other social settings be considered outrageous. Knowing all this he decided, unwisely as it turned out, to deflect or defer these inquiries which though made casually almost always have a practical objective, such as touching you for a little of the ready, as one example." J.D. stopped for breath, sipped some cognac, and went right on.

"In fact now, as the brandy was being passed around pretty freely and the conversation took a lighthearted turn, he decided to 'counterattack.' Reminding King Kong of his failure at Gela, he asked him, above the casual conversation, to explain its real cause. At that point *all* conversation, including that which had been going on at adjacent tables, stopped at once; it was like one of those odd moments when a room full of chattering people suddenly falls silent (my mother used to tell me when I was a small boy that at those moments God was calling for our attention—I always wondered why he never spoke, but was afraid to ask).

"Almost immediately Salvatore laughed heartily, and as if this were a cue the other two joined in his merriment. King Kong sat there as if turned to stone as Salvatore patted him reassuringly. The newcomer (your father) though a stranger to them, this Salvatore said, obviously was "*un uomo discreto*" who could be trusted with the most intimate information. He insisted that the fat man tell his story. Salvatore's friends, who looked a little puzzled, nonetheless quickly seconded his importunity. Charley's impression was that the newcomers, having heard the story, thought it worth telling, and he joined in the spate of encouragement. King Kong, perspiring freely and seemingly under a terrific strain haltingly began to speak.

"When he drove to Gela and looked over his land everything seemed to be in his favor, he told Charley, with frequent nervous glances at Salvatore. His uncle had even arranged for payment of the inheritance taxes. There was a building on the land which with some modification would serve his purpose. Best of all the location was at the junction of the main roads to Catania and Agrigento. Joyously, he drove home to tell his wife the good news, and to offer a proposal of managership to his brother-in-law. Early next morning he started again for Gela to begin his arrangements." J.D. took another sip of his brandy as he looked at his companion portenteously, then he went on.

"He did not get very far. They were waiting for him in

ambush near a small bridge a few miles from Gela. He wasn't even sure how many of them there were; but he remembered most vividly the oily-smelling muzzle of the double-barreled shotgun, wrapped in an old US Army blanket, which was thrust under his nose as he was told what would happen to his family before he himself died if he did not sell the property he had inherited to a certain "*uomo d' affare*" in Gela; then he received a beating that left him half-dead by the roadside. Two days later, without a word to his family, he limped painfully to an address in Gela and sold the property very cheaply. Today there is a large restaurant on the site, which mainly caters expensive weddings. This "wedding palace," however, also is one of the largest outlets for illegal drugs in southern Sicily. And thus the fat man's tale ended.

"Salvatore had listened with unconcealed enjoyment, and now he gave King Kong a conspiratorial wink and urged him to tell the newcomer how his generous and loving uncle had died. The restaurateur, whose face now was gray, mumbled something about the old man being found dead at the bottom of a ravine; more indistinctly he muttered that his uncle had been the victim of an accident: while hunting rabbits he apparently had lost his footing and had tumbled into the ravine. His shotgun must have been discharged in the fall, since his face was riddled with a full charge of pellets. King Kong's chin was on his chest when he finished.

"And it was then that Salvatore turned to your father; and no longer smiling but with a very determined expression, asked, 'And now, you, *Signor di Grande Discrezzione*, just what is your business, and what do you want in this part of Sicily? I know from your accent that you are not Sicilian nor are you from any part of southern Italy. You are from the North, that we know, but now we must know the what—*what* are you?' The threat in his tone was almost palpable. And instead of taking out his American passport and so proving that he, a simple tourist, though not *un*interested in what he had heard was *dis*interested, so they need not fear him,

Charley simply said he was a writer (at the time I think he was experimenting with poetry). A moment later the three men got up and left without another word."

Wychway, who had never been able to decide whether his father was an Italiophile, an Anglophile, or both, found himself wondering what he could have been up to. Would he not produce his passport because then they'd know he was neither Italian nor English...? He brought his attention back to what J.D. was saying.

"...they were gone, King Kong, slumped in his chair, looked up at Charley and shook his head. If the *Gentiluomo* hadn't guessed earlier who these men were he should have no need to wonder now, he said sadly. He added listlessly that it didn't matter anymore what he revealed about these *mafiosi* (the other patrons had all left by this time) since in his opinion it was no odds that Charley would ever have an opportunity to publicize what he had heard that evening. I assumed it must have been then that Charley had asked for paper to write his letter.

"For three weeks I heard nothing further from Charley or from anyone else about this strange incident. I checked the newspapers for missing Americans; I contacted your embassy here in London and asked them to investigate the matter. No results, anywhere. Silence of the tomb, as it were.

"And then one evening as I was sitting in my flat reading and sipping sherry (and still reflecting occasionally upon your father's strange experience and subsequent seeming disappearance) the doorbell went. It was late and I wasn't expecting anyone. I went to the door, and by God it was none other than Charley! He just stood there with that big grin, pumping my hand, and then he asked me what I'd thought of the story!

"Yes, it was just a story! —a fiction, if you will. *Can* you imagine? After leaving Vittoria he'd taken a 'side trip' from Syracuse to Malta and had found the place so interesting he hadn't taken the time to write or to get in touch otherwise. And later, over a drink, he reminded me that just before he'd left for Italy I'd asked him to write and tell me any good story ideas he might have come across. At the time I was trying to do a little writing to qualify for membership in this bloody Scribes club, you see. And *why* was his writing in that letter so hard to read? Too much Italian brandy! —But I ask you, really!" J.D. shook his head and grinned.[1]

Wychway smiled back but remained silent. There were a lot of things about his father he'd never know, he decided.

"Lord knows your father had enough real-life adventures to last three ordinary men a lifetime, but somehow that never seemed enough for him," J.D. went on, "he had to have these imaginary ones as well. He had to make them up out of his own fancies." With this Somerville sat back and laughed out loud. "He used to come out with some of the most outrageous things. Once he told me, as we were sitting in a tin hut in Malaya under a heavy monsoonal rain—we hadn't seen a woman, well, none to speak of, for about three months—and he said, 'You know, J.D., it's not all this getting laid that's tiring me out, it's all the masturbation in between.'" J.D. shook his head. "And at the oddest times he'd mutter something cryptic about: 'If you don't get in, you can't get out—so you have to get in to get out.' I never really understood what he meant by that.... But I will say this: I think he would have been one hell of a writer—a novelist, I mean. Would have made MacLean, Le Carré, Clancy, and all that crowd look like a lot of flaming amateurs."

"Well, he did do that one—that *Twelve Days of Christmas*—about that weird experience you two had over here four or five years ago?"

"Oh yes, but that was based on actual fact. But I think beyond that one the old boy could have made up some stunners, out of whole cloth, so to speak." The Major became silent as he stared at his glass for a moment. "In any case, I

[1] See "The Texass Bar & Restaurante" in *Antipodes 10* by John Pascal; American Literary Press, Baltimore, 1995.

certainly have missed the old devil." He raised his glass. "Here's to him," he looked at Wychway, "and to you—Charley," and he drank to the bottom.

It was then that Wychway decided to tell J.D. about his recent experiences, from the accident on the Autobahn to his breathtaking discovery while playing darts at Bury St. Edmunds. He told him also, with some reservations, about Magda whom, after a little prompting, J.D. recalled from his and Charley Witchway's visit to Bumfries Hall on that Christmas of years ago.

Chapter Six

Confirmation

Wychway stayed at Somerville's place in Bayswater that night and early next morning J.D. drove him to Heathrow. There had been just enough space for Wychway's two bags in the small, powerful Austin-Healy. As they turned on to the M11 J.D. went back to Wychway's strange revelation of the previous evening.

"Tell me something else before I forget to ask: How far is this, this telescopic vision, for lack of a better description, good for? I mean, what are the limits, short and long?"

"It's like using field glasses, well, more like a telescope—monocular I guess the word is. I don't know how I'd rate the power, but it's pretty good. But like field glasses or a telescope it's only good beyond about eight or ten feet—less than that everything's a blur. I definitely don't get microscopic vision. Telescopic is as good as any other way of saying it."

"Truly and utterly strange; one could say, bizarre, even—like in a science fiction novel. Are there any ill effects? I mean, do you get headaches or anything like that?"

"No, not anymore anyway. After I got out of the hospital, before the onset of this, this super eyeball thing, I used to get these terrible headaches, and sometimes my vision would blur. Once or twice I got this awful vertigo feeling. I guess the demon was trying to assert itself. But now, now that I know what my eye can do and I can control it, most of the time anyway, no more headaches, vertigo, or anything else like that."

"He gave her the big eye," J.D. muttered as he looked at the road and reached for a cigarette.

"Wh-what?"

"Just an old expression—American, I think—from my youth." He glanced at the younger man, "Sorry. Didn't mean to make light of the situation.—But you'll undoubtedly be finding out more about it today. What time is your appointment with this German doctor?"

"At three this afternoon."

"I'd be interested to know what he has to say." And with this J.D. fell silent, and remained so until they reached the airport.

Wychway found J.D.'s expression of interest reassuring. It was good to know there was someone he could talk to. And Magda also would be waiting to hear from him. He reflected on how few friends, acquaintances really, he had in Europe, or for the matter of that, in the States or anywhere else. And in the last couple of days he'd met two people with whom he'd felt a greater intimacy (aside from the sex he'd shared with Magda) than he'd ever experienced with any of the rest of the people he knew. A likely factor contributing to this was his unspoken fear about his condition. He had wanted to be near someone, as a child does when it is afraid. He'd tried to act nonchalant, but he actually was close to being terrified. His mind (such as it was, he reflected, after all the hammering his head had taken) kept going back twenty-five years, to his head wound and its aftermath. He remembered hearing about headshot cases where the victim suddenly experienced some phenomenal power, attributed generally to a derangement of the nervous system but usually inexplicable, and then died, just as suddenly, soon afterward. Wychway wasn't ready to die, not yet anyway. Life would have to get a hell of a lot worse before he'd start feeling it wasn't worth living. Of course, he told himself, it has been said in a number of different ways for centuries that if we could know the future our sanity wouldn't be worth an hour's purchase.

If Wychway hadn't been so deep in his own thoughts he might have noticed that Somerville wasn't merely glancing occasionally at the rearview mirror: from time to time he seemed to be studying it.

Wychway arrived at the Frankfurt international airport at a little after ten-thirty that morning, and after retrieving his luggage took the shuttle bus around to the US Air Force MAC Terminal, to which his ID card gave him access, and retrieved his Ford Escort from the long-term parking lot. He drove south and was in Mannheim around midday. There he decided to have lunch at a Hungarian restaurant which he favored.

As he sat in a quiet corner eating some of his favorite dishes, but somehow not enjoying them as much as he usually did, his mind not unnaturally went to Magda, and he found himself wishing she were with him. After all, he thought, she *was* Hungarian. He wanted some wine, but Sibelius had instructed him not to drink anything alcoholic for twenty-four hours prior to his appointment. Well, he thought, fifteen would have to do—he and J.D. had sat up with nightcaps and talked until past midnight.

He was back on the road to Heidelberg in less than an hour, and at ten till three he was entering the university hospital where Sibelius's *Neurologie Klinik* was located. The burly German he collided with at the entrance, when Wychway, mistakenly thinking for a moment that he'd left his keys in his car, suddenly stopped and turned, was effusively apologetic.

The visit with Sibelius was surprisingly short. The doctor was alone in his office, and without any preamble other than a perfunctory handshake asked:

"How are you feeling, Herr Wychway?—Please, remove your jacket and sit down."

Wychway hesitated, not sure whether he should blurt out the truth immediately or wait for a more specific question. As he removed his jacket he decided on a vague answer to the doctor's innocuous query.

"Not too bad, under the circumstances." As he seated himself he tried to maintain eye to eye contact, but the man was busy with a sphygmomanometer.

"Please, roll up your sleeve," Sibelius directed, seemingly ignoring Wychway's reply, and proceeded with his cursory examination of blood pressure, pulse rate, ears and throat. When the doctor reached for an ophthalmoscope Wychway decided this was the time to come out with it.

As he related his strange experience in the pub at Bury St. Edmunds and the subsequent confirmatory evidence of his uncanny visual ability Wychway sensed in a way he would have found difficult to define that though Sibelius's reaction of amazement and incredulity ostensibly was what normally could be expected there was something else, something which under ordinary circumstances shouldn't have been there (always taking into account that there was nothing ordinary about these circumstances). There was a subtle, perhaps suppressed, gleam of exultation in the man's eyes. Perhaps, Wychway told himself, he was imagining things. But Sibelius now was firing questions at him with machine gun rapidity, questions which for the most part Wychway had already been asked by Somerville, or earlier, by Magda. When Sibelius stopped for breath Wychway asked:

"But how in hell could it even be *possible?*"

"The universe is not only queerer than we imagine, Herr Wychway, but perhaps queerer than we *can* imagine," the Doctor intoned portenteously. Wychway knew he'd heard this somewhere, or had read it, but couldn't remember where. It sounded like something Carl Sagan or Arthur C. Clarke would say.

"Truly incredible," Sibelius now was saying, "there was a case... but no, nothing like this, nothing so clearly defined, so—accomplished, so consistent!" he was busy with the ophthalmoscope as he talked more to himself than to his patient. Finally he straightened up and stepped back.

"I have learned from your medical records that you live here in Germany—in Stuttgart, is that not so, Herr Wychway?" he put down the instrument and looked keenly at Wychway.

"Yes, Stuttgart, well, Vaihingen, it's—"

"I know Vaihingen very well, Herr Wychway," the doctor interposed politely and enthusiastically. "Years ago, after the war, I worked for your Government. A long, long time ago. I was at Kelly Barracks—"

His tone had become nostalgic when Wychway gently interrupted him; despite his usual good manners he was not in the mood for social chat.

"Look, Doctor Sibelius, in a minute we'll be showing each other family pictures, and that would be very nice, under other circumstances maybe, but—"

"Yes, yes, of course you are right," Sibelius apologized hurriedly. "Please forgive me, Herr Wychway.

"That's okay, Doc, it's just that this has been a pretty spooky experience." To his own annoyance Wychway realized not for the first time that when he was excited or upset he reverted to slang. "What I mean to say is that this is not just a bizarre experience for me. I must confess that I'm really worried about what *else* might be going to happen. I don't mind telling you that I'm more than just worried, I—"

"Please! Herr Wychway," the other interposed sympathetically, "I understand. Your fear is only natural. No doubt this was a terrifying experience for you. And from what little I know of it your previous medical history—the wound in Indochina and its unfortunate consequences—can only serve to compound and intensify your fears. But let me assure you that from what I know at this point you have no reason to fear for your life—of that I am certain—or that some other similarly frightening condition will manifest itself."

"But how can you know this? You've hardly examined me. Aren't you going to make any other tests?"

"Of course there must be other tests," the doctor replied soothingly, "and they will be performed today, before you leave. We must have a CAT scan, and perhaps even an MRI, as soon as possible. Then there will the more routine x-rays, blood work, and of course an electroencephalogram. All this will be done this afternoon."

"Will I have to be admitted again—to the hospital, I mean?" Wychway asked apprehensively.

Sibelius was thoughtful for a moment.

"No, I do not think that will be necessary. But let me not give you a definite answer to that question until after I have seen at least the results of the CAT scan, which we shall do first. May we leave it at that for the moment?—Good." And with that he began scribbling authorizations for the tests and the interview ended.

It was after five that afternoon before Wychway saw Sibelius again. He was seated in the Doctor's waiting room when Sibelius bustled in with a sheaf of papers in his hand and beckoned Wychway to follow him into an inner office. Having seated himself at his desk the elderly and scholarly professor motioned his patient to a seat, then leaned back and put his fingertips together.

"I have good news, which you will wish to hear first, I am sure," he smiled a wintry little smile. "You are in no danger. We need not re-admit you to the hospital or detain you in any way, at least not for the present. It will take some time to go over all these test results," he waved at the papers he had dropped on his desk, "but I will begin to study them immediately, and I will be in touch with you as soon as possible. Meanwhile—"

"Doctor," Wychway broke in impatiently, "is there nothing you can do to correct this thing, to make me—normal again? Maybe you could operate on the optic nerve: is that the problem? Maybe—"

"The optic nerve is not the problem. That is merely a conduit, to use simple language. Something else has been deranged, a distortion of the eye wall—I could even see this when I made a casual examination of the fundus earlier today.

And the lens also..." he trailed off, then began again. "Herr Wychway, the surgery I performed on you was extremely risky, but it was absolutely necessary; I had to do it to save your life. But now, to go in again..." he spread his hands expressively. "Could you not endure this, this aberration, at least for a time? After all, I have not even seen these as yet," he patted the x-rays, computer printouts, and charts, which he had placed neatly on a corner of his desk. When Wychway, staring down at his folded hands, didn't respond Sibelius went on. "Give me a few days—two days perhaps, *ja*? Then we shall see. You will do that?"

Seeing no alternative Wychway could do nothing but agree. Sibelius then advised his patient to try to "take it easy for a few days," not to worry, to remain calm, not to drink or smoke too much, and gave him a prescription for a mild sedative. Then, having given the doctor his address and telephone number, Wychway left.

And as he walked down the corridor he found himself wondering how Sibelius could have expected to get into touch with him if Wychway hadn't given him the particulars. Well, he assumed, perhaps through the Embassy... or perhaps the old man was just absent-minded.

Wychway went straight to the Monokel, a bar and restaurant on Bergheimerstrasse, and ordered a large brandy. Goetz Göttler, the owner, was behind the bar and brought Wychway his drink.

"Hallo, Cholly, lonk dime no zee!"

"I've been in England, Goetz. Needed a rest."

"Nize place, Englandt, eggszept now dey go broke again, *ja*? Göttler laughed. "You know, ven I vass a liddle boy, durink de var, ven dose Nazi cherks took over Franz, people vould zay, 'Dere vill alvays be an Englandt, but Hitler vill be the kink!'"

Wychway reflected unhappily that if anyone in Germany could cheer him up it was this man, and still he felt bleak and cheerless.

"Cholly, vot's wronk? You lookink like you lost your

last friendt."

Wychway, who had knocked back his drink in just two swallows, looked up with an unconvincing smile and said, "Just got something on my mind, Goetz. It'll pass."

"You like anudder trink? Dot vun I chust giff you, I dun't dink it even douched de sides goink down," the jolly, red-faced German chuckled. Although he knew Wychway spoke very passable German Goetz Göttler loved speaking his own brand of English—learned from the occupation forces in the US Zone after the war—to anyone who was willing to listen.

Wychway thought of Sibelius's injunctions for just the merest moment before he answered, "Why not?"

"*Gut.*—You know vat I alvays say, Cholly— 'Half trunk iss vasted money'!" Goetz laughed as he went for the Asbach.

An hour and three more brandies later, after more mainly one-sided chatting, Wychway left for Stuttgart. He'd refused dinner, which he knew would have been "on de *haus*," with a promise to return soon.

He made the drive to Stuttgart very carefully, being fully aware that the Germans were hell on drunken driving. But somehow he didn't feel drunk in the least; he felt wide awake and his senses were very keen, his coordination as good as it ever was. As he bored along the Number 4 Autobahn at 150 kilometers per hour he felt completely relaxed. Nonetheless he was very careful about keeping both hands on the wheel and both eyes open all the time. Somehow he didn't feel oppressed anymore about his freakish eye. In fact he began to feel a little elated, telling himself he was possessed of a new ability, not a disability, as he had thought of it before. Just think of what you did at that dart board! he told himself aloud.

When he let himself into his flat in Vaihingen he stepped on an envelope that had been thrust under his door. He picked it up and stuffed it in his jacket pocket, and by the time he got his bags into the sitting room he'd already forgotten about it. He looked at the clock on the mantel of his inoperable fireplace. Almost nine o'clock. He wondered if he should call Magda, or maybe even Somerville. Then he realized Magda would be at Oxford by now, and he hadn't got her phone number there, or even her address for that matter. As for Somerville, he would wait until he had more information to give him. He took his bags into the bedroom and hung up his suits; the rest could wait until tomorrow. He stretched out on the bed and was asleep in less than five minutes.

When he awoke an hour later he decided to go out to a nearby Gasthaus for a late supper. After a month in England he missed German food, which wasn't much of a testimonial to English food, he told himself wryly. He was thankful that his sense of humor and irony was reasserting itself, even if he had to admit that Goetz's Asbach undoubtedly had had a good deal to do with this.

He remembered the letter as he sat waiting for his food in the Gasthaus restaurant. He'd been alternately thinking of Magda and wondering if there would still be enough of an edge on his social appetite after supper to justify calling an attractive German woman he knew in his apartment building and inviting her to his place for a nightcap. These more or less pleasant musings were immediately dispelled when he saw the signature scrawled boldly across the bottom of the single sheet of paper: "Browning," who would arrive, according to the note, at Wychway's flat on the morrow at "1600 hours." How typical was that "1600 hours"! thought Wychway. From this moment his elation, tentative as it was, left him, to be replaced for a reason he couldn't define by all his earlier curiosity, anxiety, alarm, and outright fear, which now he felt even more keenly.

An hour later, as he lay in bed again, but this time unable to sleep, Wychway remembered the tranquilizers Sibelius had prescribed—then he realized he hadn't even gotten the prescription filled....

Day was beginning to break when, utterly exhausted, he fell into a restless sleep.

The man who had been watching the entrance to Wychway's building dozed off behind the wheel of his BMW at about the same time.

Chapter Seven

Inquisition

While Wychway was eating dispiritedly at Der Goldener Schwan Herr Doktor Professur Joachim Manfried Sibelius found himself closeted in a brightly lit room with three other men. Browning, a swarthy, grizzled, compact, tough-looking man in the late-sixties and one of the two Americans present, said in his characteristically forthright way:

"Tell us how you did it, Doc."

Sibelius hesitated a moment before answering.

"I do not wish to insult your intelligence, Herr Browning, but without the necessary scientific knowledge it would be very difficult, almost impossible, to explain even in the layman's language." Browning looked annoyed. "May I say however," the doctor hurried on, "that 'it' virtually did itself? There was a pre-condition of the brain, and there is no doubt that this was caused in some way by the two massive head injuries the man sustained. The first of these he suffered in the Vietnam war; and that, incidentally, must have produced some interesting, if different, phenomena of its own. Based on what he has told me I wish I had his old medical records and could confer with the military doctors who attended him.... You see, it has to do with the hemispheric—" he interrupted himself when he saw the look on Browning's face. "What I am trying to say is that his brain was, let us say, predisposed to manifest this, this capacity, this incredible ability.—There is so much we still do not know. There have been experiments, mainly in what was the Soviet Union, but still, no really conclusive data ever showed how such a condition—"

"What you're saying is, you don't know what the fuck caused it, right?" Browning interrupted rudely.

Sibelius flinched a little at this coarse, if valid, question.

"Well, if you must put it that way, I—"

"Right. Anyway, the point is, he can do it, right?" I mean, Christ, that Limey watcher we put on him said if he'd had a mirror he could have been throwing those darts over his shoulder and he couldn't miss."

"Oh, yes! I have conducted tests which showed he is capable of incredible telescopic vision. —But you did not let me finish! You think I did nothing? The second injury, which would have resulted in his death if I hadn't operated, gave me the opportunity to 'improve' on the preexisting condition. There was the necessity of replacing the lens, and the moving back of the retina—I am oversimplifying all this in the hope it will be more clear for you. Yes, admittedly there was a condition which was highly receptive to the stimulation of the optic nerve, but the stimulation had to be continued, and it is the microminiaturized 'stimulator'—to use a layman's term—which I implanted that makes this possible. Yes, replacing the lens, and the moving back of the retina, otherwise although the man might have this incredible capability it would be latent and unpredictable. The experience would occur from time to time, but no one, not even your man himself, would know when it was going to happen. That is what I do not understand: what causes the phenomenon in a 'natural' way, if I may use that imprecise way of—"

"Okay, okay, as long as we know it'll work, whenever he wants it to," Browning cut him off again.

"Of that I can give you a perfect assurance. All he has to do is close his left eye and—"

"Okay, right. How'd he take it? What'd he say?"

"*Mein Liebe Gott!*" Sibelius reverted momentarily to his

native tongue, "What did he *say*? He was terrified! He wanted to know what would happen next. My heart went out to him. I—"
Browning gave the man a disdainful look. "Yeah, yeah— okay, okay, my heart bleeds, too," he broke in without conviction. "Now, what'd you tell him?"
"Tell him? I told him there was no immediate cause for alarm, that we would make these tests, and I would let him know the results in a few days—"
"Did he ask if you could correct the, uh, situation, the condition?"
"Yes. Yes, he did. I told him I could make no judgement on anything until I had studied the test results."
"Good. Don't worry about any of that shit, and don't get in touch with him any more unless I tell you to; and unless the tests show he's got some other kind of disabling problem, forget about them. I'll take care of the rest. I'm going to see him tomorrow."
"Then he will know that I, that I..."
"Don't worry about it. I'm taking the rap for everything. But if it makes your candy ass feel any better I'll tell him I held a gun on you until you agreed to do it, how's that? —But he's okay, right? I mean, except for his new eyeball he's physically in good shape?"
"Oh, yes! He is in marvellous physical condition. The long rest he had was just what he needed. As to his psychological status, however, I can not—"
"Forget that. —Now," Browning went on relentlessly, "nobody else was involved, right?"
"Yes, and no," Sibelius held up a hand to forestall the inevitable objection. "I could not conduct such delicate surgery totally unassisted; but still, I was careful, and fame has its advantages; when one is at the top of his profession one can do—"
"Uh-huh.—A license to steal, eh? Believe me, I hear you loud and clear," he grinned at the other American in the room.
"I would not put it that way," the doctor replied, making an obvious effort to control his annoyance, "but have it as you

wish. —In any case, I explained to my assistants that the implantation was necessary to assist the damaged optic nerve—and it *was* damaged somewhat—to ensure that 'normal' vision was restored. I added the proviso, however, that the technique was experimental, and to that extent certainly I was not lying. A crude comparison of my rationale would be the use of a Pacemaker-type device to assist in controlling the pulse of a defective heart.

"When the patient returned to me I was able to see him and examine him in complete privacy; and when I wrote up my report for my assistants and other colleagues in the field I of course made no mention of having achieved the desired... phenomenon. And no one but myself was permitted to analyze today's test results. —Of course, henceforth I shall live in dread of someone coming to me with a *legitimate* case, requesting that I reprise my performance," the doctor ended on a note of doubtful resignation.

In his explication Sibelius had omitted to mention that at least one of his assistants had been extremely curious, perhaps even suspicious, about the entire surgical procedure. The renowned neurosurgeon had no way of knowing that in making this omission he probably had saved the young man's life, at least for the time being.

Browning, seemingly satisfied with what he had heard, went on:

"So what can you compare him with—a pair of six by thirty field glasses?"

"More like seven-fifty recon binoculars, if I read the Doc's report right," broke in Ward, Browning's general "dog robber," before Sibelius could reply.

Sibelius ignored this last comment.

"The effect produced is more like that of a telescope. There are limits to the near as well as far ranges. Objects closer than about eight or nine feet are merely blurs; magnification qualities at the extreme distances are virtually identical to those produced by use of a telescope. And of course, like a telescope, he does not have stereoscopic vision in the one-eyed mode; but if he wants to judge distances all he has to do is go back to using both eyes—after all, telescopic rifles do not have stereo vision; the hunter sets his sights based upon his judgement of the distance to be fired over before he looks through his telescope and —"

True to form Browning brushed him off once again, but this time he had a thoughful expression as he looked at Sibelius and said:

"Right, right—never mind all this bullshit about telescopic rifles. And it might be a good idea to use a different analogue in the future, not that you're going to be discussing this with anyone other than the people in this room, right?"

"Of course not, Herr Browning. My position has been made very clear to me." He glanced at the third man in the room, a German civilian known to him only as "Hamm," who had been standing quietly near the door with his arms folded across his chest. Sibelius knew Hamm was some sort of German official—it had been Hamm, with an official letter signed by the Minister of the Interior himself, who had approached Sibelius initially about this strange project—but that was all he knew. And the more he thought about all this the less he wanted to know about it. He was experiencing an increasing feeling of unease, a feeling that despite all the assurances he had received he had, in accepting the strange commission which had been thrust upon him, placed himself in a position of serious potential jeopardy. Sibelius was purely a scientist, but he knew enough about the affairs of men to realize that in the accomplishment of certain aims, aims directed from the highest levels of the political-economic world, individuals, even eminent men such as himself, counted for little or nothing. They were mere pawns in a game where the stakes were too high to permit anything but lip service to what men once called the Cardinal Virtues. He found himself feeling thankful that he had no family.

Browning's harsh metallic voice was intruding on these thoughts.

"... see about the medical costs, Ward?"

"No problem. The usual dummy insurance company in Zurich—S.O.P.," Ward replied laconically.

The interview (Browning had insisted on calling it a "debriefing") was being conducted in of all places the main building of the US Army Community Center, Heidelberg, in a room which normally served as the office of the Provost Marshal of that euphemistically named organization. Browning, who had wanted to have the meeting at EUCOM headquarters in Stuttgart, had been assured by the P.M. that the room was "secure" after Sibelius, fearing he might be compromised by going to such a major military installation as the US European Command headquarters in Stuttgart, insisted they meet in Heidelberg, preferably at some civilian facility.

Browning, who had compromised only so far, now walked to the window, and as he gazed out at the mainly female shoppers scurrying in and out of the adjacent commissary and post exchange, said musingly in a voice which was slightly more caustic than usual:

"Of all the people we pay, it has to be him! To think: all the mother-fucker does is read Arabic newspapers to see if some raghead has put a secret message in the personals... Christ, he doesn't even spell his friggin' name the same way his old man did!" He looked at Ward as something else suddenly occured to him. "And what in the goddam hell was he doin' drivin' around with $20,000—out of some poor unsuspecting bastard's confidential fund, no doubt—in a fucking money belt, no less, since he wasn't even remotely connected with ops?"

"His combat record in Nam was damn' good, at least until he got hit," Ward offered digressively. I mean, he's got all the training we could want and—"

"That's enough about that shit, Ward," Browning turned on his man with a glare after having thrown a meaningful glance in Sibelius's direction. Ward, having prevented with his interruption an indiscretion on Browning's part now had to endure the indignity of being admonished for the same thing. Despite his unswerving loyalty to his superior he found himself thinking, and not for the first time, about early retirement, and why he'd ever gotten into this ball of snakes which was referred to, rather childishly, he thought, as "The Company."

"The Herr Wychway seemed a nice enough fellow," Sibelius put in innocuously. —But may I ask you a question, Mr. Browning?" he added quietly.

"You can ask, but whether or not you get an answer depends on the question. Go ahead," Browning finished impatiently.

"I realize my part in this, this..." he searched for a word.

"Operation," Ward offered helpfully, and received another glare from his chief, which did not go unnoticed by Sibelius.

The doctor spread his hands, "It does not matter what you call it; but how in Heaven's name did this poor man become chosen for this, this experiment? He could not have volunteered—he was still unconscious when they brought him to me! And you could not have known he would have this accident, or that he would survive. Even *I* did not know if he would live or die for the first three days...." he ended with a gesture of bewilderment.

The three other men in the room all looked at each other in silence.

Chapter Eight

QHR-242

Browning was thoughtful for a few moments before he broke the silence; then he said, more to himself than to anyone in the room:

"I guess it's all right.—Shit, why not?" He turned to face Sibelius and spoke in his normal voice, "Look, Doc (Hamm winced every time this diminutive was used), you're in research; do you know what a 'requirement' is, in R and D talk?"

"R and D...? Ah, yes! of course. Research and development," Sibelius replied, ignoring the other's rudeness.

"Well, there're all kinds of requirements—mostly they're called QMRs, Qualitative Matériel Requirements. Then you got SDRs, Small Developmental Requirements, for the little stuff, the 'quick fixes.' All these requirements are based on concepts and doctrine, objectives, and— well, I'm not going into all that horseshit. Anyway, all kinds, mostly matériel requirements, anything from tanks and airplanes that can do certain things down to special kinds of food. Christ, I remember one during that Vietnam clusterfuck where they wanted a 'device' that would give a soldier the ability to go out on patrol and operate with no food or water *for ten fucking days*! Jesus! I can remember the exact words: '...and be able to accomplish his mission with no detrimental physical or psychological effects'! One like that we call a 'latter-day, solid-state, blue fairy.'[1] He shook his head.

"And that's exactly what we used to call this one that you just pulled off. Except this one's called a Q*HR*, a *human* requirement. It's been on the books for years, like the one submitted hy those signal assholes about mental telepathy. I gotta give you this much, Doc: even if Wychway did most of it himself, it's like a miracle, a fucking miracle! Usually—shit— *always*, after a long, long time and after millions of bucks have gone down the rat hole—you get an answer from the labs or the pud pullers at some university who're supposed to be working on a requirement—and pocketing jillions in the process—that what you want is 'presently beyond the state of the art,' which means, in plainer words: We knew going in we couldn't do it in a hundred years, but we took your fucking money anyway.'" He looked at Hamm, who had just glanced at his watch.

"Well, I know this is becoming a goddam speech so I'll cut it short and try to keep it simple. This guy Wychway works for us, in a manner of speaking, so he's been a volunteer from day one, whether he likes it or not. When we heard what happened on number Eleven Autobahn that night—and in case you're wondering, that *was* a genuine accident—and that our boy, 'Mario Andretti' Wychway, had a fifty-fifty chance of surviving we decided to take a shot at solid-state blue fairy QHR-31/10/85/242 which, loosely translated, means that on Halloween of 1985 Ronnie Reagan's boys, at a place in Virginia which shall remain unnamed, djinned up the two hundred and forty-second requirement of that year, and the requirement was one dealing with human subjects and specifically, eyeballs. The last thing I'm going to tell you about this is that Wychway isn't our first candidate for the Mister Megamonocle title. We tried in '89, in Boston. That was also one of

---

[1] See "The Latter Day Solid State Blue Fairy" in *Antipodes 10* by John Pascal; American Literary Press, Baltimore, 1995.

our volunteers who'd busted his skull. It didn't work. He started hallucinating, went completely ape shit, and finally (thank God) died."

"Of course," Sibelius put in deferentially, "I dare not ask what the purpose, the objective of this 'requirement' is, which as you have described it seems rather a general one?"

"No, you dare not," was Browning's terse reply.

Sibelius was thoughtful.

"Do you not think it would have been wise to have told me about this earlier—experiment, to have provided me with the medical records and—"

"Uh-uh, no," Browning, true to form, interjected unequivocally. We considered that, but decided against it for two reasons: one, we didn't want you to meet the other doctor, the Boston one, and discuss this matter—that's called compartmentalization in our business—and if you got his records you'd definitely want to talk to him; and two, we thought if you knew how that first one went, and believe me, it was a real fucking horror story, you might just throw up your hands and refuse to have anything to do with this." Browning reflected. "I just wish that one in Beantown had panned out; that poor bastard would have been just what we needed—"

"But if we may go back to Herr Wychway for a moment," Hamm, breaking his long silence, interjected diplomatically, diverting Browning from the potentially dangerous ground over which his thoughts seemed to be taking him, "does he not also screen the news reports and the opinion pages for trends and include this in his reports? It is my understanding also that he took a good degree in political—"

Browning, the consummate enemy and transgressor of conversational priviledge, if not rights, cut Hamm off in this sensible and laudable attempt at fairness.

"Trends?" he fairly shouted as he turned towards the rest of them, "fucking *trends?*—There's only one fucking trend among those sand niggers...." He looked heavenward as if seeking the strength to go on. "I can't believe Charley Witchway was his father," he whispered hoarsely almost to himself. "When I think of the shit *he* did…"

"Charley Witchway was a great operator in his day, in and out of the Army, but you gotta admit, Boss, he never agreed with you about the A-rabs (he pronounced the word with a hard "A")," Ward offered. "I remember he used to talk about the injustice of lumping them all together as a bunch of bloodthirsty, religion-crazed terrorists, especially by the news media…" he looked around as he trailed off, apparently embarrassed that he'd said so much. Browning, who had been staring at him with an expression of combined mock patience and incredulity finally broke the silence which followed. Sibelius's presence seemed to have been forgotten for the moment.

"All I can tell *you*, smart ass, is that whatever Charley Witchway's private convictions were, whenever he put his harness on he was a mission machine; no matter what it was or what he thought about it personally he'd break his ass trying to get it done. And sometimes it damn near did—break his ass, I mean." He glanced at Sibelius as he said these words, as if he felt the elderly German needed this final ocular emphasis. When Sibelius turned his face away in distaste, Ward's voice preempted the remark, undoubtedly nasty, with which Browning was about to attempt to regain the doctor's attention:

"Witchway was shot in the head too, in Nam, like his kid, wasn't he, Boss?"

Apparently not minding this diversion, Browning laughed harshly.

"Yeah. The standing joke in those days was that if he'd been hit any place else he probably wouldn't have made it. The Dinks he worked with in SOG put it out that he couldn't be killed, and if he could, he'd come back. Charley used to tell the Buddha heads that if he got zapped he wanted to be reincarnated as a girl's bicycle seat!" Browning shook his head and snorted again which—to his own embarrassment, Ward's amusement, and Sibelius's disgust—caused a quantity of mucus, accompanied by a large, glistening bubble, to shoot out of his fleshy nose. Hamm remained phlegmatic as Browning tried to suck the mess back up into his nostril while he dug hastily for a handkerchief.

Sibelius, who had been sitting with his elbows resting on his knees, slowly lowered his face into his hands.

Chapter Nine

The Scribe and the Pharisee

When Browning arrived Wychway was sitting on the balcony of his leased apartment on Waldburgstrasse in the Vaihingen district of Stuttgart, drinking a bottle of Corvo and listening to Verdi's *Sicilian Vespers*. He had left the front door ajar so he wouldn't have to get up and let Browning in. He disliked Browning intensely, especially when the man made familiar references to Wychway's father and "the good old days." They'd met just once, but Wychway's father had spoken of Browning on more than one occasion and not infrequently had referred to him as "that shit." Others in "The Community" had mentioned him also.

Whatever else might be said about Browning, there was no gainsaying that he was a consummate professional in his field. He was intelligent, resourceful, virtually fearless, and once launched upon a mission had the singleness of purpose of a pit bull terrier. His colleagues, subordinate and superior alike, seemed awed by him, and it was these traits that, at least in the minds of his superiors, compensated for his coarseness and those even less desireable qualities, mainly social, which he exhibited so freely. Browning was more than just a trouble shooter: he was, on the operations side of the CIA house, what was informally referred to as a "Special Agent at Large in Charge of Special Projects"; once given a mission or project he became what could almost be described as a free lance.

This charter enabled him to utilize all the assets of the Agency as well as other organizations, both in and out of the intelligence community, both in the US and among other nations more or less allied to US interests and objectives.

Now, as Browning came through the sitting room calling his name Wychway put his wine glass down and slowly closed his left eye and concentrated on Browning's face, seeing every blemish and blackhead, bristles missed by the razor, even the pores, which exuded an oily sweat. He dropped his gaze two feet, and was sure he saw traces of urine stains in the crotch of Browning's trousers. Satisfied, he went back to normal vision, feeling a little better about his newly found ability.

"Come in. —Care for a drink? Cigarette?" Wychway turned off the music.

"No, thanks," Browning replied tonelessly, and without waiting to be asked lowered his stocky, powerful body into the chair opposite Wychway, who smiled and said:

"I've noticed there's a lot of that going around."

"What's that?"

"People who don't drink or smoke."

"Goddammit, Wychway, don't be flip with me," with which Browning fished a crumpled pack of Camels out of his pocket and threw it down on the table between them. Looking around he asked, "Where's Dorian Gray?"

Although Wychway had hired his handsome Alsatian houseman, Florian Greflich, wittingly and without predjudice, he knew that the efficient, unobtrusive, and uncomplaining young man, given his "alternative lifestyle" was the butt of endless jokes among most Agency people who knew of the situation. Florian, who had been driven from the family hearth when he had admitted his "different sexual orientation" had, upon returning home to retrieve his few possessions a week after Wychway had hired him, told his staid, uncompromising father how he felt about his new employer: "He is as 'straight' as you are, and yet he never discusses our differences, and he certainly never preaches to me about anything. I think I could love this man (you needn't sneer; I didn't mean it in that way), in fact I wish *he* were my father." And with that he had left home for good.

"There was no sense in keeping him here while I was mooning around England getting back on my feet," Wychway told his surly visitor. "He and some of his friends went to Austria looking for the early snow. He's a great skier, you know."

"I'll bet," sniggered Browning. I'm sure he and his friends are having a ball—at the very least!" he rolled his eyes around suggestively. "When's he getting his sweet little ass back here?"

"He should be back tomorrow or the next day," the other answered with obvious annoyance.

"Good. I don't want anybody walking in here tonight, right?" he raised an inquisitive eyebrow.

"There's no fear of that."

"Good," Browning repeated. "Now…"

Wychway waited, gazing levelly and seemingly calmly at the other but experiencing an almost irresistable urge to close his left eye again. Browning's smile never reached his eyes as he said: .

"I'll bet your wondering why I asked to see you."

"I'm wondering why you've bothered to use 'asked' when it was made clear to me that this was a command performance." Browning's battered face became nasty as Wychway went on. "But yes, I'm mystified. I thought you were still on the ops side…"

"What makes you think I'm not?"

"Okay, fine, but I'm not."

"You are now, kid," Browning said brusquely and obviously enjoying himself, "in fact you're working for me now."

Wychway no longer was mystified—he was appalled: everything he'd ever heard about this man went through his mind as he sought for an answer, a reason. Could it possibly have anything to do with…? But Browning was going on.

"But before I get into that I've got a couple of other items I want to clear up." He reached for his cigarettes, fingered one out, lit it, and blew a stream of smoke across at Wychway.

"Wychway," he hesitated as he shook his head with a look of distaste, "what in the fiddle fuck did you think you were doing when you went to that poor asshole Jennings in Berlin and euchered twenty-thousand bucks in confidential funds out of him? Do you see yourself as the Lone Ranger, or Batman, or something?"

Wychway looked out over the balcony railing and said nothing. Without being fully conscious of it he was practicing his newly found ability on the surrounding buildings. As Browning's harangue went on Wychway discovered an attractive woman who was changing her dress in an apartment 200 yards away.

"Besides being illegal," Browning continued, "what you did has really fucked up friend Jennings to a fare-thee-well. I guess even you can figure that out. If it doesn't end his whole goddam career, which I seriously think it might, the best the poor bastard can hope for is an assignment to some armpit like Ouagadougou.—Well, you got anything to say?"

Wychway brought his attention back.

"No."

"No, huh? I'll bet a dollar to a doughnut you're dying to tell me what a lucrative source you had down there in Moonshintown. What was that dirt bag gonna do, tell you where all the secret weapons were stashed in Iraq?"

Wychway felt he had to say something before Browning buried him completely. He decided that using some typical bureaucratic jargon might help.

"He convinced me he had information which was vital to our future interests in the Middle—"

"No shit! And you, as the big fucking Bob Cratchitt-scribbler-extraordinary of the Agency were fully qualified to assess this source and just how much the info was worth, right? So off you go with about as much direction as a fart in a whirlwind, and in the process goddam near get yourself killed; which, I'll admit, would probably have been doing the world in general and the intelligence community in particular a big-assed favor." He hesitated a moment, "As it turns out it's good you *didn't* get killed, not for your sake but for mine—but more about that later....

"Now, speaking of that money, numbnuts, I'll tell you this: Before many more suns have passed you are going to Munich with the proper ID and that receipt they gave us and you're going to claim 'your' money; and then you're going to crawl into that embassy building in Berlin and you're going to turn that money in, to the station chief personally, and you're going to apologize for your asshole antics. And you better hope you don't run into Jennings while you're at it, or if you do you better pray he's not armed. Are you getting all this, Wychway?"

Wychway merely nodded his head. He'd stopped listening after Browning had interrupted him. Now he was wondering what the policy and procedure was for resignation from the Agency. And he was trying to remember how much money he had in his savings account at the Commerzbank which, since the economic disaster in the States, was paying twice the interest he could get at home.

"Right," said Browning as he lit another cigarette. He looked at the half-empty Corvo bottle and then looked around generally, "Do you have a decent drink around this goddam hutch (he pronounced it 'hootch')?"

Wychway was astonished. How could the man expect hospitality after what he'd just done, what he'd said? He looked at Browning indecisively, not knowing whether to accept this added indignity or to speak his mind. Browning gave him no chance to do either. Incredibly, the man smiled, almost good-naturedly.

"Listen, the ass chewing's over. You knew it was coming, from somebody, and you also knew you had it coming, so let's have a drink and I'll get down to what this visit is *really* all about. You can hate me all you want, Wychway; just try to keep it to yourself during our future relationship."

Incredible, thought Wychway, as he went for something stronger than wine. He felt cold, and got himself a sweater while he was at it. He decided he wouldn't be civil enough to ask Browning if he wanted to move into the sitting room.

Now, Browning, who had chosen to remain on the balcony and had accepted a large scotch with a little water, looked contentedly across at Wychway, who continued with the wine.

"It works, doesn't it?"

"What works?"

"Don't give me that coy bullshit, I saw you squinting at my crotch when I walked in here."

"No offense, Mr. Browning—"

"None taken; and by the way, if we're going to be working together, you can start calling me 'Browning,' or 'Lew,' or 'Sir', but don't call me Mr. Browning."

"Is that your real name—Browning, I mean?"

"Jesus Christ, Wychway, gimme a break! What the hell difference does it make anyway? If you call me Browning, I promise, I'll answer to it. —Now, let's knock off the chit-chat and get down to it." He drank some scotch, then said, "You have filled the requirement, Wychway, beyond our wildest dreams; you have become 'The Man.' You saw the Doc a couple of days ago—Sibelius—right?"

It took him several seconds to assimilate this, but as the enormity of the revelation dawned on him the anger and resentment he had been stifling now burst from Wychway:

"You son of a bitch! *You* did it, didn't you?"

"Well, Charley—may I call you Charley? I used to call your father 'Charley.' No, *I* didn't do it, but I am going to *use* it, with your cooperation, of course. Actually, the Doc did it, with a lot of help from you, if what he says is true. And the inspiration came from on High, but more about that later. But just think: if nothing else comes of it, you'll still be the world's champion dart shooter!"

Again, it took a few moments as Browning sat looking at him with a Cheshire smile for Wychway to connect this statement with his experience in the pub at Bury St. Edmunds the previous week. By now he was really shaken.

"That kid I played darts with in England—*he* was on

the payroll?"

"Indirectly. He was on loan from the Brits."

"And the old lady on the train, her too, I suppose?—and that German guy I bumped into at the clinic?"

Browning nodded smugly. "By the way," his face grew more serious, "did you say anything to that old crock, what the hell's his name, Somerville? when you stayed with him in London?"

"No," Wychway lied, not really knowing why. "Goddammit, Browning, what do you want with me?" he spilled half his wine getting the glass back on the table, "Why did you, they, no, *you*, do this to me? What *did* Sibelius do to me?—When I asked him he said it was something to do with my old head injury; that combined with this accident and all the work he had to do to bring me out of—"

"That was all bullshit—necessary bullshit at the time, but still bullshit. —What else did he do?"

"They took a buncha tests. He was gonna call me about the results in a coupla days." Wychway, among a host of other emotions he was experiencing, was despising himself again for breaking out into all this slang. He knew he did it when he was frightened or upset, and he knew that being with a vulgarian such as Browning lent itself to brutalizing the language; but he was beginning to suspect that part of the reason also was his cowardly concern that people like Browning, as much he despised them, would judge him pompous if he spoke the standard English he'd learned to love and respect, especially since he'd left the service.

"Don't worry about those tests they took yesterday," Browning was saying, "that was mostly bullshit, too. I already heard from the Doc: you're okay. Except for this supereye he gave you you're just like anybody else." Wychway had risen and was standing nervously behind his chair with his hands resting on its back. Still, he couldn't deny the sense of relief those last words had given him. He let out a lot of air as Browning commanded, "Siddown, goddammit! and hear me out."

Wychway sat.

"Now, what's happened to you," Browning continued in a more reasonable voice, "the 'Big Eye' I'm going to call it—in fact, that's not a bad name for the whole fuckin' operation—Operation Bigeye... Yeah, I like it!" he muttered to himself, then: "Look, Wychway, what happened to you is something which I for one used to call a pie in the sky. I never in hell thought it would ever happen—not in *my* lifetime at least. But here it is, here *you* are; it's happened, and I'm going to jump on it with both feet because it might just be the key I've needed for over a year." He looked hard at Wychway, who was sitting staring at his clasped hands. "You getting this, Charley?"

Wychway looked up.

"Yeah, I'm getting it, more or less," he replied morosely.

"Good. Stay tuned," the irrepressible Browning said as handed Wychway his empty glass.

Wychway went and got him another drink and then refilled his own glass with wine. He was beginning to feel extremely uneasy. In fact he was beginning to get the same feeling he always used to get when he'd climb aboard an aircraft to make another parachute jump: a hollow sort of feeling at the pit of his stomach. Now as from a distance he heard Browning's flat, harsh New England accents.

"I've had an ongoing mission for over a year and I'm overdue. Overdue? Shit, the election's around the corner. —But never mind about that," he censored himself. "Anyway, if I don't get the genii out of the fucking bottle soonest my ass is gonna be grass!"

"You have my deepest sympathy, Mr. Browning," Wychway said drily as he sipped his wine. He was far from feeling the self-possession he was trying to exhibit.

"Listen, smartass—I'll talk and you listen," Browning bristled.

But Wychway, partly from fear, partly out of a sense of righteous outrage, was through listening.

"No, Browning, you listen," he rasped as he leaned forward, and the intensity of his expression silenced the other, at least temporarily. "I don't know what you want from me, but I know this much: it's something you can't order me to do, otherwise you wouldn't have wasted your time coming here, to me, and I know it must be pretty goddammed important.— Important? shit, that doesn't even come close, does it? You *need* me, you need what I've got—thanks to you and your twisted friend, Sibelius, you son of a bitch—to help you do it, whatever it is, and knowing you're part of it I have no doubt that it is of the nastiest. So I don't feel threatened, at least not for now. You can't afford to let anything happen to me, can you?" He didn't wait for, much less did he expect an answer to this last question. "Are *you* getting *this*, Herr Browning?" (Browning's contempt for the Germans and all things German was common knowledge in the Agency.)

When Wychway stopped for breath Browning licked his lips and leaned back in his chair.

"Keep talking, hotshot," he intoned cooly as he kept his gaze leveled at Wychway.

"Okay, so now I'm going to tell you what *I* want, before I even agree to listen to the rest of your undoubtedly bizarre scheme."

"Be careful, Wychway, Browning held up a hairy cautionary hand. Once you're briefed on this, there's no going back. If you change your mind you get put on ice, maybe permanently. You know the drill, even if you're *not* in ops."

"We'll get to that later. Right now, like I said, this is what you've gotta do before this goes any further."

"Yeah?—What?"

"First, you've got to make it known in all the right places that you encouraged me to trade with this Iraqi guy in Munich. Also, that you made a 'bootleg' phone call to Jennings ordering him, unofficially, to go into the 'grab bag' for the twenty K, without telling the station chief. I know you've got that much authority; and besides, Jennings is scared shitless of you—he told me so. And I'm not going to the *Stadtpolizei* in Munich to claim the dough, *nor* am I going to crawl into the station chief's office to turn it in. And, I want all this in writing, your own writing, and signed. We won't need any witnesses, you're handwriting'll be good enough." Wychway couldn't help smiling as he saw how Browning was taking this: there was a possibility, he thought, that the man would crush the glass he was clenching as he stared across almost apoplectically.

"That's all piss and wind, you jumped up, half-assed, feather merchant! (Browning had been a Marine sergeant before joining the Agency; many of his colleagues assumed he thought he still was, at least philosophically). Who in the fucking hell do you think you're talking to?"

"I know exactly who I'm talking to. —There's no use your blowing a gasket over this; I'm not going to change my mind, and that's flat. As you yourself would be likely to say, 'Be reasonable: see it my way'." He smiled as he shook out a cigarette, "Look, Browning, you're a big rabbit in the Agency; besides, this shit goes on all the time, you know that better than I do, and in your racket you're used to lying." He lit his cigarette and exhaled a plume of smoke, glancing at the other out of the corner of his eye. "After all, it's no big deal compared to some of the crap that goes on—e. g., Iran-Contra, a scam which I'm sure has your fingerprints as well other highly notable ones all over it." He paused and looked at Browning who though obviously still furious just as obviously was giving all this some thought. Wychway raised his glass in a mock toast, "Well, sir, do we have a deal, at least to that extent?"

Browning shrugged, then stretched and said:

"You know, I don't like to break balls (I'll bet you don't, thought Wychway), but I gotta tell you how much I wish your old man was sitting where you are right now. He not only was a great operator; he had a sense of humor!" He paused, assumed a martyred expression, and finally said, "Ah, shit,— why not?" It came out as a sort of yawn. But almost immediately he sat up alertly and waggled one large forefinger. "But nothing in writing. I'll do what you said, but I won't sign any goddam statement. You can stick that where the sun never shines, asshole."

"A neatly turned phrase, I'll admit, but that doesn't get it. Uh-uh, It's gotta be in writing. You see, it's a pretty simple equation with you and your kind: you just couldn't be a man of your word and still draw your pay. I think even the little kids who watch TV know that much about people like you."

Browning seemed to reflect for a moment (was there the trace of a smile playing on his lips? Wychway wondered) then he drank the dregs of his scotch, put down his glass, and said:

"I'll tell you what I'll do, jerk-off: I won't put that horse-shit about 'encouraging' you and 'ordering' Jennings and so on in writing—Christ, anybody who's known me for fifteen minutes would know I wouldn't be a party to any asshole scheme like that; besides, what would I be doing dicking around with the likes of you? —but what I will put in writing is a statement to the effect that you're off the hook on your simple-shit operation in Munich. I'll say it was some cover dodge for what we're really going after or something, and now it's a dead issue and anybody who brings it up will be risking putting the big casino in jeopardy, while putting his own dick in the wringer, and so on.—Will *that* make you happy, or are you going to keep playing games?"

Wychway was sure this was as much as he could expect. Even if Browning were to agree to the original terms it wouldn't put him, Browning, in any difficulty—some slight embarrassment perhaps, but no serious trouble—especially if this mission were as colossally important as he'd made it out to be (and as Wychway himself was beginning to believe it must be). Browning just had to save *some* face. Wychway nodded his agreement, upon which, after warning him not to discuss any aspect of this matter, including his wonderful new ability, and telling him he would be notified where and when to report "for the next phase of his briefing," Browning took his leave.

Two days later, as Browning had promised he would, Wychway received the exonerating statement by special courier. He stood there by the door reading after the man had left and though reason fairly shouted the phrase "fool's paradise" at him, he clung to the belief that it still was not too late to back out of this, whatever it was. After all, he had this statement from Browning....

As he walked back through the apartment to find a safe place in which to secrete Browning's testimonial (if any place was safe from these bastards, he mused as he went) he found himself wondering why—since undoubtedly they'd followed him from the time he'd been released from the hospital—why Browning had never mentioned Magda, or at least wondered who lived at the cottage where he'd spent that weekend in Ipswich. He started for the phone, then changed his mind, and went to see if he had another bottle of Corvo. With a thoughtful look on his face he absentmindedly turned the record player on as he went by.

Ten minutes later he was at the phone again, but the number he rang was in London's West End, not Ipswich.

Chapter Ten

The Sadducee

Margaret Ursula Feldon, of the psychology department at Somerville College, Oxford, was a very imposing forty-year-old woman: an intellectual atheist, egoist, dedicated feminist—she was all those things. And she was a striking figure physically as well: blond, blue-eyed, almost six feet tall and very well-proportioned; when well-dressed she could be described as stately. If she'd been endowed with a different personality she might have been called, especially in her salad days, "a thunderingly attractive English rose." Even now that her hair was more gray than blond her still-fresh complexion and regular features gave her an undeniable attractiveness.

But mainly she was a ruthless realist. She espoused no "causes," not because of any sense of impartiality or objectivity in her view of matters or events, but merely because she didn't care. It mattered not a jot to her whether South Africa was run fairly or by white supremacists, or whether the Israeli's would ever agree to a Palestinian homeland in the occupied territories. She received with detachment reports of the Africans who were dying in their millions annually from starvation or disease. She was utterly uninterested in what party controlled the United Kingdom as long as her personal and professional life was not interfered with. Although she would have been too young to have done so at the time Hitler threatened to invade and occupy the British Isles, it was generally agreed (rather jocularly in these less threatening times) among those of her colleagues who knew her best that she probably would have collaborated cheerfully with the Nazi occupiers had that calamity befallen the British.

All this had been taken into consideration before she was approached and recruited by two conservatively dressed men who came up to Oxford from London in the spring of 1988. Since obviously in Professor Feldon's case it would have been patently foolish to have made a peurile appeal to any sense of patriotism, it had been wisely decided that money, hard cash, would be the medium of solicitation. Their offer had been made in the morning; and had been accepted before tea time. The people at the "The Circus" realized that they wouldn't have to concern themselves with Feldon's defection unless she were offered more money by another intelligence organization—if penetration were to made in her case the lance would have to be tipped with pounds or, with the Russians now virtually out of the picture, more likely in Saudi riyals, or dollars in the hands of Britain's American "cousins." But with the tight surveillance they kept on the Saudi agents and the economic situation in the US—which was becoming more dire almost daily—forcing budgetary restraint, this was seen as no serious threat. The Germans, still living under the onus of Nazism and the Holocaust, wouldn't dare, and the French in their isolationist arrogance didn't care. The Italians of course didn't have the money. And after all, what did it matter? Such a link as Dr. Feldon would provide in the intelligence chain would be of the smallest and least important and, barring the odd foreign faculty member, would have no international ramifications.

Professor Feldon's rather innocuous and routine task was to report periodically on the political inclinations and, if such existed, the political activities of the other members of the faculty of Somerville in particular and, if available, on those of the remainder of the university in general. Occasionally special reports or other duties might be required of her, she was told.

Her student, Magda Karolyi Tisza, fell into this latter category. Though of noble birth Magda was relatively poor. Also she had not yet acquired the British citizenship which she wanted so badly. And so it happened that Feldon, who in addition to her tutorial responsibilities had become Magda's sometime lover, had acquired the girl as a sort of sub-agent, an amateurish one to be sure, but one who nonetheless had proven herself to be effective, especially in this latest matter of the American, Charles Wychway. And now for a highly classified reason to which neither woman was privy Magda had suddenly become extremely important to The Circus. Feldon had been informed very recently that because of Magda, her new handlers now would come from the "E" Division (Foreign Nationals) of MI5. All Feldon knew was that Magda had been given the mission of gaining the confidence of this "Wychway."

And therein lay the rub. Margaret Feldon's only concession to her emotions lay in the self-realization that she was passionately, almost desperately in love with the young and beautiful girl who now sat with evident composure on the opposite side of her large mahogany desk. And Margaret was becoming increasingly afraid lest she lose her lover, however tenuous and occasional their affair had been thus far.

Now in a voice she strove to control she asked:

"You've been *with* the man, haven't you?"

"How do you mean, 'with'?"

"Must I use plain words? Did you let him *screw* you? Ha!— Perhaps I should have asked: Did you *want* him to screw you?"

"What possible difference would it make? I mean, would it matter as long as I did what I was instructed to do?"

In a voice that barely reached across the desk the other asked:

"Did you kiss him— 'down there', I mean?"

"Margaret, please!"

"Did you?" the woman fairly shouted.

"No. —Yes! Why are you doing this? I have my own life. You can't—"

"All right!" the other broke in angrily, "I don't want another row, let's just leave that for the moment."

"Why can't we just leave it, full stop?" Magda murmured looking away.

There was silence for at least a minute before Feldon shook her head impatiently and changed the subject:

"Have you read my monograph yet, the one I gave you last week?"

"The one on relative guilt, or guilt relativity, or whatever it was? —I haven't had time yet."

"Perhaps if you spent less time in bed with unattractive men—"

"He's not unattractive," Magda cut her off, "and I was only doing what you told me to do."

"Up to a point, yes. But all right. Enough. Since you're here ostensibly as a student, and I spoke of unattractive people, let me paraphrase just a part of the introduction of that paper for you." She lit a cigarette and smiled, as if at some secret joke.

"Yes, publicly it's known as 'The Theory of Relative Guilt', but privately I call it 'The Theory of Relative Assholes'—marvellous, these expressions we've been picking up from the American television programs, are they not? In this case, anyway, the classification, however coarse, is extremely apt, I think. But, to get on with it:

"There are three groups of people in this world, Magda: a relatively small group of assholes who have become successful by their own ability and effort, or just fortuitously, or by a combination of all these things; and two other groups of assholes. One of these latter groups, though larger than the first, also is relatively small and consists of people who, though not as powerful or authoritative as the first group, somehow, by their own efforts or otherwise, have achieved a state of credibility with the last group, which comprises the remainder of mankind.

"The assholes in this last group, a vast sea of humanity, are controlled by the first two groups: generally by the first group, who are elitest and control economies, polities, and, deities;

and particularly by the second group because they tell the last group how to live. As one example, when you hear an unattractive, unintelligent, uncoordinated, in short useless, person say, "I can do anything if I want to badly enough!" you can be certain that that person has been convinced by a member of the second group (a 'professional counselor' or an 'expert' of some kind, often for a high fee) that this nonsense is true. This of course is all part of the black divinity of the 'I'm okay, you're okay' travesty which has been perpetuated for any number of selfish reasons since its sinister appearance in America in the 1960's.

"The first group is amused and permits this to go on; people are easier to control if they're happy, or at least if they think they are (the old bread and circuses, and so on). The second group, seen as authoritative on the subject of "How one should live one's life," achieves fame and money in any number of ways: by "treating" members of the third group on an individual or "encounter group" basis, as guests on television or radio 'talk' shows, by publishing books, or by contact with the lumpen proletariat in some other way. It doesn't matter whether they, the members of this second group, believe in what they're saying and doing or not—the harm will be done.

"The third group stumbles through life full of anxieties, confusion, and frustration, not understanding what they're doing wrong—why they do not become beautiful, adept, popular, successful, rich, and all the rest of what they've been told they are capable of achieving—because, after all, they've been told they can have the very best of everything, all they have to do is *want* it. Ultimately they feel guilty about something they cannot define. This kind of baseless 'guilt' is nothing to the guilt the members of the first two groups *should* feel but have habituated themselves to override, thanks mainly to their vanity, pride, avarice, and greed, and to a lesser extent their ignorance...."

Magda, who though she despised Feldon's easy coarseness, had been listening with interest. Now she let out her breath.

"Good Lord! Do you really believe all that?"

"Believe it? It doesn't take an act of faith. It's true!"

Magda sat silently staring at the desk in front of her, and Margaret, sensing Magda's disapproval and wishing to avoid another squabble, went back to Wychway, doing her best now to be impersonal.

"Well, if you have no further questions let us leave this mainly depressing subject and get back to your friend, the American." Magda looked uncomfortable, and Feldon hurried on. "This Wychway, did he tell you about something remarkable that he'd experienced, something to do with his eyesight?"

"Yes. He said he had this ability of seeing, seeing things magnified somehow. He was playing darts, or something, in Bury St. Edmunds, and that was when he discovered it."

"Do you think he's told anyone else?"

"I don't think there would have been an opportunity before he told me." She hesitated. "He was going to see a friend in London, actually a friend of his late father's; he may have told him. It was an Englishman, an older man, a Major Somerville. That's all I can tell you."

"What was his state of mind," the older woman, having regained her composure, asked.

"How do you mean?"

"Well, was he very concerned about this, this freakish quality of his? Was he apprehesive, frightened, what?"

Magda was thoughtful as she said, "Well, he seemed to be trying to make light of it, but underneath I'm certain he was frightened. My God! who wouldn't be? Especially as he has a history of head injuries—he was badly wounded in Vietnam, and had some strange after effects."

"So, he told you about that, did he?"

"He told me many things about himself. —I, I think he is not a very happy man." Magda took her cigarettes out of her bag, lit one, and inhaled deeply. She threw the crumpled pack on the desk, and the Professor reached across and helped herself.

"His happiness is not your concern," the other said pointedly. "When do expect to see him or hear from him again?"

Magda picked a minute piece of tobacco (Wychway had been delighted to notice that she smoked non-filtered cigarettes) from the tip of her pink tongue before she answered.

"He said he would get in touch with me from Germany after he knew more about his condition. I assume he meant he would telephone me." Magda raised a hand to forestall the obvious question, "No, he has not contacted me yet. You shall know it when he does—if he does."

"And that's all?"

"That's all."

"So far as your assignment is concerned, yes...." Margaret Feldon sighed as her voice trailed off. Finally she shrugged and said, "I'm sure you realize the sensitive nature of this information? —I'm talking about the incredible visual ability of this, this Wychway person, of course. I have no idea where it all will lead...."

"What are they going to do with him? Do you know? Can *I* know?"

"I have no idea what purpose he will serve, and quite frankly I couldn't care less. Whatever it is they are up to, this is what is called a 'close hold' operation, extremely close hold. — God, what disgusting English these people use; I'm sure they acquired that one from the Americans—and I've been told that if any information about this man gets beyond us, you and me that is, the consequences will be dire. *There's* a word for you: 'dire.' I'm sure what they meant to convey is that the consequences would be dire not merely for the mission's sake, whatever in the bloody hell that is, but for us, you and me, as well."

As Magda resignedly nodded her understanding Margaret rose from her desk and her face softened. She wanted to change to a previous, more personal subject, and she knew that her earlier approach had been the wrong one. She walked around to Magda's side, raised the girl's chin, and kissed her full on the mouth.

"I do love you, you know," she whispered huskily. She then went to the door and locked it.

When she returned she kicked off her shoes and fell on her knees before Magda's chair, her hands on the girl's knees. When Magda drew back slightly and turned her head away the older woman gazed at her imploringly and began murmuring incantations of love while caressing her feverishly. Magda frowned her annoyance, but only slightly, and then, uncrossing her long, slim legs and reaching for the hem of her dress, slid forward towards the edge of her chair as a faraway look replaced her little frown. In a few moments her face had assumed a bemused, almost mystical expression, then this expression became fixed as gradually her eyes become glazed. Her knuckles turned white as she gripped the arms of her chair and her mouth became convulsed in a spasm of ecstasy.

When a few minutes later Magda fell back in her chair with a long shuddering groan Margaret raised her head, took the limp girl by the shoulders, and once again kissed her fully and lingeringly on the mouth. She then rose and backed to her desk, with the fixed light of genuine passion in her eyes, removing her skirt, pantyhose, and panties as she went. She sat well back on the desk and brought her heels up on its edge, and as Magda approached she spread her knees wide and lay back, disarranging a number of small objects as she went.

Not many minutes later both women, now completely naked, were on the floor, striving so passionately neither of them heard the discreet knock on the door, or Feldon's secretary's voice, rising in volume each successive time she called out that the professor was late for an important conference.

PART TWO

THE PILGRIMS

Chapter Eleven

The Eremite

Except for two brief walks in a nearby wood Wychway didn't leave his apartment during the time he waited for more explicit instructions. For one thing he didn't want to chance the possibility of meeting someone in whom he might be tempted to confide; for another Browning had made it clear that he should have as little contact as was feasible with anyone, to include the other Agency people with whom he worked and who had been told that Wychway had been ordered back to the States on an extended, indefinite assignment and that a "suitable replacement" to cover his absence would be forthcoming. And Wychway didn't have to be told that in an operation of this one's seeming importance any inadvertant revelations would be dealt with harshly, perhaps even fatally. Several times during this period he'd considered calling Doctor Sibelius and "telling him off," but each time he'd rejected the idea as foolish and non-productive.

If Florian had noticed his preoccupied manner and his

manifest edginess he'd been discreet enough not to mention it. Since the young man's return from the Austrian Alps Wychway's anxiety had been patently obvious, but nothing had been discussed; and if Florian thought his employer's reclusive new habits also were strange he kept these thoughts to himself. Thankful for Florian's polite restraint, Wychway cursed Browning anew for the unjust calumnies he'd heaped upon this intelligent and faithful servant.

On Halloween morning Florian brought him the plain, uninscribed envelope which must have been thrust under the door sometime during the night. Wychway tore it open and read the terse message:

Kneipe Zum Schlossquelle 011500 Nov.

The next afternoon at three o'clock Wychway entered the Zum Schlossquelle, a low-class pub three blocks from his flat, and met Ward, Browning's bag man and general factotum. The meeting lasted less than ten minutes. After telling Wychway, essentially, that he was to vanish from his present locale within seventy-two hours and reappear at the Hohenfels Infantry Training Area in Bavaria shortly thereafter, Ward put down his half-finished beer and left Wychway sitting there, digesting these terse orders which would lead him to the next phase in his orientation program.

According to his instructions Wychway packed one small bag. Everything he would need, he had been told, would be furnished as he went along in the preparation phase of the operation. He called a number Ward had given him and arranged for the storage of his car at Eucom headquarters. Luckily he was able to arrange temporary employment for Florian with an American couple he knew at Kelly Barracks who were looking for a housekeeper. Although he had a good general idea of the type of operations Browning usually controlled he would not let himself dwell on the ominous possibility that his absence well might be permanent rather than temporary.

Arrangements had been made for him to be flown to

Bavaria in an Army courier plane. Browning didn't want to chance Wychway's being seen on any public carrier, surface or air, and he didn't want to have to worry about another Autobahn accident, whether Wychway or someone else was driving. Magda was increasingly on his mind those last few days. He fought the urge to call her   and lost He called from the telephone exchange at the local *Postamt* the evening before he was to be picked up for the drive to the airport at Echterdingen. Since it was a Sunday he called her Ipswich number. She answered almost immediately.

"Oh, Charles, I am so glad you have called. I was beginning to be so worried about—"

"Yeah, yeah, I know," he interrupted her gently, "but listen, I can't talk very long (her phone might be bugged, he thought, recalling Browning's confirmation of the watchers in England). I just wanted you to know I'm all right—looks like I'll be a freak for life, but otherwise I'm okay. I might get a second opinion when I get a chance—"

"What do you mean, when you get a chance?" she interrupted in turn.

"Well, I've got to go away for a while, I'll be kind of busy."

"Away? Away where—can you tell me?"

Just as he was about to tell her he would be in Bavaria for a time Wychway realized the last half of her question was a little odd. Considering the ordinary description he'd given her of his job and duties why shouldn't he be able to tell her? For a reason he couldn't have explained he decided to stick to Browning's script:

"Oh, I've gotta go back to the States for a while. I'm told it's a 'special assignment,' but I'm sure it'll be more of the same boring old jazz—same atmosphere, different hemisphere, that's all," he quipped.

"Can I see you before you leave?"

"I'm afraid not, Magda. My plane leaves tomorrow." That much was true, he reflected.

"Please let me hear from you when you get to the US,"

Magda was saying.

"Yeah, I'll write, don't worry." Wychway knew things like that were arranged routinely in situations like this. In fact one of Browning's flunkeys probably already had typed a dozen phoney letters and postcards for him to copy, sign, and address. These would go back to the States in the embassy pouch, to be posted there periodically from any number of different places. "Well, I gotta get off now," he finished lamely, "got to pack an' all that crap. I'll be in touch, Good Lookin' — And for Chrissake don't worry about me" (he secretly hoped she would).

"All right, Charles, I'll try not to," she cleared her throat, "I didn't think I would miss you so much, I—"

"Don't worry; maybe I'll be able to sneak a quick trip back over here to Germany. If I can, I'll book through Old Blighty and come up to Oxford or Ipswich for a day or two; but I've got to get to the States before I can check all that out. Right now I don't know what the hell is going on." Which was true enough, he thought.

"All right then. I will say 'Goodbye' for now, Charles, and please, please take care of yourself!"

"'Bye, Magda, and I'll be thinking about you, you can be sure of that." And with that he hung up. And he *was* thinking of her, but perhaps not in quite the way that she would have wanted him to.

He was almost out of the building when he stopped, thought for a moment, then went back and put through a call to J. D. Somerville's place in Bayswater.

That night the third and last sealed envelope was thrust under his door; it told him to walk out of his apartment building the next morning "at 0700." A white BMW would be there waiting to take him to the airport.

Next morning he stood in the entryway for ten minutes scanning the street before the BMW surged up and stopped with a squeal of rubber. The man at the wheel opened the door on the passenger side and beckoned him to hurry. There was another man in the back seat. As Wychway stood there momentarily the driver snatched his old battered valpac (actually a vintage B-4 bag passed down from his father) and threw it over the back of the front seat. The man in the back cursed as he settled the bag on the seat next to him and Wychway got in.

"Gawddam', Doowane, Ah had a cigarette in mah mouth when you done thet!"

"Fuck it, we're late," was the other's laconic answer as he drove off with more protestations from the tires.

Wychway remembered something his father used to say about "getting the edge" on people, especially at the first encounter.

"Damned right, you're late. I was told I could walk out of my place and the car'd be there."

"Don't yew worry about it, good buddy, that bird ain't goin' nowheres without *us*. Now let's can it, I got some drivin' tuh do."

They were on the Autobahn before the driver broke the silence.

"Name's Link, C.D. Link," he announced without taking his eyes off the road. He jerked a thumb over his shoulder, "That there's Larry Ledbetter in the back seat. We used to call 'im Leadbelly, till he found out that other Ledbetter wuz a nigger singer," he added with a self-satisfied chuckle. —So you're Wychway, huh? Heard a' you, Wychway. We was in Nam about the same time. I 'uz on my fifth tour when you wuz on yer first."

"Yeah, well, I couldn't make it over there any sooner. I had to grow up first." He had intended this to be ironic, but as he spoke it seemed rather lame.

Link snorted. "Yeah. An' I heard y'all didn't stay very long neither. Yer career got kinda cut off, didn' it?" When Wychway merely nodded Link glanced at Ledbetter in the rear view mirror and added, "Yeah, we got the word from Lew Browning about you, Wychway. We're supposed to treat y'all like a piece of Moorano glass—especially yore haid." He glanced again in the mirror, "Course, with all the trainin' Ah got to put yew through that ain't gonna be so easy."

"I know you'll do your best," was all Wychway could think of replying.

Link's annoyance at this remark was obvious as he glanced across at Wychway.

"Yeah, well, anyway, from now till yore deployed I'm gonna stick to you like shit to a blanket, y'all kin bet yer last pair a' jump boots on thet."

Ledbetter didn't improve Link's mood when, a few minutes later, he contributed an old joke which even Wychway remembered hearing about Link who, mainly because of all the time he had spent in Southeast Asia rather than his doubtful record there, had achieved a certain notoriety, if not fame.

"Was Link ever an MIA in Nam?" the voice from the back seat chanted the query; and then the reply, "I don't think so, why?"—followed by the punchline: "'cause then they could've called him, 'The Missin' Link'!"

Yes, Wychway had heard about Charles Duwayne Link (Link and his pals pronounced it Doowane) from Attessuc, Georgia. He must be about fifty now and undoubtedly still was the red-necked, prejudiced asshole who'd thoroughly enjoyed serving at all those oases of coarse and orderly dullness, surrounded by their vast cultural deserts, which the US Army had to offer—places like Forts Benning, Bragg, and Campbell. A retread who'd bullshitted himself into the Agency and ultimately had become one of the lesser instruments of Browning's policy. When Wychway was at Ft. Bragg waiting for his medical discharge in the spring of 1975 he'd heard the rumour that Link had cashed in handsomely on the panic that accompanied the final American pullout. As the Armed Forces Radio Network played "White Christmas" over and over (the signal for the hurried bailout) Link, through his contacts at the US Embassy and Than Son Nhut Airbase, on the outskirts of Saigon, was pocketing thousands of dollars per head from wealthy, terrified Vietnamese—who were certain to be on the communists' "black list"—to fly them out of Vietnam. It was rumored also that it was Link who had originated the "Special Forces Prayer": "Yea, though I walk through the valley of the shadow of death I will fear no evil— 'cause I'm the meanest son of a bitch in the valley!" But, no, thought Wychway, the story almost certainly was apocraphal; the man didn't have the wit even for that.

Now as they pounded along the Eleven Autobahn on the southern outskirts of Stuttgart Link asked over his shoulder:

"Larry, d'ya remember how far that fuckin' turnoff fer the Flooghaven is from here?"

"Shit, C.D., Ah on'y been there the onc't..."

Wychway, who had never been to the Echterdingen airport, closed his left eye and scanned the level stretch ahead, taking the next two blue and white direction signs in turn. The second sign was more than a mile away.

"Take the one after the next one; it's about a mile and a half from here," he said with assurance.

Link glanced at him as if he were about to speak, then with the merest of nods began moving over into the right lane.

Link drove to a remote part of the airport, on the opposite side from the terminal, where a US Army Twin Beach awaited them, the two pilots standing by its door. As Link and Wychway approached one of them looked at his watch and nodded to his companion but said nothing as they climbed in and moved up to the cockpit. Larry had already driven off in the BMW.

In a little more than forty-five minutes they were taxiing up to the operations building at the Fürstenfeldbruck Luftwaffe base where a blue US Air Force mini-van awaited them. The van took them to a helipad.

A half-hour later their helicopter landed them in front of the headquarters building at the Hohenfels Infantry Training Area. It began snowing as Wychway went inside.

Chapter Twelve

Exegesis

"Well, Charley-my-boy, we meet again, as they say," Browning affected with false geniality as Wychway entered the room.

It was still only eleven in the morning when Wychway, having stowed his few possessions in the billet which had been assigned him, met with Browning in a "secure" room which had been set up as an operations center for what had now been dubbed officially Operation Bigeye. Browning nodded to a chair near the field table at which he was seated. They were alone.

"Not much in the way of comfort, I know. But we just got set up, and we'll be getting some more furniture in here today. But we've nailed down a secure area for ourselves for the duration of Bigeye; anybody tries to get through our perimeter fence gets wasted, with no questions asked. —Siddown, siddown," he added enthusiastically as briskly he went through the motions of washing his hands.

Wychway's dislike of Browning went up a notch as he sat and lit a cigarette. It was little wonder, he mused, that the man had people such as Link around him.

"It's okay to smoke, I suppose?"

"Smoke? —Personally, I don't give a shit if you burst into flames; but in your case, I'd begin to take it easy on the weeds for a while. We've got a hell of a training program set out for you. But more about that later. Now," he picked up some papers from the table, "I've been going over copies of your old

201 file and your DD 214" (Wychway's army records of his qualifications and experience), he tapped the papers with a blunt finger, "and my wondering eyes behold that you're not only airborne qualified but a Pathfinder as well, and when you were in the Special Forces you had a primary MOS in light weapons and a secondary in demolitions. Also, I see you spent six months with MACSOG, and only left because you got hit pretty bad. —Verrry interesting." Browning took his cigarettes out, lit one, and tried to settle himself more comfortably in his unyielding wooden chair before he went on.

"How you feeling, okay?"

"Yeah, I'm all right, I guess."

"Way outta shape is all, right?—And you've still got 'it,' if what Link told me about you reading signs on the Autobahn is right," Browning went on without waiting for an answer," or did you know where the airport was?"

"No, Link was right—it, uh, still works, but I prefer to pretend it isn't there. I just don't wink anymore," Wychway said resignedly. "But look, can I know what the hell is going on? What am I doing here?"

"Obviously, you're getting briefed, Wychway."

Wychway was sure he wouldn't want to hear what was coming, but for that reason wanted to get it over as soon as possible. A phrase from P.G. Wodehouse passed inconsequently through his mind: "The surgeon's knife, what?"—which in his case also was a terrible pun. Trepidation mixed with impatience as he almost pleaded:

"Well, can we get *on* with it?"

Browning ignored the question.

"If you were with MACSOG I shouldn't have to tell you what a maximum security operation is all about, and this one is so close hold it goes beyond 'close to the vest'—this one we gotta keep under our skin. —Got it?" He made eye contact, and when Wychway nodded he went on.

You ever read a book called *The Day of the Jackal?*"

"Yes."

"Remember the equipment he needed? All that pain in the ass routine with the car and crutches and hollow tubes and all that shit? Jesus, what a crock! —Do you remember that?"

"Yeah, I remember. What about it?"

"Well, there's an easier way now."

"How, easier?"

"You could do it with any good, long-range rifle, and you wouldn't need a scope; and even with a scope, to get a head shot or any other killing shot, you'd have to be within a couple of hundred yards. And then, it's hard to 'pan around' the general target area with a scope; you gotta 'find' your target first, then go back to the scope and zero in with that—all that bullshit. With the magnification you've got it wouldn't matter, you could stand off a thousand yards—"

"What the hell am I supposed to be *doing* at a thousand yards?"

"Knockin' somebody off, asshole, or didja think this was gonna be an international small arms competition we were gettin' you ready for?"

Wychway leaned back in his chair, slowly shaking his head as he said: "Uh-uh. You've got the wrong boy. Vietnam was one thing, but this? Uh-uh, I'm not gonna be anybody's button man. Why not get some 'local asset,' a guy from in-country—whatever country it happens to *be*—to be the shooter?"

"We were trying, but then you came along with the bug-eye—too good an opportunity to waste, especially with those R & D guys breathing hard about finally meeting the requirement. Besides, you know the conventional wisdom about using your own talent if you possibly can." Browning's controlled patience was obvious as he continued. "This ain't a volunteer mission, Charley. You're it. There's no 'if' about your doing this, just when, and maybe a few more details about how, and where. You don't think we went through all that Sibelius bullshit just in the hope you'd say 'yes' do you?"

Wychway was thoughtful for half a minute before he looked back at Browning; then drumming his fingers on the field table he said:

"Anyway, it wouldn't work, even if I were Buffalo Bill Cody and had a buffalo gun. There's a major problem with what you're saying. It just wouldn't work."

"Why in the hell not?"

"Because I wouldn't be able to focus on the sights. I just couldn't get sight alignment, let alone sight picture."

"What the fuck are you talking about? Sibelius told me—"

"Never mind what Sibelius told you. Listen to me for a minute!"

"Awright, spit it out."

"O.K—Did this latter-day goddam Dr. Frankenstein say anything to you about minimum and maximum ranges, especially minimum ranges?"

Browning looked thoughtful. "Yeahhh, I think he did...." Then his expression froze. "Holy Mother of Fucking Pearl!—that just didn't register. God*dammit!*"

"Yeah, there it is. I can throw killer darts, as long as the board's at least the regulation distance away, but anything closer than that and—"

Browning was already on his way to the door. "I'm gonna have to think about this; I'm sure we can work it out. I gotta go talk to Link. —Wait here!"

"You do that," said Wychway, who suddenly felt better as the door slammed shut.

Left alone for twenty minutes Wychway wandered around the dingy room. He was thumbing through the large assortment of dirty, dog-eared, back numbers of multinational 'skin' books and magazines he'd found in one corner when Browning bustled back in.

"Wouldn't work, would it?" Wychway dropped the large, soft-backed Italian publication of pornographic movie stills he'd been perusing with increasing interest and ambled back towards the center of the room.

"Siddown. Now shut up and listen. —We got it."

"Got what?" Wychway sat down again in the same uncomfortable chair.

"You'll use a light machine gun. Not one of those two-bit Uzi's or Tech Nines or Tens, or whatever the fuck they're callin' them now: a real one, like maybe an M60—. Naw, not an M60," he corrected himself, "too heavy, and they're all probably in the Smithsonian by now, anyway—something better, if we can get our hands on it in time, good for a couple of thousand yards, and solid tracer, no one-in-four bullshit. You gotta be able to see the bullets, or whatever, strike. You're gonna get the son of a bitch when he's in the open, anyway. Besides, his security is so tight, dense might be a better word, you couldn't get anywhere near him, even in a suicide attempt."

Wychway winced at those last few words.

"Can I know who the 'son of a bitch' is at least?"

"We haven't decided yet. I mean, it's down to two of 'em and I don't have the final decision yet which one we're going after. It won't matter as far as the first part of your training goes anyway."

"Oh, really? Well, as long as the bids are still out can I suggest a candidate?"

"Who'd it be, me?" Browning smiled archly.

"No, that fucking ape of yours, Link."

And as Browning's grin widened Wychway realized that there are people who can smile all day long, but it never comes through; their eyes are devoid of any expression, like a shark's or a snake's. Browning, very businesslike now, went on:

"You'll be working for an oil company, not an American one, maybe Italian or German. What language do you speak best, besides Arabic, I mean?"

"English?"

"Goddammit, Wychway—"

"My Italian's pretty good, but I guess my German is a little more precise, even though I've been told my accent still ain't what it oughta be."

"You can be Austrian, or maybe a Swiss; then, if you speak shit German they won't know."

"An Austrian would know."

"There won't be any fucking Austrians around."

"How're you gonna know that?"

"That's on my end of it, let me worry about shit like that."

"Swell. A minute ago you were talking about who 'we're' going after. So where do you get this 'we' shit? Are you going with me on this little detail?"

"Cool it, Wychway. You know what I'm talking about. And I *gotta* know what I'm talking about. You think we can afford to send you in there on a deal as big as this and let your cover get blown over some dumb-shit mistake like that? —We thought about passing you off as a Brit, but if, just if, you did get your dick stuck in the wringer our Limey friends would raise a million dollars worth of the purest hell over it. No, your gonna be a nice, neutral, Austrian oilfield worker looking for a job."

"So, it'll be a Son of the Desert I'm going after, whoever he is, right?"

"Let me worry about that for now."

"Bestimmt, Sie ist ein richtige Esel."

"What the fuck's that supposed to mean?"

"I was just practicing my Austrian German."

"For the time being I'm gonna have to put up with a certain amount of your shit, Wychway, but don't push me too far."

Wychway, who was just beginning to assimilate what it was he was going to be expected to do and for whom this entire scheme was beginning to assume a quality of nightmarish unreality, answered in the gravelly voice of Jack Benny's Rochester:

"Yezz, Boss." He suddenly felt giddy, almost drunk, as he began to grasp the implications of what the other man had been saying.

Browning mistook his reply for professional sangfroid, or at least bravado.

"That's the spirit, Charley. But you don't have to call me 'Boss,' make it 'Lew,' whydoncha?"

By this time Wychway was in a cold sweat.

"What if I'm not buying this, 'Lew'; what if I just say, 'No'?" he asked very seriously.

Browning shook his head disappointedly as he raised both hands in mock exasperation. Now he leaned forward and spoke earnestly:

"We're beyond that, Charley. And you know better than to ask that. Aside from what I said before about all we've done to get you this far, there's been too much said already, you know that. Christ, we're halfway through this briefing. You already know too fucking much about what's in the mill. And it wouldn't take a goddam genius to see that an operation of this seriousness has to come from the top, Charley, and I mean the *top*—the fucking *penthouse*, Charley!"

"Yeah, I see," said Wychway, whose fear now was turning to anger, "and if I know so much *now* that I would have to be put away if I flat refused to go, what about if I went? Shit, I'd know even more, wouldn't I? Talk about being a foremost authority! So tell me I wouldn't be an even bigger threat to you guys then, assuming of course that my happy ass makes it through this lunatic drill. Oh, yeah! —How about them fuckin' apples, Lew?"

Browning's chair scraped as he twisted his body to look out the window before he answered. His back was turned as he said:

"No, no, no, Charley. You're not thinking, or maybe you just don't know enough about this kind of stunt. Win, lose, or draw, you can't hurt us. See, if you were ever to start shooting your mouth off we'd just disclaim any knowledge. Shit, it's happened a hundred times, a thousand times. We'd give 'em 'Script Three,' or whatever. We'd just say, 'Yeah, sure, the guy *did* it (or tried to do it). So what? He's just another crazy. Sure, he was with the CIA for a while. He was a feather merchant, a candy-assed reporter in Current Intelligence who must have had delusions of grandeur. Didn't he try, on his own and without authorization, to play games with some Iraqi rag head in Munich? He must have gotten completely carried away to think he could pull off assassinating, let's say, 'X,' on his own that way. Of course, there was that terrible head wound he received in Vietnam, poor boy. His friends said he never was quite the same after that, etc., etc....' Like that, simple.

"We're experts at lying through our teeth, Charley. It's become a way of life, not just for us who are paid to lie, but unfortunately for the Great American Unwashed and Unannointed, for every son of a bitch inside the Beltway, from the Oval Office on down. And if you were to start shooting your mouth off now, assuming we let you, we'd just say you were crazy. Sibelius has phony medical records that would back us up. That, connected to your existing medical history, would put paid to you and your 'bullshit'—and bullshit is what it would be seen as by every 'right-thinking' Westerner who's gotten so used to believing *our* bullshit he wouldn't think twice about yours."

"*Si fecisti, nega!* " muttered Wychway.

"What'd you say?"

"Nothing, just thinking out loud."

"Think all you want, just listen. —Now, if you tried to blow the operation while you were in the target area we could take care of that, too. You don't think you're going to be the only asset we'll have in the area of interest, do you? And it'd be a bitch for you to spot him because he ain't gonna be a Westerner, that's for shit-sure. But you can bet your ass he'll be one of the best. Oh yeah, he will. He will be on *this* one. You getting this, Wychway? Excuse the goddam speech by the way, but obviously it's time you learned a few of the hard facts of this rotten life." He paused for breath, and as Wychway stared over his grizzled head and through the dirty window at the few brown leaves blowing across the dusty compound in front of the headquarters building he went on:

"Also I guess I better remind you of the papers you signed when you joined this outfit," he raised an admonitory hand, anticipating Wychway's protest, "I know, I know. You came in with a medical profile, and with the understanding that you had no committment to field duty or special ops. — But see, you've gone beyond that now. And you did agree to

perform duties for which you had a special aptitude, don't
forget that. So now, it's a whole different ball game for you.
It isn't as if now, being 'normal,' you can be considered for
unlimited duty; it's that you've got a special qualification for
a special job."

"Yeah, thanks to you, goddammit—and that quack,
Sibelius."

"Not altogether, Charley," Browning said as he turned
around. "You'd also have to say 'thanks' to that Dink who shot
you in the head in Nam, and thanks to yourself for ever joining
the Company and for trying to straighten out a curve in the
Autobahn at a hundred and sixty miles an hour while in the
process of trying to do something you weren't getting paid to
do and had no business trying on your own, and even thanks to
the eggheads who came up with QHR-242—never mind what
that means for now.

"You know, Charley, if a guy started looking for reasons
why he found himself in a certain place in this fucked up
world he'd go crazy, or at least get goddammed frustrated." He
sighed, scratched his fleshy nose and added, "Anyhow, there's
no way out of it now. You gotta go, unless something unfortunate happens to you during the orientation and training phase,
and we don't expect anything like that. I've made that clear to
everyone involved."

"I've heard."

"From Link?"

"Yeah, it was among his first gracious words."

"Don't let that Cracker bother you. He's a pain in the ass
and off duty I couldn't stand being around him for thirty seconds, but he knows his onions as far this phase of the operation is concerned. He'll be in charge of your training program,
the physical outdoors shit, but—"

"Jesus Christ! Lew—"

"Now wait a minute. *I'm* in charge of this operation, and
so I'm reponsible for administration, training, deployment,
everything, overall. But I can't be here all the time, and even if

I could I'm sure as hell not in shape to run your ass all over Hohenfels. But be advised: *all* Link is reponsible for is training, and just the outdoor stuff at that; area studies, briefings, and so on will be in other hands. I may ask his advice on ops from time to time, but that's all it is: advice. *Watashiwa*, I, will make the decisions, about everything, and that also goes for your training, too, no matter what that hayseed says. Keep that in mind. But unless it's something absolutely outrageous, especially if it has to do with physical risk, most especially to your head, even more than that, to your eyes, do what he tells you. Think of him as a training aid, nothing more. You don't have to socialize with him."

"Give me a break!"

"I know. It makes you wonder sometimes whether the Agency shouldn't hire somebody from a finishing school, like they did for the first astronauts."

"What the Agency should do is stay out of zoos when they do their recruiting," Wychway replied. He had taken out a ballpoint pen and was busily scribbling with it.

"For Christ's sake, Wychway, you're not making notes on any of this, are you?"

"Notes? No, no.—Just doodling."

"Doodling what?"

"I'm designing a new American flag...."

"Oh? You fill me with interest. Go on."

"Well," said Wychway as he continued drawing, looking critically at the result from time to time, "a diagonal bar sinister will bisect a pristine White House (or penthouse, if you prefer), which is centered. On one half there'll be a crushed beer can, Bud, I guess, suspended in the cup of a jock strap; on the other an electric guitar and one of those one-size-fits-all baseball caps with the adjusto-strap in the back. Across the bottom, on a flying pennon, will be inscribed: '**Si Fecisti Nega**!' I'm not sure we can keep the red, white and blue color scheme, though. See, we'd need four colors, and—"

"What's this 'see fascisti neighgo' shit, anyway?"

"It's Latin. It means, 'If you did it, deny it'—stonewall!"

"What put all that crap in your head?"

"Oh, what you were saying a little while ago, and thinking about that ape of your's, Link."

"Yer losing it, Wychway. And this ain't the time to lose it."

"Chances are you're right. On both counts," said Wychway as he threw down his pen and looked across at Browning. Both men were silent for a full minute before Browning asked:

"Feeling any better?"

"No, but you've made it pretty clear that doesn't matter a hell of a lot."

Browning looked at his watch as he bent over to open the black Samsonite attaché case which was on the floor next to him.

"You know, the first time I was in Saigon, in '62 I think it was, you could get one of these steel Rolexes for 125 bucks." Anyway, Mr. Rolex tells me the sun is over the yardarm." He took out an unopened bottle of Johnny Walker Black Label scotch, twisted the cork cap out, and handed the bottle to Wychway. "Here. No glasses yet. Goes with the shoddy surroundings. —By the way, what did Sibelius tell you about booze?"

"Not to overdo it," answered Wychway before he took a good long pull.

"Right, I checked with him about that and a few other things concerning your lifestyle."

"Christ Almighty; then why the hell did you ask me?"

"Just checking. —By the way, I know you never got the results of all those tests they took on you, but I did. He cleared you for special ops—no limitations." As Wychway groaned Browning smiled and reached for the bottle, wiped off the neck with his hand, and took a drink. He smacked the cork back in the bottle, which he left on the table as he rose, sighed once more, picked up the attaché case, and said:

"Enough of this shit already. Let's go get some chow. We'll hit the German *Kantina*. The food in that GI Burger King they put in here for the American kids makes me wanna puke, to say nothing of that half-frozen, shit French wine in those little bottles. If we're lucky," Browning continued, brightening, "the Krauts'll have goulasch with *Spätzle* today. And the wine is that good red stuff from the Rheinland Pfalz. They've even got wine glasses, no styrofoam cups."

Wychway reflected momentarily on this hypocricy from the German hater, but merely said: "Jesus, I would've thought with your rank and pay you'd have seven-course French meals, catered."

"Are you shittin' me? As far as anyone knows, we're not even *here*. We gotta blend in with the fuckin' woodwork."

As Wychway followed him to the door he found himself wishing he could be hungry. Or that he were Browning. Or someone else, maybe even Link. Or that he'd never been born.

My God, no, not Link! he thought as the door slammed. What an argument for the pro-choice people! Better never to have been born at all!

Chapter Thirteen

Apotheosis

Despite the fact that he wasn't hungry Wychway thought it an ill omen that the *Kantina* had run out of goulash just before they had had a chance to order their lunch. However, he and Browning settled on what turned out to be a very creditable *Schwein Schnitzel*.

"Your records say you were married once, but you're single now, right?" Browning reopened the conversation as they began to eat.

"Yeah, that's right."

"Any kids?"

"No, you?"

Browning seemed surprised at the question.

"I got nine, here and there, to speak of, as they say. No problem. They're all grown up now. Well, my youngest boy's in college, but he's pretty self-reliant. I just send him a few bucks once in a while. My wife died a few years ago," he added, seemingly as an afterthought.

Somehow this personal aspect of Browning's life made Wychway feel a little more relaxed. He ate a bit of his cutlet, sipped some wine and said:

"Sorry to hear it. You must have been together a long time."

"Nope. She was my second wife; we were only married a couple of years. And don't be sorry, she was a world-class pain in the ass, and my kids hated her. My first wife was all right; she didn't give me any trouble, just kids." He looked up and grinned with his mouth full of food, "I kept her chained to a pipe in the cellar."

Wychway couldn't resist a chuckle as he said, "Groucho Marx supposedly once said to a man with eleven kids: 'I love my cigar, but I take it out of my mouth once in a while.'"

Browning didn't respond to this remark as just then a tall, long-legged, dark-haired young woman came up to their table with a manila folder tucked under her arm. With a perfunctory nod at Wychway, who was still staring at her legs, she leaned over Browning and spoke quietly:

"You said you wanted to know as soon as this came in. I just got it over the scrambler from Langley five minutes ago," she handed the folder to Browning. "I put today's one-time code in there too," she added, then stepped back, and with her weight on one beautiful leg crossed her arms under her ample bosom and waited.

"'Today's one-time code' won't get *this*," Browning said portentously as he extracted a small piece of paper from his wallet, then tore open the sealed envelope, and without taking his eyes off the brief coded message it contained made a vague gesture in Wychway's direction and said distractedly:

"Gloria, this is Charley Wychway. Charley, meet my secretary, Gloria Mundi...." Ball point pen in hand, he had already begun decoding.

Gloria Mundi nodded and flashed an attractive smile at Wychway, who smiled back as Browning finished his decoding, raising one eyebrow as he did so. He replaced the slip of paper in his wallet, closed the folder, handed it back to Gloria, and said simply and somewhat grimly:

"Shred it, then eat the shreds."

Gloria nodded, and with another dazzling smile at Wychway, she left.

"It's firm," Browning looked across between mouthfuls.

"I'd say it's a little more than that," Wychway agreed as he watched Gloria Mundi walking briskly away in her well-tailored olive green mini-skirt. "From behind it looks like two teddy bears screwing under an o.g., blanket. What's her name again?"

"My fucking oath! (he pronounced it oaf). You're gonna do just great on this little trip if every time you see a good lookin' piece of ass your brains drop down to your balls."

"Just trying to cheer myself up. And you gotta admit, she *is* a gorgeous woman. —Well, are you going to tell me? What the hell *is* firm?"

"They've selected the target. It's locked in, final."

"And—?"

"And nothing, Wychway," Browning gritted. "Like I said, you'll know when it's time for you to know and not before, so in the meantime don't be a pain in the ass. You're gonna concentrate on your training program, which starts, under the guidance of your esteemed colleague, Link, tomorrow morning."

Wychway threw his fork into his half-empty plate, sighed, and leaned back in his chair, all the while staring at Browning's set features. Finally he looked away and said:

"Why can't all this just be a bad dream...."

"Shit happens, as the Taoists say."

"Yeah. I'd rather be a Buddhist, though."

"Why a Buddhist?"

"Because they'd say, 'If shit happens it's not really happening.'—Or better still a Protestant: 'Let shit happen to someone else,' I think that's their approach." Of course actually I'm fucked, because I'm nominally a Catholic, and *they'd* say, If shit happens I deserve it...."

"You're losing it again, Charley. Let's get the hell outta here," Browning frowned as he pushed his chair back.

"Yeah.... " Wychway rose, drained his wine glass and threw his napkin on the table, all the while muttering, "If shit happens it is the will of Allah. Yeah, that's it...."

Back in the office Browning opened the conversation before even sitting down at his "desk."

"We're going through another world swing, Charley. Did

you know that *Mein Kampf* is number eight on the Swedish nonfiction bestseller list this week? The Neo-Nazis are getting stronger every day." Browning became thoughtful for a few moments, then added, "Yeah, but that ain't all. The Outfit's been in the shit for too long, what with that Aldridge Ames fiasco, which doesn't seem to *ever* wanna die; and then the disinformation scam right into D.O.D. and the White House. Feeding all that KGB shit in, *knowing* it was shit, just so the defense contractors could stay on the gravy train —"

"*What*?" Wychway fairly shouted, "you mean to tell me that that was done on purpose so that—"

"C'mon Wychway, grow up. Why the hell *else* do you think they did it? I mean *nobody* could explain it, right? Congress's intelligence committees were 'at a loss to understand why,' and so on, the media couldn't explain it, and so forth—*Bullshit!* Nobody *wanted* to explain it, because they *knew*, going both ways: the Agency knew they were getting inflated facts and figures on the Rooski's military capabilities, and the bosses in Defense *and* the Head Shed knew it! It's called, You throw it, and I'll eat it. Oh, yeah. We had the full Kremlin Orchestra playing just the tunes we wanted to hear." With a meaningful look at Wychway Browning ended this diatribe. "And now that *you* know it, Charley, you can forget it. *Verstehen Sie?*"

Wychway responded numbly, "Yeah, I got it. But, Jesus Christ..!

"Never mind Him. It wouldn't surprise me if *He* was in on it, too. What's important *now* is that we do something *good* for a change. So let's get back to this friggin' mission which, I'm told, the guys in the back room are banking on to redeem us in everybody's eyes and, what is infinitely more important, save next year's fucking budget—to say nothing of getting our esteemed President reelected. —So let's get on with the program."

Browning paused again, then announced portentiously:

"It's Saddam Hussein. We're going after Saddam. Most of the latest polls show that the majority of Americans think we should have gotten him when the getting was good: during or right after Desert Storm, nailed him in Baghdad or hung him as a war criminal right after the war. Khaddafi was the other candidate, but I guess he got lucky this time." He waited while Wychway digested this.

"Now, aside from all that other shit I just told you to forget here's some more you're going to lose your memory over. The reason we're doing it *now* is political. The US economy is on its ass, no matter what else you hear to the contrary, and matters otherwise are so bad—like what the hell we're supposed to do about all those guys getting blown away on that "peace keeping" force in Bosnia. On top of that we're almost into another election year, and all the talking heads seem to agree that our boy in the White House ain't gonna make a second term unless he turns the economy around, which even God couldn't do, or he gets credit for something really spectacular elsewhere. So they need a diversion. By the way, I'm telling you all this before you have your mandatory, self-induced amnesia attack because no matter what kind of a shit you think I am I've never sent anybody in harm's way without giving the poor bastard some inkling as to why there's a good chance he's going to lose his ass. Got it?"

Wychway nodded, looked heavenward, and sighed. "Isn't there a law about killing heads of state—the 'Kennedy Law' is it?" He saw Browning's expression and added hastily, "Okay, okay, more gallows humor. But, how about the Mossad? They could handle it on their lunch hour. In fact, if they'd had our approval when—"

"You're missing the whole point. Weren't you listening? *We* gotta do it. We'll never admit we did it, openly; it'll be leaked, an open secret, but we'll get the credit, an' public opinion will be on our side. — But never mind that crap, and just stay with me." Though Wychway found this reasoning rather specious, he remained silent.

"Your training period'll last four weeks: three weeks of basic stuff like weapons refresher, an update on new demolitions equipment you probably never heard of, commo, land navigation, much PT—mostly, longer and longer runs—jump refresher training, and at night, area study, to include map and aerial photo recon. We even got access to Russian spy satellite photos from *Sovinformsputnik* after the Soviet breakup. We could zoom in on the toilet paper roll Saddam uses if we wanted to. Can you believe that people in the States and other countries—private citizens, I'm talking about—have been buying photos of their houses and the cars parked in their driveways, for anything up to $5000? The Russians are so hungry for money they'll sell almost anything—forget the 'almost'!

"Okay, to get on with it. The fourth week'll be devoted mainly to language refresher, with a little on Iraqi dialects and customs, and intensive final briefings, and work with the weapon of choice until you feel like it's part of your body, and until using that special eyeball o' yours becomes second nature. You'll keep up your runs that week, too. Any questions, so far?"

"Yeah. Did you say something about 'jump refresher training'?"

"Yeah, so what?"

"So here's some nice inoffensive Austrian oilfield worker going to Baghdad looking for work, and he decides not to land with the plane and the rest of the people but to just skydive in with his carry-on luggage? What the fuck is going *on*?"

"Stay cool, Charley. The jump training is just part of S.O.P. contingency planning."

"What the hell's all that mean? I never took the long course in Agency gobbledegook."

"That means that in case we should decide we don't want you going through Iraqi immigration or customs formalities at your point of entry, even with your phoney identity, you might have to use different transportation to enter the country. That way, unless your 'controlled' by a spot check somewhere, there won't even be a record that you're in-country. Also, going in 'normally' like any other civilian asshole there might be a bit of a problem at the customs check, like explaining some of the weird shit you'll have in your luggage. Got it?

Jesus! you're enough to make a *martyr* look for a way out."

"Christ Almighty! then there a real possibility that'll happen—that I'll have to jump in?"

"There's a possibility, but the decision ain't up to me; it's with the head shed back at Langley, maybe even higher."

"Yeah, sure, but don't tell me they aren't even gonna ask for your recommendation. And if they do, what're you gonna tell *them*?"

"I don't feel one way or the other about it right now. Stay tuned."

"There's something you seem to have almost studiously avoided talking about."

"What's that?"

"How do I get *out*—or do I?"

"If you go in through the airport like any other visitor, you might come out the same way, unless you really step on your dick getting the job done. If that happens, or we decide to go clandestine on the whole operation, we got an extraction plan, which you'll hear about if it becomes necessary. Of course, your gonna have your phoney Austrian passport, so if we put a phoney entrance stamp in it and you *don't* step on your dick maybe you can come out like a white man, with no sweat after all."

Wychway was silent as he sauntered seemingly aimlessly to a far corner of the office. Then he turned to face Browning, and closed one eye.

"What the hell are you up to now?" Browning asked petulantly.

"Since I can't see if you've got any hair in your ass, I'm counting the ones in your nose," replied Wychway irrelevantly (Browning would have said irreverently).

Silently Browning passed a hand over his face, reminiscent of the old comedian, Edgar Kennedy; then he said with restrained anger:

"It ain't *my* ass that's in question here, you fucking clown, it's yours. Did you get what I was telling you?"

"I understood what you said; it's just that your sense of

political correctness left me almost speechless for a moment,"
Wychway sighed deeply as he reapproached Browning's desk.
"So when do I start tap dancing?"

"Tomorrow morning. Tonight's your last night off,"
Browning said quietly as he pushed the almost-full scotch bottle he'd left on the field table across to Wychway. "Here; I'm
sure you'll be in the mood for a little of this tonight. But I
wouldn't hit it *too* hard if I were you; your pal, Link, or one of
his hoods, will be scratching on your tent about zero-dark-thir-
ty or so." He chuckled, "If I know Link he'll want to do the
honors himself. —And, oh, yeah, I almost forgot. The 'family
physician' will be coming down on a weekly basis to check
your secret weapon, and your general physical condition."

"Sibelius?"

"Who else? By the way, we've given him a code name for
this drill. You said it as a joke this morning, but it ain't a joke
anymore. Whenever he comes through the gate he becomes
Herr Doktor Professur Victor Frankenstein. He's even gonna
have the ID to prove it."

"You gotta be kidding."

"Hell, no. It's S.O.P. on any operation as sensitive as this one:
anybody coming in from the outside hasta have a phony name."

"Jesus. Couldn't you have used a little more imagination?"

"Like what?"

"Well, for openers, Cyclops comes to mind," Wychway
said mock-seriously as he reached for the bottle and pulled
out the cork.

"God*dammit!* Dr. Cyclops! Why the hell didn't *I* think of
that? Well, it's too late now.... Anyway, you got any more
questions?"

"Just one."

"Shoot."

"Where does Gloria Mundi hang out?"

"Lay off, Wychway, that's private stock," Browning growled.

"Sorry!" Wychway spat out ironically, "but I thought one
of the Company's rules was 'Staff doesn't screw staff'."

"*What* fuckin' rules? the other snorted, and then sat looking at his companion as if considering something for a few moments. Finally, with a sardonic smile, he said:

"Oh, hell, why not? If you pull this off, Wychway, you're gonna be a real hero, a celebrity. Christ, you're gonna be a *god*! Hell, who knows? If you pull this off there's always Khaddafi—"

"We were talking about Gloria."

"Okay, just this once, because of the special circumstances, you got the green light. I'll put in the word for you."

"Something like the condemned man's last meal?"

"You could say that. She's eatin' stuff, all right. But try not to make too much noise; her quarters are right next to mine."

Wychway and Gloria had lowered the level of the scotch significantly by the time they headed for her bedroom, taking the bottle with them.

As they were settling into bed Gloria asked casually about his 'sex life'; and suddenly, with uncharacteristic recklessness, Wychway decided to try something new.

"I've pretty much given up chasing women," he lied glibly, "what with this AIDS thing. Then of course there's herpes, yeast infections, and all the other—what do they call 'em now, SCDs or STDs?" He gave her a sheepish look as he turned to her and put his arm around her beautiful white shoulders, "I don't like to admit it, but you look like the kind of person it'd be hard to lie to," he broke eye contact, "so I gotta admit that I, well, barring rare notable exceptions—like you—I usually just play with myself once in a while," he ended with false embarrassment.

To Wychway's satisfaction, Gloria's response was positive and extremely enthusiastic.

"Great! So do I!" her face sobered a little as she added, "whenever I can keep Browning's paws off me, that is." She hesitated a moment, then brightened again and asked, "But have you ever tried the mutual thing?"

Looking her full in the face with the expression of a ten-year-old who had been asked the same question Wychway slowly shook his head, No.

From this point onward Gloria took matters into her own hands, so to speak, and they had arrived at a point where she was explaining (demonstrating, to be more precise) how she "got her vagina off," when Wychway, seeming to recollect something he'd read, suggested that another method which apparently had good results was anal intercourse.

It wasn't long after this that Browning started pounding on his wall.

In a quiet and tender moment before leaving her in the small hours of the next morning Wychway—as a result of too much scotch, the unusual (for him at least) sex, and Gloria's assurance that she was cleared for "access to anything Browning is"—told Gloria who the target was. And under the circumstances he didn't notice the extreme thoughtfulness this information produced in the girl; nor did he reflect at all on the fact that if Browning had wanted her to know what the message contained he wouldn't have used a different code breaker.

Chapter Fourteen

Sic Transit Gloria Mundi

Not much later that morning Wychway felt as if his head had just touched his pillow when there was a pounding on the thin panels of his unsubstantial door. Added to the pounding in his head this was almost more than he could bear. He had barely managed to croak an inarticulate response when the door opened; and bleary-eyed he found himself staring almost uncomprhendingly at Link who, fully dressed in his field uniform, leered at him from the doorway.

"Come on, Wychway! Drop yore cock an' grab yore socks! It's just a case of mind ovuh mattuh: We don't mind and you don't mattuh!" he guffawed lustily.

"Oh, God!" groaned Wychway with a malevolent stare at Link. He sat up in bed with his elbows on his knees, then slowly lowered his face into his hands.

While Wychway was stumbling into his sheetmetal shower stall, Lew Browning was seated at his newly-installed desk, drinking coffee with his assistant, Harry Ward. Browning sipped some hot coffee, put his cup down and said:

"You know, if it wasn't for his record in Nam I'd say let's lose the son of a bitch and go back to the drawing board."

"A little late, isn't it, after all that Sibelius shit? —And, you know, I keep thinking about how great his father was at stunts like this."

"Yeah, there *is* that. Charley Witchway had the balls of a

blind burglar. —But still, I don't think this squirrel would make a good pimple on his ol' man's ass.

"Look at it this way, Boss: we're gonna get paid, whatever happens, once we get him in there—"

"Oh yeah? And what if he decides to defect? I wouldn't put it past the liberal-minded bastard."

"Our in-country boy offs him, no?"

"Great, and what about the target—the *real* target now, not Saddam, but the new one we got on the scrambler last night, Asshole?"

"Yeah, yeah, I know; but you said we weren't supposed to talk about that. We're supposed to make believe Saddam is still the target, ain't we?"

"Jesus Christ, Harry! Who the hell do you think I am? That's for everybody else's consumption."

"Yeah, yeah, I know, but these fuckin' walls are thinner than in a Japanese whorehouse. And I'm sure your beautiful-assed Gloria's got her ear glued to the door. —By the way, what's *she* so happy about this morning?

"I think Wychway must've pushed all her joy buttons last night," Browning replied sourly without looking up.

"Jesus! he didn't waste any time, did he?" Ward made a gesture, "Bada-bing!"

"With Gloria you don't have to waste time," Browning breathed philosphically. "Judging from the noises that were coming through my wall they achieved lift-off, the first time, around ten. After that it got steadily worse."

"Or maybe, from their point of view, better," Ward leered.

"Yeah," admitted Browning grudgingly, then abruptly went back to the previous subject.

"You know, speaking of the real target," he intoned musingly in a quieter voice, "Wychway didn't know how close he came when he asked me yesterday why we didn't just let the Mossad take care of Saddam." He looked across at his assistant. "Wouldn't they just love to, if they thought they could get away with it."

"How're you gonna handle it, by the way? If Wychway thinks it's just Hussein, an' with that calibrated eyeball he can hardly miss, even if they're standing in a group, I mean, how the hell—?"

"No sweat. Just before he goes, at his final briefing, we're gonna tell him that our bleeding heart Secretary of State, Wilbur Claxton, will be there in Baghdad on a special visit, djinned up by the White House on the spur of the moment, to talk Saddam around to our way of thinking—something like Sadat's trip to Israel back in the '70's. Anyway, I tell Wychway: 'Just shoot; if Saddam's in a group, even if it includes Claxton, shoot 'em all—we can always get a new secretary of state, but they can't replace Saddam'." Browning chuckled. "You know, it's kinda funny, but it was our boy Charley who triggered this whole thing on Claxton. We were going to make it a surgical shot at Saddam with a high-powered rifle. But then, when I heard that that calibrated eyeball of his couldn't handle that kind of shot, we went to an automatic weapon, a crowd killer—which brought the guys at Langley to Claxton, whose ass they've been wanting to burn for years. They saw a heaven-sent opportunity."

"Especially since Claxton's pro-Arab and, most especially, pro-Palestinian, right? I mean, it was his urging that got us to reestablish this half-assed relationship with Iraq, wasn't it? The CNN correspondents have gotta go through the Algerian Embassy in D.C. to get in, an' through the Poles in Baghdad to get out, right?" Ward shook his head. "Yeah, but even Wychway's not gonna buy that 'shoot 'em all' shit. Why the hell would we be sending Claxton over there to make peace overtures just when we're planning to put Saddam's lights out?"

"Yeah, he will. That's the beauty of it. Think about it a minute. We send Claxton, the Arab ass kisser, to lull Saddam into a sense of false security; Saddam would have to think he couldn't be safer—from us, anyway—unless he was standing next to the President. Of course Claxton doesn't have the vaguest idea what the fuck we're up to, in spades. Got it? — Beautiful, ain't it?"

"I got it. A double cross for Saddam, and a *double* double cross for Claxton. And even a kind of a double cross for Wychway, I guess."

"Don't worry about it, Harry. It's just business as usual."

"Yeah, ain't it ever," sighed his companion.

Ward got up, wandered across the room, then came back and stood in front of Browning's desk. "Okay. I got one last burning question.

"Yeah?" Browning replied a little impatiently.

"Does 'You-Know-Who' know about this?"

"Stop soundin' like a fucking owl. You mean the President?"

"Uh, huh."

"Well, that's a good question, Harry," Browning said non-committally as he reached for his coffee, grimaced at finding it had gotten cold, and pressed an intercom button.

"Is that all you're gonna say?"

"Uh, huh," Browning smiled mirthlessly as Gloria Mundi came in with an electric coffee pot. As she beamed at Browning and poured more coffee Ward asked innocuously:

"When's Sibelius due in?"

"Thanks, Gloria," Browning said tonelessly and narrowed his eyes at her as she left the room. He turned back to Ward. "You mean 'Frankenstein,' don'tcha?"

"Christ! Yeah, okay, Frankenstein.

Browning drank some coffee.

"He should be here in a day or two. He's gotta 'deliver a paper' or some such shit at Tübingen University this week. By the way, is our little song bird still working in the good Doc's lab?"

"Oh, yeah. 'Igor.' That's his code name. Yeah, I got Charley Moore checkin' in with him a couple of times a week."

"Have Moore check every day from now until this is over. And make *sure* Igor accompanies Frankenstein on his visit here. Got it?"

"Right, Boss. —Uh, there is one more thing."

"Yeah?"

"Well, I was wrong. I got *one more* burning question."

"Nobody's perfect, Harry," commented Browning tolerantly as he examined his fingernails, "shoot."

"Well, I know the Claxton thing's close-hold—just you'n' me, right?—but I guess you figured it was okay to tell Gloria about Saddam, right?"

Browning dropped his feet to the floor and came bolt upright, spilling his coffee and almost falling out of his chair in the process.

"*What?*"

"She *knows* about Saddam. Jesus, you didn't tell her? Well, at least that's the impression I got—that she knew—when I was out there bullshitting with her while I was waiting for you this morning."

"Get that goddam Wychway in here!" Browning ordered grimly. —"No, wait a minute. *Just what did she say?*"

"Well, it wasn't flat out, like in so many words, I mean. She said something about, 'Well, it looks like we gotta finish the job for Schwartzkopf, after all', something like that....'"

"My fucking oaf!" Browning muttered through clenched teeth as he waved Ward out of the office.

Late that afternoon, still wearing his sweat-stained, dirty fatigues, Wychway stood next to his jeep at the entrance to the Hohenfels Mortuary and stared gloomily at the small sign someone had pinned to the door with the neatly printed and brutally pragmatic message:

**However Fair and Smooth the Skin
Stench and Corruption Lie Within.**

As a black Audi sedan drove up and parked next to the jeep, Wychway tore the sign off the wall and dropped it on the ground. The sedan driver held the door as Browning, frowning grimly, got out and approached. He stood for a moment, hands in pockets, staring down at the sign, then said curtly:

"Well, let's not stand here; I'm freezing my pills. Let's go see what the fuck happened." As they went in he stepped on the sign and ground it into the snow.

"Some kind of poisoning. Hard to say until I get in there," the Army pathologist Captain said laconically. "Might be food poisoning," he added, looking down at Gloria Mundi's rigid and ashen face.

"Like ptomaine, you mean?" Wychway asked.

"Naw. Assuming it *was* an accident, probably not. That's a mistake almost everybody still makes: ptomaine's the old misnomer for food poisoning. The ptomaines are strong alkaloids that're formed by bacterial action in decaying animal or vegetable matter. They're in a separate class. But food poisoning's caused by bacteria toxins, or sometimes just certain bacteria, or even food that's just poisonous, like certain mushrooms, or what we like to call toadstools." He shook his head, "The Germans with their weird sense of humor have a little joke. They say, 'You can eat any kind of mushroom, you know?' And when some jerk responds with, '*Any* kind?' they say, 'Yes, but some you only eat *once!*' Sick."

"I told her to be careful of that fucking goulash in the *Kantina*," growled Browning with a look of disgust.

"I thought you recommended it," said Wychway, giving Browning an unpleasant look. —"Well, maybe she just swallowed her 'L' pill by mistake, thinking it was her birth control pill," he added ironically, at which he received a sharp kick in the ankle from Browning, sharp enough to be painful despite the fact that he was wearing field boots.

With a quizzical look at the two men the doctor said:

"Too bad she couldn't talk before she checked out; we'd know a lot more. Boy! even with that ghastly Hippocratic smile on her face you can tell she sure must've been a beauty," he apostrophized as he replaced the sheet.

"Hippocratic smile?" Wychway wondered.

"*Risus sardonicus.* I know she didn't die of tetanus, but these symptoms are similar. The facial muscles are in spasm— the raised eyebrows, the drawing up of the corners of the mouth—whatever it was, produced that grotesque 'grinning' effect," he nodded towards the body.

"When'll you know what the story is?" Browning cut in brusquely.

"Well, I oughtta be able to give you something definite by late tomorrow morning, okay? By the way, how do I get in touch with you guys?"

"You don't. We'll call you before noon, tomorrow," Browning threw over his shoulder as with a hand on Wychway's elbow he headed for the door.

Once outside Browning released his car and driver and headed for Wychway's jeep.

"What the hell *happened?*" Wychway asked as they got in.

"Beats the shit outta me. I know she went down to Hohenfels village for something. Maybe she ate down there."

"That's always assuming it *was* food poisoning."

Browning disregarded this logic. "She took off around noon. Told me she had something she wanted to do in Hohenfels, Christmas shopping or some such shit. I told her, Okay, take the rest of the day off. That was it; she jumped in her little BMW, and took off. That was the last time I saw her, alive. Then about three o' clock I got this call from the German cops who found her dead in her car between here and Hohenfels."

"Which way was she heading?" asked Wychway as he pulled up in front of their "headquarters."

"This way, towards the Base."

"Did she have an accident? I mean, could the car have spun around maybe, and just *looked* like it was coming this way? It's a two-way road, you know, and if she lost control—"

"So what are *you* now, Wychway, a fucking cop?" Browning sneered as he got out and stood with his hands in his pockets waiting for Wychway to walk around the jeep.

Back in his office, as he hung up his overcoat Browning commented tactlessly:

"Well, Charley, at least you had your brief moment of

glory, or Gloria, or whatever."

"You just don't give a rat's ass, do you? I mean, her body's hardly cold yet and you don't feel a fucking thing for her, do you?"

"I feel pissed off that now I gotta go back through the pipeline and get another secretary with the right security clearance and who isn't a moron," Browning answered without emotion as he went into the outer office. As Wychway was removing his jacket Browning returned holding several sheets of paper.

"Balls! She never finished the after-action report on Sibel... I mean, Frankenstein. And nobody else has access— Where the hell is Ward? He can do it."

Wychway sighed and sank into a chair. He was mentally and physically drained. He lit a cigarette and exhaled a long plume of smoke. He didn't care where Ward was; and if he'd known he wouldn't have told Browning anyway.

"How'd you get to the morgue so fast, anyway? You should have been up to your ass in running snow trails under the guidance of your pal, Link."

"Link had a radio. I think it was Ward who called him. There was a young GI following us in a jeep. When Link told me what happened I took the jeep."

"Just like that, you took the jeep?"

"Not exactly. The driver saw my point right away, but Link seemed to lack the proper feudal spirit. He seemed to think his charter covered all my movements, in and out of training. I saw it differently, under the circumstances."

"So where *is* Link?"

"As we speak I would imagine he's somewhere between, uh, Training Area 13 B, I think it was, and the base camp."

"Walking?"

"Pigs can't fly. —But since he's not an absolute idiot, although he comes close, I imagine he got on his handy-dandy radio and called for transport."

At that moment a single-sideband radio which was on the floor next to Browning's desk and which had been emitting a steady, low, hissing sound suddenly announced:

"Bigeye Six, this is Bigeye Three, over."

"Speak of the trolley and you hear the gong," said Browning as with a severe look at Wychway he reached for the handset.

"This is Six, over,"

"This is Three," Link replied in the semi-breathless voice of a man walking and transmitting simultaneously. "Is that son of a bitch, Wych— I mean, Bigeye—hell, you know who I mean—is he at your location? Over."

"Affirmative, Three. I know what's on your mind, and you can save it till you get back. How're you doin' on transportation?"

"Ain't got jack shit, Six. They was supposed to be a jeep out here 'fore now, but meanwhile it's just 120 steps per minute. Can y'all assist? Over."

"This is Six. I'll get somebody out there right away, over."

"Send *him*, Six, he's the one I wanna see!"

"Can it, Three. Just cool it till I get somebody out there. Out."

"He'll cool it all right," said Wychway with a smile. "When I left it was already below freezing out there. —By the way, do *I* have a call sign?"

"Sure. I'm Bigeye Six, Ward's Five, Link's Three, Gloria—may God rest her beautiful ass—was Two, and you, the real star of the piece, are just plain Bigeye. The base commander, Colonel Kane, is on the net, but only for support and admin reasons: he's Four; and Bigeye One is reserved for any big wheel that might come out from Washington. Got it? —So, let's see if Brother Kane *is* on the net" Browning turned back to the radio, called Bigeye Four, got Bigeye Three-Four (Four's Sergeant Major), and ascertained that Link was being picked up at that moment. As he swiveled to face Wychway the latter said:

"Thanks for the commo lesson. Now could we get back to the late Bigeye Two for a minute?"

"Let's wait till we hear from the doc tomorrow, okay? Otherwise we'll just be pissing into the wind. —Speaking of tomorrow, what's Link got on your schedule?"

Sprawled in his chair, Wychway stared at the ceiling and sighed:

"The daily run—he says I gotta be up to five miles in two weeks—then I get into the pre-jump refresher; there's a thirty-four foot tower we ran past this morning and he was leering at it. I swear, his mouth was watering. He says I'll make my first practice jump in two weeks."

Browning nodded.

"If you wanna know about the post mortem check in with me around noon tomorrow. I'll wait for you here. *Don't* try to get me on the radio. No matter what she died of, I wanna keep this in the family, understand?"

"Do I have to steal another jeep to get back here?" Wychway asked unsmilingly.

"No, asshole, I'll brief Link tonight."

Wychway merely nodded as he rose, picked up the beret he had thrown down next his chair, and walked out. As he went through the door Browning shouted after him:

"Leave that jeep outside your quarters. I'll have someone from Kane's office pick it up."

Wychway turned in the doorway.

"Why don't you just get Kane to authorize a vehicle for me on a twenty-four hour dispatch. I mean, who knows, I might want to go to the Club and have dinner one of these nights. I do still get to eat once or twice a day, don't I?"

"Yeah, yeah, okay. It's already in the mill. Oh, yeah, and your Mickey Mouse ID and some other shit'll be ready tomorrow, maybe. You're getting a new identity for this stunt; your new monicker's gonna be Carl Wolff, so if you got your initials on anything, like luggage, they'll still work—Carl, with a "C" 'cause you had an English mother, see? Anyway, it'll all be in your reading file, and I want you to start using it now." Browning shook his head, "Goddammit, I gotta get another secretary," he added parenthetically.

"Also, Dr. Frankenstein should get in tomorrow afternoon or evening to check you out. I suggest you lay off the booze tonight." Browning grumpily waved a hand of dismissal as he picked up a paper from his desk.

Once outside Wychway got in his misappropriated jeep and drove to his quarters. He stayed there just long enough to shower, change his clothes, and drink a large whiskey. As he left his small suite of rooms he glanced at the Class "C" telephone on a small night table next to the bed and nodded grimly to himself.

He stood in the small parking area outside the BOQ and casually lit a cigarette as he looked up and down the seemingly deserted narrow street. Scanning with his extraordinary vision he saw nothing at first; and then he spotted the other jeep, parked two hundred yards away, with a man, bundled up against the cold, leaning against its side. He got back into his jeep and drove to the Officers' Club.

Once inside the Club Wychway didn't stop, but went straight through towards the rear of the lobby. Partly concealed behind a sign showing the way to the rest rooms, he watched as his shadow came in and looked around the crowded lobby; then continued back and found the door which gave the kitchen workers access to the rest rooms. He walked quickly through the kitchen and out the rear service door, then ran to a corner of the building and looked back. No one followed. He ran around the building to his jeep, and under a lowering sky headed for the main gate.

By the time he reached the small town of Hohenfels he needed his headlights as he drove slowly down the main street looking for the local *Postamt*.

At eleven-thirty the next morning, after some warm-up exercises, his run, and commencement of airborne refresher, over which Link's assistant, Larry Ledbetter, presided, Wychway drove over to the headquarters building in his "new" jeep. When he had gotten back to the BOQ the previous evening it had been parked outside with a GI lounging against it waiting for the "old" jeep. And in his room there had been a message from Browning, telling him that henceforth he had to get approval from him, Browning, personally, whenever he wanted to go off the Base Camp area.

Browning was not in his office, and as Wychway sat waiting the phone rang. Since there was no one in the outer office, Wychway answered it after the fifth ring. It was the pathologist returning an earlier call from Browning.

"Yeah, this is, uh, Carl Wolff, I'm the guy who was with Browning yesterday at the mortuary. The post mortem? Yeah. Hell, yes! I'm his right-hand man. Go ahead."

The doctor's voice had a metallic sound:

"Okay, it could have been food poisoning, but I'm beginning to have doubts. For one thing there was hardly any food in her stomach. Apparently, she did coffee in the morning, with maybe a cookie thrown in; but there was no breakfast to speak of, and certainly no lunch. But it was a strong alkaloid poison that did it. Now, that's a little pale compared to what else I found." The doctor hesitated. "Are you sure I can talk about this over the phone? What I gotta say is a little sinister."

Wychway glanced quickly over his shoulder as he heard a vehicle pull up outside.

"Yeah, yeah, go ahead. This phone's secure," he lied rapidly.

"Well, on her leg, way up on the inner aspect of her thigh, there was something written. And, get this—it was written in lipstick!"

"Quick, what'd it say, quick!" Wychway urged as he heard the outer door of the building open and close.

"Just three words — 'He did it.' Then there was what looked like the letter 'P,' writ large, which sort of trailed off and—"

"Okay, fine, thanks," Wychway broke in, "keep all that to yourself till further notice." He replaced the handset quickly but quietly just as Browning came through the outer office.

"How in the hell did *you* get in here?" was Browning's surly greeting.

"I just walked in. The door was wide open."

"My fucking oaf! I'm gonna kill that goddam Ward," he stormed as that individual calmly strolled in. Where in the goddam fucking Christ you been? I told you not to leave until I got back!"

I didn't leave, Boss, I was down the hall in the latrine. What the hell are you so steamed about?"

With slightly less heat Browning asked:

"Did the doc call back?"

Ward glanced at Wychway. "Not while I was here. And I wasn't gone longer'n five minutes." If the phone rang I think I would've heard it from the can, though," he ended a little lamely.

"My fuckin' oaf," Browning repeated as he ran a hand over his brow. "Wychway, when did *you* blow in here?"

"Just a few minutes before you walked in—and you did get a call," this time Wychway glanced at Ward, "it was that medic we saw at the mortuary yesterday."

Browning gave him a level stare.

"What'd he say? I left word he wasn't supposed to talk to anybody but me," he said sternly.

With another glance at Ward, Wychway cleared his throat, then returned Browning's stare.

"I think you oughtta talk to him yourself, Lew. I could hardly understand what the hell he was burbling about," he said quietly.

"Listen, you can talk in front of Ward if that's what's..." he trailed off as Wychway's eyes never left his. "Okay," he went on thoughtfully, "I'll give him a call. —Now," he said briskly as he moved to his desk, "you got a date this afternoon. Dr. Frankenstein is coming in. He'll have one of his lab boys with him, and they're gonna give you a complete run-through at the base dispensary. Then we'll all meet at the Club for dinner," he included Ward with a glance.

As Wychway left Browning was directing Ward to "see to the notification of Gloria's next o' kin."

That evening, after Dr. "Frankenstein's" examination had given him a clean bill of physical health generally and had confirmed that his newly acquired and fantastic visual ability was constant and unimpaired, Wychway (now Carl Wolff), along with the Doctor, "Igor," his not-so-faithful young assistant, (Ward's "mole," Klaus-Dieter Hoffmann), and Browning all drove to the Officers' Club for dinner. Ward, who met them in the lobby, guided them to a small private dining room.

A waiter brought in drinks, and Browning engaged Sibelius-Frankenstein in earnest conversation while in a far corner Wychway-Wolff stood with a large scotch and looked out a window at the falling snow. He sensed more than saw someone at his elbow.

"*Entschuldigung*—excuse me, please, Herr, ah, Wolff, is it not?" a voice asked hesitantly and deferentially in excellent German.

"Wolff" turned to see "Igor" smiling rather sheepishly at him.

"*Ja, Ich bins*," he smiled back ruefully, using the trite, quaint proletarian phrase, "but could we speak English? —my German's a little rusty. I've spent most of my life with my mother and her people in England."

"*Ja*, sure! it gives me the chance to practice," the young man answered enthusiastically and in adequate English; then with a continued hesitancy he went on. "I, um, I know this matter is very hush-hush as you English say, but the Herr Professor certainly performed what is almost a miracle in your case, is it not?"

Wolff gave him another rueful smile.

"Yes, I suppose that's one way of putting it. Of course, miracles usually work for the good, but in this case I don't—" he broke off as he realized he was beginning to tread carelessly. But let's not talk about that right now, especially so soon after you and the good Doctor put me through that wringer at the dispensary."

"Yes, we will leave the subject if it is distasteful to you. But first," "Igor" held up an admonitory finger, "a word of caution. You must remember what the Herr Doctor told you. Under no circumstances must you sustain *any* severe blow to the head, especially in these early stages, *verstehen Sie*? I do not know what they are putting you through, here at Hohenfels, but please, be careful or you can destroy all our very good work!" He smiled engagingly and added, "And you *Englisch*, like the Americans, are sometimes too ready with the fists, *ja?*"

Wychway-Wolff returned Hoffmann's smile.

"Not to worry; I absolutely abhor violence. Now, what about you? I understand you're on the way to making some little reputation for yourself, working under such a great man."

"Ah, perhaps someday. Who knows?" the young scientist replied diffidently, but it is the Professor who will achieve great fame once the scientific world becomes aware of what he has achieved." He glanced quickly at his companion, "Of course, I realize that that cannot be for some time because of the secrecy which in this case is necessary. But he has been reassured by Herr Browning that someday all shall be revealed, and then—"

"Right," Wolff interposed with a polite smile, "but for now I think the less said about the whole thing the better, okay?" He was thoughtful for a few moments, then looking directly at Hoffmann added, "And I say that in the Doctor's better interests, as well as Browning's; and perhaps even in yours and mine as well. So really, why don't we just talk about something else?" he ended pleasantly as he drained his glass.

"Igor" nodded slowly and with appropriate seriousness, but somehow still giving Wolff the impression that they shared a portentous secret. For a few moments he just stood looking at Wolff with a tentative, speculative expression, as if he were trying to make up his mind about whether or not to say something more. Then his face cleared, and with an engaging smile he changed the subject.

"Do you read mystery stories, Herr Wolff?"

"Oh, once in while I suppose, when I'm in a certain mood," Wolff answered pleasantly.

And with that Klaus-Dieter Hoffmann, aka Igor, who as it turned out was an avid fan of English mystery writers, launched into some of his favorite theories on the perfect crime, specifically, insoluble murders. He listed as trite the icicle which when driven into the heart would melt, thereby leaving no murder weapon, and in the same vein Roald Dahl's celebrated frozen leg of lamb which when defrosted and cooked had ultimately and ironically been eaten by the hungry and grateful policemen at the very scene where it had been used as the matronly murderer's "blunt instrument." He deprecated the needle-in-cheek and suction technique of drawing the air out of one's lungs so suddenly as to cause immediate asphyxiation. And then he spoke of the poisons which Dame Agatha Christie had loved so well, and hinted darkly that all of them were as nothing compared to what he had come up with in his spare time one weekend in "Frankenstein's" laboratory.

After admitting that his idea of killing someone and then seating the body in a locked stall in a public toilet had merit—with uncaring people going in and out of the facility and no one else but the occasional attendent coming in to clean, and a certain malodorous quality being normal in such a place, the body, even after it had begun to decompose, might not be discovered for days, or even weeks—Igor proudly described his masterpiece. Through not a great deal of experimentation, he told Wolff, he had produced a chemical agent which when placed in water, even chlorinated water, was harmless enough, but which when combined with *human urine* instantaneously produced a gas of such lethality as to be fatal, within seconds of being inhaled, to anyone in close proximity—that was to say, a meter, a few feet—to the chemical reaction. What was more, he added rubbing his hands in self-approving glee, the gas was so non-persistent as to dissipate itself in less than thirty seconds; and best of all, it would leave no trace in the toilet water, even assuming it hadn't been flushed away!

As they went to the dinner table together Wolff mused that whatever the future held for this young scientist, chances were excellent that his name would be in the headlines some day, for *some* reason.

Wolff's surmise was absolutely correct, although there

was no way he could have predicted the imminence of his prophesy, still less the form it would take.

It was not until the next morning that Wychway-Wolff heard about Lufthansa Flight 742, which crashed inexplicably enroute from Munich to Frankfurt and which, he was to read on the front page of the *International Herald-Tribune*, carried all eighty-three passengers and crew to their deaths, including Herr Doktor Professur Sibelius and his assistant, Klaus-Dieter Hoffmann.

Chapter Fifteen

Offices of the Priesthood

Sitting over his morning coffee at the Officers' Mess, Wolff put his newspaper aside and extracted the envelope the mess steward had handed him as he'd entered the lobby. A glance had revealed it was nothing official, so he had stuffed it in his leather jacket, taken a copy of the *Herald-Tribune* from a near-by rack, and gone to a table where with his attention riveted to the headlines and their accompanying story the letter had been forgotten.

The envelope was addressed in neat block letters to "Herr Karl Wolff, in care of the *Offiziere* Mess, Base Hohenfels, To be called for." Wolff hurriedly tore it open and found a brief message, unsigned, and something else. The message, written in English, read:

> *My Dear Herr Wolff,*
>
> *It was so much a pleasure to talk to you yesterday night. You are such a good listener!*
>
> *I will include with this letter the secret to my little "masterpiece," as well as a small quantity for analysis. Who knows? Perhaps in your business someday this could be useful!*
>
> *But, if I may make bold, if it is accepted by the*

people for whom you are employed, I would like to
have credit as its originator, if that would be possible.
I hope some day we shall meet again, and soon!

Wolff experienced a small *frisson* as he read this last sentence. The note was signed, "Best regards from your Friend, 'Igor.'" The "something else" which accompanied the note on a separate sheet of paper was a chemical formula, along with a small hermetically sealed plastic packet, about an inch square, whose contents seemed granular, like sugar crystals. Neatly printed in German on the packet were, on one side, the words, "For up to two gallons H_2O," and on the other, "Shelf life: indefinite." Wolff glanced back at the cryptic and formulaic text, and with a rueful chuckle crumpled the paper and looked around for a trash basket; seeing none, he popped the ball of paper, along with the packet, into the ashtray. A moment later, unsure of what the fate of objects found in ashtrays at the Club might be, he retrieved the packet and slipped into his pocket. Besides, he thought with grim humor, if he ever got into a real corner, assuming he had enough time to pee and "Igor" wasn't just a quack scientist after all, it would be a more interesting way to go out than with the prosaic "L" pill.

He drank coffee and smoked for several minutes, telling himself that the less he dwelt on the recent violent and tragic deaths of these three people whom he had known only briefly the better, especially considering what lay in store for him in the all too immediate future. But his eyes kept going back to that little crumpled ball of paper, and when a young German waitress who had come to tidy his table reached for the ashtray Wolff put his hand over it protectively. When the girl shrugged and walked away he retrieved the paper, smoothed it out, folded it carefully, and put it in his pocket. Who knew, maybe "Igor" was right, he mused, maybe the Agency would be interested in this. But if they were, he told himself, he wouldn't just give it to them out of some newly found stupid sense of loyalty: he'd trade it for something.

A few minutes later he picked up the note and the envelope which had been lying on the table in front of him; then, after a few moments of further reflection, he fished out the formula paper. On his way out of the Club he took all three items to the men's room, where he went into a stall, burned them, and flushed the ashes down the toilet. By the time he walked out of the Club he'd already forgotten about the packet he'd slipped in his pocket.

Browning had said no more about the Gloria Mundi incident, and Wolff sensibly hadn't either, until Browning summoned him from the training area on that same morning after the Lufthansa tragedy.

In his usual brusque manner Browning opened the conversation without a conventional greeting as Wolff entered the office.

"So what're your thoughts about that call from the Doc yesterday—about what he said, I mean?"

Wolff shrugged as he kicked snow off his boots, then replied monosyllabically:

"Weird."

"C'mon, Charley, I mean Carl, gimme me a little more'n just, 'weird'."

"I'm with operations, Lew, not security," Wolff stalled.

"Cut the shit. Whatta you *think*?"

"Well, for openers, has any of this been reported to Colonel Kane at Base Camp Headquarters? I mean, this *is* an Army-run base, so shouldn't the CID get plugged into this if there's been an indication of 'foul play,' to use a horseshit phrase?"

"I told you an' Ward yesterday I want this kept in 'the family'."

"Yeah, good, Lew, but what about that pathology guy? How long do you think you can keep him bottled up?"

"Forever, if I have to," Browning answered ominously.

"What're you gonna do, Lew, bump *him* off?"

Browning gave the other a long look of appraisal before answering.

"That might've been okay, even funny, without the emphasis. Why didn't you just put a 'too' on the end of it?"

Wolff went to the door, closed it, and stood with his back to it.

"Okay, Lew, cards on the table time. Did you have her knocked off?"

Browning shook his head slowly.

"Assuming I did, and of course I'm not admitting a fucking thing, what's it to you, anyway?" he forstalled Wolff's reply with an upraised hand. "But before you answer *that* one, answer me this: Why would I? Why would I off my perfectly good secretary, who incidentally, and as you well know, also was one of the greatest pieces of ass east of New York?"

For a moment Wolff seriously considered overturning Browning's desk; with a visible effort he controlled himself, then replied tersely:

"As to your first question, there's no sense in trying to answer it, because you wouldn't know what the hell I was talking about; but as to the second, here's an answer even you can understand. How about: 'Because maybe when I was about five-thirds drunk and had my nose buried in her beautiful crotch I might've told her about who I'm going after'?

"You know, Lew, I never was very good at math, but I can add. That 'P' could have been the beginning of a 'B,' couldn't it? She just didn't have time, poor baby. What's it take for that shit to work—ten seconds? twenty, max? And the lipstick? Why the lipstick? Well, maybe that was all she had, maybe; but drunk or not I remember her telling me how she *always* kept one of those little notebook and pen combinations handy, pen attached so she wouldn't misplace it. Christ, she *showed* it to me that night! It was right there next to her bed! So the lipstick. Did anybody run a chemical analysis of that lipstick, I wonder? And the German cops. I also find myself wondering about the German fuzz. This happened on *their* turf. How are *they* handling it, or are they? Let's see: Who was that German agent at Sibelius's debriefing that Ward was telling me about? Hahn, or Hamm, something like that, wasn't it? Do I smell the dirty little hand of the *Abwehr,* or BND, or whatever they're calling themselves now, in here covering up this shit from the German side?"

When a low rumbling growl escaped the other's lips at the mention of Ward's indiscretion, Wolff rightly assumed that Browning was making a mental note for his next conversation with his much-beleaguered assistant.

He went on.

"They seem to be dropping like flies, Lew. First Gloria, then Sibelius. I guess he won't be needing his code name anymore, will he? What was *his* sin, by the way? Was he going to deliver a paper on Bugeye to his egghead friends? And his assistant, Hoffmann, poor bastard. Who's next? The Doc at the mortuary, I guess. Then who? Colonel John Kane?—if the Doc gets to him before you get to the Doc? It's a lot like certain lies, isn't it, Lew? Once you've told the first one you gotta tell a hundred more to cover your ass."

When Wolff stopped for breath, Browning, who had maintained an icy silence throughout this tirade, spoke quietly and calmly.

"Feeling better, Charley, now that you've had your big anal period?"

"Better out than in, my old lady used to say," the other responded shortly.

"Okay, I got two things to say to you," Browning leaned forward and intoned seriously, "One, this conversation never took place; and two, if you ever so much as hint at the shit you been comin' out with in the last few minutes you'll regret it. I swear to you, you'll wish—"

"What're you gonna do, send me on a suicide mission to Baghdad or something?" Wolff interrupted caustically.

Browning picked up a pencil from his desktop and rolled it between his hairy fingers a few times before he spoke again in the same tone.

"All these accusations of your's are just bullshit; you know that, don't you? Well, *I* know it, and that's all that really matters," he paused reflectively, "but assuming, just for the moment, that there's anything at all in what you say, just *assuming* there is, then your little hit list isn't quite complete. You remember that kid—what was her name, Magda?—the one that picked you up in England?"

Browning remained perfectly motionless as Wolff took two angry steps towards the desk, then stopped, shook his head slowly, and with a deep sigh sank into a chair.

"Yeah, Carl," Browning said soothingly, "everything's gonna be just fine. You're doin' great! You just let me worry about the nickel and dime shit, okay? You do the heavy lifting an' I'll take care of the tidying up."

Except for those times when he went off the Base, Charles Duwayne Link's unvarying "uniform" during Wychway-Wolff's sojourn at the Hohenfels Training Area consisted of faded blue jeans, a brown leather World War II-vintage airman's jacket over an olive-drab army-issue sweater, a black Basque beret, and brown "Dingo" cowboy boots, of the "leather lowers and synthetic (Naugahide) uppers" variety. Sewn on the leather jacket were two patches. One, black with a RANGER tab over a grinning death's head and crossed M16 rifles, bore the motto: FUCK WITH THE BEST-DIE LIKE THE REST. The other, on a bright red background, proclaimed: AIRBORNE, in black letters on a yellow pennon across the top. Beneath this was a grinning death's head, adorned with a lavender (!) beret, centered in a pair of white jump wings which supported a bloody dagger. Emblazoned in yellow under the jump wings was: WE KILL FOR PEACE. He often carried a swagger stick, with a .50 caliber cartridge case at its butt end and a .30 caliber cartridge, with base and primer removed, at its point. The .50 caliber cartridge case was inscribed with the motto: Protect the Innocent - Convince the Undecided - Kill the Rest. Like most American professional soldiers, or as in Link's case, former soldiers, he kept himself scrupulously neat and clean.

He was almost pathologically stingy, and at every opportu-

nity cadged cigarettes from Wolff or anyone else who happened to be in his company. He would declare breaks at intervals during the training day, saying, "Take ten. Smoke if you
got 'em; if ya ain't got 'em, get one from the man next to
you," and turning to Wychway-Wolff with a leer that the latter
soon came to despise would add, "Well, Witchy-Wolfy,
whatya know?—*yore* the man next tuh me!" He brooked no
interference with his training schedule or regimen. Even
Browning had difficulty from time to time when for reasons of
"briefing updates" or other matters he had to break Link's star
pupil away from the training at hand.

Gradually Wolff became convinced that in Link he saw a
classic example of the three traits that comprised Freud's anal
triad, traits which according to the revolutionary Viennese
neurologist grew out of mismanaged toilet training in child-
hood and which constituted an "anal character": viz., obstina-
cy, stinginess, and pedantic orderliness.

Link's favorite dish, at least during this period of time
when he was in Germany, was "chicken fried steak" (his name
for *Wienerschnitzel*) accompanied by hominy grits, which he
called "Georgia ice cream," whenever he could get them. His
favorite pastime when off duty was getting drunk on American
beer (never using a glass)—in a country renowned for the
unparalled excellence and variety of its beer—while listening
to the coarsest Richard Pryor or Eddy Murphy recordings and
pointing out (unnecessarily) the "best parts," as in, "Hey, listen
to *this*, you guys, this is the good part—yew know, when he
talks about 'the feets'? Ah tell yuh, these niggers're better'n
those ol' minstrel shows. 'Course those were *white* guys in
them minstrel shows." He often would expound on what
apparently was one of his life's ambitions— to enter a
"midget-throwin' contest" which, he claimed, was held annually "somewhere down in Australia." He also was prone to
decscribe his sexual exploits in great detail.

One evening, when Wolff went to Link's quarters to discuss something about the next day's training programme Link,

with a can of Bud in hand and in full flower, was entertaining his sycophantic cronies with a story about his last visit to the town of Hohenfels.

"... an' when that *Strasse* queen laid her hot li'l hand on mah laig mah dick wuz harder'n Chinese algebra, an'—" he broke off his narrative and scowled as Wolff knocked and came in the door.

"Y'all don't wanna lissen tuh this, Herr Wolff," he drawled at the new arrival. "It's liable tuh corrupt yore morals," he added and leered hugely at his companions.

"You know, Link, guys that talk about it as much as you do usually end up with Mary Hand and her five sisters at the end of the evening, but they'll never admit it," Wolff responded cooly.

"Listen, big shot, you couldn't get laid in Scully Square with a fist fulla twenties on Navy Day," Link shot back with a conspiratorial glance at his friends.

"They don't call it Scully Square any more," Wolff sighed. "Call me when you're through debriefing yourself on your exploits among the finer class of people in Hohenfels, okay? I gotta talk to you about the drill for tomorrow," and he left before the other could respond.

"Whut evah y'all say, *Charles!*" Link shouted at the closed door after he had recovered his composure. Though his own given name was Charles Duwayne, Link insisted on "Duwayne" or "C.D." "Charles is a candy-ass name," he told his friends, and berated anyone bearing the name, especially Wolff, née Wychway.

It was so cold on the old now seldom used known-distance rifle range that after the first fifteen minutes, Wolff had to replace his gloves with "trigger-fingered" mittens with wool inserts in order to retain any feeling in his hands.

Using solid tracer ammunition from the 500 yard line where they started it was child's play for him to blow out the very center of the bull's-eye, using first an old AK47 which Link produced from somewhere. When they moved back to the

1000-yard line the result was much the same. Wolff had always been pretty good with a rifle, either semi- or fully automatic, but this was incredible. Later, when the regular maintenance personnel were permitted back on the range, they were surprised (and pleased) to find that after all the automatic fire they'd heard that day not even one round had struck any of their target frames. To Wolff, with his new and bizarre visual ability, even at 1000 yards the bull's-eye looked like a large black beach ball.

In the early afternoon, after they'd had what Browning ironically called "a catered lunch"—which meant standing around consuming coffee and sandwiches and stamping their feet to keep them from freezing—they went to the machine gun range, where Link's men hauled two M60's and several boxes of belted ammunition out of the weapons truck. Meanwhile two men checked, adjusted, and in some cases replaced "E"- and "F"-type silhouette targets[1] at various distances down range. Wolff would be firing long and short bursts at targets which were arranged singly or in groups of up to six at ranges of from 300 to 1500 yards. The targets were designed to fall over backward when hit solidly.

After more than an hour of this, again with excellent results, Link called a break and walked back to a truck which was parked about twenty yards behind the firing line. Wolff rose from the prone firing position he'd been in, stretched as he walked a few steps away, and lit a cigarette. He watched as Link unloaded a strange looking weapon from the truck and came towards him.

"Care for a cigarette, Duwayne?" he asked, aware that both the other's hands were occupied.

"Naw, not now. Hey, Wolfy, I bet yew never seen one o' *these* babies."

Wolff looked critically at the weapon Link held up for his inspection. He drew on his cigarette, exhaled, and said:

[1] See Glossary.

"That wouldn't be one of those experimental flechette models I've heard about, would it?"

"Yew got it!" Link singsonged. "Whatta piece!" he looked at the firearm almost lovingly. "Murder Incorporated, that's whut Ah call it. Fires a cloud of death, Wolfy, with *darts*, would yew believe it?"

"Very impressive. Do I get to fire it?"

"Hell, yes! Didja think this wuz jus' show an' tell? Lew Browning told me to let you try it out today," he said importantly as he handed Wolff the sinister looking weapon. "Here, check it out. Yer supposed ta be an ol' weapons man. Familiarize yoresef. I'll get the 'star wars ammo' an' ya kin start bangin' away in ten minutes," he looked at his watch, "Browning oughta be here by then. He's comin' out tuh watch."

However much Link was prone to exaggeration and hyperbole, the automatic, air-cooled, belt- *or* magazine-fed flechette gun, known in R&D circles as the XMG 95F (Experimental Machine Gun, vintage 1995, Flechette firing) was everything he'd raved about. From the prone position, with the weapon resting on its spring-loaded, collapsible bipod, Wolff literally tore the heads off any and all silhouette targets at which he was directed to fire. Since each cartridge contained three finned (for stability in flight) steel flechettes, or darts, instead of a single conventional, jacketed lead bullet the volume of fire was effactually trebled. Somehow however, Wolff discovered, nothing was lost in accuracy. Using his telescopic vision and firing solid tracer low over open sights, as he'd done earlier with the AK-47 on the KD range (to compensate for the short-range visual disability he'd described to Browning) he would bring the beaten zone up into the targets, getting a bonus richochet effect as he did so, with devastating results. The flechettes though lighter than the standard cylindro-conoidal service bullet were as effective, since with a muzzle velocity of 4600 fps they more than achieved the requisite fifty-three foot-pounds of terminal energy necessary to "incapacitate" the average man. Another quality of the gun, less dramatic perhaps but no less important, was that in firing two full boxes (500 rounds) of ammunition not one stoppage or malfunction of any kind, in either the belt-fed or magazine-fed mode, was sustained.

A final advantage lay in its compactness. Since all its parts with the exception of the bolt and barrel were manufactured from a newly-developed high-stress plastic, the weapon, which was no longer than an M16, weighed less than eight pounds. It could be broken down quickly into three main components to fit—along with such other necessary equipment as a lensatic compass, maps, ammunition, utility knife, compact first aid kit, emergency rations, and possibly even a micro-miniaturized transceiver (CW)—into a specially designed general purpose bag used mainly for parachute special operations. In turn this GP bag easily could be converted into the type of inoffensive-looking civilian backpack that is in such common use today.

Following Wolff's final tour de force, as he burned up the last belt of ammunition and which left only two of the original fifty targets standing, and those drunkenly and precariously, Browning approved the XMG-95F on the spot as the "primary weapon of choice for the mission."

Wolff's training continued apace. Barring rare trips into Hohenfels town, always accompanied by Ward now, he stayed on the Base and trained hard for the mission. During the short late-November days he was almost constantly in the field: running at least five miles every morning—now without pausing for breaks—along snow-packed roads and rougher trails; navigating through varied terrain using a map and compass in daytime, and a map, penlight, and the stars by night. And it was on these night problems that he discovered his right eye gave him more than just magnification in the dark—he judged he could identify objects, at all ranges, at least twice as well as with his normal left eye. He assumed it had something to do with more rod cells coming into play, as in the case of cats, which with more rod-shaped than cone-shaped optical cells can see roughly six times better at night than humans (well, normal humans anyway, Wychway sighed inwardly).

Since his military records revealed that he'd had extensive survival training as a Special Forces soldier and even had gone through a course in desert warfare and survival in California's Mohave Desert, the week of desert indoctrination and training in northwestern Egypt which had been proposed earlier was replaced by more "classroom" study of Iraq's geography, especially the area from Baghdad south to the Kuwaiti-Saudi border, to include its flora and fauna.

To Wolff's ineffable dismay the final decision to parachute him into Iraq was made during his second week of preparation. This decision was based upon the fact of the equipment he would need for his mission, not least the assassination weapon. Without absolutely assured access to his equipment the mission would become, as Browning so typically would have it, "An exercise in fucking futlility." Now that the US no longer had access to military airbases or even an embassy in Iraq the simple expedient of shipping in what would be needed on a military plane or in the official embassy pouch did not exist. Consideration briefly was given to air dropping the equipment at some predesignated remote location where Wychway, after having entered the country "legally" under his "Austrian" passport, would await the drop aircraft. This proposal was rejected almost immediately as being fraught with too many unforeseen risks and uncertainties.

Now, already having had a few days of jump refresher training and familiarization with new or unfamiliar parachute equipment, he began making day and night jumps with the ram-air-canopied, feather-light (seven-pound) Pterdactyl—a highly maneuverable, civilian sport parachute he'd never seen or even heard of let alone used in his earlier days as a soldier-parachutist. This specially modified Pteradactyl—canopy, suspension lines, harness, everything including its harness hardware—was made of "self-destructing" materials. Produced by Swedish R&D scientists years earlier the materials precluded the parachuted agent's having to bury or otherwise hide or destroy his 'chute so as to leave no traces of his infiltration in the drop area. A small vial of a chemical compound, when spilled anywhere on the parachute assembly, began a chain reaction which reduced the materials to ash.

Although the fundamental decision had been made to "insert" Wolff by parachute, the specific method of his infiltration had not been decided upon and now became the subject of much discussion. Link, who was considered the expert in this phase of the operation, proposed two possible choices in what he called Wolff's "deployment": HALO; and a variation of LABS.

Testing had been done years earlier (in fact, back in the early 1960's Wychway's father had been one of the volunteer HALO test jumpers at El Centro, California) with the high altitude (exiting the aircraft at altitudes exceeding 43,000 feet)), low opening (deploying the parachute at about 2000 feet or less) technique as a means of infiltrating national borders. Leaving the aircraft at such an extreme altitude enabled an experienced parachutist to sail laterally as far as five or more miles in any direction (depending on shear winds) in his free fall before pulling his rip cord (or having it actuated by some automatic ground-sensing—barometric or radar—device), thereby enabling him, in theory at least, to leave the aircraft over one country and land in another. The major drawbacks of such a system were threefold: first, the fact that hostile radars mainly were located along borders; second, the prohibitive quantity and complexity of the life support equipment required for the parachutist in the initial stage of the jump; and third, the geographic restriction (especially in the case of a large national land mass, such as the former USSR) of having to land on the fringe of "the country of interest."

The low-altitude bombing system also was not new; and so, in the age of the Cruise missile and its variants as well as other missile systems and because of the growing obsolescence of strategic bombing in general, was seldom talked about. Nonetheless it was thought that this technique might be adaptable for the requirement at hand.

LABS, for whatever it might be worth in view of what has been said, in its "infiltration mode" envisioned the use of three low-level jet bombers (for Bigeye Browning had obtained B1Bs)—two loaded with radar jamming equipment, one modified to carry one or possibly two parachutists—using computerized TFR and streaking towards a hostile country at tree top level, flying "nap of the earth," or "contour flying" in tight formation until they reached the border. At or near the border one aircraft would turn left and another right (at this time one or both also might release anti-radar chaff or even a small HIMAT diversionary drone), while the third, the "payload aircraft," continued straight in towards its prearranged drop zone. At a predetermined distance from the "insertion point" the "drop airplane" would go into a steep climb, thereby slowing appreciably, and the parachutist would exit (or be ejected) in free fall at a precalculated altitude, much as a bomb would be lobbed in a conventional LABS strike. When the parachutist reached a certain point and had slowed to a suitable speed somewhere along the path of the parabolic arc into which he had been projected he would deploy his parachute, or if he was temporarily incapacitated due to disorientation or some other manifestation of this unusual procedure, his parachute would deploy automatically at a safe distance above the ground. If all else failed and he still was able to use it he always had a conventional ripcord. Assuming all went according to plan he would get his opening at an altitude of between 500 and 1000 feet. Although deeper penetration than can be achieved by the HALO technique is possible with LABS, obviously distances still would be limited, as the deeper the aircraft attempts to penetrate hostile terrain the greater the chances of discovery and disaster. Understandably, the advent of Stealth-type aircraft had been a key reason for renewed interest in the technique. So although it was somewhat antiquated LABS ultimately was chosen as the means of Wolff's "insertion."

The three black unmarked airplanes would take off from the Fürstenfeldbruck Luftwaffe base outside Munich and fly to an airfield in the Kuwaiti desert where they would refuel and wait for darkness. Then they would fly north to the southern "no fly" boundary (at 33° north latitude[2])—established as part of the United Nations sanctions following the Persian Gulf War—where the diversionary aircraft would peel away, fly diversionary patterns, and eventually return to Fürstenfeldbruck, overflying Jordan and Israel on the way. Meanwhile, the "hot" plane would continue north between the Tigris and Euphrates Rivers, drop Wolff within twenty miles of Baghdad, cross the northern "no fly" zone (36°), fly on into Turkey, and land at Incerlik NATO Air Base, near Adana, where Browning would be waiting to debrief the aircrew. LABS also was considered favorable for this mission since in taking advantage of the zones forbidden to Iraqi aircraft the drop airplane would have little problem crossing the national frontiers and would have to fly only about a hundred miles—at close to Mach one a mere matter of six minutes—illicitly over "sovereign" territory before dropping its precious cargo. Chances were considered excellent that the Iraqi's would never even know an "insertion" had been made.

Finally, when Wolff inquired about his mode of *egress* from Iraq (assuming he got through his mission safely) he was told that his emergency "extraction" or "exfiltration" plan would be put into effect "on a contingency basis only," and would be explained to him just before mission departure time. He was left to wonder, and hope, that there might be a chance he could come out like any other visitor ("a white man," as Browning had so typically put it), using a commercial airline. Just one more thing to worry about, he told himself.

On the evenings when he wasn't committed to field train-

---

[2] Changed from 32° in September 1996 when tensions again flared between Iraq and the US.

ing he studied the language, culture, politics, economy, and geography of "the area of interest" under the tutelage of John Evans, an area specialist who had been flown in from Langley (accompanied by Wendy Foxley, Browning's new secretary) for the purpose. He studied maps of certain areas of Iraq until he could reproduce rough but accurate copies from memory. Supplied with the necessary papers and documents, he was rehearsed repeatedly by Browning and Ward in his role as Carl Wolff, the Austrian oilfield worker. An oil man was even brought in from somewhere to give him a crash course in oilfield operations (Wolff hoped the poor innocent would make it home safely after he finished his teaching chores).

All in all he did well. Following a routine progress report from Evans one day Browning grudgingly admitted to Ward that "Wolff" undoubtedly "had it," however slightly, over his father, Colonel Witchway, in the area of that quick intelligence necessary for missions such as the one at hand. Of course he was impelled to dilute the compliment with, "Blood tells, Ward, blood tells." Ward's muttered and unintelligible response was, "Genes, genes."

Nothing more was done or even said about Gloria Mundi or about the untimely deaths of the two scientists. Once, when Wolff raised the subject of Gloria's strange death to Ward in a private moment, the assistant mission director simply left the room without saying a word. Less than a week after the Lufthansa crash, while having a drink at the Club bar, Wolff (who now was known at Hohenfels simply as "Carl") discovered that both Colonel John Kane and Captain Simonetti, the mortuary pathologist, had been transferred, not merely to another post in Germany or even elsewhere in Europe, but back to the CONUS.

After what the newspapers reported as "an exhaustive investigation," the German commercial aviation authorities' report on the Lufthansa Flight 742 tragedy was "inconclusive as to the exact cause of the crash." A Bavarian farmer who claimed he had seen the plane come down said he'd heard an explosion while the plane was still in flight; this report was unconfirmed, however, and therefore not given any serious credence.

Wychway-Wolff read this newspaper account just after his penultimate briefing the night before he was scheduled to be dropped into Iraq. At that briefing Browning had explained about the Claxton "complication," but not in the same way as he had explained it to Harry Ward.

Chapter Sixteen

The Missing Link

There was no urgency about getting to Fürstenfeldbruck since they'd have to wait for darkness in Kuwait anyway, so on the morning of Wolff's departure he found himself in Browning's office receiving his final briefing.

The matter of security for the experimental machine gun Wolff would take in with him was discussed. The first idea, to bury the weapon well enough so it would not be found, was abandoned in favor of transferring it as quickly as possible after its use in the assassination to an agent already in-country.

Wolff was told to get to an "English-style" pub in Baghdad, the Kamin Klause, owned and operated by an expatriate German with the unlikely name of Salah Amin Schwartz. In conversational German with Schwartz Wolff was to interject the phrase "No sweat" several times, which would, Browning told him, establish his bona fides with Schwartz who then would introduce him to Wolff's in-country CIA contact. This man would suggest to Wolff the best time and place for the "hit." When Wolff asked the agent's name Browning shrugged and smiled:

"You'll get it from Schwartz or the man himself. Right now, all you need to know is what you need to know."

"Like in case I'm nailed and questioned by the Iraqi authorities before the main event, right?"

"That's right, smart ass. Which brings me back to the little complication caused by the Claxton visit that we talked about last night. Right now all you mainly need to know and remember is, wherever the Christ the shoot is—maybe at a mosque someplace, I think somebody said—but anyway, when you start shooting let 'em really have it, don't hesitate, Claxton or no Claxton. If he's standing there, tough shit. Get the whole fuckin' bunch of 'em that're on the reviewing stand, or wherever the hell they are, Claxton along with 'em—he'll just be giving his life for his country like any good soldier, an' like I told you, he'll be no big loss. secretarys of state are a dime a dozen in D.C. "

"I swear to Christ," Wolff interposed, "this gets more and more weird as it goes along. So now can I assume I've got clearance to kill *our own Secretary of State* in furtherance of this great and noble cause?" he asked, and received a nod and another of those mirthless smiles he had come to detest. He thought for a moment and then asked:

"Will you be 'in-country,' uh, like with the Claxton party as a strap hanger or something, while I'm 'deployed'?"

"Hell, no! The Iraqis got a dossier on me an inch thick they got from the Soviets years ago, and I wouldn't be surprised if the Russians have been updating it. The ragheads won't get a chance to identify anybody who's even remotely connected with the Company during this drill. Unless of course they're so good they keep book on minor people like you who do newspaper translations for us," he chuckled. "No, Charley, I'll wait for you here, or maybe in Turkey, depending on how you get out of there after your big moment."

"Which now brings us, I hope, to—"

"Right," Browning broke in, "your extraction, if it's necessary to do it covertly."

Wolff waited while the other shook out a cigarette and lit it deliberately and reflectively. With his suspicions about Browning's part in the deaths of Gloria Mundi and Sibelius and Hoffmann, suspicions which now were almost certainties, he thought miserably that any talk of his getting out of Iraq would be superfluous. He supposed it would be more a matter of whether another Agency man "wasted" him before he could get out, or what was more likely, based upon the denials the US Government was ready to use in the event of his being caught, that Browning would compromise him to the Iraqis. Nonetheless he listened carefully as the other went on.

"There are a couple of ways we can do it. One *good* thing about Iraq, at least as far we're concerned, is all its wide open spaces. Chances are we'd send in a STOL aircraft or maybe even a high speed chopper to scoop up your ass out of the desert. Or, there's even the old Fulton Recovery System. You remember that?"

"Yeah, I remember it. I got 'snatched' one sunny day at Bragg when we demonstrated it for a bunch of Congressmen. But how do I get all the equipment in there—the balloon, the harness, the gas bottle, and all that shit?"[1]

"You don't. We drop it to you one night and pick you up the next day. Oh, yeah, another thing, by the way. As to any wanderings in the desert, be advised that there are still land mines all over the country, left over from Desert Storm — around sixty per square mile of terrain, I'm told."

"Wonderful. What about commo? Do I keep in touch with you guys on my CW set, use BTBs and all that?"

"That's a last resort. If you gotta transmit, don't worry about that Mickey Mouse BTB crap. I don't think those sand niggers have anything in the RDF line that'd zero in on you. But anyway, I don't think any o' that shit'll be necessary. Salah Schwartz—God, what a stupid fuckin' name!—Salah Schwartz'll relay by land line both ways, and that 'in-country guy' we talked about will be his conduit to you. *Verstehen?*"

"Land line? You mean Schwarz is gonna be taking messages and calling you on his *phone*, don't you? That's real sophistication, isn't it? Jesus, Lew, are you sure we got enough money to pay the phone bill?"

---

[1] See Glossary.

"One of the cardinal rules, asshole, is: If you can keep it simple, do it. The dirtbags know Schwartz calls Germany all the time; as long as he isn't compromised they couldn't give a shit less. Most of 'em—except the real old farts from the British Mandate days—don't know any English, let alone German, anyway," he gave a short barking laugh, "and I think it was the Germans who put in their telephone system. Jesus, what an opportunity! If it had only been us!"

"I fully agree with that 'keep it simple' bit. If I'm not compromised, or at least even if I don't *think* I've been compromised, I'm going to the airport and getting a commercial flight out of there like any other sane person."

"Stay sane, Charley, at least until this is over," Browning advised patronizingly.

Wolff-Wychway gave a short bitter laugh.

"Will it *ever* be over, Lew?"

Browning sighed and swiveled his chair to look out at the snowy landscape. He spoke to the window.

"Well, if we keep stepping on our dicks it might well be over, at least as we know the gravy train now. Some people, insiders, are calling the Agency a 'self-eating ice cream cone!' I'm talking about the *big* picture. How long do you think those Congressional oversight committees are going to take the heat they're getting for our screwups? I hear that fifty percent of our daily briefings back at Langley are devoted to 'damage control' now; all about our cocaine smuggling operations; Aldridge Ames, the spy who'll never die; Daliberti and Barloon, those two happy 'airplane mechanics,' wandering aimlessly and blamelessly across the border. Then it's revealed that the Agency hired Toto Constant to discredit Aristide in Haiti, and that this 'CAS' supplied the phoney report on drugs and manic depression that got Jesse Helms all fired up. In '93 Clinton sent the Harlan County with US and Canuck troops aboard to Port Au Prince to cool the situation; paid Constant to put on a phony demonstration at the pier—with the understanding no US people would be hurt—so the Harlan County

unasses, to our disgrace. Then there were those big juicy headlines about the KGB disinformation scam, and right after that
the fact that the Company and DoD had spent twenty mil in a
little less than ten years on *psychics*. Of course, we 'spill' that
much every day, but *psychics*! My fucking oaf!" He swivelled
to face the other.

"You know, our record ain't that great anyway, when you
come right down to it. I mean, look at how we missed the boat,
royally, when the Soviets collapsed, as one grisly example, to
say nothing of that Bay of Pigs clusterfuck back in '60. And so
since we get little enough done under the *best* circumstances
what the fuck are we gettin' accomplished when most of our
time and energy is spent plugging holes and shorin' up the bulk-
heads? It's like somethin' out of a bad French farce, ain't it?"

When he paused for breath Wolff spoke so softly that his
voice hardly carried across the desk.

"Has it ever occured to you that maybe we, I mean the
Agency, has outlived its usefulness?"

"Since you're still on the payroll, Wychway (this was serious enough to Browning to drop the use of code names), you
shouldn't be heard sayin' things like that."

"Oh, really?" replied the other flippantly, "and *I* particularly really should care, shouldn't I?" He laughed cynically, "And
that reminds me of something. Do I get an 'L' pill, if they're
still calling them that?"

"Hell, no! What for? Like I told you, nobody's gonna
believe you anyway, no matter what you tell them, and even if
they did we'd deny it and say you were just another crazy, a
rogue agent, or better still, a rogue clerk."

Oh, well, I've still got Igor's piss packet, remembered
Wychway with grim humor.

Browning became thoughtful, then added:

"And then again, maybe if you pull this off they'll thank
you—I mean, Joe Raghead in the street—maybe they've wanted to get rid of Saddam all along, but just couldn't get their act
together. I mean, just think of those goddam sanctions they've

been living under; all that would blow away the minute that big jerk was gone. Then you'd be *their* hero, too. How's that for a scenario? 'L' pill my ass, you'd be the next Caliph of Baghdad!" he glanced at Wolff and laughed loudly, "whatsa matter, no sense of humor?"

If this were a movie, thought Wychway, Ernest Borgnine would have to play Browning.

"You're about as funny as Mothers' Day at the orphanage, Lew," Wolff replied laconically as again he thought that no matter how much Browning might laugh the humor never reached his eyes; they were dead, like a shark's.

As he watched Wolff's expression Browning became serious again.

"Okay. Go back to the 'Q' and get your shit together. We'll check you out when we pick you up there," he looked at his Rolex, "in say, thirty minutes. We still got plenty of time."

As Wolff picked up his cloth cap—which, along with the Italian leather jacket, Levis, and the excellent Austrian boots, he would wear into Iraq—and started for the door Browning stopped him with:

"There's one more thing."

Halfway through the doorway Wolff stopped, and asked over his shoulder:

"What's that?"

"Keep an eye on Link."

Wolff turned to face the other more fully.

"What the hell is that supposed to mean?"

"Just do it, never mind why."

Wolff reapproached the desk.

"Now, just a minute. What's with Link—I mean, other than his odious and repellent qualities in general?"

"He came in earlier this morning. I wasn't surprised. He's been throwing some pretty broad hints around for the last couple of weeks about how he's better qualified for this job than you, and so on, and so forth."

"And?"

"And, I told him to stop being a juvenile asshole and get on with his job and let you do yours."

"Incredible," was all Wolff could think of to say.

"Yeah, I know, but just watch it anyway. I thought about getting him outta here, I mean like right now, but he's in the pattern and we need him on the infiltration; he knows more about the LABS routine than anybody we got. I don't think it'll be a problem; it's just talk. You know what a bullshitter he is. But just in case, watch your ass."

"Wonderful. Like, I don't already have enough on my mind, right?"

"I honestly don't think it'll ever happen, but if he gets any funny ideas while your out there cool 'im off. You got that Beretta I gave you, right? Just ice him, abort the mission, and we'll do it again, without him. And for Christ's sake, *don't* get into any punchouts! Remember what we got invested in that computerized head a' yours!"

"My fucking oaf!" muttered Wolff to himself as he went out the door shaking his head.

From conversations Browning had overheard it had come as no big surprise when Link came to him with his proposal earlier that same morning.

Link had launched himself immediately into the reasons for his replacing Wolff as "the shooter."

"Ah don't need all that area study shit. Y'all can't trust that candy-ass. Ah'll do it if I gotta get within five feet of the target!" Link of course, like Wychway, had no reason to think the victim was anyone but Saddam Hussein.

"Now listen to me, Duwayne. If you count all the R&D money that went into Bigeye and all the other stuff that went into this operation we're probably talking about maybe half a billion dollars of investment in this guy. Besides, it's just too goddam late to make such a radical change. I mean, if he'd been disabled in training or something like that we might have had to consider a replacement. But I'd still have to get clear-

ance from the back room boys and all that. Be reasonable,"
Browning put in equably.

"Y'all coulda had *me* for free! You still can!" Link raved
on, disregarding this logic. "Besides, I think he's a 'fear
biter'," he said with a cunning look, "if he's got any 'bite' in
hlm at all. *You* know, like some dawgs? Ah just think he's a
yeller dog, sir."

"Maybe. Maybe you're right; but even dogs that bite out of
fear have their uses. And they can tear your ass just as bad as
those that don't. No, Duwayne, this shit just won't flush, and
that's it. Now start concentrating on your part of the mission,
will you? We only got a few hours before station time for
Christ's sake! Now get your ass outta here," Browning
declared with finality.

And with that Link, somewhat like his adversary, Wolff,
had stalked off muttering to himself.

Browning's eyebrows rose skyward.

"*What?*"

"I'm tellin' you, Boss, *he left the goddam plane*," the pilot-
cum-mission leader was explaining to him on the runway apron
at Incerlik. "Link wasn't on the bird when we landed. The mission went smooth as silk. Ejection went off right on the dime.
We hit that DZ like we were laser guided. And the whole time
we were over Injun country our sensors showed we weren't
being radared, not once. —They *both* must've gone. The only
people aboard when we came in were me 'n' Steve, here," he
nodded at his observer-copilot. "After the drop we tried to raise
Link on the intercom, but no dice. When Steve crawled back
there to take a look they were both *gonzo*. All he found was a
nine mike-mike Walther. —Show 'im, Steve."

The co-pilot stepped forward and handed Browning the pistol.
"I don't think it's been fired recently, sir," he said deferentially.

Browning's face was a study in rage, frustration, and even
fear as he snatched the pistol away.

"I knew I shouldn't've sent that dumb fucking red-neck

jerk!" he hissed under his breath as he unloaded the pistol, cleared it, then sniffed its muzzle.

"What, Boss?" the pilot asked.

"Nothin'. Get this friggin' plane outta here. The goddam Turks've been askin' too many questions already. Move it!" He walked away, stuffing the Walther into his overcoat pocket and muttering to himself as he went.

The co-pilot picked up the cartridge Browning had ejected in clearing the pistol; he threw it up in the air and caught it a few times, then dropped it into his pocket as he followed the other pilot back to their plane.

Wolff didn't find Link until sunrise. He would never have found him at all if it hadn't been for his extraordinary sight advantage. The body looked like a bundle of rags someone had discarded on this remote desert hillside some twenty miles outside Baghdad. One of the Dingo boots was gone. As much as he had despised the man, Wolff was grateful for the fact that Link almost certainly must have been dead or at least unconscious before he hit the ground. Now, as the sun's orange crescent appeared over the eastern horizon of this rugged and deserted landscape, Wolff shook his head and shivered a little, not entirely from the cold. Although Browning's final words had prepared him at least to some extent for what had happened, he still found the bizarre events of the previous night incredible.

Shouting over the noise of the aircraft, Link had started his tirade just minutes after their takeoff from the remote desert airfield in Kuwait. There were just the two of them in the bomb bay area. There was no need for a crew chief or "static jumpmaster" since Link knew the aircraft intimately, having made dozens of similar "infiltrations" at El Centro.

"I know more about this mission than you do, Wychway, and can do it better, an' *I* ain't worried about comin' back! Ah'll kill the bastard if'n I gotta strangle 'im with mah bare hands! An' they'll nevah fergit me fer what I done!"

It was at this point that Wolff, already encumbered in a quarter of a million dollars worth of equipment, noticed Link was holding a pistol loosely at his side. Now Link raised his arm and leveled the weapon at Wolff's head. Wolff noted almost irrelevantly that the pistol was an old German P38, already cocked and ready to fire.

"Take thet shit off an' lay it on th' floor, an' thin move away from it," Link ordered as he moved a step closer. A B12 air force parachute, which under other conditions a crew chief or "static" jumpmaster would wear for reasons of safety during more normal airborne operations, lay on the floor near Link's feet.

The aircraft, a vintage B1B bomber converted for the purpose, carried a CARP system; the display module was bolted at eye level to the bulkhead. From the cockpit the pilot would switch on its red light precisely three minutes before the drop; at drop time its counterpart, the green "Go" light, would wink on. The CARP box remained unlit as the two men stood confronting each other. With a detached part of his brain Wolff strove to remember as he locked eyes with Link what he'd heard about distances, aircraft speeds, and times at the recent LABS briefing. He calculated quickly that the red light should come on in about two minutes, which meant the bomb bay doors would open in roughly five minutes. Fighting off the panic which was rising into his throat, he tried to reason with Link. He took a step forward, holding up a peaceful hand, palm outward.

"Goddammit, Link, use your head—you're not even wearing a 'chute, an' that light's comin' on in just seconds!" he screamed over the noise of the aircraft.

Link's only reply was an animal snarl as he dropped his eyes to Wolff's chest.

Because a reserve parachute would be useless at the low altitude his main 'chute would deploy, Wolff carried none; in its place, just below his sternum and the quick release mechanism for his harness, was the "black box": the radar controlled device which would deploy his parachute when it sensed the ground was 1200 feet away. Suddenly, just as the red "three minute" warning light glowed red Link reached across and grasped Wolff's parachute harness just above the "black box." Now, with both men standing on the bomb bay doors, Link desperately tried to work the harness release. Wolff grasped Link's gun wrist with his left hand as with his right he fumbled for the Beretta he'd shoved into a jacket pocket under his harness.

They were still grappling when the red light died and the green one came on and the bomb bay doors opened, and for a second or two Wolff wasn't even aware they'd left the airplane. Link, holding onto the "black box" with his left hand, dropped his pistol, grabbed at the spare chute at his feet, and missed. They went out together, with Wolff, his Beretta now in his hand, falling backwards and Link hanging on to his harness with both hands.

Somewhere in their cartwheeling and parabolic free fall Wolff managed to put a bullet in just under Link's nose (later he would bless himself for having cocked the weapon before putting it in his pocket—perhaps Browning's final admonition had had its effect after all). But as Link fell away he managed somehow to tear off the "black box" as he went. Although Wolff never totally lost consciousness it took him many precious seconds to reorient himself, and he was well into the downward and now seemingly fatal arc of his parabolic decent when he pulled his ripcord and audibly prayed he was not too late. His parachute canopy finally opened at less than 200 feet.

A moonless night had been chosen for his insertion, but there was plenty of starlight, and his Special Forces parachuting experience told him that even on the darkest nights, when visibility on the ground was restricted to just a few yards, it always was significantly better from the air. He had hoped to use his special vision to scan the DZ from about 1500 feet, and using the highly maneuverable Pteradactyl land exactly where he chose. But almost as soon as he'd gotten full deployment his feet slammed into the ground. He'd tried to go limp from the waist down and do the standard PLF, but it was too late; he hit the rocky ground very hard, a little too hard as it turned out (like a sack full of piss clams, his father would have said), and when he managed to get to his feet he was still feeling dazed.

After he became sufficiently sensible again he destroyed his 'chute, then found a crevice between two large boulders and bedded down uncomfortably to wait for first light. The adrenal surge resulting from his recent experiences and from thoughts of what lay ahead finally subsided, and after two sleepless hours, exhausted, he dozed off. It was getting very cold.

He awoke in that "beginning morning nautical twilight" time—which sometimes is referred to as "Dawn's left hand of God" and which has been crucial to military and naval operations for millenia. He got up feeling very stiff and sore and with a vile taste in his mouth. Shivering with cold, he drank some water, and then relieved himself.

Since he was north of Baghdad the area should be relatively free of those mines Browning had spoken of; it was in the south, especially in the southern approches to Baghdad City, that the greatest concentrations lay. Still, he decided, he must be wary.

After checking the immediate vicinity to ensure he'd left no traces of his visitation, he climbed a few feet to a higher vantage point, intending to sweep the surrounding terrain using his telescopic sight. When he closed his left eye he experienced a wave of nausea and dizziness so severe that he went reeling off the rocky outcropping he'd climbed. He ended in a sitting position, and remained there with both eyes closed and his head between his knees for several minutes while the sensation subsided; then he cautiously raised his head and opened his eyes. It took him a full fifteen minutes after the nausea and dizziness had gone to make himself try again. Still sitting he chose a rock about a hundred yards away, and very slowly closed his left eye again, almost clutching at the ground as he did so.

Although there were no ill effects this time, *the rock remained its normal size!* With every nerve on the *qui vive* he opened and closed his left eye several times. No change! He was looking at a ten-inch rock as it normally would appear at a distance of a hundred yards.

His first reaction was panic. What was he to do? The mission hinged on his visual ability, and now if he'd lost it (that damned hard landing!) how could he go on with... And then another thought edged out this dutiful, mission-oriented concern. What if he *had* lost the ability? It sure as hell wasn't *his* fault. Could he be expected to go on? What was the use of all that specialized training? No, too bad, but the S.O.P. would demand that the mission be aborted, scrubbed, washed out— the words sounded delicious as he said them to himself. Oh, yes. He would go to this nonsensical Kamin Klause place in Baghdad, contact the ridiculous Arab-German Salah Schwartz, and through him send the message to Browning. It was over! Oh, if only he could see Browning's face and hear what he'd say upon receiving the bad (great!) news!

While these thoughts were racing through his mind he had been sitting in the same position, his left eye still closed, his right still focused on the rock. Suddenly, he experienced a startling popping sensation in his head, an almost audible "snap!"—like a powerful electrical current jumping a gap, and just as suddenly the rock in his field of vision ballooned into an object at least ten times its actual size....

After having checked several other objects at various ranges in the immediate area, Wolff, now deflated in inverse proportion to the rock's sudden "inflation," got to his feet, and with a long shuddering sigh found his cigarettes (Fatima's, bought earlier in Baghdad by someone he'd never know), leaned against the rockpile he'd climbed, and finished pulling himself together.

He had backtracked more than a mile along the plane's flight path, scanning at intervals of 500 yards, and moments before sunrise had seen the Dingo boot. Thirty yards away behind a little hummock he had found the body. Link must have hit the ground at over 100 miles an hour.

Now, holding the boot loosely and thinking rapidly, Wolff stood looking down at the corpse. Link still had the Pteradactyl's "back box" clutched in both hands. The poor bastard, Wolff thought grimly, I guess he was desperate to hang on to *something*.

Wolff dropped the boot and went in search of something to dig with. Fifty yards away he found the abandoned broken "leg" of an old camel saddle studded with rusted nails and which, he discovered to his dismay, was harboring one of the only three varieties of poisonous snake in Iraq. Having induced the snake to seek other accommodations, he retrieved the saddle leg, and using it as a shovel and his utility knife to unearth obstructive rocks, he dug a shallow grave and buried what was left of Link, Dingos and all. He had been a little concerned about the absence of Link's beret; but was relieved to find it under the body. Before he left the relatively secluded gravesite he carefully removed any traces of fresh surplus spoil from his excavation and spread it around the area to dry and blend with the rest of the terrain. He buried the "black box" a hundred yards away.

Following a quick visual reconnaisance to ensure that he was unobserved, he moved to a spot half a mile away, from which he could observe the grave site and at the same time check the traffic on the distant highway to Baghdad. Barring the occasional vehicle, and of course the snake he'd displaced earlier, Wolff had seen no live movement of any kind since he'd landed. He was grateful the drop area selected was barren and therefore free of any "locals" tending their grazing sheep or goats. As the sun rose higher he was grateful also for the heat after the frigid night he'd spent among the rocks. He drank some more water. He was becoming ravenously hungry, which he thought likely was a good sign that his adrenal system was getting properly reorganized.

Keeping the location of his observation post in mind he selected a place sufficiently distant from Link's unobtrusive grave to cache the items he'd have to leave behind when he went into Baghdad. From three easily identifiable locations, which he mentally numbered one, two, and three, he took compass bearings to the spot; then with an indelible felt pen (purchased in Vienna) he printed the azimuth numbers neatly and sequentially next to the stamped logotype, **Wäscherei Strauss, Salzburg,** inside the collar of the otherwise unmarked shirt he'd been issued "to wear for job interviews." The final result looked like a typical laundry mark, except perhaps for the rather unimaginative name given the laundry. Out of the hundreds of Austrian names he could have come up with, Wolff thought ironically, leave it to Browning's Neanderthal brain to come up with The Waltz King's!

He cleaned the Beretta (that was one thing he could thank Browning for—his own personal piece), replaced the round he'd shot Link with, and secreted the pistol and an extra magazine load in the special holster sewn into his left boot; in the other boot there was a pocket for the compass. Then he stored the XMG-95F—broken down into three parts in its compact case—its ammunition, his microminiaturized CW transceiver, the utility knife, certain maps, papers, and documents (including his own genuine passport, which Browning had expressly forbidden him to take into Iraq), and most of his emergency rations in the cache, wrapping all of this first in waterproof plastic. Then he quickly converted the nylon GP bag with which he'd jumped all this in into an innocuous-looking civilian backpack.

He spent the remainder of the morning resting, checking his other papers and maps, and timing the passage of the Baghdad-bound busses on the main road in the distance, all the while speaking aloud to himself in idiomatic Arabic.

Baghdad was about twenty miles to the southeast. In the splendid physical condition he was in (one thing he could thank Link for) he was reasonably certain he could have run all the way to the city, but decided to try stopping a bus instead. If for any reason he were questioned he could say that he had been hiking back to Baghdad from the ancient and historic town of Samarra, had become tired, and had decided to take a bus the rest of the way. (The "Iraqi" visa stamp in his passport showed he had arrived in-country two days previously.) He had seen Samarra on one of his maps and now from the top of his rocky observation post he could see the town itself about five or perhaps even six or seven miles to the north (he kept reminding himself to compensate for the fact that objects always appeared closer than they actually were when seen from an elevated position). To the east was the main northwest-southeast road, with its sparse, high-speed traffic, which followed the Tigris River into Baghdad, and still closer was the Baghdad-Mosul railway line.

At noon he started towards the highway. Two busses had passed at three hour intervals, and the last had gone by at ten o' clock. As he waited by the roadside he felt ravenous. He considered opening one of the two cans of spiced lamb he carried in his backpack (another purchase by some faceless agent of Browning's), but decided he'd try to get something in Baghdad. Perhaps there would be food at the Kamin Klause.

At ten past one he stopped an old, dusty, Mercedes bus which was lavishly and brightly decorated in Islamic style and which carried "third class" passengers, along with their luggage and parcels on its sturdy fenced-in roof. The elderly-looking driver (who likely wasn't over fifty) gave Wolff a gold-toothed smile of welcome as he climbed aboard, then waved away the money he proffered, telling him he could pay when he reached his destination. Wolff took an immediate liking to this leathery-faced and jolly man.

Chapter Seventeen

The Hajj

As the festively painted old bus, swaying alarmingly, bowled along towards Baghdad, with the people on the roof—whose collective weight along with their baggage unboubtedly was responsible for the swaying—holding on for dear life, Wolff reflected upon the "missing" Link, and decided that there were at least seven ways in which the man could be considered to be "missing" or to have "missed" something.

In misjudging Wychway-Wolff, and consequently his reaction to the abruptly proposed mission substitution, Link had missed the opportunity of shooting him dead as soon as conveniently possible after they'd taken off from the Kuwaiti airfield. Had he done so he would have had plenty of time to take over Wolff's equipment and concomitantly his mission, before the drop. He'd missed the parachute he'd grabbed at as the bomb bay opened. Though less important, he even had missed his appointed time to take Wolff-Wychway to Echterdingen airport.

Less concretely but perhaps as important as anything else, Link had missed any number of things. He missed the point of any conversation which dealt with the less material aspects of life, and therefore missed—to use a hackneyed and much abused phrase— what many would call the finer things in life in general. Alternatively, there could be no question about the fact that he "missed" the "great life" in Attessuc, Georgia. And now having been buried in the desert, and assuming he would never be found, he would always be among the missing.

Yes, there was all that; but, Wolff consoled himself, with the possible exception of his mother (assuming he had one) Link probably never would be really *missed*, at least not by anyone of consequence who had ever really known him. And these thoughts led him to brood over the bizarre series of events, misfortunes actually, which had placed him in this situation; here, in this ramshackle old bus in a hostile country, with an insane task he must accomplish. Insanity. That's what this was—a form of insanity. He tried to remember that famous quotation about the Gods making us crazy before they killed us. What was it? —Oh, yes, good old Euripedes: Those whom God wishes to destroy, he first makes mad. That was it. Great, just great...

He looked through the window at the barren terrain. When he closed his left eye he experienced a mild aura of dizziness, not nearly as great as it had been when he'd started searching for Link hours earlier, and this time there was no nausea, but *it* was still there, and he had trouble focusing. The movement of the bus didn't help. But as he persisted in searching out distant objects on the desert he was relieved to find that the dizziness passed. Now he wasn't quite sure *how* he felt about his "normal" telescopic vision having returned.

Fifteen minutes later the flamboyant old bus dropped him off within three blocks of the Kamin Klause. With a "thank you" as he paid the cheerful old driver, Wolff got down and looked around.

The streets seemed unusually crowded with vendors and other trades people for a Sunday as he made his way to the address which he'd been given; then he remembered that Friday is the Islamic "Sabbath." He stopped briefly to ask an old shopkeeper, who sat amid myriad cheap brass-plated coffee pots of all sizes and who was fondly stroking a large Afghan cat, if he was headed right. Still petting his cat the kindly old man smiled and nodded affirmatively and with a graceful gesture offered his wares. Wolff declined politely and went on.

Outside the Kamin Klause a street vendor offered what appeared to be lukewarm slices of pizza and cans of that syrupy variety of Coca Cola which is produced especially to suit Middle Eastern tastes. With a smile Wolff again politely declined. As he entered the German-English-Iraqi pub a muezzin in a minaret outlined against a slate-gray sky was calling the Faithful to prayer over a loudspeaker system.

After Wolff's first few desultory remarks in his "Austrian-German" to Salah Amin Schwartz at the small bar of the Kamin Klause the bald, burly proprietor smiled and hazarded:

"*Österreichisch, ja?*"

"*Ja, von Salzburg*, Wolff replied, and ordered a beer. Then he asked if the name, 'Kamin Klause,' didn't mean something like, inglenook, in English.

"*Ja, bestimmt, ganz richtig!. Sprachensie Englisch?*"

"*Natürlich, und Sie?*" Wolff smiled.

"Yeah, sure," the other replied easily in what Wolff could have sworn was a New York accent, " I lived in the States five years." He glanced over Wolff's shoulder. 'Scuse me a minute, I think somebody wants a drink."

"No sweat, Wolff answered mildly, I've got nothing but time."

Schwartz stopped and turned around.

What'd you say?"

"I said, 'No sweat.' If you lived in the States you must know what *that* means. You know, like, no *sweat?*"

"Yeah, I know. I thought it might be you when you walked in here," Schwartz said quietly. What's your boss's name?"

"Browning."

"That ain't his name."

"It's the only one *I* know."

Schwartz smiled as at some secret joke.

"Okay, you're all right. Now, watch where I go when I deliver this drink, okay? I'll be right back."

"No sweat," Wolff answered sourly as he picked up his beer glass.

Without turning around he could see Schwartz in the bar

mirror as he took a glass of white wine to a serious-looking young black man who was seated alone at a booth-table and who seemed to be cracking nuts.

Wolff was looking appraisingly at the two English dartboards in a far corner where two men were having a game when Schwartz returned with his empty tray.

"Pretend you just recognized him," the big German said *sotto voce.* "He'll pick up on it; then go over and give him the big 'Hello.' His name's Hajji.

"Okay, Salah. One more thing. You got any real food in here, I mean besides nuts? I can't remember when I ate last."

"Sure. I'll bring somethin' over to you." He left the bar and went through a beaded curtain into another room.

Besides the dart players there were only two other people in the place, but Wolff performed as if playing to a full house. As he stared in the mirror his face assumed an expression of surprised pleasure; then he wheeled around, looked hard at the man in the booth, and with a broad smile and outstretched hand went to him. The other rose, and with appropriate smiles, gestures, and words of greeting (in Arabic) the two "friends" were "reunited."

When they were seated the black man said quietly by way of genuine introduction:

"How do you do? You go by Wolff, right? I am Hajji Abdullah No Sweat. I had better know your given name, just in case."

"Carl, with a 'C.' Doctor Frankenstein didn't give me a middle name."

"Doctor Frankenstein?" the other asked, obviously mystified.

"It's a long story," said Wolff with asperity, "which can wait till later."

"In any case," the black man smiled, "welcome, welcome to Baghdad!"

"Thanks," Wolff said tersely.

"And your arrival was without difficulty, I trust?" the other said significantly, "no problems with immigration, customs, or other such trivial but nonetheless pestilential formalities?"

Wolff winced as he shut his eyes tight, reopened them, and muttered:

"Uh, not exactly; but again, that'll have to wait, if you don't mind."

Hajji Abdullah No Sweat merely smiled and shrugged his assent.

"Right," Wolff returned the briefest of smiles. "But, Hajji Abdullah *No Sweat*? That's your *name*?"

Hajji beamed, revealing the biggest, whitest, most even set of teeth Wolff had ever seen. These were set off to even greater advantage by their background: a large, round, milk chocolate-colored face with very good skin. He was gracefully slender, about thirty-five years old, Wolff judged, and obviously in the very pink (if that's the word he wanted in this case) of health. When he'd stood to greet his "old friend" the man had been a few inches under Wolff's height.

"That's what my friends call me. Somehow I just can't stop using that expression, 'No sweat'," he said in the rapid Iraqi dialect of Baghdad, "I just love it. It's my only concession to American slang, I hope. But let's speak English," he went on in that distinctive, cultured British voice which Americans like to call "the Oxford sound" and which the British refer to as "the gentle voice."

Wolff repeated the name quietly a couple of times, as if trying it out on his tongue.

"It is a bit of a mouthful," his companion went on pleasantly, "but you can cut it to just Hajji if you'd like. I'm proudest of that, you see; I've made the Hajj—the pilgrimage to Mecca, you know—five times"

Wolff looked across and smiled. "I'll call you Hajji, then. But what I was thinking about was 'Hans'."

The other's jet black eyebrows went up. "*Hans*?"

"H.A.N.S. It comes out Hans, see?"

Hajji clapped his well-shaped hands and laughed aloud.

"*Ham'd'Allah*! Wonderful! Why haven't I ever *thought* of that? Of course, Hans is a German name, and Germany isn't one of my favorite countries—the dust bins are all alike, and they make the flowers and trees grow in orderly ranks—although the language is very precise and descriptive. But then, there also was that marvellous fellow from Holland, Hans Christian Anderssen. Hans it shall be, dear fellow! No sweat! " He poured some wine for Wolff into the extra glass Schwartz had left on the table.

"Good! So can I take it you speak German, too?" Wolff asked with growing regard for this amiable and engaging young man.

"Absolutely. I'm a bit of a linguist, you know. Italian's my favorite though." He lowered his voice, "That's where I was recruited by your people, by the by, in Florence."

"You lived there, in Florence?"

"Oh, yes, for a time. Wonderful place; a veritable museum in its own right. Originally I'm from Upper Volta, from Ouagadougou, the capital. My uncle is minister of tourism there. But I left when I went off to school as a young boy, and I haven't been back since, very much. I prefer Europe, and the Near or Middle East."

"May I ask what you were doing when you were, ah, recruited?"

"Very foolishly, as it turned out, I was trying to get an American agent—never suspecting his real identity of course—to buy certain items for me in the US-NATO Base Exchange at Leghorn so I could flog them off on the Mercato Nero."

"You? *You* were dealing in the black market in Italy?"

"I? Of course. You don't suppose I spent all those years at Charterhouse and then at the University of London's School of Economics learning nothing, do you?" He looked across with a wryly humorous expression. "But I wasn't among the best and brightest after all, was I? They, your exalted *Cia* (he gave the Agency its Italian pronunciation: Cheeya), realizing through this agent—whom, I thought, was sincerely interested in becoming wealthy under my auspices—realizing that I possessed some useful and attractive qualities (my languages for a starter) blackmailed me into going to work for them! More unfortunately, there was a witness to my conversation with that misbegotten agent (may a camel defile his father's grave!)—a weak person who was coerced into signing a deposition attesting to my little effort to obtain a few paltry personal computers at the Leghorn BX. So there you have it.

"In sum," he continued, "the agreement was that I would give them three years of my valuable time, in lieu of their turning me over to the US *and* Italian authorities (infinitely worse). However, I am pleased to tell you that all this happened almost three years ago; therefore this, dear fellow, will be my last hurrah, as the Americans would say. And if it hadn't been for the Americans I wouldn't have spent all this time in Iraq, which I have come to love more than Italy, actually. I now have an Iraqi passport, by the way. The fact that I am a Muslim plays a very important part, of course, but mainly it's the people I've met and dealt with here. I've come to love them. I plan to stay in Iraq after my indentured servitude is over." He sat back and sipped more wine, looking thoughtful.

"What's your cover? I mean, what's your overt reason for living here in Iraq?" Wolff asked quietly.

"I work for a travel agency, ostensibly Syrian, but actually owned by an American company, a dummy, of course, controlled by *the* 'Company.' I can't say its been all beer and skittles, but the experience has had its rather interesting moments, and they *have* paid me extremely well; even though my controller, on those unfortunate occasions when we must meet, looks at me as if I were something he'd just scraped off his shoe. Ah, you Americans! You may lack grace and significant culture perhaps, but you have such a never-ending supply of the ready!"

"As a matter of fact, we're broke, or haven't you heard?"

"Oh, yes, quite so. I *am* an economist you know. You're 'broke' all right, as you put it, but not so you could *notice* it, not yet anyway. It will be your grandchildren, if you happen to have any, who will pay the bill for Reagan's and his successors'," he paused momentarily, "largesse, shall we say? Your budget deficit gets plenty of attention, and has been corrected, but what about that *seven trillion dollars* of national debt? The interest alone that your government pays! Do you know how much *one* trillion dollars is? If Socrates had been given that much and told he could spend a million a day, and had lived to do it for the last 2,500 years, he'd still be doing it!"

Wolff merely nodded somberly in agreement and emptied his wine glass as "Hans" glanced around the pub and became more serious.

"But to business, I suppose, eh?" he said briskly as Salah Schwartz arrived with food and, Wolff was pleased to see, a bottle of Omar Kayam, an excellent red wine. They were silent until Schwartz left, then Wolff reopened the conversation.

"Go ahead, Hans, but I gotta get on the outside of some of this food, so 'scuse me while I have at it."

"No sweat, old man" the other replied reaching for the white wine, "time is one asset we have in sufficiency."

They fell silent again for a few minutes as Wolff voraciously attacked his food and Hans went back to his own simple repast, which consisted of dried figs stuffed with the almonds he'd been shelling when Wolff first saw him. Occasionally he would wipe his lips, sip some white wine, and look across at his companion as if he were making an appraisal. Hungry as he was Wolff wasn't completely oblivious to this, and when he stopped eating for a few moments and raised his wine glass in a mock toast he said softly:

"Hans, how much do you know about this caper?"

Hans peered quizzically at the remnants on Wolff's plate. "'Capers', Mr. Wolff?"

"Carl, call me Carl. —No, not *those* capers, Hans—*caper*. Stunt. You know," he lowered his voice another decibel, "mission, assignment, job," he hissed.

"Ah, that! Yes, well, I was told I know just what you know, barring those 'in-country' aspects, which I know and you don't, and with which I am to help you."

Wolff was amused by the careful placement of the preposition, "with." Most of the time, unless he chose not to, this man, like Randolph Churchill, spoke as precisely as most good writers write, giving his speech a pedantic flavor, he decided. But he asked seriously:

"Then you know who, let us say, the object of my attentions is?"

"Oh, yes. That I know," Hans paused thoughtfully a moment, "but," he stopped again, then looked straight at Wolff, "well as told you I am an economist; but perhaps I should have told you that more precisely I am a *political* economist; my field actually is macroeconomics." He held up a hand to forestall the other's interruption, " and I have given much thought to the plan, as it was explained to me, and—"

"Just what the hell are you driving at, 'old boy'," Wolff now interjected impatiently. "Just say it, okay?"

"In a word," replied Hans as he leaned closer, "I am not convinced that 'the object of your attentions,' as you like to call him, is the real object of *their in*tentions." He sat back staring at a point in space just above Wolff's head as he let this sink in.

Despite the hot spicy food he had just eaten Wolff felt something turning cold in the pit of his stomach.

"Meaning, just what?"

"Your Secretary of State, Claxton, has a reputation for favoring the interests of the Arab nations in the Middle East, has he not? He strongly advocates more warplanes for the Saudis, increased foreign aid for the Egyptians, massive aid to help the Palestinians develop their new State in Gaza and in the West Bank, and, most recently, the lifting of sanctions and the subsequent establishment of economic relations with this country, Iraq, leading to full diplomatic relations within a year or two. Despite the grave concerns which the Israeli hard liners continue to express over these matters and despite the pressure from their Jewish-American supporters, Claxton has a strong following in your country as well as throughout the international community. Aside from those relatively few Westerners who see the issue as one of principle, and of course the vast majority of Islamic peoples, his main and most significant approval comes, not surprisingly, from the world of business and international finance. Multinational businesses throughout the world have given him their discreet but tangible and potent support, mainly through their influence in the US Congress." Hans paused and looked levelly at his companion.

"All right, fine, and thanks for the interesting lecture; but what the hell does all that have to do with," he glanced around the pub, "with the matter at hand?"

On the 6th of December, which happens to be St. Nicholas' Day—not that that means much to a Muslim such as myself, but still, he *was* from these parts—in any case, on December 6th, just six days from now, Saddam Hussein will officiate at the reopening and rededication of the newly restored, famous and ancient mosque at Al-Basrah, in southern Iraq—the one that was almost totally destroyed in the Gulf War. On December 5th Secretary of State Claxton is scheduled to arrive in Baghdad on a state visit: the first overture, so to speak, in the new US-Iraq relations. The Iraqis have invited Claxton to be guest of honor at the Al-Basrah ceremony."

Wolff was shaking his head.

"Are you saying that that's when I'm supposed to 'do my thing'?"

"Yes."

When Wolff remained silent Hans asked:

"Tell me, if you can, and will, just how were you planning to do it? The technicalities are what I'm interested in."

Wolff considered for a few moments, and then he told him in the briefest terms possible. When he was finished Hans smiled mirthlessly, revealing no teeth this time.

"Well, old boy, that does nothing to allay my suspicions; but it goes a long way towards confirming them. In fact, I see now that what they may have in mind is to get what you Americans used to call 'two for a nickel'—in those distant days when one *could* get something for a nickel, of course," he chuckled.

"But—are you really *serious*? I mean, Jesus Christ! *Clax-*

ton? This is beginning to sound like a fucking Oliver Stone movie! —I hope the expletive doesn't offend your sensibilities," he added with less heat.

"No sweat, dear fellow. But I hope *you* are not offended if I use that same colorful Anglo-Saxon adjective as a gerund to say that I think it is *you* who is getting the fucking, from your own people."

And it was just then that Wolff, whose seat faced the pub's entrance, saw J.D. Somerville walk in—ruddy face, trench coat, trilby hat, walking stick, and all.

It had been from the German *Postamt* in Hohenfels that Wolff, late on the day Gloria Mundi had died, had called J.D. Somerville. Already highly suspicious of the circumstances of her death, he felt impelled to not only apprise J.D., at least in a general way, of what was going on, but also to ask him to contact Magda and give *her* fair warning. Anyone he'd been in contact with since this *Todtentanz* had begun, he reasoned, might be in jeopardy.

Being aware also of the probable complicity of the German authorities in Browning's machinations he'd been cryptic in his phone conversation, trusting to Somerville's quick intelligence and experience in clandestine operations. He had opened the conversation by announcing himself (and feeling a little silly about it) as "that Lone Wolf" who'd been Somerville's dinner companion several weeks ago in London. There was the briefest of pauses as J.D. mentally identified him, and then:

"Yes, old chap! How are you?"

"I'm fine, so far. But, uh, apparently there's a dangerous little epidemic going around over here. I haven't gotten it yet, and I don't know if it's gotten over to England yet, but for Christ's sake be careful; you know, especially at your age, sir."

There was another brief silence, then J.D.'s cultured drawl replied:

"I see. Well, that sounds like good advice, and I'll take it. Anything else?"

"Well, I'd appreciate it if you gave that girl I told you about a call for me; I'm afraid I won't have a chance to call her myself. You remember her, don't you? Good. Okay, just tell her I miss her and to take good care of herself—you know what I mean? Do you want me to give you her phone number?"

"That won't be necessary," J.D. replied curtly.

"Good. Okay, and be sure to tell her about that flu epidemic, will you?"

"Most certainly. Is there any way I can get back to you?"

"Uh, no, I'm afraid not."

"Are you still in Germany?"

"Yes, but not for long; I'm going off to find new work, towards the end of this month, actually."

"Where are you off to *now*?"

"I can't really say."

"I see. Anything else?"

And then Wolff had a minor inspiration. He remembered what J.D. had told him about never going to the movies, which left so little to the imagination, he'd said, and how he preferred to read instead. "I'd rather read books, you know," he'd explained, "they have better 'pictures'."

"Oh, yeah, one little thing. I know how much you like movies, especially the older ones. Well, the other night I watched an oldie with Tony Curtis, one of his first pictures, when that Bronx accent of his was really thick, you know?—the name escapes me just now, but I'm sure you've seen it. Remember that scene where he's up on a sandhill or someplace with the beautiful girl? Then he points down at the city in the distance and says, 'Yondah lies da palace of my foddah, da Caliph a' *Baghdad*.' It's really too much, if you know what I mean."

"Not *Casablanca* you're talking about, is it?"

If anyone *were* monitoring this call, Wolff hoped it wasn't a movie buff.

"No, no, no. That was the one in Morocco, with all those classic lines people are always quoting. This is *Baghdad*, back in the days when Iraq was part of Persia. See?"

"Oh, yes. I see. Very interesting place, Baghdad."

"Yeah, maybe you could check it out—on video tape or something."

I'll see if I can do that."

And there the conversation had ended.

Now, here in this unlikely pub in Baghdad was living proof that Wolff had not underestimated Somerville's perspicacity. Unfortunately he also had underestimated his initiative and his astuteness in starting his search in "British" or "American" bars and restaurants, and inquiring about a man who called himself Wychway, or "Wolf." The Kamin Klause had been only the third place J.D. had visited.

Although he was delighted to see his father's old comrade, as anyone in a similarly lonely and dangerous situation would be happy to see anyone who wasn't a potential enemy, Wolff cursed himself inwardly. He had meant his telephone call to Somerville merely as a warning, to keep him (and he hoped, Magda) safe, not as an invitation to join him in Baghdad! Now he realized with misgiving that he really *had* put the genial old soldier in jeopardy. *Why* had he not said something like, "I'll see you when next I'm in England, or even just, "I'll be in touch, J.D.!'"?

As Wolff deliberated about the adviseability of even acknowledging him in Hans's presence the matter was taken out of his hands as J.D., with a cursory look around, saw Wolff and came straight to the table. With a courteous little bow he offered his hand.

"How *are* you, old boy?" he greeted Wolff cheerfully but anonymously.

Chapter Eighteen

Confession and Apologia

After introducing J.D. to Hans (as simply 'Hans,' and leaving out all that "No Sweat" business, which seemed to relieve the so-named individual immeasureably) Wolff excused himself and went to the men's room. As he'd expected, Hans joined him almost immediately; fortunately the place was empty, and during a hurried conference Wolff tried to calm the agent's understandable trepidation about Somerville's bona fides. The black man also wasn't pleased with Wolff's friend per se.

"Besides, he looked at me like I went to the wrong school, or my clothes didn't fit," Hans complained inconsequently.

"At least he didn't give you a fleeting glance and ask me, 'Who's the Wog?' when he walked up to the table. And stop quoting from P.G. Wodehouse. J.D.'s a great man, Hans; he was one of my father's best friends—solid gold. And a very good man to have around when you're in a strait, from all I've heard about him. It's just that he's a little old fashioned."

"Longs for those palmy days before London was infested with 'second-class citizens'?" Hans opined cynically.

But in the end he acquiesced to Wolff's wishes. It was decided that they would part company from Somerville, at least for the time being, and resume their conversation (understandably Wolff was very keen to hear more of Hans's views about the Agency's real intentions) at the place where Hans had arranged accommodation for Wolff during his brief stay in Baghdad.

Back at the table Wolff explained to J.D. that since, unfortunately, he and Hans had business to attend to he would contact his friend later at his hotel, the Baghdad Hilton. Without delay and with characteristic bonhomie J.D. extricated himself from the booth. Wolff rose with him. They ended face to face and only inches apart, and J.D. almost had to lip read his friend's muttered:

"Did you contact Magda?"

"Yes," J.D. nodded, "all's well," he mouthed back. "More later," he added noncommittally in a normal voice as with a smile and a quick handshake for his friend and a curt nod for Hans, he left.

A few minutes later Wolff signaled Salah Schwartz to the table and, over Schwartz's objections, insisted on paying the bill; remembering what Browning had told him about the phone contact he promised he would keep in touch. The big German amicably suggested he come in sometime for a game of darts. In fact, he added, the Anglo-American community, or what was left of it after the Gulf War, had a dart league which met on Wednesday nights. Wolff thanked him for the invitation, complimented him on the food, and again said he'd keep in touch.

When he and Hans went outside a light snow was falling.

"I don't think they've had snow here in twenty years," commented Hans as he pulled up his coat collar.

"I haven't been here during the last twenty years," Wolff rejoined gloomily as he stopped and knelt as if adjusting one of his boots. When he straightened up he said:

"Do me a favor, would you Hans? I might be able explain what I'm doing with one or the other of the items I'm carrying in these beautiful boots, but not both. Besides, I'm not supposed to be surveying any prospective oilfields yet, so would you please stash this compass for me?"

"Stash…?"

"Hide, Hans, secrete, if you please," Wolff replied with a tolerant smile. "I'm sure you've got a 'Hong Kong pocket' or two in that overcoat you're wearing."

"No sweat," said Hans as he took the compass.

By the time they arrived at their destination the snow had stopped, leaving just a light dusting on the pavements. Hans had booked Wolff into a small, clean, inexpensive hotel, where he was required to leave his passport at the tiny "front desk." Once in the small and austerely furnished room Hans produced a bottle of brandy from the depths of his voluminous overcoat, and with Wolff sipping out of a tooth glass and Hans drinking from the bottle they resumed their conversation. Hans had reassured Wolff about possible surveillance. "No sweat about bugs," he'd told him, "my 'colleagues' can't wheel and deal here like they can where they've got an embassy establishment with an entire country team and all their cherished electronic equipment. And even if they had they wouldn't get much cooperation, if any, from the Iraqis. Besides, I changed hotels. This isn't the one you're supposed to be staying at."

Not long into their talk Wolff, who had been lounging on the bed while Hans occupied the only chair, sat up sharply when the other almost casually revealed that he had known Gloria Mundi. Gloria Mundi, the beautiful Circassian whose real name had been Nahla Maturboff, actually had been an Iraqi agent, Hans now told Wolff.

"Somehow," Hans smiled meaningfully but without rancor, "she found out about Saddam, but she suspected there was more. We'll never know why or how, but she did."

"How did *you* find out? Was she on *your* private payroll, too?" Wolff asked sarcastically.

"Before I answer that, I'd like to know how you really feel about this assignment, at least *your* part of the brief: what you were told you must do. Forgetting morals or ethics—which we are told to do on page one of the Agency handbook—do you think eliminating Saddam Hussein would serve the better interests of your country, and of course the interests of countries friendly to the US in general?"

Wolff sipped his brandy as he gathered his thoughts.

"No, not now. The time to have gotten rid of the man was

during or right after the Gulf War. Either we should have taken him out during the war, or gone on to Baghdad and had him deposed or otherwise eliminated. I don't think anyone, in or out of Iraq, who counted for anything would have batted an eye if we'd tried him as a war criminal and hanged him in the public square. But getting rid of him *this* way now, now that he's had a chance to re-entrench himself, could well lead to a 'palace coup,' maybe civil war and anarchy, and who knows if we'd be any better off with what followed *his* regime—it could be worse. If, for example, the Shi'ites ever came to power we could have another Iran on our hands, and what would be even more dangerous is that this could lead to a *rapprochement* between Iraq and Iran, maybe even a coalition or pact—greater Persia all over again, maybe, despite the language difference—and then our shit would really be in the street, to say nothing of the Israelis'. Kuwait would become a nonentity overnight, and taken together with the other two we're talking about a third of the world's oil. I think Claxton's right in that sense: better to deal with the devil we know."

"And how do you feel personally about what you've been sent to do?" asked Hans gently.

"I know Saddam Hussein is a power-mad, opportunistic, self-seeking bastard and that he should pay for all the nasty things he's done. But I don't see myself as the avenging angel, or his agent. I didn't want any part of this," Wolff answered flatly; and he went on to explain the bizarre events leading to his optical phenomenon and to describe, briefly and generally, the coercion he'd been subjected to by Browning.

"Is it truly so phenomenal, that effect they produced in your vision?" Hans asked digressively.

"Oh, yeah," Wolff passed a hand gently over his face, "it works all right. I thought I'd lost it for a while after I augered in out there in the desert last night," he shook his head with a wry look as Hans raised his eyebrows at this. "My arrival didn't go exactly as planned," he mused, "but the eyeball seems to be okay again. I don't use it any more than I have to. It makes me feel like some sort of a freak." He paused for a few moments. "You know, I think their using me on this job is a lot of bullshit. I think they're just field testing this thing—they call it Bigeye—using me as their first working test model. If they wanted to kill Saddam I'm sure they could have used a more conventional approach. As I pointed out to Browning early in the game, the Mossad doubtless could have handled it during one of their coffee breaks."

"Which brings us back to what I was telling you when your friend, Colonel Blimp, showed up," Hans looked across at his companion, "You have put your trust in me, and I will reciprocate." He looked thoughtful as he sipped some brandy.

"I've become more and more convinced that Saddam is not the primary target after all. Oh, in their zeal to satisfy American public opinion and to produce a coup for your politically ailing President they'll be happy to see 'the Hitler of the Middle East" (what nonsense!) go down, but I think it's deeper than that. And you, I'm afraid, dear fellow, are just a pawn. You certainly are right in that they want to test their new scientific breakthrough—more like a freak accident if you ask me, but let that go for the moment—but that, I think, is just a part of it, that and getting Saddam out of their hair, so to speak. I'm convinced they want this man, Claxton, out of the way. Are you aware that there's talk of his resigning his post as Secretary of State and running against your exalted imbecile of a president (I hope you'll pardon the indiscretion) in next year's primary election? And, oh, yes—since we seem to be putting all our cards on the table—about Nahla Maturboff (Allah be kind!), or as you knew her, Gloria Mundi. No, she was not on *my* payroll; but, in a manner of speaking, we both were on the *same* payroll, or I should say, pay*rolls*."

Wolff sat up again, and this time he swung his feet to the floor. "You're a double... You're working for the *Iraqis*?"

"Yes, and no. I'm *not* working for the current regime. I *do* represent the interests of a group of Iraqi dissidents who hope to change the polity of this country to one of true democracy one day. These are not the Shi'ites you spoke of, they are not reactionary Islamic fundamentalists, nor are they the Kurds, who have such great grievances against the established dictatorship. 'My people' represent no one sect or group. What they do represent—and if I were not convinced of this I would not have agreed to help them—what they do represent are the better interests of *all* Iraqis. Incidentally, that Iraqi fellow you were going to see in Munich when you had that terrible smash on the Autobahn? —Yes, he was one of our people."

Wolff, having decided that nothing would surprise him anymore, said simply: "*Was?*"

Hans gave the other a knowing look.

"He was killed crossing a street a few days after your accident. —But let me go on. What they, these dissidents, hope to do eventually is form a peaceful coalition of all the groups I mentioned, including the ruling Ba'ath Party but *ex*cluding Saddam Hussein. But they want to *depose* Saddam, legally and if at all possible, peacefully, to preclude the occurence of the probable chaos you so wisely described a little while ago. Assassinating Saddam now would almost certainly throw all their plans and preparations into disarray. Losing Secretary Claxton as an influential friend and key figure in the West, and especially in the only superpower left on earth, would be a great setback also, though probably without the prompt and dire repercussions Saddam's killing would have." Hans lit a cigarette and made himself a little more comfortable in the hard straight-backed chair.

"Does Claxton know about this, this movement you're working for?" Wolff asked as he idly fingered his watch.

"Yes. On his last visit to Jordan six months ago he was told, discreetly, by King Hussein. Hussein has agreed to act quietly as an 'honest broker' in the preliminary and understandably extremely delicate negotiations to determine the kind and amount of support, if any, which would be forthcoming from both the West and the other Islamic nations. Discus-

sions thus far have been conducted by selected individuals—
Claxton being one—but not on the official, state levels.

"So you see, I *do* trust you; I must, because now that you
know I oppose your assassinating Saddam—oppose it only for
practical reasons, mind you— now that you know that, there is
every chance that you would have to kill me. I'm sure you are,
at least potentially, extremely proficient at killing. Or, if you
did not do it yourself you could have me removed by some
other means (I know also about your direct phone contact
through Schwartz at the Kamin Klause), to preclude my probable interference in or betrayal of your 'sacred' mission. But I
do not think you are sufficiently dedicated to what you have
been sent to do to do that. You would simply have innocent
blood on your hands; and I have a very strong feeling that you
do not want *anyone's* blood on your hands if you can possibly
avoid it. So I am willing to take that risk. And for whatever it
may be worth I give you my word that I will do nothing to hin-
der you, other than of course my very best to try to dissuade
you from going through with this ill-conceived, depraved, and
as it applies to you, deceitful scheme. *En fin*, if this trust I
spoke of still exists between us let us try now for a kind of
mutual accommodation." He forestalled Wolff's interruption
with a well-manicured hand.

"Now let me tell you something else. In 1968, after the Tet
Offensive (Allah be merciful!) I was in Vietnam for several
weeks. I went at the invitation of a chap I'd known in England
who had become the senior advisor to the South Vietnamese
minister of finance," Hans squirmed in his chair and actually
giggled. "All that money the Americans poured into that
wretched country, and it was a Brit telling them how to spend
it! When I think of all the hundreds if not thousands of 'advisors' in Vietnam who were American, except for this cove...
Well, anyway, not to digress. While there the Brit introduced
me to an American officer who was staying at my hotel in
Saigon—the old Cavalier of French colonial days. This Ami
was in Saigon for a few days to brief the high command on a

subject he had become expert in over years of study, both in and out of the army. Although we'd just met and I was still tired from my long journey, what this fellow had to say was so fascinating that despite my weariness I listened eagerly while he talked long into the night.

"The subject of his briefing was something he called 'pol-war,' an acronym for political warfare (a rather misleading title as it turned out), which he defined as a systematic process of ensuring the loyalty of a given military organization to a legitimately constituted govenment, realizing that whomever controls the armed forces of a country, especially an 'emerging' one, has a good chance of staying in power (witness Saddam Hussein as one unfortunate example). Historically this polwar had its roots in the Soviet political commissar system, which as I'm sure you know was superimposed by Trotsky on his new Red Army to keep the soldiers in line. Later the Chinese communists adapted the Russian system for their own use. Rather ironically, when Chang Kai Shek and his loyal friends rather unceremoniously were chivvied off the mainland to what we now call Taiwan in '49, they, the Nationalists, took the polwar idea with them; after all, as was too painfully proven by Chiang and company's unceremonious removal, it had worked extremely well for Mao and *his* colleagues.

"The system, with a major modification which I will tell you about shortly, worked beautifully for the Chinese Nationalists, and was a major factor in keeping Chiang and after his death his son and their cohorts in power and helping to lead them into the economic prominence they enjoy today, because *the polwar system kept the Nationalist regime stable*, especially during those first few crucial years of settling into the new homeland. After all, the Chinese Nationalists still had an army of several hundred thousand men—and women of course, to be politically correct. So now, we have one polwar system in the Soviet Union; a somewhat different system, adapted to the needs of masses of agrarian peasants, in Mainland China; and yet a third system practiced still differently (more democratically, I might hint) on Taiwan.

"But there was an even more dramatic and important distinction about the Taiwan system. It was being practiced on the '*right*' side of the iron and bamboo curtains. It was being practiced in the 'Free World'! So Chiang and his minions, unwittingly or not, gave the thing an aura of legitamacy. And today, with communism more risible than anathematized, and only to be found perhaps in a theme park in Cuba or Albania—as one astute observer has put it— the Soviet and Chicom taint doesn't mean much, if anything, anymore.

"Now, after the French colonialists in Indochina were ignominiously shown the door by the communists in '54, and after the 17th parallel arrangement gave the South Vietnamese a country, more or less, they, the RVN, began looking at what the Chinats had accomplished in just a few years in Taiwan. Since the Americans, who were trying to help stabilize the new country, had nothing much more than platitudes and what they called 'psywar' or 'psyops' to offer, the shaky South Vietnamese govenment turned to the Chinats, who very willingly sent polwar advisors to help the RVN establish a system of their own, which was ambitiously christened the Republic of Vietnam General Political Warfare Department, or GPWD, as it became familiarly known."

At this point in his lengthy disquisition Hans levered himself out of the uncomfortable chair, took a long pull out of the brandy bottle, and went to the tiny sink where, since Wolff was in possession of the only glass available, he drank deeply straight from the faucet. After a quick glance in the tiny mirror he came back and stood looking down at his newly-found confidant.

"I hope I'm not being tiresome with all this, but it is highly important. I'll do my best to end it now without omitting anything of consequence.

"Try to imagine a grid," he said as he gestured with his hands, "metaphorically speaking, laid over the entire RVNAF, the Republic of Vietnam Armed Forces—army, air force, and navy, such as it was. This was the GPWD, superimposed over the ordinary military hierarchy, from the very highest level right down to the squad or equivalent unit. And here's the difference, which I alluded to earlier, instituted by the Nationalist Chinese when they adapted the Chicom system: In addition to the mainly pragmatic and largely negative Soviet or Chicom approach—the political indoctrination, the spying, informing on and weeding out of dissidents, the execution squads, and so on—the highly successful Chinat approach, and the unfortunately fruitless and virtually stillborn Vietnamese approach, included positive elements of troop welfare, recreation and morale, and so on—those elements which keep a soldier loyal or at least keep him from deserting every time his wife has a child or the crops must be harvested, or what is more important, keep him from being induced to turn on his own leaders, to include those who head his government.

"In short both approaches included all those bits and pieces, important bits and pieces, which tend to keep a soldier, sailor, or airman if not completely happy then at least content. It is axiomatic that soldiers will always bitch, no matter how good they have it. The corollary also is valid: you can start worrying when they stop bitching. In any case, these services, the bits and pieces, are included under one central organization instead of being relegated to special staff functions or ancillary agencies—such your Red Cross (our Red Crescent), the chaplains, emergency relief for dependents, special services and sports activities, and so forth—as they are in most Western armies. And that's the main reason why the US couldn't contribute much if anything to this effort in Vietnam. Since they *presume* the loyalty of their forces, they see, justifiably to some extent, no need for a central rigid organization of this kind.

"Of course the less desireable elements I've mentioned— the spies within the ranks, the political indoctrination, the political officer alongside the commander—must be there also. But in the 'Free World' system brought to Vietnam by the Chinese Nationalists that political officer at the commander's elbow was there not merely to ensure that the commander was loyal and that government policies were adhered to, but also to see that the troops were given reasonable leave time and were fed and paid properly, among other things.

"Also, and interestingly I think, the system included what the Americans called psyop or psywar. In addition to propagandizing their own forces there was a section of the GPWD which targeted the enemy with propaganda and which conducted other, more subtle and clandestine activities against them. In theory at least the program was extremely efficient and had great merit. Unfortunately for the South Vietnamese, though they gave it a real try—with their Chinese National advisers and the Americans helping all they could, mainly with money—under the circumstances there was no way they could get the system working effectively while they were fighting a fully-fledged war at the same time. That was one disadvantage the Chinats hadn't had to face; they'd already lost their war, and were no longer in a hostile environment—all they had to contend with were their own people."

Hans poured what was left of the brandy into Wolff's tooth glass and went back to his chair; then he looked across at his companion and said:

"Given the right circumstances I think such a system, honestly administered by a reasonably honest government, could be instrumental in Iraq's salvation."

Wolff sat with his elbows on his knees, staring at the amber fluid in his glass for a few moments. The only sound in the room was the creaking of Hans's chair as he resettled himself. Then Wolff glanced at his watch and asked:

"What happened to that officer you met in Saigon—the polwar expert?"

"He survived the war, and not many years later he retired and taught political theory and philosophy at a small college in New England. He retired again, and now he spends his time in private scholarship and writing. As a matter of fact," Hans continued with a smile of genuine pleasure, "through my efforts he has agreed to come to us, at the appropriate time, as an advisor to Iraq's future government on the very matters I just spoke of." Then he interrupted himself, addressing Wolff for the first time by his "given" name:

"Carl, you have checked your watch no less than four times in the last half-hour. Do you have another meeting today? I do hope my little polemic didn't bore you too much?" he ended with a trace of sarcasm.

"No, no, no. Actually I found it very interesting," Wolff hastened to apologize. "Sorry, Hans, I didn't know it was so obvious. And I *have* been listening. I remember hearing about that GPWD outfit when I was in Nam, but I never got the real story on what the hell they were supposed to be doing. That's a little odd, because I was in special ops myself, and after hearing what you've just told me I'm sure that there could have been an overlap in some of our operations."

"Such as the Chieu Hoi and Phoenix programs, for example?"

"Exactly. My God, that Phoenix Program! We must have killed tens of thousands of innocent Vietnamese citizens, claiming they were VCI, just to supply the body count figures the CIA wanted to send to Washington. Jesus!" Wolff shook his head, then went on:

"Well, all that's what the Italians would call *acqua passatta* now; but it certainly sounds like this polwar thing would be right up the street of some of these 'developing nations,' as we patronizingly like to call them—Iraq included—if what you and your friends are trying to pull off is successful." Now he looked openly at his watch and added, "No, I just thought I'd give Major Somerville a call; there's something personal, and to me, important, I want to talk to him about. Nothing about 'the job,' Hans, I assure you. Can we go down and make a call?"

When Hans, using the public telephone in the hotel lobby, had gotten through to Somerville at his hotel he turned the phone over to Wolff.

"Yeah, it's me. I take it you got in touch with Magda, right?"

"Oh, yes, just after your call, in fact."

"Well, how is she—is she okay?"

"Why don't you ask her yourself?" J.D. chuckled, "she's right here. I brought her along."

"*What*? You brought her *with* you?"

"Yes. She insisted."

With this Wolff leaned against the wall and groaned.

"Hallo! Are you there?—*Hallo!*"

"Yeah, I'm here...." mumbled Wolff, as once again he cursed himself inwardly and wholeheartedly.

When around seven o' clock that evening they met in the lobby of the Baghdad Hilton Wolff, despite his misgivings, gave Magda a hug that might have cracked the ribs of an older or frailer woman.

Somerville insisted they all have a drink at the hotel bar (which Wolff, after several glasses of wine at the Kamin Klause and half a pint of brandy at his *pension*, could have done without) after which while Hans escorted Magda to the main dining room J.D. took Wolff up to his room where he could have a proper shower and a shave. In the bar Wolff had been delighted by J.D.'s cordiality, a trifle forced perhaps but still welcome, towards Hans. A half-hour later they all were seated together at dinner.

They made desultory conversation through the first and second courses, all rather stilted of course, as when four highly intelligent people are trying to be polite but are unsure of each other's trust. Finally Somerville, seated at the head of the table and acting more or less as *pater familias,* gently threw down his napkin, looked around at the other three, and said:

"I think it's time we cleared the air, don't you?"

With a glance at Hans Wolff immediately spoke up.

"I second the motion. Go ahead, J.D.," at which the older man nodded and looked across at Hans.

"I want to tell you what *I* know about all this. Magda can speak for herself, but I must admit that we discussed the situation on our way to Baghdad. Then you can think about that and decide if we should go further. Does that meet with *your* approval, Charley?"

"It does. —But maybe you'd better use 'Carl' from now on, okay?" He tried to catch Magda's eye as he said this, but she was busy impressing little designs on the tablecloth with her fork.

"Fine," J.D. smiled. Well, Hans—may I call you Hans?"

"Of course you may, Major. Let us not be formal." Wolff was amused to notice the paradox of Hans's polite conventional response for what should and would have been a simple, "No sweat!"

"Let us not," agreed Somerville pleasantly, "J.D.'ll do. — Well, have you had enough time to reflect, Hans?"

"Yes. Please tell me what you know, or suspect, Maj…, um, J.D."

Based upon the few facts he already knew added to Wolff's cryptic phone call and the very fact of *where* they were, and drawing upon his very considerable personal experience in such matters, J.D. had the mission pretty nearly taped—barring Hans's subtle suspicions about Secretary of State Wilbur Claxton being the real target of the assassination. When he finished he looked at both Hans and Wolff in turn.

"Well?" he asked curtly.

Chapter Nineteen

A Passion in the Desert

Hans looked across at Wolff who merely shrugged and with a resigned expression cocked his head in J.D.'s direction by way of congratulation. Hans looked at the old soldier and nodded twice.

"You'd think me an imbecile if I tried to deny it, so I won't deny it. On the other hand I won't confirm it," he added hurriedly. "That would be madness, here, under these circumstances." He waited for a reply.

Instead of answering, Somerville turned to Magda, by way of introducing her to the conversation. When he saw that she seemed to be in some distress, he quickly amended what he had proposed to say.

"Are you feeling all right, my dear?"

"Perhaps I ate something which didn't quite agree with me," Magda answered with a wan smile. "And then the trip in that crowded airplane... But I'm fine, really," she added as she managed another, more convincing, smile. In view of the fact that they had traveled first class, as Wolff had learned in casual conversation with J.D. up in his suite, this last comment seemed a little odd. But Magda was going on.

"I must say I haven't thought the matter out as thoroughly as all that," she said picking her words carefully, "but, yes, it makes sense. But it is all rather, rather frightening I think, is it not?" she ended rather lamely as with a distressed expression she looked around at her companions.

Wolff, who for the last few moments had been sitting silently shaking his head in seeming frustration now spoke up decisively.

"It's up to you, Hans, old man, but I think it's time to put *all* the cards on the table, don't you?"

"Which would mean," Hans replied unmoved, "that—assuming there is any truth to what has already been said, and of course I am not admitting that for a moment, you understand—but if there were, you must realize, Carl, that we would be placing two innocent people in the direst position of danger by discussing this any further?"

"For Christ's sake, Hans! Isn't it a little late to be trying to get the cat back in the bag? The mere fact that we've all been seen together—I'm sure you won't deny that we're all under surveillance? Do you think we haven't been 'made' already? Do you want us to think you're the only Company man in Baghdad?"

"*I've* been watched since I went to wait for you at the Kamin Klause. Whom do you think those two idiots were who were playing darts in the corner? And we're being watched now. So perhaps these two innocent people, while they're still relatively innocent, would do well to get on the next available flight back to London. Do you not think that would be wise?"

"Sure, Hans, and then tomorrow or the next day we can pick up the *Herald-Tribune* and read about another mysterious plane crash? Bear's ass! Better they stay here, now that they *are* here. And keep this in mind: the closer they are to us, the safer they'll be. No, our illustrious leaders aren't going to risk cocking up the whole operation while it's still cooking. Got it?"

"And when it's 'cooked,' done with, what then?"

"We'll save that for 'then'."

"You mean you're actually going to go through with this? Because if you're not we're going to be faced with even greater dangers. You see that, don't you?"

"This isn't the time to talk about that," Wolff said emphatically enough, though he glanced self-consciously at Magda and J.D. in turn. "But I'll tell you this much, Hans: we *are* going south." He was thoughtful a moment. "In fact, we're going to take Magda and Major Somerville with us—that is, if they agree. —J.D., Magda?"

"In for a penny, in for a pound, I always say. Of course I'll go," J.D. answered unhesitatingly.

"Rebecca West was right—all men are lunatics and all women are idiots. But yes, I will go, too," Magda replied in her turn.

"*What*! Have you *all* gone insane? I won't take responsibility for—"

"Hold on now, Hans. Let me finish," Wolff broke in brusquely. "We've got a natural cover story. Four friends, one of whom *is a travel agent and owns a car*—better still, an *old* car, right? —and meet adventitiously in Baghdad and decide to go and see the sights, especially the newly-restored mosque at Al-Basrah." He broke off his speech to shoo away the morose waiter who had come to clear the table, then he went on:

"Anyway, Hans, you heard me. Just tell your people at the Polish Embassy,[1] or wherever the hell those embassyless clowns hang out just now, about this great cover story we've got now. But we're going to do it my way—about which more in a minute. Right now you're going to tell J.D. and Magda that bit about what you think the real object of this exercise is." He held up a hand to forestall Hans's objection. "Goddammit, don't argue with me! Somebody's gotta make these decisions from now on anyway, and I just appointed myself as him. Now *tell* 'em!" he ended almost viciously.

During this conversation J.D. Somerville had been listening with great interest; now he beamed with pleasure.

"Chip off the old block, by Jove," he muttered in Magda's direction.

---

[1] With no direct diplomatic relations between Iraq and the United States, an arrangement existed whereby US citizens desiring to enter Iraq applied for visas through the Algerian Embassy in Washington, D.C.; in Iraq those who needed exit visas or other aasistance from US authorities were instructed to go through the Polish Embassy in Baghdad.

And then, with a look of great misgiving, Hans told them his worst fears.

After the brief and somewhat stunned silence that followed this appalling presentation, J.D., with typical "British phlegm," divertingly referred to Wolff's cryptic telephone call to him in London, and this led Wolff to tell them, more seriously, about the bizarre events attending the sudden and tragic deaths of "Gloria Mundi," Sibelius, and his young assistant, Hoffmann.

Hans's dreams and plans for a new and democratic Iraq were not to be revealed until they were on the long road to Al-Basrah.

Now that they had "cleared the air," to use J.D.'s phrase, their discussion was continued in what J.D. called his "billet." Magda had gone to her room, saying that if she were going to stay in Iraq longer than the few days on which she had planned she would have to call her College and let them know. She dismissed with a gesture Wolff's suggestion that she take some aspirin and lie down, saying that she felt much better now and would be back to hear more as soon as she could.

Meanwhile, seated comfortably with the other two in his own suite on the seventh floor of the hotel, Somerville was demanding to know, point blank, just what Wolff did intend to do about his mission. On the way to J.D.'s rooms Hans had repeated the gist of what he'd told Wolff earlier about the Agency's surveillance limitations here in Iraq, so J.D. wasted no time readdressing the subject.

"Well, Charley—Oh, all right then, Carl!—just what in the bloody blazes *do* you have in mind? Keep in mind that, as you so rightly pointed out, the girl and I, whether we like it or not, are in this thing now up to our armpits. So I, and she, even if we do not have what your people like to call a *need* to know certainly have every *right* to know. So let's have it—do you actually plan to go through with this insane scheme? And now, what about this very sensible theory Hans has suggested? In my mind, you know, for whatever it's worth, it makes very good sense."

"I know it's asking a lot, especially on such short acquaintance, but do you trust me, J.D.?"

"Of course I trust you. The mere fact that you called me in London shows the trust you've placed in *me*. Yes, of course I trust you. Now, what are you trying to say?"

Wolff got up and walked to the window, from which he could see the lights of Baghdad arrayed panoramically. Happily the great destruction caused by bombs and missiles during the Gulf War had almost entirely been repaired. The view was beautiful and somehow evocative in a strange, almost mystical way. He thought of the bus driver who had taken him into the City and of the old shopkeeper and his cat outside the Kamin Klause. He had felt much the same emotions when he'd first seen Cairo (under much pleasanter circumstances) and now he decided that all ancient Islamic cities in the Near East had this same ineffable, mysterious, even mystical quality. As he gazed over the city he tried his special vision. He achieved it immediately as he closed his left eye; then, for a nanosecond, he experienced a blackout, much as sometimes occurs on a television screen. Then full sight, with magnification, reasserted itself. He noted once again that his night vision under magnification was extraordinary, much like the "light gathering" quality of a pair of good field glasses. Without turning around and in a voice that barely carried across the room he said:

"I don't know *exactly* what I'm going to do, J.D., but I'm going to go through with this at least up to a point, at least as far as Basrah. I have to see... I've been lied to so many times I'm not sure *what* I'll find down there." He turned and came back to stand before the two men. As he spoke he looked down alternately at them.

"I'm pretty sure I'll know when I get down there." He forestalled J.D.'s protest with a gesture. "And on reflection I'm not sure I was right about you and Magda going along. Actually I think it might be better after all if Hans and I went on alone. Hans has good friends here in Baghdad. I'm sure he can find a place where you two can hole up until we get back," he smiled ruefully, "or at least until the smoke clears."

"What is it I will do, or not do?" Magda, who had quietly let herself in using the key J.D. had given her, asked from the doorway.

"You're going along to Al-Basrah—as am I—and that's flat," declared J.D. in a voice and with an expression which in his soldiering days undoubtedly would have brooked no further discussion, to say nothing of contravention. And even now—barring a few minutes of fruitless protest from Wolff—with Magda's complacent approval and with Hans pretty much washing his hands of the entire issue, saying he thought they were all crazy, the old soldier's Gibralter-like decision was carried, and they went on to discuss the details of their "strange odyssey," as Hans described it.

After deciding that they would depart Baghdad for Al-Basrah on the second of December, two days hence, they agreed that this was enough discussion for one night—especially since Hans had to "check in with his people." Wolff saw him to the door, and as they shook hands asked:

"How do you feel, Hans?"

"If they don't give me a lie detector test I should be all right; and since they've hardly got office space over here, to say nothing of all their usual exotic electronic equipment, I don't see that they can." He assumed a gallows look as he added, "and it's too early in the game for them to start torturing me, don't you think?"

"Stop worrying, old Hans. Like I told you, they can't say 'No'; or I should say, they can *say* it, but there's nothing they can do to stop us."

"Whatever you say, Chief," the other replied with woeful sarcasm as he turned to leave. Abruptly he turned back with a pensive expression.

"By the way, there *is* one more thing that still bothers me."

"What's that, Hans?"

"What, actually, does 'bear's ass' mean?"

Not much later Wolff and Magda bid a tired Somerville good night and went to her room. Wolff realized when he finally and thankfully closed his eyes to sleep an hour later that the last time he had slept, barring that couple of hours cat-napping in the desert, was in his bed at the Hohenfels Base two nights ago.

Since the first order of business dealt with retrieving the items Wolff had cached in the desert, and not wishing to implicate the others even further unnecessarily, Wolff and Hans had decided to meet at a coffee shop near Wolff's hotel in the morning to discuss ways and means. After that, assuming Hans had not met with an adamant (and threatening) refusal on the part of his handlers to go on with Wolff's cover scheme, they would contact J.D. and Magda and begin preparations for the trip south.

At mid-morning the following day Wolff, sitting with his thick black coffee at a small table with a good view of the street, watched as Hans parked his dusty old Fiat at the curb, and after a glance up and down the street came into the café.

As he removed his overcoat and sat down he greeted Wolff with, "They gave me a message for you from Browning."

"A great way to start the day. What'd he say? Mission aborted, I fervently hope? —By the way, Good morning!"

"Oh, yes. Sorry! Good morning! No such bloody luck, old man. I'll give it to you verbatim, as 'they' gave it to me. —He said, 'Tell him he's walking very close to the edge'." Hans signaled for a waiter.

"And what about taking J.D. and Magda with us to Basrah?"

"No sweat, as long as you keep that cautionary word from Browning uppermost in your mind, I was told, that was provisionally approved, reluctantly I might add, at least as far as Basrah, then you must separate yourself from them. That's what prompted Browning's message—they had to get approval from him."

"Typical," said Wolff disgustedly. "You *know* the chubby son of a bitch, don't you? Salah Schwartz told me, when I first met him yesterday, that 'Browning' wasn't his real name."

"Right, on both counts. I met 'Browning' in Cairo, during the Gulf War. They sent me there in early January of '91 to wait out the fireworks display in Baghdad. I saw him in Alexandria, also. In addition to his lavish flat in Garden City, near the US Embassy, he had a place near the beach there, in Alex. Living very high off the hog, he was.

"Well, one day I sneaked a dekko at his dossier in the station chief's office at the Embassy—I was on very friendly terms with one of the chief's secretaries, a beautiful girl named Fatoumata, from Cote d' Ivoire. She absolutely hated Browning. He was such a bad lot, especially among the local people he dealt with—my Muslim brothers and sisters, you understand—calling them 'dirt bags,' 'rag heads,' 'sand niggers' and worse, that I felt I wanted to know more about him. You never know *what* information might come in handy some day in this game of snakes and ladders....

"Anyway, his name actually is Alfonso Abbandonato. He was born in 1930 to a poor, but honest, Italo-American family in Boston. When he was twelve or thirteen and had just finished grammar school his parents died, and there was no other relative to care for him. When he was placed in a state orphanage he ran away. But although he was homeless and destitute he also was shrewd and resourceful, and lived mainly by his wits (he would accept no charity) in a cheap rooming house in the North End, the Italian district of Boston. This, incidentally, was in 1945, towards the end of the war.

"For a time he made a lease-hire arrangement for a horse and wagon, and in season bought watermelons at the big open air market (a species of Covent Garden, I suppose) and sold them house-to-house. The old Italians jokingly called him *Il Principe degli Mellone*, the Watermelon Prince. In winter, using the same horse and wagon, he sold coal. He never went back to school. Interestingly, though undoubtedly all the usual temptations lay before him, he had an absolutely clean record with the police; not so much as a misdemeanor is on file.

"And so he went on until he was about sixteen. An interesting anecdote, though possibly apocryphal, was that at about this time he hitchhiked to Boys' Town, in Nebraska, but was turned down by Father Flanagan. No reason was given, but it seems odd, if in fact the story is true, in view of his faultless police record in Boston."

"Knowing Browning I imagine he killed everybody who kept the records," Wolff commented cynically.

"In any case, " Hans smiled briefly, "this record of trial and hardship, with no known depredations along the way, was to pay big dividends later, as you shall see.

"When he was sixteen or seventeen he managed, somehow, to get into the Marines. This marked the beginning of a remarkably successful career, especially in view of the almost overwhelming disadvantages he began with. He was sent to Korea, in 1951, where he was wounded twice, won two citations for valor, and was promoted to the rank of sergeant. After the armistice, and after he was fully recovered from his wounds, he went back to Korea, still as a Marine sergeant, where he was assigned to a highly secret UNKMAC unit which handled Korean line crossers—spies, in common parlance—for the Eighth US Army G2. According to his dossier, on several occasions he went himself across the 38th parallel into North Korea to confirm information he'd received from his local agents. He'd been so successful at his job that when he returned to the States after his sixteen months in Korea he was recruited by the CIA. And it was his 'clean bill of health' as a youth, under the worst possible circumstances, combined with his native intelligence (certainly not his educational background), his gritty determination, and of course his ruthlessness that has led to the power and success he enjoys today. Incidentally, although he's a widower he was married twice, and has any number of children, not all of whom are legitimate."

"That I know about," Wolff interjected, "but do go on."

"All right, now back to the present. On one occasion I was sent to his place in Cairo—to deliver some important papers by

hand, as I recall. Well, the place was on Dar el Shifa, near Air
France's beautiful Meridien Hotel, and was one of those palatial
six-storey piles with walls two feet thick the Italians built in the
1930s. When I gave my name and asked for Browning, the
boab, a species of *concierge* as you know, who met me in the
lobby escorted me to a small private lift with an intercom next
to it. He spoke briefly in Arabic and waited; when approval
came he pulled open the gate and stood aside. The lift went
straight up to a penthouse, there were no other stops, and
opened directly into Browning's flat. A tall, slender, and very
dark *sufragi*—undoubtedly a son of the Nubian Desert—in an
immaculate white *galabiya* and *kufiya* opened the gate, and with
a humble bow bade me enter. Then he said, astonishingly and
archaically: "Browning Effendi will be with you soon." Then he
left me, padding quietly away into the cool dim silence.

The place into which I walked could only be described as
lavish—I don't say exactly tasteful, but absolutely lavish.
Ceilings five meters high, each with its slowly rotating teak-
wood fan, highly polished floors of either granite or hard-
wood, depending upon which of the dozen rooms one found
oneself in, an Eighteenth-century Italian marble fireplace large
enough to walk into, several servants milling about unobtrusively, and to top all this off (terrifyingly, for me) a huge Russian wolfhound which came lumbering inquisitively up to me
shortly after I'd entered.

"When to my infinite relief Browning finally made his
appearance—in a velvet smoking jacket, no less!—and got the
dog away he seemed smugly gratified by my obvious astonishment at all this baroque splendor (which in some cases, such
as the gold, pink, and white 'early King Farouk' furniture, was
somewhat bizarre actually). He was positively gloating in fact.

"Abruptly and without the least display of courtesy or hospitality he led me into a sort of den or studio which was off
one of the main rooms. I gave him the papers, and stood silently by until such time as he would see fit to dismiss me. As he
opened the dispatch case and laid the documents out on a low

table in front of a 'Faroukian' settee and began to go over them I could hardly conceal my amusement. Suspended from the towering ceiling by a length of cheap, common, cloth-insulated, twisted green flex was what I judged (by its brilliance when he snapped it on) to be at least a 250 watt naked light bulb. The only other furniture in the room was a sideboard loaded with prodigious quantities of liquor.

"Hunched over the table, his coarse peasant face a study in obtuse concentration, with his mouth hanging open in seemingly doltish stupefaction, I found myself wondering, rather naively I suppose, how the United States could have risen to a state of such preeminence in world affairs with products like Browning holding such sensitive and key positions. I should have mentioned that although he was down on the Embassy roster ostensibly as some sort of political attaché, actually he was the CIA Deputy Chief of Station in Cairo. How did he explain this ridiculous room, a room which E. Phillips Oppenheim, even in one of his worst spy thrillers, would find risible? Then, doing an extrapolation in opulence, so to speak, I found myself trying to visualize what the *station chief's* place must be like!

"But be that as it may. At the time of which I speak Browning's dossier also had revealed that he was being watched by his own people; not so much as a security risk, understand, but because he was suspected of dealing in the cigarette black market in Alex. So now all this grandeur began to make some sense. Browning was doing himself well, all right, but, I was sure, not merely on his government salary. After he had dismissed me—rather peremptorily, the blighter!—I walked very thoughtfully the few blocks back to the Embassy with the receipt for the documents he had given me.

"Being a bit of an authority, as you know," Hans permitted himself the ghost of a smile, "in such business negotiations, I took a trip to Alex one day with a Cairene friend who was acquainted with *all* the markets there, legitimate and otherwise."

Abruptly Hans interrupted his narrative to glance at his watch.

"But I think all this, though perhaps interesting, is taking up too much time. Shouldn't we, rather, get on with the business at hand?"

"No, no, no, Hans. We've got all kinds of time. Please, go on," Wolff, who by this time was almost spellbound, hurriedly importuned.

"I'll be brief then. Alexandria, being a port town, is a hub of smuggling and black market activities. With an Egyptian customs duty of one hundred percent, you can imagine what goes on. In a word, although I couldn't arrange to get 'our friend' into really serious trouble, I could, and did, with the help of Gamal, my Cairene friend, put an end to the very lucrative traffic in the illicit sale, on a wholesale basis mind you, of American cigarettes in which he, Browning, was engaged. Before I left to come back here I heard that he had given up his beach house in Alex; and from what I saw on the Embassy bulletin board the day before I left Cairo he was in the process of selling any number of valuable art objects and," Hans chuckled wryly, "even a large, pedigreed Russian wolfhound. Oh, yes! There was another interesting entry in his dossier. Although it never was proved, it was alleged by more than one of Browning's colleagues that in that terrible April of 1975 he, Browning, had made a small fortune getting wealthy Vietnamese and their families out of the country, *at $4000 a head*, on American aircraft. He worked it with some sergeant named, Lang, or Ling, I think it was."

"No, as a matter of fact I think the sergeant's name must have been Link, Hans." Wolff had been sitting silently nodding his head, like a man whose suspicions have been confirmed, and now he told Hans about Link and what had happened on the infiltration drop.

When he had brought himself back to the present he said:

"Okay, let's get down to it, Hans."

They decided they would get Wolff's 'stash,' as he called it, that night, or actually, early the next morning, during the hours of darkness. Wolff told Hans the moon phase should still be right since they'd dropped him on the first night of the new moon. Later in the morning, some time before noon, they would rendezvous with J.D. and Magda and drive south.

While Hans finished his coffee, Wolff went to telephone the Baghdad Hilton.

"We'll meet them at the Hilton at around eleven tomorrow morning, before check-out time," he told Hans when he returned. "J.D.'s richer than Croesis, I think," he grinned, "but I know from what my father told me that he'd bitch about paying another day's tariff. We decided that for the rest of today it might look good if we did a little sightseeing. Do you think that crate you've got parked out there can handle it, or should we rent a decent car? Wolff chaffed his companion, "I've got all kinds of taxpayers' money they gave me out of the confidential fund...."

Hans looked offended as he rose and got into his coat.

"Not only will that 'crate,' as you so unfeelingly call it, handle the sightseeing, but it will also get us to Basrah. That car of which you speak so disparagingly is my sweetheart!" he said with an air of exaggerated dignity.

"Well, whether it handles today's little outing or not, I guess it's going to *have* to get us to Basrah after all, Hans. I don't see getting those toys I parked out in the desert down there in a rented car. Have you made the arrangements with your mechanic friend, by the way?"

"No sweat. It is all arranged for early tomorrow morning."

"You know, this isn't so different than *The Day of the Jackal* after all," Wolff mused to himself.

"What? Did you say something about a 'jackal'?" Hans asked mystified.

"Oh, nothing really, Hans. I was just remembering one of Browning's many put downs. Sometime when we have absolutely nothing to talk about I'll tell you about it."

Hans's "sweetheart" did "handle it," and they spent a convivial day visiting places of interest in this, one of the oldest cities in the world (according to Hans as old as 6000 years). After an excellent late lunch in a Lebanese restaurant they dropped J.D. and Magda off at the Hilton and Wolff went to his hotel for some more needed rest before that night's activities in the desert and all that was yet to come.

Using his luminous-dialed lensatic compass Wolff located the cache after only two sightings. Hans, who had driven off after dropping him at the roadside, was there waiting on the deserted highway with his lights off when Wolff returned with his equipment. Fortunately, the Iraqi trucks which in defiance of the UN embargo hauled contraband down from Turkey virtually every day traveled mainly during daylight hours.

By three A.M. they were back in Baghdad. After dropping Wolff at his hotel Hans drove himself home, taking with him the items Wolff had retrieved in the desert.

Four hours later he was at an auto repair shop, owned by an Iraqi friend of his, where he supervised the considerable work which needed to be done on his superannuated but still sturdy Fiat prior to their departure.

Before noon that same day, together with J.D. and Magda, Hans and Wolff had cleared the outskirts of the ancient city and were headed south.

As Hans drove the old car along at a good pace Wolff half turned in his seat, and with his arm extended along the seat back threw a grin over his shoulder at Somerville.

"So here I am—with my ultra-secret, ultra-momentous mission blown sky high—in a broken-down '85 Fiat, while the paper shufflers I work for get chauffeured to their offices in limousines!" He transferred the grin to Hans as he muttered *sotto voce*:

"I take it everything went okay at your friend's place, old Hans?"

"Quite satisfactory." Hans replied as quietly if a little stiffly, "Old Hans's 'broken-down Fiat' now has dual mufflers and dual exhaust pipes (whatever all *that* means), only one set of which actually work, however. Still, I think the asthetic effect is rather good. Gives the old bus an air, a certain *diablerie*. It also meets the requirement admirably, and I was provided with a satchel of certain special tools which may be needed for 'future adjustments'," he ended more seriously with a meaningful glance at Wolff.

" Am I to assume that our little act has gone from a duet to a trio, Hans?"

Hans's briefly puzzled expression quickly changed to enlightenment:

"No, no worries, Carl. He wanted no part in our performance."

"Well, okay, but I'll be interested to know how you managed it."

"And shall *I* take it we are not to know what it is you two are discussing so arcanely? J.D. inquired quietly from the back seat, "although I think I could hazard a good guess."

"Yes, Major, you are not to know," Hans replied with cheerful finality.

It was when they had crossed the Tigris into that great plain which the ancients called Mesopotamia that Magda expressed a keen desire to "go to the ladies' room," and Hans, somewhat nonplussed, glanced at Wolff and suggested quietly:

"Well be in Al Hayy in a half-hour...."

"Naw," just pull off the road anywhere around here—but not too *far* off the road, okay?" Wolff instructed. He was sure they were in mine country now; not US or Coalition mines, he felt sure, but Iraqi mines, not that it mattered.

Wolff got out and held a back door open for Magda, who was attractively dressed in a skirt and blouse under her expensive beige leather jacket. Standing there shading her eyes against the desert sun she looked truly beautiful, he thought. He now also scanned the area, with an efficacy at least ten times greater than Magda's, but saw no one.

With Magda following closely behind him Wolfe picked his way carefully as they went off into the rough and, in places, marshy terrain. The area they had been driving through was interspersed with irrigation canals and small lakes, with here and there a small village. He recalled now from his area studies that most of Iraq's fifteen million inhabitants lived in this vast alluvial plain between Baghdad and Basrah; but that figure must include both those cities, he reasoned. As they trudged along in silence he remembered also having read how Robert Byron had cursed this area in his *The Road to Oxiana,*[2] describing it scathingly as a "land of mud deprived of mud's only possible advantage—vegetable fertility." Of course Byron had been writing more than sixty years ago, and one had to take into account the man's characteristic, and very British, arrogance....

In the distance, to the west, Wolff could see a lake. Perhaps not the best place in the world to deploy tanks, he noted critically to himself, but there would be mines along the access trails and roads. The real "tank country" was to the west, beyond the Euphrates, in the great Syrian desert, which extended west into Jordan and south into Saudi Arabia.

Now with only his normal vision he was certain he saw two partially exposed antitank mines about twenty yards off to his left; then in his magnification mode thought he saw the circular pattern of smaller antipersonnel mines which had been sown protectively around them. He said nothing about this as Magda trudged along behind him. They had gone about a hundred and fifty yards before she found a place which suited her behind some rocks.

Hans and J.D. waited more or less patiently for five minutes, then got out of the car, crossed the road, and went to find their own rockpile. Five minutes after they'd returned they saw the other two, holding hands as they slowly retraced their way back. With every few steps Magda reached down, seemingly to brush away an insect from her knee.

---

[2] *Oxiana* refers to the country of the Oxus, the ancient name for Amu Darya, the river in northeast Afghanistan.

When finally they were back on the road and on their way to Basrah, Somerville had to suppress a smile when he noticed that Magda, as unobtrusively as possible, was picking bits of debris out of her hands, elbows, knees. And it took all his self-control to stifle a guffaw when he noticed that in the front seat Wolff was vigorously brushing his trouser knees.

Chapter Twenty

Epiphany

The Fiat was beginning to overheat and Magda was tired so they decided to spend the night at a small inn Hans knew near the ancient ruins of Nippur and continue on to Basrah early next morning. Wolff and Magda had abandoned any pretense as far as Hans and J.D. were concerned, but in deference to this more traditional (Islamic) and rural society booked a room as husband and wife, while the other two took separate single rooms. Except for the four of them there seemed to be no other guests at the inn. The rooms were small, clean, and generally adequate for an overnight stay. There was a common bath, which no one objected to. As he followed Magda and the young Arab boy who carried their bags up to the room Wolff thought ironically, My cover grows daily; now I'm a *married* Austrian oilfield worker!

After they had freshened up a little they reassembled in the common room-cum-restaurant for an early dinner. Since there seemed to be no one in attendance they chose a table and seated themselves. Then they noticed the young Arab "bellboy" who now, crouching in a corner of the large room with a slender metal tube, was blowing the embers back into life in a large stone fireplace.

They sat smoking and talking quietly until the proprietor—a lean, wizened old man wearing a light gray woolen *thawb*,[1] and with a face like creased leather and a nose like an eagle's beak—came to their table and with a polite bow welcomed them to "Mesopotamia," the name of his inn (as well as the ancient area through which they were traveling). Having heard them chatting among themselves in English, he spoke to them fluently in the same language.

They accepted the old man's suggestion of roast lamb, and after he had placed the order with his cook he returned to ask what they would like to drink. Somerville, rubbing his large freckled hands in anticipation, suggested genially that a light red wine to accompany the meat seemed right. Chagrined, the proprietor expressed a thousand regrets, and explained that he had no license to sell anything alcoholic. Things were different here in the country, he said, than they were in Baghdad where the Islamic laws were "a little bent in favor of tourist money," evoking a smile from Hans. Then with a furtive little look around the room, which except for the boy was virtually empty, he added hesitantly and with an engagingly conspiratorial smile:

"However, if you really would enjoy some…" he held up a long brown index finger, "let me see what I can do," he ended as he hurried away. While he was gone the boy of the luggage and the fireplace shyly served them appetizers of *hummus* and *baba ghannou*.

The proprietor reappeared within a few minutes, obviously pleased with himself and with four Coca Cola cans on a tray. He placed a can in front of each of them, then stepped back and surveyed the group of faces looking up at him.

"I assume you are all Christians," his gaze lingered fleetingly on Hans, "thus we must not forget the wedding at Canaan where, it is written, Christ himself transformed the water into wine!" He smiled benignantly down on them and

---

[1] A long, loose cotton (woolen or worsted in colder months) gown reaching to the ankles, akin to the *galabiya* or *djellaba* of other Arab countries.

added genially, "I think you will find the lamb quite good," as he left them.

"What the hell...?" Wolff began, mystified.

J.D. glanced at the can in front of him and said:

"You'll notice these tins have been opened, old man. I suggest you try a little," he smiled as he reached for his 'Coke'."

"Not a *great* Coke," smiled Wolff with mock connoisseurship after he'd taken a sip, "but definitely a *good* Coke."

J.D. toasted him solemnly, and drank deeply. "What about you, Hans? Off limits, I suppose?"

"Oh, don't worry about me, old boy," said Hans as he reached for his drink. "Hamd'Allah!" he exclaimed when he'd tasted the excellent wine. "I'm a *progressive* Muslim, you see!"

Within moments they all were enjoying their "Cokes" and chatting animatedly. Wolff felt the relief of being in real human company again after those grueling weeks at Hohenfels.

"You should use your napkin *before* you drink your wine, Charles, as well as after," Magda murmured disapprovingly to Wolff.

"It's 'Carl,' Magda", he advised, then asked, "even when you're drinking it out of a Coke can?" Then he wiped his mouth, raised his 'Coke,' and looking her straight in the eye lisped affectionately, "Here's looking at *you*, kid."

As they waited for their food conversation lagged for a few moments, and Wolff's eyes wandered around the large room. He noticed that hanging here and there on the mainly blank distempered walls were pictures of such religious figures as Abraham, Isaiah, Jesus Christ, the Holy Mother, and Moses. In conformance with Islamic Law of course there were no pictures of Mohammed. Magda, who had been following his gaze and almost reading his thoughts, commented:

"A little odd, no? Those 'others' in a Muslim place, I mean."

"Oh, no, not at all," Hans, quick to follow this drift, put in. "Those were great people. We venerate them. Jesus Christ, for example, was a great prophet, and his Mother, therefore, also is greatly respected."

At that moment, with the old proprietor in attendance, the cook himself arrived with a huge tray heaped high with a steaming, rice-stuffed, aromatic lamb, roasted whole, and surrounded by circles of flat, unleavened bread. They all were ravenously hungry, and they occupied themselves with the business of eating and drinking for the next half-hour. The 'Coca Cola' cans were taken away to be replenished by the Arab boy who, all smiles now, seemed to be caught up in the convivial mood of these interesting strangers.

When their strong black coffee was served J.D. asked the old proprietor, who had introduced himself simply as "Yakob," to join them, and with another gracious bow he did so. Mainly because he felt they would have little in common to discuss with this genial but no doubt illiterate "son of the desert" Wolff revived the subject of the religious pictures. But he was wrong about Yakob, who was not reticent about speaking and as it turned out was anything but illiterate.

Islam was tolerant of other monotheistic religions, he told them, religions such as Christianity and Judaism which were held to contain the main tenets of the true doctrine, though in more or less distorted form. Those religions enjoyed considerable autonomy under the authority of the Muslim state.

"I'm paraphrasing Maxime Rodinson of course, the famous French Marxist Orientalist, about whom I once wrote a monograph when I was an exchange student at the Woodrow Wilson School at Princeton University in America (Magda almost boggled at this). I wrote on Rodinson because I had found that most Americans, other than certain scholars, were in total ignorance of the man. Yes, the children of Mohammed protected the children of Abraham and those of Jesus of Nazareth."

Not surprisingly there also was a large picture of Saddam Hussein, hung prominently and in solitary splendor away from any of the other pictures. Wolff asked Yakob if he would give his opinion of the Iraqi leader. The old man hesitated for a moment;

then, as if he had made up his mind about something, said:

"I am too old to care any more what happens to me if I speak the truth. —Saddam Hussein? One's first impulse is to say that someone should kill him. But then, what would become of this poor country immediately afterward? There would be absolute chaos, and for God knows how long." He fell silent for a few moments.

"Ah, Saddam Hussein, our beloved *Führer*," he sighed ironically and invocatively, and then quoted Aristotle:

"'The tyrant who impoverishes the citizens is obliged to make war in order to keep his subjects occupied and impose on them the permanent need of a chief.' This could be Saddam's motto of state," he smiled wryly. "Ironically, we have the Arabs to thank, indirectly of course, for such truths. Forget not that it was the Arabs, mainly in that magnificent library of Alexandria, who preserved much of the greatness of the Greeks.

"My God, that Gulf War! he expostulated. "As Wellington rightly put it: 'Next to a battle lost nothing is so dreadful as a battle won.'

"It isn't that people are stupid, or that they are ignorant about what is going on; it is that they are mainly helpless to do anything about it. Those in governance must protect them. I subscribe to your Samuel Johnson who, quoting from the Romans as he often did, said: 'It is better to save a citizen than to kill an enemy.' That says it all, I think."

Wolff looked at Hans, who nodded and asked:

"Are you of the Shi'ia faith, Jacob?"

The old man smiled broadly and waved a hand towards the wall behind him.

"Do you think that with Isaiah, and Moses, and even Abraham looking down upon me I could deny my faith?"

"Do you mean to tell us you're a *Jew*?" Wolff, realizing now that the small, brimless white cap he'd seen when Yakob bowed was not a *kufiya* but a Hebrew *yamulka*, was astonished nonetheless, "I mean, with your fervor about the Arabs and Iraq, and..."

"'Hath not a Jew passion'?" the wise old man declaimed histrionically ("My God! now he's quoting from Shakespeare," Wolff heard Magda mutter under her breath). I am a citizen of this country; I have my Iraqi passport and I am proud of it. Religiously I am a Jew, but can I not be an Iraqi also? Is not a Jew born in America an American? For centuries my ancestors drew water from the same wells as their Muslim brothers; as do I, still.

"How were the Jews actually treated where Islam was dominant, over the centuries before the establishment of the state of Israel? Mainly, they were protected. Before I gave up in despair and came back here, to the desert, when I was actively striving, mainly in academia, for an Arab-Israeli *rapprochment*, I taught classes at both Hebrew and Muslim universities about the subject; I hope someone is still doing that.

"But then one hears, 'This is my grandfather's axe—my father put a new blade on it, and I replaced the haft.' This is a way of describing the continuance, the perpetuation of a belief or an attitude which has been handed down from generation to generation, like the Arab-bashing and antisemitism over the centuries, since the Crusades, and more recently the stereotyping and even persecution of Arabs in particular. If you are a free-thinking person you should take pride in 'making your own axe,' and in swinging it at a different tree. You cannot fight terrorism with indignation.

"No, he ended with a sigh as he rose to leave them, "if there is ever to be *real* peace in this region we, Arabs and Jews, must go back to the wells—together." He rose from his seat, gently pushed his chair in, and rested his gnarled hands on its back.

"Will you see the ruins of Nippur before you go on?" he asked solicitously. The archeologists—from Germany, I think—were busy there last fall. They are trying to estabish the relationship between the Babylonians and the tenth or eleventh dynasty of Egypt's pharonic Middle Kingdom of 4000 years ago."

"We may tomorrow, before we continue on to Al-Basrah," Wolff lied politely, and received an equally polite nod from Yakob. And with that the old man bowed, blessed them, and left. Wolff watched as Hans fumbled for a handkerchief and blew his nose loudly.

There was silence at the table for a few minutes as each had his or her own thoughts; then Magda excused herself to go upstairs and Hans went in search of the old man. Undoubtedly he was interested in discussing Iraq's future more fully.

Not many minutes later Somerville stubbed out his cigarette and pushed back his chair, all the while holding Wolff's eyes.

"Let's get some fresh air," he suggested," but it was obvious he wanted a private talk.

They walked away from the inn to the far side of the courtyard, which was enclosed by a wall, and stood by Hans's Fiat. Wolff noted gratefully that the double gate had been closed and locked for the night. It had grown very dark, but the desert stars looked huge and brilliant. J.D. turned up his collar against the night chill and then gazed up at the dense panoply of heavenly bodies. They stood silent for a few minutes. Wolff leaned against Hans's "sweetheart" and lit a cigarette; and then J.D. opened the ineveitable conversation.

"So what *are* you going to do, old boy?"

"I don't know yet."

"There isn't the deuce of a lot of time left, is there?"

"That I do know,"

"You shouldn't go any further with this, you know. If Hans is right, and I think there's every chance that he is, this whole thing is absolutely insane."

"J.D., it's insane even if Hans *isn't* right."

"Of course, you're right, but—"

"Just between you, me, and those great big fat fucking stars up there—if you'll pardon the expression—I don't think any of this matters, as far as I'm concerned, one way or the other. Whether I do it or not, *whoever* the real target is, I don't think I'm going to get out of Iraq alive. And if somehow I do, I don't think I'll stay that way very long."

"What if you had Hans tell his people in Baghdad you just won't do it?"

"Aren't you forgetting what Browning threatened to do?— Oh, Jesus! you don't know, do you? He's got me by the balls, in a couple of senses. I never told you what he said, well, hinted, about Magda: If I don't go through with this *she* picks up the tab! Even if we can protect her for a while that vindictive bastard will get to her someday, someplace, just to get his revenge, if it accomplshes nothing else. I *know* the son of a bitch, J.D.!"

"The point is well taken," J.D. said soberly, "So, it seems this two-edged 'Sword of Damocles" is rather a personal one. Would you say that if it were someone other than this *emminence gris*, Browning—who's beginning to seem like the evil shade in some tiresome morality play—if someone other than he were 'directing this scenario,' as the Americans like to say, might your position not be so dire?"

Wolff "field stripped" his cigarette end and let the wind blow it away before he replied with a mirthless smile:

"Could be. So let's put out our own contract on Browning and I'm in the clear, right? Bear's ass! If it weren't Browning it'd be some other son of a bitch just like him. I keep trying to tell myself that maybe if I do get Saddam and get away with it, (*Ensh'Allah*), everything'll be okay; it'll be over. They never said anything about Claxton. I'd just be doing my job *as I know it*, and..." He shook his head. "Of course, that goddam weapon I'm supposed to use is a crowd killer, and Claxton's bound to be standing right next to Hussein. Yeah, I remember Browning saying something like, 'Get 'em all, if you have to....'"

"I'd like to hear more about that weapon, by the way—" J.D. was saying as Hans, a little breathlessly, came trotting up to them.

"I just got off the phone to Baghdad. Browning's there," he announced without preamble.

Wolff and J.D. merely looked at each other for a moment, and then silently followed Hans back into the inn.

By ten o'clock J.D. had gone to bed, Hans was sitting near the now cold fireplace reading a copy of the Koran he'd borrowed from Yakob, and Wolff, with a Coca Cola can at his elbow, was sitting at one of the dining room tables studying a map. Magda, who had been wandering around the large room getting a closer look at the pictures which had evoked such interesting conversation earlier, now went over and stood behind Wolff with her hands on his shoulders. Without turning he patted her hand as she started humming then singing in a small clear sweet voice the beautifully evocative old German song, "*Liebe Wahr es Nicht*.[2]

Without looking up Wolff incanted softly, "A can of wine, a map of southern Iraq—and thou beside me, singing in the wilderness."

"Can't you be serious?"

"If I took this seriously I'd start screaming in stark terror. What I'm doing is called 'whistling in the dark.' I'm trying to tell myself it's all a charade, a play, just theater—"

"But this Browning, who is he?"

"Just another s.o.b."

"But he seems to hold your fate in his hands...."

When Wolff merely nodded his head slowly in agreement Magda sighed and kissed him on the top of his head.

"Well, goodnight; and don't stay up too late—we must leave early tomorrow," (playing the role of the little *Hausfrau* already, thought Wolff wryly but not unhappily).

Hans, who had been hovering in the background came up when Magda was out of earshot and spoke to Wolff's back.

"This sudden appearance by Browning, what do you think it means?"

"I just don't know, unless it has something to do with J.D.

[2] Known to Americans as "Take Me in Your Arms," the composer of this haunting melody, a Czech by the accident of war, would once as a Bohemian have been considered a compatriot of the Hungarian Magda.

and Magda coming with us," the other answered tersely without turning around.

Hans was silent for a few moments, then:

"Speaking of your beautiful Magda," he said without irony, "there's something I think you should know." He waited until Wolff had turned and given him his full attention before he went on.

"When I used old Jacob's phone to check in with Baghdad I came away without my notebook, and as I started back to get it I heard Magda's voice. She was on the telephone. I stopped and waited politely, not wanting to interrupt her conversation. She couldn't see I was there since she was around a corner of the corridor. I couldn't help overhearing part of what she said, and after the first few words I was all ears.

"All I heard was, 'He's using the name Wolff now. That's right.' Then there was, 'You *knew*?' followed by, 'You're going to do *what*?' like she had received a couple of big surprises. And at that point the other party must have rung off rather abruptly. I crept away silently. Luckily whatever she heard kept her there, at the phone, thinking for a while, otherwise she might have found me standing there dumbfounded."

As he stared hard up at Hans Wolff's face was a mixture of shock, disbelief, anger, perhaps even fear.

Now he remembered that earlier he had overheard Magda asking the young servant boy, who doubtless thanks to Yakob spoke a little English, if there were a telephone she could use. At the time, he thought she merely was making another routine call to Oxford. But this... Also now he considered more seriously the fact that she had seemed extremely troubled, beyond her concerns about Browning, just before she'd gone up to bed.

"Can you check her out with your people in Baghdad?"

"I hardly think that's feasible. If she's with them they'll of course deny it. If she's working for other interests we quite probably would get an order to 'take immediate action,' if you get my drift. Immediate and *drastic* action, meaning we deposit your beautiful Magda in a deep convenient well somewhere along the road to Basrah."

Wolff merely nodded his acceptance of this irrefutable logic and said:

"Have you said anything to J.D. about this yet?" Hans shook his head negatively. "Good. Let's keep it that way for now."

He sat quietly for a full minute, then he put his maps away, bade goodnight to an obviously troubled Hans, and went slowly upstairs to the onerous task of confronting Magda with the disturbing facts he had just heard.

The next morning they had a hurried breakfast of very sweet tea, *pita*, hard boiled eggs, fruit, and for those who felt adventurous enough to try it at this hour of the day a mixture of cooked beans and onions heavily laced with cumin. Magda, who looked tired and distracted, drank some tea but hardly touched her food.

At a little after eight o'clock they were back on the road to Al-Basrah.

This time, with Hans sitting next to him, Wolff drove.

After five minutes of silence Wolff glanced at Hans.

"I think J.D. would be interested in what you were telling me yesterday, Hans—about Iraq and its future, remember? Especially that bit about 'polwar'."

Hans said nothing for a few moments, then nodding to himself a couple of times he half turned in his seat, and prefacing his exposition with the hope that he wouldn't prove tiresome gave J.D. and Magda a condensed version of what he had explained in detail to Wolff the previous day. When he had finished, Somerville, without hesitation, heartily approved of the goals Hans had outlined, and said that based upon his many years of soldiering he saw great merit in the "polwar scheme" ("…for countries such as Iraq, of course," he couldn't help appending). For her part Magda asked several incisive and intelligent questions, which pleased Hans and even evoked a respectful (if grudging) glance in the mirror from Wolff.

They all were thoughtfully quiet for a time as Wolff pushed the old Fiat along at a good pace. In the back seat

Somerville went back to leafing through a thick, soft-backed book he'd taken from his old and cherished BOAC shoulder bag while Magda, who had been gazing listlessly out at the drab terrain and now apparently with nothing else to occupy her, tried unobtrusively to read the book's title. J.D. smiled tolerantly as he held the thick volume up for her inspection.

"Vera Brittain," she murmured, "the tragic young Englishwoman of the first World War?"

"Yes," replied J.D. quietly, "what she endured during that terrible time is almost beyond comprehension—her fiancé, then her best friend, and ultimately her brother, whom she loved so dearly, all were killed in the war—but she *did* endure it, and she survived to bring some order out of the shambles of her young life. Just one hell of a woman."

Then he went on in a voice they all could hear:

"You know, I haven't been able to forget what that wise old son of the desert, Yakob, was telling us yesterday, and it made me think of this book I brought along: it's Vera Brittain's *Testament of Youth*. I've been looking out some of her quotations. Listen to this for a moment; I'll try to paraphrase it. She's speaking of war, of course. She knew little else in her young life:

"' How can we be so insistent on the rights and claims of every human soul,'" he read in his cultured voice, "'and yet at the same time countenance this wholesale murder, which if it were applied to animals or birds or indeed anything except men would fill us with a sickness and repulsion greater than we could endure? ... Soldiers are sent to regions where they will probably be slaughtered in a brutally degrading fashion in which we would never allow animals to be slaughtered. Public opinion has made it a high and lofty virtue to countenance this, but to the saner mind it seems more like a reason for shutting up half the nation in a criminal lunatic asylum.'" J.D. paused momentarily, then went on:

"'The philosophy about the ennobling effects of suffering, that tells you your soul grows through grief and sorrow, is right, ultimately. But I don't think this is the case at first. At first, pain beyond a certain point merely makes you lifeless, and apathetic to everything but itself.'

"Despite all this pacifist fervor," J.D. appended, "she went through the war as a V.A.D. nurse—absolutely loyal throughout."

With this last phrase Wolff glanced in the rearview mirror and caught Magda's eye.

"Loyalty!" he grated, with a bitterness that made Somerville look up. Keenly perceptive as always, he noticed that Magda, who looked infinitely troubled, quickly resumed her survellance of the fertile but seemingly deserted landscape.

PART THREE

MISSIONARIES

Chapter Twenty-one

Redemption

The breakdown occurred at the 226 KM marker, about halfway between Baghdad and Al-Basrah.

Wolff, who had been looking under the hood, came back and announced:

"I'm afraid your cherished Fiat has drawn a line in the sand, Hans. You've got a broken timing chain; and as if that weren't enough, I think the head's buckled, probably from driving overheated all this way. But even if it isn't you'll need a new head gasket."

"I cannot believe it," Hans moaned. "My friend, Youssef, the mechanic, said it was in very good condition for so old a car!"

Somerville, who had taken the opportunity to go off and relieve himself, came up behind Wolff and asked:

"What's the form?"

"Hans's 'sweetheart' just shit the bed," Wolff told him curtly.

"Well, that's a colorful way of putting it," J.D. sighed. "Can we repair the old girl?"

"Not a prayer. Not out here, anyway."

"Well, what now?"

"A good question. We can only hope someone will come along who doesn't hate *all* Western devils. Now I'm glad we got all that Evian water from Yakob before we left.

"I wish I had a box of dynamite," said Hans sorrowfully.

"What on earth for?" J. D. asked in amazement.

"Have you never had a favorite hunter which broke its leg in a bad jump?" was the mournful reply; which had the momentary effect of lightening their collective gloom, until Wolff said thoughtfully:

"I'm afraid even if you had a box of dynamite, Hans, I couldn't let you blow her up. Aren't you forgetting something?"

"Great Scott! I forgot about the—" but Wolff, with the merest of glances at Magda, didn't let him finish.

"That's *right*, Hans," he chanted, nodding his head. "One thing's certain. We can't leave old Sweetheart out here in the desert, not unaccompanied anyhow. We gotta get her towed to where they can put her back in shape, at least for another hundred and fifty miles' worth."

"Something about that rakish dual exhaust system you had installed back in Baghdad, Hans?" J.D. commented cryptically; but any reply Hans might have made was preempted by Wolff's exclamation as he stood shading his eyes and looking back up the road in the direction from which they had come.

"Hold on! —here comes a vehicle!" he announced. Then as he closed his left eye he amended, "No, two vehicles: a station wagon and a truck right on its tail—looks like at least a ton and a half or two tonner—loaded with wooden crates. The wagon looks like it's a new Mercedes." To the others, as they followed his example and shaded their eyes against the dazzling sunlight, the first vehicle was a mere dot on the distant horizon, and the truck a slightly larger one just behind it.

It was Hans who suggested that however typically "Western" Magda might appear, no rational eye could ever possibly see her as the "Great Shaitan"; and so it was she who gamely if not enthusiastically stood out from her three male companions and flagged the approaching station wagon down. The heavily loaded truck swerved around the slowing passenger car and continued down the road for another fifty yards before it pulled off with a squeal of brakes and came to a stop in a cloud of its own dust.

The station wagon *was* a new Mercedes and pulled off the road a little beyond where they were standing near the disabled Fiat. The driver opened his door and stood half in and half out of the car and shouted to them in Arabic:

"Do you need help? Is your machine broken?"

At a nudge and a glance from Wolff Hans went towards the man.

"Yes, it is hopeless. It must be gotten to a garage. Perhaps if you could take me to the next town, or if you just send someone to help us…" Hans left the plea unfinished as the man got out of his car and approached. Wolff noticed that the driver of the truck had dismounted also and was on his way back to them. Two small children peered through the back window of the Mercedes, and there was someone else in the front passenger seat.

The entire episode turned out better than anyone could have expected. The couple in the station wagon, Ekbal Amin Mahmoud and his wife along with their two children were on their way to Al-Basrah. The truck which accompanied them was loaded with dried dates.

To J.D.'s manifest relief English was quickly chosen as the *lingua franca*, in which introductions and suitable explanations were made. (Wolff's group had decided that Magda now would play the role of Somerville's niece, Wolff his Austrian friend, and Hans the tour guide they had acquired in Baghdad.) Now Mr. Mahmoud, taking his decision on the advice of his truck driver, who was introduced simply as Bashir, decided they *all* would go to Basrah. There was adequate room in the station wagon, and they could tow Hans's car with the truck. Luckily the Fiat was equipped with a rear wheel drive system, and in the truck along with any number of other useful items there was a towbar.

In less than twenty minutes, with Magda and J.D. already seated in the Mercedes and with Hans looking on (in wistful dejection, as J.D. described it later), Wolff and Bashir had the towing arrangement in place. Earlier, J.D., with Magda's help, had transferred the luggage from the trunk and roof rack of the Fiat to the Mercedes' capacious rack, where he and Bashir secured it with rope. When they were ready to leave Mahmoud said a few words to Bashir, who went to the back of the truck and busied himself there for a few moments. He returned quickly and with a smile handed his employer's wife a neatly wrapped parcel.

Hans chose to ride in the truck, mainly for reasons known best to himself and Wolff but also, and in keeping with his considerate nature, in order to provide more room for the others in the station wagon. In that vehicle Mahmoud and his wife resumed their seats in front with Wolff and his two companions behind them, while the children, a boy and a girl aged about seven and five respectively, played quietly in the rear luggage space.

Within little more than half an hour of their having stopped Mahmoud and company, the four travelers were once again on their way south, with the truck following as before. Only two other cars, going at extremely high speeds, had passed them heading south during that time.

Not long after they had gotten underway Mahmoud's wife—who, by the time they reached Basrah they would come to know and address by the rather unlikely name of Camille and who they were to learn taught at a middle school in Baghdad—undid the parcel she'd taken from Bashir, and turning in her seat with a smile offered the dates it contained to those in the back seat.

"We are going to Basrah to the mosque," she said in accented but readily undertandable English. "You have heard of the rededication?"

Wolff nodded politely and affirmatively as he helped himself to a date, throwing in a gratuitous "*Danke!*" as he did so ("Take more, more," the woman urged.)

"Yes, it is in three days. Our President and many other important people will be there."

Having ensured that J.D., Magda, and the children (who accepted them politely from Magda) had received what she considered an adequate supply of the dried dates Camille continued:

"Yes, we are going to the ceremony at the mosque, and while we are in Al-Basrah we will sell our dates, which have been drying in our warehouse since the harvest. All those which are on the truck, one hopes!"

"*Ensh'Allah!*" Ekbal Mahmoud sighed without taking his eyes off the road. "At this time of the year there is a great demand in Western countries for figs and dates. Germany and your country, Herr Wolff, were two of our biggest markets. Would that we could still ship these dates out of the country!"

"We have even heard that Mr. Claxton, the American foreign minister, will be there," the woman went on undeterred. "We hope this can mean a resumption of the good relations which were established between Iraq the United States in 1984, before all this horrible war."

And during that *other* horrible war, the one with Iran, Wolff mused; and those great relations were established for purely pragmatic reasons; *Realpolitik*, again, as usual. But he felt *some* sort of reply was expected, so he said with oblique relevancy as he gazed at the passing landscape:

"There are still a great number of mines out there. Do you have many people injured accidentally?"

Camille huffed a little and said:

"Oh, yes! Occasionally a farmer or a goatherd sets one off, with horrible results."

"Yes," interjected J.D. grimly, "a mine is the most impersonal weapon ever devised—perhaps *indiscriminate* would be the better word. They're a curse, Madame Mahmoud, especially the antipersonnel types. Most of them are designed to

wound—to maim—not to kill. The idea being that a dead soldier can be left unattended, but a badly wounded one must be
assisted, and usually that takes at least two other soldiers away
from their duties."

"I've heard there are currently about 100 million armed
mines in sixty countries throughout the world," Wolff put in.

"There are eight to ten million—that's one for every person—
in Cambodia alone. And for nine years the US dropped about a
million dollars worth of antipersonnel mines all over Laos
every day."

"But that is not the worst result of the war," Camille went
on dolefully. "I will not argue the politics, but almost half a
million Iraqi children have already died as a result of the sanctions since the Gulf War; two and a half million more are suffering from malnutrition. And the inflation of prices! We have
been fortunate," she cast a fond glance at her children, "but
many people cannot even feed themselves anymore."

Ekbal Mahmoud now broke his silence, in even better
English than that of his wife:

"These poor travelers don't want to hear all that, Camille."

"Oh, no," Magda said animatedly, "I am very interested in
this. There has been so much controversy over these sanctions.... Please, go on, Mrs. Mahmoud!"

During this conversation the children had been silent.
Now, glancing over his shoulder, Wolff noticed that they were
kneeling quietly with their hands on the back of the seat; and
Magda was holding the little girl's hand. Somehow this tender
little demonstration brought back the inner confusion, the
uncertainty he had been experiencing about Magda all day.
This virtual turmoil of emotions had been palliated by the
breakdown and subsequent events, but now it returned to tor-
ment him. Now he noticed that Magda was looking at him
strangely, as if she were studying his face.

Camille Mahmoud's response to Magda's urging came fil-
tering through his thoughts:

"... that it is mainly the United States that insists that these sanctions be kept in place. They have this, this, what is the word I want?"—she said it in Arabic—and Wolff supplied the English. "Thank you! —yes, this implacable feeling about President Hussein. They will not rest until he is gone."

Wolff was certain that she would not be speaking so freely If she were aware of his true identity, at the very least as that of an American.

Camille went on:

"But meanwhile we must suffer—especially the children, and the old, and the poor. But we *all* suffer, because it is unjust that we, the people of Iraq, must be cut off from the rest of the world because of this one man, and this, this *vendetta* against him. We hear that the Americans have no quarrel with the Iraqi people. But what would they have us *do*? They tell us we must *somehow* depose the President. Allah be merciful! Even if we knew how to do that and had the will, there would be a bloodbath in this country such as you could not imagine!"

When she paused for breath J.D. interjected:

"Yes, but aside from this animosity towards Hussein, which is very real, I admit, in my country as well as in the States, there is the very serious matter of these weapons that supposedly are being or at least *were* being developed. I'm talking about the nuclear and biological and chemical weapons that—"

"Such as that fabulous milk factory in Baghdad which according to the Americans was actually manufacturing chemical agents?" Mahmoud interposed with a snort as he hit the steering wheel with the heel of his hand. "Please believe me when I tell you that those children who are listening so intently behind you received their milk supply, indirectly of course, from that very factory!"

"Yes, well, I never did believe all that gas (please pardon the pun; it was absolutely unintentional!) we heard about that factory during the war. But, what about the nuclear programme? There *was* one going on, at least for a time; of that I'm certain."

"Yes, there was one," Mahmoud admitted soberly, "but I am convinced it exists no longer (Hans was to confirm this later). You must understand that Hussein would gladly come to terms now, if he could do so without losing too much face. When those two sons-in-law of his defected to Amman they revealed that over half a million documents relating to the weapons programme existed (they were stored in a chicken coop, if you will believe it!). The U.N. inspectors found those documents, so now Saddam Hussein has no choice—the existing weapons will be destroyed, and no new ones will be produced. No matter what my wife says about there being no will for change in this country even Hussein has cause for concern now. There are those in this country..." he tailed off here.

"But let us not talk of this," he smiled (a little nervously, Wolff thought) into the rearview mirror at no one in particular, "and I beg of you—please do not repeat any of this conversation, at least while you remain in Iraq." There was silence for a few moments; then, following his own advice, Mahmoud changed topics.

"Are you aware," he asked cynically, "that not one SCUD missile was shot down by Patriot anti-missile missiles in the Gulf War?"

"That's as may be, but it didn't alter the outcome, did it?" J.D. responded rather callously, to which Mahmoud mumbled another aspiration to Allah.

Until they arrived at a security check point at Az Zubayr, just outside Al-Basrah, late that afternoon, the rest of the trip was uneventful. They had made topical conversation, in great part about the ancient history of the area; then Somerville went on at length about Sir John Baggot Glubb, a British soldier who had commanded the Arab Legion in this area from 1938 to 1956 and whose scholarly books about the Arabs he'd read avidly. At one point, since they were nearing Iraq's second largest oil producing area Wolff thought it would be appropriate to ask Mahmoud about employment opportunities, and did so. The anticipated reply was that the sanctions had virtually put an end to hiring for the time being. Mahmoud, rather astutely, expressed surprise that Wolff had not foreseen this. But Wolff was ready for this: With so many Palestinian workers having left the country during and after the Gulf War, he said, he thought there would be a good chance of employment—which reply, though possibly not doing much for Mahmoud's opinion of Wolff's perspicacity, put a plausible end to this brief conversation. Later, when the conversation again had flagged, Wolff, to everyone's great amusement, tried singing a little song in Arabic along with the two children. From time to time everyone ate more dates and drank some of the Evian water. Still later and shortly after an unspoken agreement between Magda and Camille they made one brief "rest" stop at An Nasiriyah.

As it turned out they couldn't have been more fortunate at the check point (one of many established to provide additional security for the forthcoming ceremony). Their circumstances couldn't have been better if they had been devised. Here were, the check point guards undoubtedly told themselves, four tourists who with their old (disreputable) car had been stranded on their way to Basrah, when along came these good Iraqi citizens (in their beautiful new Mercedes) to rescue them. Passports or identity cards were summarily checked, the Fiat given a cursory (and openly disdainful) look, and they were waved on. Wolff noticed that although they were available, mirrors were not used to check under any of the vehicles in their small convoy. Since they had met the Mahmoud's, he thought gratefully if a little uneasily, their luck had been exceptionally good.

They were well along the Shatt al-Arab now, the confluence of the two great rivers, which continued on into the Persian Gulf with, to the north and east, its huge 6,000-square-mile marshland that extends into Iran.

On the outer precincts of the town Mahmoud pulled over, signaling Bashir to do the same, and a brief conference was held about what to do next. Bashir said he knew of a garage which boasted an excellent mechanic who specialized in Fiats and Alpha Romeos. He suggested that he go right on there, before unloading his cargo, so that work on the Fiat could begin without delay. Hans of course said he would go along. He would meet his friends later, he said, at a hotel where he had arranged for all of them to stay he told them with the merest hint of a wink at Wolff.

At this point Mahmoud excused himself and took his wife aside for a brief consultation. When after a minute or two they rejoined the others he announced that since they had a house in Basrah (in addition to their permament residence in Baghdad) which they used on occasions such as this, Wolff, Magda, and J.D. would be more comfortable waiting for Hans there. If it was necessary they could call their hotel from there and explain their delay, Mahmoud said. Or for the matter of that, he told them with genuine enthusiasm, they could stay on with him and his family for the few days they would be in Basrah. There was plenty of room to accommodate all of them. Camille smiled and nodded her approval of this.

Wolff and Hans exchanged significant looks at this point (and at which Wolff found himself thinking inconsequently that apparently the date business in Iraq was not to be despised), and after suitable expressions of gratitude it was agreed that Wolff, Magda, and J.D. would avail themselves of at least the first offer. Hans received the Mahmouds' local telephone number and address and went on his way with Bashir in the truck, with his cherished sweetheart still in tow, while the other three went with the Mahmoud's to their Basrah residence, where their two part-time servants who had opened the place in anticipation of their arrival awaited them.

They were comfortably ensconced when Hans telephoned to Wolff.

"Well, Bashir took me to this repair shop he knows and told his mechanic friends to take care of my needs. He'd like you to tell his boss he's gone to park the truck in the warehouse, wherever that is. Now, I have good news and some not so good, old boy," Hans's voice sounded tinny over the line.

"Let's do this in German, Hans," Wolff bit off the words in that language, "just in case we're 'not alone,' if you get my meaning."

"*Zu Befehl, mein Führer!*"

"Don't get carried away, Hans. Okay, what's the good news?"

"No buckled head, it just needs a new, um, thingummy—gasket, is that the word? But the timing chain, whatever that is, does have to be replaced and then the car will be ready to go."

"And the bad news?"

"The two mechanics say they'll need another day to finish the work. They've been very busy because of all the visitors in town."

Wolff glanced over his shoulder to ensure he was alone, then cupped the mouthpiece with his hand and said just above a whisper:

"There's one thing that worries me, Hans."

"What? I can barely hear you."

Wolff raised his voice an octave:

"The goddam *timing chain*. The head gasket's no problem, but to put in the new timing chain I'm pretty sure they're going to have to put her up on a lift. Can you hear me?"

"No sweat, I can hear you all right now."

"Okay. Hans, do they have a hydraulic lift in their shop?"

"A hydral... Wait a moment...." Wolff could hear Hans muttering to himself, then he was back. "Nooo.... Ah! I see. There's no lift, but there's a pit, an oblong pit, in the floor. They must drive the cars over it and—"

"Right. A grease pit," Wolff cut in. "Okay, now listen carefully, Hans. You're going to hang around while they work on the car, right?—Good. Okay, tell these guys they can replace the gasket today, but tell 'em that tomorrow, when they do the timing chain, you're Austrian friend—me—wants to see how they do it. Tell them I like to work on my own car, tell 'em anything, but I want to be there when they get under that car. You got that?"

"*Kein Schweiß*,"[1] Hans answered with less than his usual enthusiasm.

"Stay there until they've finished with it for today, okay? They're working on it now? Good. Now, where's this hotel you had us booked into? The Mahmouds have been all over us with hospitality, and I guess Magda and J.D. would be okay here for the next day or two, but this isn't the time for us, you and me, to split up—not yet, anyway. And I've gotta get out of here—there's a lot to do in the next couple of days. Besides, our hosts shouldn't get any more involved with us than they already have. They're innocent (I hope), and who knows what the hell's going to come down before this is over. So now, give me that address." Wolff pulled a small notebook and ballpoint pen out of a pocket and wrote while Hans talked. "That sounds like it's near the *souk*. It is? Right, I'll find it."

"May I ask if you've gotten that business with Magda resolved? I noticed she was rather subdued this morning, so I assume you spoke to her last night?"

"You bet your ass I did," Wolff broke emotionally into English. "I mean, *natürlich, alles in Ordnung.*" "Well, it's not as bad as it might have been," he went on in German, "and she won't be making any more phone calls. I can't be too explicit right now so all I'll say is that she was on the same team you're on, or supposed to be on, but sort of playing in the—the bush leagues (Wolff spoke these two last untranslatable words in English). If you're not getting this don't worry. I'll fill you in when I see you. —And oh, yeah, another thing. I'll brief J.D. on all this before I leave here. I think she's following the true faith now; but just in case, he'll keep an eye on her while I'm away."

"I think I follow you, Carl—but, 'bush leagues'?" a mystified Hans inquired timidly, " I don't even follow *European* football. "

---

[1] "No sweat," although almost certainly no German ever used such a grammatical construction.

"It's baseball, but don't sweat it, Hans," Wolff assured him amicably in English and in Hans's own coin. Then he ended the conversation in German:

"Call me when you're about to leave the garage and we'll meet at that hotel. And for Christ's sake Hans, make *sure* Sweetheart is parked for the night before you leave." He hung up and went back to the Mahmoud's spacious but austerely furnished sitting room where with a servant in attendance everyone including the two children was sipping tea.

The Mahmouds insisted that their guests stay for dinner which, Camille told them graciously as she went around offering a box of Turkish cigarettes, was almost ready. Wolff felt they could hardly refuse after all that these people had done for them; in any case, he and the others having eaten nothing barring the dates since early morning were famished. With a nod of acknowledgement from Magda and J.D. he accepted in polite Arabic for all three. He explained that Hans was engaged with the car repair and would not join them. Hans now would also have to wait for him a little longer; if he became anxious he could always call again, he told himself.

Wolff was to tell himself later (with a loud belch and a wry grin) that if he'd given the matter any thought at the time, the variety of pungent aromas emanating from the back of the house might have given him an idea of what the Mahmouds had in store for their newly-acquired Western acquaintances. He had been thinking in terms of the usual hour or hour and a half for a typical Western (at least, European) meal; but by the time they had gone through the soup, thick with lamb chunks and spiced with cinnamon and cardamon; the *ful*, or broad beans cooked in tomato, onion, and oil; the *sanbusak*, a thin triangular pastry stuffed with ground meat, onion, and a local type of garlic called *kurrath*; eggs gently cooked on a bed of fried onion, green peppers, and tomato; then the main dish of *kabsah*, consisting of chicken sauteed with garlic, onion, tomato, grated carrot, and grated orange rind, served atop rice simmered in the meat sauce and all of it garnished with raisins and almonds; a choice of either large fat-fleshed grouper laid open and covered with the by now predictable onion, tomato, and garlic, as well as hot pepper and cumin, and served with lemon, or baked king mackerel with a sweet-sour sauce made from dried tamarind; and finally, after a brief rest, an elegant *muhallabiyah*, a delicate pudding of rice, flour, and milk, lightly flavored with orange blossom and rose water and decorated with almonds and pistachios, more than three hours had elapsed.[2]

By the end of this gargantuan meal it had been decided that Magda and J.D. would spend the night at the Mahmoud house, but that Wolff, who was to accompany Hans to the garage early next morning, would stay at the hotel where by this time Hans undoubtedly had booked in. Magda, who had become enamoured of the Mahmoud children, seemed more than happy to stay, while J.D., quickly understanding that Wolff did not want her left there alone, also readily agreed to accept the Mahmoud's hospitality.

It was at this point that Hans, understandably alarmed by Wolff's tardiiness, called once more and Wolff apprised him of these latest plans.

When he returned from the telephone Camille was cheerfully suggesting that although next day Ekbal and Bashir would have to visit the date markets, she would be happy to take Magda, and J.D. as well if he wished to go along, to some places of interest in Basrah.

When Wolff politely but firmly refused Mahmoud's offer to drive him to the hotel, insisting that his host remain with his guests, one of the servant boys was sent to find a taxi. Although Mahmoud, who undoubtedly was tired after his long drive, protested sincerely, he almost certainly was grateful to remain at home. With many thanks to his hosts and with a long

---

[2] Such a meal usually is reserved to mark the end of the Ramadan fast (the Fourth Pillar of Wisdom), which is observed during the ninth month of the Muslim year.

and significant look at Magda and a nod for J.D., Wolff took his hurried departure.

J.D. accompanied Wolff to the taxi, and as they stood facing each other assured his friend he would keep a close eye on Magda, at which Wolff asked quietly:

"Are you armed?"

"I've brought along my old service revolver," J.D. grinned. "They didn't check my hold baggage at Heathrow."

"One of those .455 Webleys? —Good Lord! the damned thing must weigh at least three pounds."

"Actually, it's a Webley-Fosbery. Yes, but one gets used to the weight, you know—and it's an old friend."

Wolff shook his head with an indulgent smile; then, after calming the impatient cab driver with a gesture, he quickly and briefly told J.D. about Magda's small but to him, Wolff, personally significant role in British-American intelligence.

Chapter Twenty-two

Clemency

The hotel where Wolff was to meet Hans was not merely near the *souk*, but virtually in it. Its redeeming virtues, as Hans pointed out, were its relative anonymity and perhaps more important its proximity to the mosque where the rededication ceremony was to take place in three days.

Wolff was himself unclear about his motivation—whether it was due to the pressures of the past month, the shock he'd received about Magda, the after-effects of the colossal (though non-alcoholic) Arabian dinner he'd consumed, or a combination of all three—but he felt an irresistable urge to get drunk, and the first thing he told Hans after greeting him and apologizing again for his delay was to find him a bottle of good whiskey.

Having cancelled the reservation for J.D. Hans had retained adjoining rooms for himself and Wolff on the top floor of the ancient building (from the roof of which Wolff was to discover there was clear view of at least the upper works of the mosque).

Now, settled in his surprisingly spacious if sparsely furnished room with Hans, a quart bottle of Johnnie Walker Black Label scotch, and two bottles of mineral water, Wolff told his eager companion about his confrontation with Magda on the previous night at "Mesopotamia."

"And so what it comes down to, old Hans," he concluded as once more he reached for the scotch, of which he had already taken significant toll, "is that she's working for the Brits, who undoubtedly are in bed with Browning and his troops on this caper. She was taken on as a 'watcher' and her handler is some broad by the name of Feldon, a professor at Oxford. And there's something screwy goin' on, 'cause when our little Magyar told this dame she was here in Iraq with me and two other guys Feldon said she was coming over here, to get Magda *outta* here. Now, what the hell's going on? I gotta ask myself. Magda undoubtedly is small potatoes in this horror show; she was just supposed to check me out and report back to Feldon that time I was screwing around in England. But even if she were more important and was ordered to come over here to keep an eye on me (and on *you*, too, I guess), why would this Felson or Feldon, whatever the fuck her name is, get on *her* horse? Christ, all she'd have to do is pick up the phone, and call *her* handler, and—" he emptied his glass and motioned to Hans for the bottle. "And if she does show up here it'll be a *real* clusterfuck! Jesus! this already is beginning to seem like a bad Italian opera—how many more goddam complications do I need?"

Hans, who had drunk very little of the scotch, said somewhat irrelevantly:

"Were you very rough with her?"

"Hell, yes, I was rough— Oh, you mean did I smack her around? No, I didn't have to; she couldn't wait to spill it. I don't think I could've done that anyway. I..." Wolff trailed off.

"That's good, on both counts," Hans murmured considerately. "Well," he continued with a philosophical sigh, "perhaps this Professor Feldon, who quite possibly is Magda's tutor, has taken a motherly or sisterly interest in the girl, especially in view of the fact that she almost certainly recruited her; perhaps she feels responsible." And with that he altered the conversation again.

"You know, after having spent the last few days in your company—your's and Magda's, I mean—I begin to see the possibility, if all goes well (Ensh'Allah!), of a den of little

Wolves someday, if you'll pardon the execrable play on words."

As Hans said this, Wolff, who had gone to the open window to urinate into the ally below, turned, and thoughtlessly closing one eye to scrutinize Hans, went reeling across the room. With a sigh Hans put the cork back in the almost empty bottle and went to help his friend into bed.

Wolff's next conscious impressions were of Hans bending over him and of the smell of steaming black coffee. Except for his boots, which Hans must have removed, he still was fully dressed. His first conscious thought was to check his "ultravision," as he'd come to think of it. Gently he brushed Hans aside, and somewhat tentatively got to his feet and went to the window which though it still was dark outside revealed, only six feet away, the stone wall of an adjoining building. For a moment Wolff dismally recalled this locale as his impromptu urinal of the previous night, then he turned to Hans and said:

"No good. Can we get up on the roof?"

"I was about to suggest that anyway. I want you to see the view; and I think you could use as much fresh air as possible today," Hans added wryly. "But do have some coffee first. I woke you early because we must get to the repair shop before they begin working on the car. But there's plenty of time yet." he glanced at his watch, "it's only six o'clock."

"God, what I'd give for a shower!" was all Wolff could manage as he went to the sink to wash his face in cold water.

As Hans led him to the stairs which reached the roof Wolff asked:

"What time did I lose consciousness last night, old Hans?"

"Fairly early—about eleven."

Dawn was breaking as Hans led Wolff out on to the windy, dusty, and deserted roof.

After ensuring that his "ultravision" was unimpaired (he'd begun wishing almost fervently that one of these times he'd find he'd lost it for good and all) Wolff sighted in on the slender and graceful minaret which towered above the mosque a half-mile away. Just as he did so the call to prayer began to boom over the loudspeakers—one of Islam's concessions to modernity in nearly all Muslim countries now.

"Well, I could 'off' the *muezzin* from right here—unless what we're hearing isn't just a recording, that is, " he told Hans drily as he went on to scan the area contained within a few square blocks of the mosque. "No offense I hope, old Hans," he added, "it's just this horrible hangover. I feel like my teeth are all wearing little sweaters."

"No offense taken, Carl. Do you see any place where you think you could, ah, set up your position, or whatever it's called? —By the by, I've got some satellite photos of Basrah they gave me in Baghdad; your friend, Browning, had them smuggled in. They're sewn into the lining of my overcoat. Do you need them?"

As Hans spoke Wolff was concentrating on a rooftop which rose above those around it, seemingly giving it "line-of-sight" on the mosque steps and from which, he estimated, those steps should be less than a thousand yards away. On that roof was a storage tank of some sort with a large green and white sign painted on its side.

"Yeah, I do; not the photos, the place, so I think we can forget the 'spy in the sky' bullshit," he pointed out the building to his friend, "and burn those goddam Russian pictures as soon as you can." He turned and looked at Hans, "Jesus! *Sewn in the lining of your coat?*" he grinned good-naturedly, "I thought *that* Mickey Mouse went out with Eric Ambler."

Meanwhile at the Mahmoud house everyone had gotten up early. Leaving the children in the care of their two servants Camille, accompanied by her guests, took Ekbal to meet Bashir at the date warehouse. From there she took Magda and J.D. to the *souk*.

Magda was examining some finely embroidered linen handkerchiefs when she felt a light touch on her shoulder. She turned to see Professor Margaret Feldon smiling down sardonically at her.

When they arrived at the repair shop Wolff was relieved to see it was still closed. This relief was short-lived, however, as he became painfully aware not long after the two mechanics arrived to unlock their shop that they seemed uneasy about something. Judging by the looks they exchanged and the glances they cast at the two strangers and a muttered word or two Wolff was certain that somehow they had discovered the phony exhaust system which the single-barreled carburetor couldn't justify. They must have begun looking the car over the night before, after Hans's departure. Now he nudged Hans into conversation with the two men while he pretended to browse around the shop, ostensibly not understanding a word, but listening keenly all the while.

Fortunately, although the two men had become suspicious they remained cordially friendly and now were somewhat forthcoming. As it turned out one of them had worked in Germany for several years (using a Turkish passport) and thus had understood just enough of Hans's telephone conversation of the previous evening to make him curious; that combined with the puzzle about the car had led them to suspect smuggling of some sort (which though rampant in Iraq because of the U.N. sanctions undoubtedly would be looked upon differently in the case of two foreigners, especially if illegal drugs were involved). To make matters worse one of the mechanics hinted that he had a friend who was a policeman. But luckily they hadn't opened up the fake assembly and discovered what it contained, so Hans jokingly told them that he had had the installation done on a whim, "merely a silly whim," to give the car a "rakish look," as he'd told his friends (indicating Wolff) earlier. Upon advice he'd received in Baghdad, however, he now was considering having a *genuine* dual carburetion system installed. After all, he told them, the major work already had been done, no? When the head mechanic agreed and suggested they could do it for him here and now Hans glibly replied that presently he could afford neither the time nor the extra money. The tourism business didn't pay him well enough. In fact, he told them jokingly, he hoped he had enough money to pay for the current repairs. Besides, he said importantly as he smiled and waved a hand in Wolff's direction, he had to act as guide to Herr Wolff and his friends. After a brief private consultation the men seemed sufficiently satisfied (no doubt putting Hans down as some sort of half-wit), and turned their attention to replacing the broken timing chain.

As they worked, Wolff, with his hands clasped behind his back as he peered over their shoulders, played the role of the intelligent, curious Austrian to the hilt: never saying a word but pretending great interest in what they were doing. As this was going on a young boy came into the shop, and without a word of greeting to anyone went to a cupboard, got a broom, and started sweeping the concrete floor.

Later, while the mechanics were busy in the grease pit, under the car, and the boy was making coffee in a back room, Wolff took Hans aside.

"Tell them you want to take the car for a test run; insist on it if you have to, and tell them you want to make it a high-speed run, so we'll have to go out of town, in the weeds somewhere. Tell them they both should go—two heads and ears are better than one, and all that bullshit, right? And insist that I go too. Tell 'em I know a little about cars myself."

"I already did—last night, remember? But what's all this about, Carl? What do you have in mind?" Hans asked a little apprehensively.

"Never mind that right now. I'll tell you later," Wolff replied evasively. "Oh, yeah, another thing—what language *don't* these guys know?"

"Italian. I found out last night when we were talking about Fiats and Alphas," Hans managed to get in quickly as one of the mechanics climbed up out of the grease pit, giving them a neutral glance as he did so.

Hans did have to insist, and finally if somewhat reluctantly the men agreed.

With one mechanic driving and the other sitting next to him they drove out of Basrah in a southwesterly direction. Both men observed a stony silence. Now with more than just a suspicion about Wolff's intentions, Hans muttered out of the side of his mouth in Italian:

"*Must* we do this?"

"Yes, we must," Wolff answered tersely in the same language.

They were driving along a wide, deserted road which ran through a disused oilfield when Wolff, sitting next to Hans in the back seat, inclined his head and said quietly:

"Tell them I'd like to drive the car myself for a little while."

Hesitatingly Hans did as he was told. They pulled off the road and Wolff and the driver exchanged places.

One thing was certain, Wolff thought as he barreled along at about seventy miles an hour: the Fiat was running infinitely better than it had the last time he'd driven it. These were good, honest mechanics (which usually was more than one could hope for in the States anymore). All the more reason to hate what he had to do. For the hundredth time he considered just ending this exercise in insanity here and now, finally. Just turn around, go back to Basrah, and with a phone call to his travel office in Baghdad Hans could have him and Magda on a flight out of Kuwait City in less than twenty-four hours....

But that was just it: Magda. That was no empty threat Browning had laid down. He would kill them both, someday, somehow; and like enough the vengeful bastard would get Hans too, and maybe even J.D. No, he had to go through with this. But he would do it his way. If he could he would just wound Saddam Hussein; if Claxton were too close he'd wait for a better shot. Of course, even if he killed Hussein it would be no great loss to anyone. Unfortunately, as Hans had wisely pointed out, it almost certainly would result in chaos through-out the country....

He tore his mind away from these despairing thoughts and back to the job at hand. Leaning forward against the steering wheel, with an ear cocked as if listening for something for a few moments, he addressed the German-speaking mechanic next to him in simple German:

"I want to stop a minute and listen to the engine," and suiting the action to the word, he pulled off to the side of the road. "You and your friend come too, in case I have any questions." With which they all got out, leaving the engine running, and assembled around the front of the car. The man Wolff had addressed though still taciturn seemed pleased with himself for being able to communicate with this Austrian in his own language.

"*Alles in Ordnung, glaube, Mein Herr*" he opined respectfully as he raised the hood.

Wolff meanwhile put his left foot up on the bumper and bent forward as if making some adjustment to his boot. When he straightened up his hands were in his jacket pockets. Hans, looking grim, had been standing off to one side and several steps away from the mechanics. Now he quickly came forward and stood between the two men.

"Is it true that with this dual carburetion one gets better fuel efficiency at high speeds?" he asked a little frenetically, "I mean, I've heard that at about seventy miles per hour the second—chamber, is it?—comes into play, and, well, I really think I should have it done. Perhaps if I can see my way clear about the money and if Herr Wolff will grant me the *time*," as he emphasized this last word he gave Wolff, who for an entirely different reason also looked grim, a significant look, "you can do it while I am still in Basrah."

With this the two Iraqis turned to stare at each other with expressions which to Wolff seemed an odd combination of relief, exasperation, and amusement, as if some niggling doubt had at last been put to rest. They responded almost simultaneously and enthusiastically to Hans's question, and from this point it was as if they had undergone a complete change of personality. With a sigh Wolff approached the other three, pretended to listen to the engine for a moment, admitted it sounded fine, and suggested they stop wasting any more of the mechanics' time and get back to Basrah.

The repairmen, now friendly and gregarious (and trusting, Wolff fervently hoped), chatted animatedly with Hans all the way back to their repair shop. When they dropped the two off Hans settled his bill, promising to "get in touch soon" on the matter of the carburetor work, while Wolff called the Mahmoud house and hurriedly told J.D. they were on their way. Wolff rang off so quickly his friend had no opportunity to tell him of Magda's chance encounter in the *souk*.

"You realize you saved their lives, don't you?" Wolff said simply as he replaced the Beretta in his boot.

"I prayed to Allah that I could do something that could keep them innocent."

"You mean uninvolved, don't you?"

As he drove Hans said simply: "It's the same thing, if you think about it."

They were silent for a few minutes, then Wolff said:

"How'd you know all that shit about dual carburetion, anyway?"

"My friend, Youssef told me. I'm surprised I remembered it all!"

"By the way, you remember that stupid conversation we had, when we left Baghdad, about the muffler work?"

Hans knit his brows a moment then said:

"You mean about duets and trios and when the Major was so curious?"

"That's it. You never told me how you got this 'Youssef' to stay 'innocent,' as you would say."

"Well, it wasn't that difficult. The items you gave me were packed so neatly and nondescriptly in those waterproof containers there was no way of identifying them. I'm sure he thought we were smuggling *something* valuable, perhaps drugs, but he merely stuffed everything neatly in the proper places as quickly as possible and then installed the new assembly on the car. He couldn't wait to be finished, however, and he asked no questions. I'm sure he'll keep quiet considering what we've already paid him from your seemingly limitless supply of money; and then there's the fact that as an extra inducement to ensure his 'cooperation' I promised I'd give him a bonus when I got back to Baghdad."

Wolff seemed satisfied with this.

"Would you have done it, Carl, if I hadn't stepped in like that, I mean?" Hans asked after another brief silence.

"Killed those two guys? Yeah. I just couldn't take the chance. But if it makes you feel any better I would have hated it. But, yeah, I would have done it. I figured we'd bury them or hide them somehow out there in that old oil field and then go back to the garage and tell that kid that we'd gone in the other direction—east, for the test ride—and that they'd insisted we drop them off out there in those Shatt al-Arab swamps so they could defect to Iran. I assumed they were Shi'ites."

"They are. Bashir told me," Hans confirmed quietly. "You know, If they *had* decided to defect they would have been smart to go like that, alone, without their wives, if they have any, seeing what happened to Saddam's sons-in law. —Supposedly they were promised amnesty by Saddam, but four days after they returned from Amman they were killed by 'family members,' because they had 'brought dishonor to Saddam, their families, and the regime'," Hans made little quotation marks in the air. "I heard they came back because their wives—Saddam's daughters—were homesick. The minute they got back the wives started divorce preceedings against them!"

"Poor pussy-whipped bastards," Wolff muttered. Then in a normal voice he said, "Speaking of borders, we were just a few miles from the *Kuwaiti* border— when I stopped, you know? Christ! if Magda and J.D. had been with us I think I couldn't have resisted the urge to drop those greasemonkeys off and just keep on going and 'defect,' myself."

There was silence again until they reached the Mahmoud residence. As they pulled in next to the now familiar Mercedes Wolff smacked Hans's knee with the flat of his hand, and with a grin said warmly:

"Well, thanks to you, old Hans, none of the nasty was necessary (inwardly, once again, he hoped he was right). —God-damit, I feel almost human!"

"That hardly describes how *I* feel," replied Hans, showing most of his snow-white teeth as he glanced at his friend and opened his door.

It was just going on one o'clock when they went in and found that Professor Margaret Feldon had, at least for the time being, joined their little party.

Not five minutes after she'd been introduced to him (with Camille Mahmoud crowing with delight over the Professor's "adventitious" meeting with Magda in the *souk*) Feldon had a disgruntled Wolff in a corner of the Mahmoud's sitting room.

"Let's not bandy words," she began imperiously in fluent German. "Magda told you who I am and what my position is, did she not?"

"Can I assume she told you what *my* position is?"

"She did not."

"So, you haven't been briefed; you're out of the loop, right?" Wolff's satisfaction was obvious.

"Apparently it was decided that I had no 'need to know.' But now that you have involved Magda in whatever it is you're doing—"

At this point the object of their brief conversation came up to them. Feldon gave Wolff a brittle smile and asked irrelevantly:

"So, what *do* you think of the feminist movement, Herr Wolff?"

"Like higher taxes, political correctness, and the general state of the world today, it helps reconcile me to death," Wolff replied readily with an equally artificial smile. Feldon's eyes flashed momentarily as he put his arm around Magda's waist.

As she gently removed his arm Magda told Wolff: "Hans would like to speak to you."

As he left them to find Hans he could hear the urgency in Feldon's voice as she began speaking agitatedly to Magda.

He found Hans pacing up and down the small terrace outside the sitting room.

"What's up?" Wolff asked as Hans turned to him.

"It is already Tuesday, Carl."

"Yeah, I know; and the ceremony is on Thursday. So?"

"Well, if you're going through with 'it' there are things to arrange, yes?"

Wolff took Hans's arm and walked him to a more secluded part of the terrace.

"There are mainly two things to arrange, Hans," he said quietly, "and if we move too early we'll just be exposing ourselves unecessarily to the Iraqi security people who undoubtedly are or soon will be swarming all over this area. One, I've got to pinpoint the shooting position; and two, we've got to get what I'll need out of the Fiat and get it to that position. I want to get out of here soon—here, the Mahmoud's house, I mean. We're *not* staying for lunch. We gotta go check out that building I saw from the hotel. It looked good: a sign on the roof says it's a hotel, another small one; and it's about a thousand yards or less away from the mosque, far enough so that chances are good it'll be out of the main security cordon Saddam's people will set up, but still well within range of the weapon I'll be using. With this six-billion-dollar eye they gave me the mosque should look like it's across the street from there. We also have to come up with some kind of escape plan; like, check out escape routes from *wherever* I set up, and so on. But one thing I found out in Vietnam, the hard way, was that you can plan very carefully up to a point, but after that it becomes meaningless. It's a little hard to explain, but what I mean is you can clutter yourself up by trying to provide for every contingency. I'm sure you've heard of Murphy's Law?"

"'If something can go wrong, it will'?—something like that?"

"Right. Sometimes, you just end up having to wing it. Now, we gotta talk about what the hell we're gonna do about Magda and J.D. The ceremony is scheduled for two in the afternoon, right?" Hans nodded. "Okay, I think they should get out of here, out of the country, I mean, early Thursday morning. Hold on a minute—"

Wolff walked the few steps back to the french door and looked inside. Magda was still engaged in intense conversation with Feldon while J.D., who fortunately was facing in Wolff's direction, was chatting amiably with Camille Mahmoud. With a jerk of his head he signaled to the Englishman and went back to Hans. J.D. joined them almost immediately, and they reengaged in intense conversation for several minutes. Among the matters they discussed Feldon was not neglected.

By the time they went in to join the others they had decided on the following plan.

Magda and J.D. would stay at the Mahmoud house one more day; Wolff wanted them away from the "scene" as long as possible, and they undoubtedly would be safer with these respectable Iraqi citizens than near him, in the heart of Al-Basrah. Since Camille had made it genuinely evident that she would like them *all* to stay that should not present a problem.

Meanwhile, Wolff and Hans would reconnoiter the tentative shooting position and later, the mosque itself. If the "new" hotel met their requirements Wolff would book a room and stay there that night and find access to the roof, while Hans would remain alone at the "*souk*" hotel one more night. The following day J.D. and Magda would move to the "*souk* hotel," into the adjoining rooms which Wolff and Hans had occupied the previous night. Wolff and Hans would spend that day making their final preparations—among them, finding a place to remove what Wolff called "the necessary" from the Fiat and booking a flight out of Iraq for Magda and J.D. They would both stay at the "new" hotel the night of the fifth. Plans for Hans and Wolff following the shoot were still vague: tentatively, and assuming they could get clear, Hans would drive back to Baghdad (claiming he had just barely escaped from Wolff's attempt to murder him) while Wolff got out of Iraq and across, somehow, to Kuwait.

Using the excuse of having to return Hans's car to the repair shop for more work and with effusive regards and apologies to Ekbal, who would be coming home soon, Wolff begged off Camille's invitation to stay for lunch. He also told his hostess that since they had already paid for their hotel they would stay there that night. Then he pointedly asked Margaret Feldon if they could give her a lift to *her* hotel (which was near the airport), hoping, unavailingly as it turned out, that the generous and gracious Camille would, uncharacteristically, not insist on her staying at the Mahmoud house overnight.

As Wolff and Hans took their leave Feldon still was protesting (though not very vigorously) that she couldn't impose on the Mahmoud's generosity, and so on, and after so short an acquaintanceship, and so forth. For his part Wolff found a good deal of reassurance in the fact that the rock-solid J.D. would be there to keep an eye on things. What, he wondered, would La Feldon think when she became aware that Magda was playing the role of J.D.'s niece?

"What are you grinning about?" Hans asked as they drove away from the Mahmoud house. "Are you experiencing one of those times when you feel that if you don't laugh you'll cry?"

"Sorry," Wolff chuckled, "but I was just thinking that I'm always leaving J.D. back to guard Magda, and that reminded me of something my father used to joke about." When Hans gave him an inquiring glance he went on:

"As a boy, in the States, along with millions of other boys, I guess, he used to listen to a radio program called 'Jack Armstrong, the All-American Boy,' a daily half-hour adventure story. The sponsor was a popular breakfast cereal—Wheaties, Breakfast of Champions (what else?). Well, there were four main characters: Jack, of course; then young Billy; a pretty young girl named Betty, who may have been Billy's sister, I can't recall; and this wise, older man they called 'Uncle Jim.' I **don't know if any of these people were really related, but maybe this older guy** *was* **an uncle of one of the other three. I** hope it wasn't Betty, because it struck my old man as strange, even as a kid, that when these people were off on one of their adventures—sort of Indiana Jones-type situations, you know?—and they were planning what to do next to get out of a scrape or catch the bad guys, or whatever, more often than not this 'Uncle Jim' stayed out of harm's way, with Betty. Sounding very wise and authoritative, he would tell Jack to go around in one direction and Billy in another while he would stay back in the cave—or shack, gulch, tree house, or wherever—and 'take care of Betty.' Sometimes Jack would even suggest it himself, as in, 'You stay back here and take care of Betty, Uncle Jim, while Billy and I see if we can—' and so on. My father told me that after a while he started hating Uncle Jim."

Hans, who had been grinning throughout this recitation, now became thoughtful. "Well, I certainly don't think you have to be concerned about the Major; I should say he's beyond reproach in that respect."

"Are you *kidding*? My old man told me J.D. was one of the greatest swordsmen on three continents, in his day."

"Interesting. But, as you say, 'in his day'!" Hans pointed out. Then after a short silence he asked:

"So, would it be safe to assume then, that I'm 'Billy'?"

Although the hotel whose roof Wolff had tentatively selected as a firing position was full due to the influx of visitors for the mosque rededication, this problem was easily resolved when Wolff with his substantial supply of "confidential" funds and with more than a hint at a substantial sum in baksheesh (with a choice of US dollars, Austrian schillings, or Iraqi dinar), convinced the proprietor that "there *must* be a room left somewhere?" He and Hans were quickly shown a large, airy room (which, amazingly, had its own bathroom) on the top floor of the old and dilapidated six-storey building, and the deal was settled on the spot.

Chapter Twenty-three

The Eve of St. Nicholas

When the porter had left their room Wolff downed a quick drink from what was left in the scotch bottle, then went straight to the bathroom and stripped off his clothes. He hadn't had a decent bathe since the one in J.D.'s "billet" at the Baghdad Hilton. On top of that he'd slept in his clothes the previous night. Meanwhile, Hans had gone prowling along the dim corridors looking for access to the roof.

As he stood under the tepid, feeble shower Wolff was astonished to notice that the water which ran off his body into the ancient but still white porcelain tub was brown! Could he have gotten *that* dirty (he pitied poor Magda) in just the last few days? Catching water in his cupped hands he was relieved to see that the brown water came directly out of the shower head.

Twenty minutes later, on the roof with Hans, he saw the catchment-storage-gravity-feed tank system which explained the brown water. (It had been the sign emblazoned on this water tank which had announced to him early that morning that this building was a hotel.) The water level in the tank, which undoubtedly had years of accumulated silt at its bottom, must be very low.

This rooftop obviously was used during the season as some sort of restaurant or café. Several folding tables and chairs (obviously neglected when the rest had been stored) were piled carelessly against the box-like structure which housed the access stairway up which they had come. Now, in the chill of Iraq's winter, the place was windswept and littered with the small debris one finds in such places when they are unattended. Wolff started nervously as a styrafoam cup, swept by the stiff breeze, rattled its way past him and came to a stop against the one-and-a-half-foot parapet which surrounded the roof.

Now he noticed that the water tank itself, mounted as it was on a two-foot concrete platform in the corner of the roof nearest the mosque, might provide the necessary visibility and perhaps even some of the cover and concealment he would want for his firing position. After ensuring that he and Hans were alone on the roof and after scanning the adjacent rooftops in a complete 360-degree arc for signs of life or any movement, he sprawled out next to the tank in the prone position— propped on his elbows to approximate the barrel height of the XMG-95F when its spring-loaded folding bipod legs were snapped open—and sighted on the mosque which he estimated was about 800 yards away. Meanwhile, Hans stood guard near the roof access door.

Wolff scanned for a full minute, until he was satisfied once more that even after such prolonged use there still were no traces of the earlier abberrations he'd experienced in his "ultravision"; then he got slowly back to his feet, nodding approvingly to himself and dusting his hands as he rose. Hans quickly arrived at his side.

"Well?"

"I've got an unobstructed view of the whole mosque front, including the steps and even about twenty yards of the terrace in front of them. If you walk over to the edge of the roof (but stay low if you do) you'll see I was looking right along the broad street that runs in front of this place and leads straight into the square the mosque sits in. —It's a shooter's paradise, Hans," he added with a barely audible sigh.

"I was afraid it might be," Hans mumbled half aloud, as

with his hands in his overcoat pockets he toed a dirty paper napkin which somehow had gotten stuck to the roof.

"Come on, Hans, we don't want to spend too much time up here," Wolff looked at his watch, "and I want to call Magda and see what that Amazon, Feldon, is up to." He rubbed his eyes, which now had begun to itch (the strain of scanning so long? the wind? his hangover? he wondered), then added as he threw an arm around Hans's shoulders, "Besides, I gotta have a little lie down. I guess I'm not as young as I used to be, and all that friggin' scotch you made me drink last night is giving me a headache."

Wolff stopped briefly to examine the rooftop door (which was secured only by a Yale lock on its inside) nodded to himself, pulled it open, and followed Hans in.

As they went the napkin Hans had dislodged scuttered to the parapet, hesitated, and then was boosted over and away by a gust of wind.

Standing next to one of the beds back in their room while pulling his jacket off, Wolff asked:

"Do you know, or at least think, we're being watched, Hans?"

"I don't know. I don't think so. I haven't noticed anyone—"

"Neither have I," Wolff interposed. "They'd be stupid to do it now that we're down here. If I were going to blow this deal I would've done it in Baghdad. And if there were any sort of confrontation between us and Browning's people it could compromise the whole operation." He reached down for the Beretta and shoved it under his pillow, then sat on the bed, pulled his boots off, glanced at the telephone on the night stand, and with a long shuddering sigh sprawled out. "I'll call Magda later...." he muttered as he rolled over on his side. He didn't even hear the door close or the lock turned as a few moments later Hans went out.

When he awoke he was completely disoriented. He had been dreaming that he and Magda, followed by the two Iraqi garage mechanics, were running through the desert towards the

Kuwait border. One of the mechanics kept calling his name, as if he wanted him to come back. He'd been annoyed, in the dream, that the man familiarly was calling him 'Charley'....

When he came to his senses he found Hans leaning over him, shaking him gently by shoulder.

"Carl. Carl! Wake up! —You've been dreaming."

"Okay, okay, I'm up, I'm up—well, awake, anyway." He pushed Hans's hand away, swung his legs around, and sat on the edge of the bed kneading his eyes with the heels of his hands. "What's up, old Hans?" He took his hands away and looked out the window. "Jesus Christ, It's dark outside! What the hell time is it, anyway?" He found an almost-empty bottle of Evian water and drank it off.

"It's nine o'clock, but you needed the sleep. I wouldn't have awakened you, but you were thrashing around in your dream so much—"

Wolff shook his head, then scratched it vigorously.

"What the hell's been going on? What have you been up to? Did anybody call from the Mahmoud house? Did you—?"

"Calm yourself, Carl," Hans held up his hands, "please, relax. You can believe it or not, but the world continued to turn without you."

"Cheeky bastard," Wolff muttered sulkily to himself.

"What? Really, Carl, there's no need to be abusive. I merely thought—"

Wolff looked up with a grin.

"No, no, Hans, not you—the guy in the dream; see, he— oh, shit, never mind, it's too crazy. But anyway, fill me in. — Jesus! I can't believe I slept that long—what's been going on?"

"Calm yourself, Carl," Hans advised again. "You've been driving yourself rather hard and have been under great pressure. The tension over sparing those mechanics (Allah be praised!), the unexpected encounter with Margaret Feldon, and I did get you up very early this morning—and after all that whiskey you drank last night—"

"Lose the sermons, okay, Hans? Now if you're through with

the introduction, *please* fill me in!" Wolff growled irritably. "There is no cause for alarm. Nothing sensational occurred during your much-needed rest. I have three things to tell you; and having mentioned Feldon, let me say first that I took the liberty of calling the Mahmoud house—from a public telephone downstairs—as I thought you might want to know what was happening there. It seems there was a bit of a *contretempts* after we left. According to the Major, Magda and this Feldon harridan had a terrible row, out on the terrace, during which she, The Feldon, flew into a rage, slapped Magda, and left, presumably to return to her hotel. Camille Mahmoud tried to reason with her, *en fin* tried to send for a taxi, but she would have none of it; and so she left, in a fury"

"You fill me with interest and possibly, joy. How did Magda take all this—do you know?"

"I'll paraphrase what your friend, the Major, said. He said that he went out to Magda on the terrace after it was all over, and in his humble opinion, and this is almost a quotation, although he doesn't understand women as much as he'd like to, he was convinced that Magda's tears were inspired more by frustration and rage than by any feelings of guilt, remorse, or loss, and certainly not love. He stressed that. When she'd settled down somewhat he took her in and gave her drink from that great flask he carries about with him. When she was fully herself again she went to Camille Mahmoud, apologized, and explained that it was all to do with her schooling."

"Good. And Hans, although it may be hard for you to bear, I'm sure '*my* friend the Major' would like to be *your* friend, too." He gave Hans a significant stare. "Now, what else is on your agenda?"

Hans cleared his throat. "I found a place where we—actually it will have to be *you* since *I* have difficulty even replacing a light bulb or hanging a picture—a place where you can do what is necessary to retrieve your, what did you call it?—your 'stash'?"

"Yeah, my stash," Wolff affirmed glumly. "Where?"

"Just here, behind the hotel. There is a closed-in courtyard where, I have been assured by the manager, you can work undisturbed. I told him that as being an oil field machinist you were also a fair dab at auto mechanics and had agreed to do a small repair for me."

"Cool," the other glanced at Hans approvingly, then amended pensively, "I hope."

"It should do. I've looked at the place. There are only two doors giving access from the hotel and both remain locked from midnight until eight ack emma each day. The large gate giving access to the alley which runs behind the hotel remains locked, except twice a week when the rubbish wagon comes in to collect the dust bins. The manager will give me the key, and we can drive the car in through that gate."

"Sounds okay."

Wolff was thoughtfully silent for a time, then he said:

"You know, we were damned lucky today, or maybe I should say those Iraqi grease monkeys were." He glanced up at Hans, who gave him a quizzical look. "You know that bag of tools I'm gonna need to unlimber that exhaust system, the ones your mechanic friend in Baghdad gave you? —Well, they were in the trunk of your 'Sweetheart' the whole effing time those guys had it in their garage. If they'd seen them it might have been a dead giveaway."

"No fears, Carl," Hans smiled agreeably, "I took them to the hotel with me when I left the repair shop last night."

With an admiring look at his friend Wolff stretched and said:

"You're a winner, old Hans. By the way, how come you hardly ever use 'no sweat' anymore?"

Hans swallowed self-consciously.

"To be perfectly honest I've been afraid that if I kept saying it when alone with you I'd forget and come out with it when J.D. was there to hear."

"What a pity. I'll miss it; it was a great part of your charm, Hans," Wolff grinned good-naturedly (secretly he was glad to have heard Hans address 'the Major' as 'J.D.'). "Now, what's the third thing you wanted to tell me?"

"I booked airline tickets to London for Magda and the Major, and I booked one for Carl Wolff to Kuwait City. I forgot to ask you what destination you wanted, but I reckoned that the main idea was to get you out of Iraq, and from Kuwait International you can go on to anywhere you want. 'My travel agency' does have an office here in Basrah, but all international bookings have to go through Baghdad; still, I should have confirmations by late tomorrow morning."

Wolff nodded understandingly and then was briefly thoughtful again.

"Look, Hans, I want you to book another reservation. It'll be under the name, Charles Wychway—Christ, it'll be nice to become 'me' again," he apostrophized—"that's W-y-c-h-w-a-y, pronounced 'which way,' as in the question—got it? I'm not going to write it down, so you'll have to memorize it, okay?"

"No sweat— no problem. Can I assume that the passport bearing that name has no entry visa stamp?" Wolff returned a sour affirmative nod. "I'll need it then, for several hours tomorrow. In fact I'd better have it now. I *wish* you'd given it me in Baghdad: I could have had it done *there* in less than a half-hour—"

"First of all, I can't 'give it you' now—it's in the frigging Fiat with the rest of the stuff. And I couldn't 'give it you' in Baghdad, after we bailed that shit out of the desert, because I didn't want to have it on me all this time, *verstehen Sie?*"

"Yes, of course; but we'll have to get it out now, tonight, or very early tomorrow, if you want that entry stamp. I've only got tomorrow in which to do the necessary, and since I'm operating in *terra incognita*, so to speak, I'll have to make some inquiries first, and so on—"

"Okay, okay. Let me think a minute," Wolff stood and walked around the room, then looked at his watch and confronted Hans. "Is it too late to get that key from the manager?"

"No, I think it's all right. He mentioned that he usually plays backgammon with his friends till at least midnight; and he'll let us keep the key overnight."

"Good. I guess you better go get it. Tell him we want to get an early start tomorrow and the car work has to be done first. As for me," he stretched again and yawned mightily, "I'm going back to bed. I feel like I could sleep for a week. Could you wake me up just before first light? We've gotta be finished before they unlock those doors at eight." Wolff started pulling his clothes off.

"That should give you another good eight hours. I'll see you then," smiled Hans, and with a wave and a *"Belli sogni!"* started to leave when Wolff called out to him. He turned to face his friend, who was getting into bed.

"Start thinking about where we're gonna stash my toys once we get them out of the Fiat. We're gonna have to sit on 'em until it's time for...you know," Wolff enjoined with a wave of dismissal.

"Hmm," was Hans's only rejoinder as again he turned to go.

"Good night, old Hans," Wolff muttered sleepily as the door closed and the key turned in the lock.

Assisted by the first feeble light of a cold, gray new day, and with Hans alternately providing more illumination with a flashlight and ensuring no one was stirring on the hotel side, Wolff, who was feeling immeasurably better after his hours of much needed rest, accomplished his task surprisingly quickly. Placing a compact but powerful screw jack under the right-hand rocker panel (which faced away from the hotel) he first raised the car as far as he could, then went to work with the tools Hans's mechanic friend had provided, which included a hacksaw and a socket wrench already fitted with the proper size socket. The dummy exhaust system came off in sizes which permitted handy storage in the Fiat's trunk, thereby precluding any problem of disposal. A short front section of pipe with no connection to the exhaust manifold was simply left in place. In less than half an hour he had replaced the jack in its trunk compartment.

To remove Wolff's "stash" from the dismantled muffler

and pipe sections and pack the items in the tool bag was the work of a few minutes. As they stored the tools in Sweetheart's trunk along with the exhaust parts it began to drizzle. They reparked the car on the street, and Hans left the gate key on the manager's tiny desk, as he'd been instructed. It was not quite seven o'clock.

After they had secreted the cache items in Hans's padlocked Samsonite suitcase and had cleaned up, they went down to the dining room where they had to wake the cook, who slept in the kitchen. While they waited for their coffee Wolff began outlining the day's plans.

"We've got to leave the hotel anyway to keep to the story you told the manager, so I'll make a recon of the mosque area and possible escape routes, on foot, or using cabs if necessary, while you go sniff out that visa stamp and make the 'Wychway' reservation. You got that passport with you?"

Hans patted the breast pocket of his well-tailored tweed jacket.

"No sw—er, no worries. I can book the reservation first and show them the passport later. What date do you wish to have entered?"

"Might as well make it the date I actually 'flew in,' yeah?"

"Why not? That way, no one can have seen you any earlier. That was the 30th of November, was it not?."

"Actually, the 29th. But it doesn't really matter since I spent the night at the 'Desert Hilton,' and nobody asked to see my papers," Wolff grinned, then became serious again.

"Now, I'm afraid you'll have to take the stash with you. One of us can't stay in the room all the time, especially this morning. We're supposed to be out sightseeing, or I'm supposed to be out looking for a job. Anyway, put the stuff back in the tool bag or use my backpack; if you walk out with that prole Samsonite bag of yours they'll think you're trying to beat the hotel bill."

Hans gave him an indignant scowl.

"*Ja, mein Füeh*— All right, Carl; I shall do as you say."

They fell silent as the coffee was served. When the servant had left Wolff went on.

"Okay. I'll call the Mahmoud's and find out when J.D. and Magda'll be ready to leave. I want to talk to her anyway— Magda, I mean—then you can go pick them up whenever it's convenient for everybody and take them to the *souk* hotel. They can move right into our old rooms. —I guess J.D. would appreciate it though," he added pensively with mock seriousness, "if you had them change the sheets on your bed...."

Wolff countered Hans's rising indignation with a smile:

"Just *kidding* ol' Hans—don't be so *touchy!*" He drank his coffee in two gulps and pushed his chair back.

"I don't mean to be a tyrant," he said as he got up, "but don't dawdle over your coffee. I don't know what time the chambermaids hit the rooms—probably not this early—but we don't want to leave that stuff unattended too long, okay?"

Hans, who was scalding himself in his haste to drink his coffee, merely nodded unhappily.

It was while walking around seemingly aimlessly in the mosque square thirty minutes later that Wolff saw Harry Ward. He stood watching as Ward, who had recognized him almost immediately, walked quickly away around a corner of the mosque. Wolff turned slowly and thoughtfully, and began walking back towards the hotel, recalling what he'd said to Hans that morning about "confrontations with Browning's people."

Midway between the mosque and the hotel he entered a locksmith's shop, where he bought a heavy brass padlock.

An hour later, after having reconnoitered the labyrinth of streets and alleys within six square blocks (or at least its equivalent in this ancient area) of the hotel and as he was stuffing his pistol under his pillow, he found a note from Hans.

Am still striving diligently (the note ran), but all arrangements should be okay and final by late this P.M., to include moving loved ones to new digs. Will see you anon. - H.

As he lay back against his doubled-up pillow Wolff lit a cigarette and at the same time burned the note. Then he began trying to visualize the events of the following day: everything he would do, or try to do, everything that would happen, everything that could or *might* happen. The next day. St. Nicholas Day....

He was thinking of the small native boats and the larger commercial ships he'd seen to the east, on the Shatt Al-Arab, from the rooftop the previous afternoon, when he felt himself dozing off.... With a groan of disgust he swung his legs off the bed. How the hell can I be sleepy when I'm thinking about what's facing me tomorrow? he thought irritably—and after all the sleep I had yesterday... He never finished the thought.

Reeling with a sickening dizziness he fell back across the bed, his teeth clenched, his body jerking convulsively and spasmodically for long seconds, until it went completely limp and he began snoring with a loud, harsh, droning sound.

At five that afternoon Hans found his friend still in a deep sleep, fully dressed, and lying crosswise on the bed. He noticed where Wolff's spittle had run down from a corner of his mouth and dried on his face. Leaning over the prostrate form he felt the wrist for a pulse and found it to be regular, but apparently a little weak. He went and sat quietly by the window. Then he took a piece of paper from his breast pocket, and with a sigh scanned it a few times. He turned when he heard the bedsprings creak.

"Wha—whaat—?" came a hoarse croak from the bed.

"I'm back. It is only I, Hans. It seems you've had another visit from the Sandman. Is it possible there are tsetse flys in Iraq?" Hans, now looking out the window, said wryly from his chair across the room.

"Who, who—is that? Hans?—you said, Hans?" Wolff's voice seemed to come from a distant place.

No longer jovial, Hans turned, and with concern written all over his face quickly got up and went across to the bed where Wolff seemed to be having some difficulty sitting up. Hans helped him sit upright, keeping an arm around his shoulder.

"Are you all right, old boy? Don't you know who this is?—I'm Hans. Your friend, Hans!"

"I—yeah, I—what the hell happened? —I just was, was—" Wolff's voice, almost a monotone, sounded puzzled, even a little frightened.

"Were you dreaming again?"

"Dream—? No, no dream. —Uh, where am I? What—"

"You're here, in the hotel room. Don't you remember?" Hans was becoming alarmed. "Do you know *who* you are—why you're here?"

Wolff stared at Hans closely with a concentrated expression. "Wychway. Charley Wychway. I—" he stopped, obviously trying hard to remember something, then just as obviously giving it up. "Jesus, I'm tired. Exhausted.... I gotta lie down...."

Hans turned him gently and eased his head down on the pillow. In doing so his hand encountered the Beretta. He slid the pistol out and slipped it into his pocket, then he stretched his friend's legs out on the bed and removed the Austrian boots.

It was night when Wolff opened his eyes again to see Magda looking down at him tenderly in the dimly lit room. She was holding his hand, and now she gave it a gentle sqeeze.

"Magda," Wolff croaked, and Hans's sigh of relief could be heard from across the room as at the same time J.D. Somerville approached the bed.

"You must have had some sort of blackout, old fellow, perhaps even a seizure of some kind, according to what Hans had to say about it. And apparently, from what Magda's told me, this isn't the first time. I *am* dreadfully sorry to have delved into your personal life like this, old chap, but unfortunately we're going through a rather serious time here, and we can't stand on too much ceremony."

When Wolff nodded with a wan but encouraging smile J.D. went on:

"Now, you've recognized Magda, and I assume you know me, and Hans, of course, but can you remember anything else?"

"I remember everything now up till yesterday, J.D. Hans and I went up on the roof, and—"

"Do you remember working on the car this morning?" Hans interposed from a distance.

"No. Everything after the roof is zilch, nothing.—Wait a minute! Yeah! yeah, the car. We had to get the... Yeah, I remember that. It's starting to come back, but give me a chance. I remember now from when this happened years ago that I shouldn't rush it with the memory drill...." He paused thoughtfully for a moment. "I remember something else too—all that booze I had.... When was that? Monday, right?"

"Better and better," said J.D. with his own sigh of relief. "Do you feel the need of more sleep?"

"No, but I feel the need for a cigarette," and suiting the action to the word pushed himself up into a sitting position and reached for his cigarettes. As he drew on his cigarette he seemed to remember something else, and he felt around under his pillow. When Hans answered his inquiring glance with an affirmative nod Wolff sighed and said in his normal, even baritone:

"Well, I guess I'm gonna live, after all." He looked at his watch. "Christ Almighty! it's ten o'clock. Has everybody eaten? Good. Somehow, I'm not a bit hungry, and I haven't eaten since that Arab *luau* Monday. Weird, but I feel okay." He turned to Hans. All right then, old Hans—what news on the Rialto?"

"Does it really matter anymore, Charley?" J.D. asked seriously.

"Yes," Hans added, "*Penso che la commedia è finita.*"[1]

Wolff looked at each of them in turn.

"No, my dear friends, it *ain't* over. And please, J.D., it's Carl, Carl Wolff—at least for another day or two. So I hope you'll all forgive me for the delay, but we're right back where we were, barring those few hours when I fell down on the job,

---

[1] I think the comedy is ended. Canio's final words in Leoncavallo's *Pagliacci*.

so to speak.''[2]

All were silent while Wolff took in the three glum (and undeniably worried) faces. Then he spoke again:

"I don't like to be rude, but I think you and Magda ought to go back to your hotel, J.D. Hans and I have some plans to make which, since they don't involve you two, you're better off not hearing." He stood up, and seemed steady enough as he extended his hand, "I won't be seeing you again, Major," he said, and after glancing at Magda's face went on quickly, "at least for a couple of days; so all I can say is a humble 'Thanks,' for everything."

J.D. took his hand.

"Good luck, old man; and if it means anything, I want you to know that in your place I should be doing the same thing. If I thought there were anything I could do to help you through this, I'd be your man, and nothing you could do would make me go." He cleared his throat huskily, "We'll have dinner again when next you're in England."

"Good old British phlegm," Hans muttered almost inaudibly.

Wolff looked up. "What's that you say, Hans?"

Hans cleared his throat.

"I said, 'I'll go with them'—take them to the hotel, I mean to say."

"No need," J.D. said (a trifle brusquely?). "We can find our way. Thanks, anyway," he added quickly with the briefest of smiles in Hans's direction.

Hans took two steps and held out his hand to J.D., who took it and shook it twice.

"I suppose we'll be seeing you tomorrow morning, Hans?"

"Oh, yes. Around nine o'clock. I'll be taking you to the airport."

Wolff gave Magda a quick kiss and embrace (*too* brief

---

[2] Undoubtedly, Wolff-Wychway is punning at his own expense. Grand mal epilepsy once was euphemistically and commonly referred to as "the falling sickness."

under the circumstances, it surely must have seemed to Hans and J.D.) and saw her and J.D. out the door. As he bid them goodbye again he quickly tried out his telescopic vision on the far end of the corridor. Once again he experienced mixed relief and disappointment in finding it was still there.

When Wolff returned from Magda's hotel at two the following morning (he'd kept the key to his old room) Hans was sound asleep. With a sigh he shoved the Beretta he'd retrieved from Hans under his pillow once again, and found there his American passport, properly visa-stamped, an open airline ticket to London in the name of Charles Wychway, and a note with something clipped to it. He put the other items aside and looked at the note which read:

With all the holus bolus going on I forgot to give this to you. I found it on the windscreen of the car when I came out from booking your ticket. - H.

Wolff examined the five- by seven-inch handbill to which the note was attached. On its front was the traditional, bordered, cruciform slogan: **Jesus Saves**, with the central "S" in "Jesus" doing double duty as the first "S" in "Saves." On the back there was scrawled an unsigned note:

Tell your friend if he doesn't keep the faith even Jesus won't be able to save him (or his).

Despite the fact that he had become convinced that Magda and Margaret Feldon had been lovers, he knew now also that whatever she may have done in the past he loved Magda and cherished her; and so it was that parenthetical "or his" that Wolff found most disturbing. He speculated ironically that if Browning subscribed to any god at all undoubtedly that god would be a harsh, wrathful, vengeful, uncompromising, and unforgiving God.

Chapter Twenty-four

Apostacy

The sixth of December dawned gray and overcast.

Wolff had awakened famished at about eight o'clock. Now while he waited for Hans who had gone to get him some food, he sat on his bed and stared at the large brass padlock he'd found in his jacket pocket. He had no idea what it was doing there.

Somewhat extraneously he thought of what little he knew about Alzheimer's Disease. Once several years ago when he'd asked a doctor to define it for him he was given an example: If you can't find your car keys, that's absentmindedness, or just plain bad memory, or perhaps what now is popularly called "Oldtimer's Disease," he'd been told; but if you found yourself staring at those keys (as he now was staring at this padlock) not knowing what they were or what they were for, that's Alzheimer's Disease. Well, this wasn't Alzheimer's Disease, he told himself dejectedly. He decided to take his own advice of last night and not try so hard. He would think about something else.

His mind turned to his parting from Magda the night before (actually, earlier that day). Now he told himself that he shouldn't have gone to her after what had happened to him; but then, after he'd recovered most of his senses, and most of his memory, here, in this room the previous night, he'd experienced an overpowering desire to be with her—not with just any woman—only her. And it had been worth it: to be with someone who loved him and knew him, knew him as well as anyone knew him, he supposed, and especially under these bizarre, almost unreal, circumstances. Someone who even knew that at any moment he might suffer another of those terrible, and terribly stigmatized, seizures.

But during those hours he'd been with her there'd been no cause for alarm, until it came to his final good-bye, which didn't bear thinking about.

After the first love making they had talked about Margaret Feldon. Magda was through with the woman, in every way, she'd told him. She, Magda, wasn't even sure she would go back to Oxford to continue her studies. Countless times, Magda said, she had considered her relationship, every aspect of it, with Margaret Feldon, and as many times she'd told herself she must break the relationship, academic as well as personal. The woman, in Magda's own words, was "a raving feminist bitch who would stop at nothing to gain her own ends." Seeing Feldon here, seeing her as she really was when she was at her worst, had made up Magda's mind for her, once for all. Of course, there was no doubt, she'd admitted to him tenderly, that he'd been a strong factor in making this final decision, but in any case it was over. She felt as if she were closing the door on a room in which she could never feel comfortable—

And now, here in his hotel room, Wolff suddenly remembered what the padlock was all about, and almost immediately he recalled seeing Ward in the mosque square! He was still sitting there weighing the padlock in his hand when he heard the key turn in the lock and Hans came in with food and news.

The food was good, but it wouldn't have mattered what it was; totally indifferent to quality Wolff ate ravenously. Hans's news was generally good, considering the rather grim circumstances. What he told Wolff rather hurriedly, since he had to leave soon to take J.D. and Magda to the Basrah airport, was: first, that the day was dim and overcast, and promised to remain that way (the better to see the tracers, Wolff muttered); second, that it seemed that virtually everyone from the hotel, guests and employees alike, intended to go to the ceremony;

and third, that a hasty (but adequate, Hans assured him) reconnaissance of the neighborhood had revealed that the hotel was (as Wolff had optimistically foreseen) just outside the main and very tight security zone or perimeter which had been set up by the Iraqi police and military forces. There were rumors downstairs, Hans added as an afterthought, that a number of US security people, understandably in civilian clothes, also were in the area.

Now, having finished a substantial quantity of food and a large pot of thick black coffee during this briefing, Wolff wiped his mouth. Considering what lay ahead, he wondered that he could have eaten at all. He said:

"I got all that, Hans—every word. It sounds like we're at least par for the course—so far, anyway. Now, I don't like to admit it, but it occurs to me that I forgot (among six thousand other things) to ask you last night where the stash is."

"You're sitting on it, in a manner of speaking. It's all under your bed. I put it there yesterday while you, while you were 'otherwhere'," Hans told him tactfully.

Wolff looked relieved as he got up, lit a cigarette, and walked to the window where he stood smoking and looking up over the adjoining building, where he could just see a patch of lead-gray sky.

"Carl?"

"Yes?" Wolff answered without turning around.

"Are you *sure* you're still up this?" Hans's voice was full of concern.

"Whether I'm up to it or not, Hans," he replied quietly, "I've got to at least try. You read that note they left on your car, didn't you? There's no turning back now. —And please, old Hans, let that be an end of it, okay?" He pulled down the window shade and turned to face his friend with a smile of genuine affection.

Hans let out all the breath he'd been holding in, and keeping his face expressionless, merely nodded.

There was no way in which the good Hans could know the

wretched anguish his friend was experiencing; how bitterly disappointed to the point of virtual despondency he was over the shattering revisitation of a curse he thought he had rid himself of years ago. Added to that was the new curse of this freakish eyesight that had been forced upon him. These aberrations, while not making life totally worthless (thanks in large part to the modern pharmacopoeia, at least in the case of Curse Number One), made it for such men as Carl Wolff, née Charles Witchway, later Wychway, son of the legendary Colonel Charles Witchway, not much more than merely endurable. As he stood there looking at his disconsolate friend Wolff found himself thinking inconsequently (but not totally irrelevantly, he told himself) that Victor Frankenstein's monster, had it actually existed, would in its terrible isolation have understood what he was feeling now.

Hans's voice interrupted these embittered thoughts.

"...still don't know anything about your escape plan. Did you check routes? Should I have the car ready to—"

"Escape routes?" Wolff gave his anxious friend a wry look as he switched on the bedside lamp. "You really don't think they're going to let me get out, do you?" He raised a hand, "Never mind about that right now. What I want you to be concerned about is getting J.D. and Magda on that plane this morning. Then I want you to concentrate on getting your *own* ass out of town before 'show time.' You can't be around me when it happens; and remember the script: you'll be running for your life, from me. You gotta tell 'em I threatened to kill you. Make up a convincing reason why—any goddam reason that sounds plausible. Tell 'em I went nuts after I augered in so hard jumping in—tell 'em anything!"

Hans began to fidget.

"Carl, please—" He checked his watch, "Listen, I've got to go now or they *will* miss that flight. But I'll be back directly. We can talk then. You—"

"*Go*, Hans!" Wolff ordered curtly as he dropped to one knee and reached for the bag under the bed. "You can stop back to let me know they got on the plane okay if you want to, but then you're gonna be outta here. —Now, go!"

When with a very unhappy expression Hans had gone Wolff locked the door and left the old fashioned key in the lock. He switched on the dim overhead light and went back to the 'stash' bag which he'd placed on the bed. After placing his Beretta close to hand he began carefully going over the items he would need later that day and replacing them in his back-pack. When he had finished he shoved the backpack under the bed; then he went to the window and raised the shade. He stood for several minutes looking out at the dreary day.

Hans quietly reentered the room an hour an a half later and found Wolff stretched out on the bed with his eyes closed, holding his pistol loosely in his right hand. Wolff obviously had heard him come in. When Hans dropped a letter gingerly on his chest he opened his eyes and gave his friend a tight smile.

"It's from Magda, Carl—and yes, everything went fine at the airport," Hans told him as he went into the bathroom.

A minute or so later Wolff's exclamation almost caused Hans to soil himself. Fearing his friend was experiencing another seizure, he hastily emerged from the bathroom to find Wolff standing at the solitary window again, holding the letter at his side.

"No problem, old Hans," he said laconically without turn-ing. "It was just something I misread in this letter. I guess I overreacted." He turned. "And now, old buddy, get on your horse—or into your 'sweetheart,' however you want to put it— and beat it outta here. You're history. And let's have no tearful farewells—just go."

Hans stood shaking his head gloomily.

"Carl—"

"No, Hans. That's it. Make it!"

Wolff came back to his friend (who now was almost in tears), gave him a quick embrace, a firm handshake, and hus-tled him to the door. As he unlocked and opened the door and gently shoved Hans through it he said:

"Oh, yeah. Thanks for delivering the mail. It *was* an interesting letter."

When Wolff went up to the roof two hours later his first act was to confirm what he'd seen when he and Hans had made their earlier visual reconnaissance. He had been puzzled then to notice the two "U" bolts, one welded to the outside of the door, which was sheathed in metal, the other to the metal door post. He reasoned that before the roof was used as a restaurant this door had been kept locked against intruders. When he tried the padlock it fit perfectly. He put it back in his pocket; he would snap it on just before he went into action. In a half-crouch he began to move around the stairway enclosure to ensure that there was no one else on the roof.

Halfway through his circuit he came upon Hans sitting tranquilly in one of the abandoned deck chairs, reading a newspaper. Unruffled by Wolff's appearance he commented urbanely:

"I see by the local paper that Mr. Claxton will be accompanied by a number of American guests."

There was no bite in Wolff's "Hans, you *son of a bitch!*"

"Perhaps, but this time you'll have to shoot *me*, if you want to be rid of me."

"I really didn't need an audience for this performance, you know," Wolff said sourly as he raised himself cautiously and began checking the area around the hotel building.

"I really don't think I constitute a crowd, Carl, and perhaps I can help you in some way—hand things to you and so forth.... Barring that, I promise to stay out of the way and do whatever you order me to. In any case, I am at your service," he finished primly as Wolff merely shook his head resignedly.

"And, oh, yes—while I was downstairs I told as many people as I could," Hans went on, "without being too obvious about it, I hope, that you and I were greatly looking forward to going to the ceremony which," he checked his watch, "my Seiko says, commences just fifty minutes from now."

At a quarter till two, after nervously having smoked two

cigarettes in quick succession, Wolff, with his backpack slung loosely across his back, went on all fours to his firing position on the water tank pediment while Hans, as instructed, remained in the vicinity of the now padlocked door. As he laid the backpack gently on the roof floor and slithered up onto the pediment and into a prone position Wolff could see, along the avenue which fronted the hotel, the stream of pedestrians flowing towards the mosque square and joining the crowds of spectators who already were gathering there.

A "U"-shaped perimeter of heavily armed guards, possibly Saddam Hussein's own "palace" guard, facing outward, towards the crowds, already was in place surrounding the mosque steps in a tight cordon. Behind temporary barricades another perimeter of uniformed police completely surrounded the outer limits of the square. While most of these guards were at static posts, Wolff noted, others patrolled assigned areas. At various points along this second cordon, mainly where the streets fed into the square, pedestrians were given at least a cursory check, and frequently were subjected to closer scrutiny (in some cases Wolff saw papers being produced) before being permitted to enter the square itself.

As he unzipped the backpack and reached in for the weapon and ammunition Wolff felt a strange pang as he recalled a line from Byron's *The Destruction of Sennacherib*:

The Assyrian came down like the wolf on the fold...

At five minutes past two, amid another large armed host, the VIP party was escorted onto the scene and began to mount the mosque steps, on the top esplanade of which seating had been arranged.

Although the XMG-95F had a front hand grip (good for close work but useless now), Wolff attached the plastic shoulder stock to the rear of the receiver so that once the bipod legs were snapped down into place this would enable him to fire the weapon much as the old obsolete Browning Automatic Rifle had been employed in one of its modes: with the firer prone and his left hand palm down over the small of the stock.

There was of course no need to "zero" the weapon's sights since Wolff (as he had explained to Browning) could not use them in the conventional way in any case.

Using his "ultravision" and looking over, not through, the lethal little weapon's rear sight Wolff did a slow pan of the VIP's who now were standing in a group on the esplanade in front of the mosque entrance.

Something he saw peripherally, noticed almost subliminally, made him snap his eye back to the edge of the group standing on the steps. It had not been so much a person that had registered as familiar to him, but a dark green overcoat someone was wearing. Now, as he concentrated on the area of interest he saw he was right. Browning! —Browning who, undoubtedly motivated by enlightened self-interest, stood somewhat conspicuously at least a dozen steps removed from the main body of VIPs. Obviously, Wolff told himself, he wanted to see the deed done, at first hand, but from a vantage point well away from the 95F's beaten zone. Also, since the Iraqis knew damned well who (or at least what) he was, and since they would probably know he was "in-country" anyway, it would give him a perfect alibi in the inevitable, ensuing investigation.

Not far from Browning stood a woman, a Western woman, Wolff judged by her stature and attire. Could it be...? Yes, it was Margaret Feldon. As he sighted alternately on the two figures his finger lingered longingly, caressingly, on the trigger....

Why did he think he heard music now? Was it Bach? He *did* hear it! It was Bach's "Sheep May Safely Graze," and getting louder all the time....

Bringing himself back to reality with a jolt (which served to stop the ghostly music) he swept his sight alignment back to the main group and focused briefly and sequentially on first, Saddam Hussein, then on Claxton, who stood next to Hussein, then he went back to Browning, lingered a moment, and this time noticed Harry Ward, Browning's bag man, with a cigarette in his mouth, standing a few steps away from Browning. Finally he went back to Saddam Hussein, and held on him in sharp focus. He must do it now! he told himself grimly; now, before Saddam and the main party began moving towards their seats.

But with sudden decision and almost choking on his own bile Wolff swung back to Browning for the third time, tapped up the thirty-round[1] magazine once more for good measure, held the picture in tight focus while he let out half his breath, held it, and fired a short burst. In the overcast gloom he clearly saw the tracer-flechettes strike the flagstones a few yards in front of Browning, then, firing a longer burst this time (chances were better than even that Browning had already taken a few ricochets), he "walked" the deadly little steel darts up Browning's legs and into his barrel torso.

Immediately, Wolff resighted on Ward, then with an oath of disgust he released the slack he'd taken up on the trigger, and quickly brought Saddam Hussein back into view. The security personnel were beginning to move already, but the absolute pandemonium which usually accompanies these events had not yet begun. Saddam was still a viable target. This time, with a better fix on the range, his first burst hit the dictator full in the right shoulder and upper arm.

When the pounding of the last burst had subsided Wolff heard someone approaching from his left. Feeling slightly dazed, he turned and saw Hans, moving as if in slow motion, coming towards him. Now he began to experience an odd feeling of unreality, accompanied by a strange but not unpleasant smell. Flowers! A beautiful aroma of flowers, getting stronger and sweeter all the time. The strong scent began to envelop him. Stronger, and very sweet, cloying. Too strong now. Too sweet. He felt he was suffocating....

Two days after the mosque shooting, at a US base somewhere

---

[1] Which provided, with three in each cartridge, a total of ninety flechettes.

in Saudi Arabia, Harry Ward, who had replaced Browning (pro tempore, but hoping for permanent confirmation), was asked by one of his agents:

" So, what are we gonna do? Do we get him out?"

"I dunno. After what the s.o.b. did to Lew Browning—"

"Yeah, I saw the body in the morgue.... Jesus, I *guarantee* you those goddam flechettes will tear up your fatigues! —But, you know, it *could* have been a mistake, Harry."

"Not with that magic eyeball of his it couldn't! Lew was at least twenty feet from the main group. And he didn't come *near* Claxton; he hit Hussein on the side *away* from Claxton. Goddammit, I gotta admit, it was a great shoot, from *his* point of view anyway, the bastard! Still, I'd love to know for sure...."

He took off his jacket, threw it on a chair, and turned to face the other.

"Fuck it! what's done is done. Let's nail the bastard! Our Baghdad guys got the magic box off Lew, didn't they? He shook his head, and without waiting for an answer added, "Poor Lew. He wouldn't admit it, not even to me, but I *know* he was gonna trigger that thing the moment Claxton got it. If 'Our Boy' was anywhere within 1500 yards of him..."

The other man maintained a respectful silence for a few moments, then said:

"Yeah." And after another pause added a little nervously: "Yeah, one of 'em got the box while the big cluster-fuck was goin' on," he snorted derisively, "Christ! that Iraqi police chief was runnin' aroun' with his thumb in his ass soundin' just like that French cop in Casablanca: 'Our beloved President has been shot! and Mr. Claxton's aide has been killed! Round up the usual suspects!'" He became serious again. "Yeah, but the point is, Harry, we don't know where the hell our boy is. He just disappeared. —Of course, he's got that CW radio, and we got that old, beat-up Fulton snatch system ready to go. Maybe he'll call in—"

"Fat chance of him asking *us* for help, after what the prick did—"

He was interrupted as another man burst into the room with:
"You can stop trying to make up your mind, Boss, at least
for now. He's gone!"

"*What?*"

"Our guys in Baghdad checked the airlines. He went out
under his real passport—Charles Wychway. And now our
Limey friends just told me he's in a hospital in London; and
Scotland Yard Special Branch is all over the place. *Our* guys,
Brits included, can't get anywhere near the son of a bitch!"

"All we gotta do is get near enough to use the 'black box'."

At this the newcomer gave Ward a grim, abashed look.

"I hate to give you more bad news, Harry, but we ain't *got*
the 'black box' anymore."

"Say *what?*"

"It's disappeared. But, hold on a minute, Boss! Even if we
had it *and* got close enough we couldn't trigger it. We ain't got
the code! it was a one-time deal and only Browning knew it.
You had to crank in the right letter-number combination to
activate it. Even if we had the goddam thing it would take even
the biggest computer back at Langley to—"

"Je-*sus Christ!* talk about the gang that couldn't shoot
straight!" Ward walked to the window with his hands clasping
his bald head.

When Wolff came to his senses he was in bed, again with
only vague recollections. He remembered having been trun-
dled around in a wheelchair somewhere or other....

Now he saw a man's face peering down at him. The man
wore a white jacket. Behind this man there were other people:
an older man, a young woman, and a black man.

"What happened?" he asked in a hoarse whisper.

"You're all right. You're in a London hospital, and you're
going to be fine," the man in white said reassuringly.

"Where am I? Am I all right?" The tone of this last question was almost pitiable. "What day is this?" he ended.

"You're in a hospital in London, and you're going to be

just fine. Today is Monday, the 10th of December. Can you tell me your name?"

"Yes," came the unhesitating reply, I'm Charles Wychway."

Someone in the background emitted a sigh of relief; someone else was sobbing quietly.

"Please close your left eye, Mr. Wychway, and look at that picture across the room."

Wychway did as he was told. "Yeah, well? I'm looking."

"Does the picture look normal?"

"Normal? Yeah, I guess so. It's a scene of some kind, but I can't quite make out what—it's too far away. Is it a landscape? What am I supposed to be seeing, anyway?"

The doctor smiled as behind him more pent up breaths were released. "You're seeing just what you should be seeing. As to the picture, it's a not very good reproduction of one of Constable's finest landscapes."

An urbane voice behind the doctor said quietly:

"Ask him if the name, Carl Wolff, means anything to him."

"You heard? Do you know a Carl Wolff?"

Wychway narrowed his eyes in thought.

"It's there, I think. It's familiar somehow, but I don't get any *face*...." Wychway watched as the man in white, obviously a doctor, motioned to the group behind him, who now approached the bed.

"Do you recognize these people?"

"Mr.—no, er, ah—*Major*, Major Some Goddam Thing—Mary? Margot? No. Magda! What the hell—" He stared intently at the pleasant-faced black man, "You're, you're—*Damn* it! I *know* you, but I just can't place—"

"Good," said the doctor with obvious relief. "It will come back. Yes, it will come back, but don't try too hard just now. You'll be with us for some time, perhaps several weeks, or longer. We want to keep you under close observation until we're sure you're completely well again; but not to worry, I'm certain you're going to be fine, just fine." The doctor turned to a grinning J.D., who took his hand and shook it warmly.

Over the course of the next several days Wychway gradually became apprised of all that had happened since the Al-Basrah
shoot. And during that time he remembered "Bigeye," and was
able to make the connection between himself and "Carl Wolff"
and between himself and Hans; and then to piece together, however imperfectly, all the major events in his double life from the
time J.D. had taken him to Heathrow months earlier.

He knew that he had been operated on (he'd awakened with
his head swathed in bandages), and had been assured by the
doctor that the entire surgical procedure would be explained to
him as soon as his mind became "sufficiently cleared to comprehend" all that he would be told. There was "some history
involved" the doctor had added somewhat cryptically.

Meanwhile, in response to his: "How in hell did you get
me out of there?" Hans and J.D. provided the narrative of
recent events.

He learned that J.D. actually never left on the plane with
Magda, but had insisted Hans take him back to the center of
events ("I couldn't resist being in at the finish of this game of
foxes and hounds," J.D. put in wryly).

They told him how after he'd suffered his second seizure
Hans had somehow disassembled and stuffed the weapon in the
backpack, picked up the expended cartridge cases, found the
padlock key(s), and somehow had gotten Wolff, along with the
backpack, down to their room. He never thought he could do it.
"I must have been like the frail little man who got his piano out
of his burning house: pure adrenalin, I suppose, but I managed."
Wychway shook his head in wonderment, not least because he
still was having difficulty with bits and pieces of his relationship with this man who in all probability had saved his life.

J.D explained how, after returning from the airport with
Hans, he'd waited downstairs in a coffee shop across from the
hotel, seated near the front window, until he'd seen Hans's signal (his bright red muffler thrown over the roof parapet, which
meant, "Come!"), and then had gone up to find Hans waiting
for him on the top landing. He told how they had gotten Wych-

way downstairs to find that, luckily, the hotel still was virtually deserted (there now being an even greater attraction at the mosque square). Having earlier abstracted the gate key from where he'd seen the hotel manager replace it on its hook behind the desk, Hans had already parked the car in the courtyard behind the hotel. The exit door presented no problem since, like all fire exits, it locked only from outside. Having gotten their friend (who now was snoring loudly in a deep sleep) into the car, Hans went quickly back upstairs and emptied the room. Now they needed a temporary, safe refuge with a telephone.

They'd driven to the Mahmoud's house, hoping that Ekbal, his wife, and the children hadn't returned from the mosque ceremony yet. At the Mahmoud house they were relieved to discover that the family was not expected to return for some time as they had planned to have dinner at a favorite Basrah restaurant (what effect the shooting would have on these plans was problematical). Hans explained to the astonished servants that they had been driving in the vicinity when their friend Herr Wolff (who was, as the servants knew, a friend of the Mahmouds) had suffered "one of his attacks," and asked if they could "bring him into the house for a few moments." In the absence of their employers the servants understandably were in a quandary as to what they should do until J.D. reassured them, using more gestures than speech, that they would remain only long enough for "Herr Wolff" to recover somewhat. The attack was not life-threatening or even serious, he managed to explain.

Meanwhile Hans was on the telephone to his Basrah office, making flight arrangements for "Major J.D.F. Somerville and his invalid friend, Mr. Charles Wychway." Yes, a wheelchair would be required, but only for boarding; and, no, a special attendant was not necessary—the Major was accustomed to taking care of his friend during their travels. And, yes, there *was* a certain urgency. Mr. Wychway's condition had worsened, though not to the extent that he couldn't travel; but it was imperative that he be gotten to his doctor in London without further delay.

Half an hour later when Wychway, though still groggy could walk unaided, they had left the Mahmoud house. A little over an hour after that Major J.D.F. Somerville and "his invalid friend," after a hurried but close scrutiny in an airport teeming with police, soldiers, and other security personnel, boarded a British Airways flight to London. Before entering the terminal Hans had taken "Carl Wolff's" passport out of his companion's pocket and slipped it into his own. After a moment's hesitation, and after being sure he wasn't observed, he gingerly extracted the Beretta and its extra magazine from Wolff's boot holster and put them in his pocket also. As an afterthought he also took the lensatic compass, which later he would dispose of in the desert.

The XMG-95F, its magazines and ammunition, and J.D.'s Webley (which sorrowfully he now wished he'd left in his Bayswater flat), along with Wolff's radio and other "mission paraphenalia," all stuffed in the backpack, were jettisoned somewhere along a lonely stretch of road between Basrah and its airport. Fortunately, there was more than enough weight to carry everything to the bottom of the Shatt al-Arab. Someday perhaps an Iraqi fisherman will be puzzled as he examines some grim and unusual jetsam he has dredged up.

As the plane leveled off in a northwesterly direction an urbane-looking Major Somerville, patting the dazed-looking man huddled on the seat next to him reassuringly on the arm, was overheard ordering a flight attendant to bring him "a large, in fact, a *very* large whisky, straight away."

Hans's adventures subsequent to leaving the Basrah airport completed the tale. On his way back to Baghdad to "face the music" from his CIA handlers, he was stopped at a checkpoint outside Al-Basrah by the Iraqi police. Now he was unsure of his wisdom in appropriating "Wolff's" Beretta. Though he'd coveted this excellent weapon since the moment he'd seen it now he wondered apprehensively if he would ever have the courage to use it, even if he were faced with a life-threatening situation.

He was recalling that ironic line spoken by Claude Rains in Casablanca: "We can't decide if he committed suicide or died trying to escape," thinking that that no doubt would be *his* fate when, amazingly, he'd been released! In a joyous daze he was told by one of the officers that they were checking the papers of all "foreigners" leaving Basrah. He almost fainted, he told Wychway, when as he was driving away from the checkpoint he remembered that he still had the Sovinformsputnik aerial photos on him! He was so anxious about this and so thankful for his deliverance (Allah be praised!) that he tore them out of his overcoat lining and burned them in the desert before he reached Baghdad. At the same time he buried "Wolff's" compass.

He had his story ready for the people in Baghdad. He told them he'd been held hostage under threat of death by "that bastard Wolff!" On three occasions, he told them, he was sure that Wolff, who had seemed to be going insane, was going to kill him. What about that Englishman, and the girl? they'd asked him. Wolff wouldn't let me go near them most of the time, after we got to Basrah, Hans had told them. The girl was his mistress, he was sure of that. As for the Brit, he didn't know anything about him except that he thought he may have been an old friend of "Wolff's" father. As far as Hans could tell, although he couldn't be absolutely certain, neither the Englishman nor the girl had known anything about Operation Bigeye.

When asked how he had escaped from Wolff Hans thought it prudent to tell a partial truth: he told them that on the day of the assassination attempt Wolff had had "some kind seizure," there, in the hotel room, and Hans had wasted no time in getting the room key out of his pocket and leaving "while the leaving was good." Still wearing his voluminous overcoat Hans stood toying with a soiled handkerchief that lay among Browning's effects on a plain deal table while he clung adamantly to his claim that he'd "had no idea, none whatsoever, whom Wolff had decided to target." With a brusque command to "stop fuckin' around that with stuff!" and with the stern injunction that he wasn't to leave Baghdad, he was permitted to go.

His surly interrogators hadn't believed him, Hans was sure of that, and he was sure that the airport and even the train and bus stations would be watched. But it didn't matter, really, he told Wychway (as J.D. looked on as if he would burst with suppressed mirth), because he'd simply booked himself on the next available flight to London, using a passport—whose photo had been replaced with one his own and in which one or two other items had been changed—that identified him as an Austrian oilfield worker with the unlikely name of Carl Wolff.

Chapter Twenty-five

Vindication

"Were we followed, do you think? Are we being watched now?" Wychway, who now was sitting up comfortably in bed and practicing his normal vision by winking at the picture on the wall opposite him, asked J.D. late the following day.

"No, to both," came the reply. "If we'd been followed I doubt we would have arrived. The hospital *was* being watched for a time, after we arrived, and very closely too; apparently your Agency's British colleagues had a routine watch on for Carl Wolff *or* Charles Wychway at all entry ports. But I had a word with a friend at the Home Office and *now* we're being watched, looked after would be the better way of saying it, by *our* people, the 'Good Guys,' as you Yanks would say—the Royal Protection Squad of Scotland Yard, no less," J.D. stretched contentedly.

"That's comforting; but I can't stay here forever, J.D., and no matter how many powerful friends you've got I don't think the Protection Squad is going to assign a detail to me *in perpetuam*. I'm on 'their' list, J.D. When I walk out of here I don't think my life'll be worth an hour's purchase, as you Brits would say."

"I've been talking to Hans, old boy, and I think we can fight fire with a little more fire of our own. This Claxton thing is a bomb in our arsenal and we've got the fuze. Hell's bells, old boy, if it comes to that I'll get you a British passport, then let the bastards think twice about trifling with one of Her Majesty's subjects!" He forstalled his friend's objection with a large freckled hand, "Just let old Hans and me see what we can do. Meanwhile, relax and get well."

J.D. rose, stretched lazily again, and made room for his friend, Albert Neville, R.C.S., the hospital's senior resident surgeon, as he said:

"And now your doctor's here to talk to you about those matters he wasn't sure you could comprehend earlier," he paused a moment, then added with a wan smile, "and which he wanted to be sure you could bear hearing about."

Dr. Neville told Wychway how his hard landing in the desert had "disarranged" Sibelius's delicate work, causing periodic malfunctioning of the desired visual effect and leading, undoubtedly, to the series of seizures he had experienced.

After a tactful silence while his patient absorbed this he went on to tell him about the explosive capsule he'd discovered, which also was part of that work.

"That German scientist who operated on you after your Autobahn smash last April operated brilliantly, I must admit, brilliantly but devilishly. If he wasn't the devil himself he certainly was his agent. I corrected the work which gave you your extraordinary visual ability, and I—" Neville paused and glanced inquiringly at J.D., who immediately nodded, Go ahead, "—and I removed a device which was, simply put, a miniature bomb that according to our forensic expert contained as much equivalent explosive, nitrostarch, I think he said it was, as a high-powered rifle cartridge. The entire procedure took me and my two assistants six hours."

"*Bomb?*" Wychway tried to sit up straighter as Neville gently restrained him. "Bomb?"

With this J.D. stepped forward and produced a small gray plastic box. "Look at this, Charley. Hans gave it me. It seems that after the shoot (please pay no attention to these particulars, Bertie; the less you know the better you'll be), while the Iraqi security chief was running around the mosque steps screaming, the American 'boys from Baghdad' found it in Browning's coat pocket. Later, when they were questioning Hans back in Baghdad, there it was, on a desk, along with the rest of the late, if not lamented, Browning's effects. Hans saw it, had no idea what it was at the time, but—thank God!—he thought If it was found on Browning it might be important, so he pinched it."

Wychway emitted a shuddering sigh: Jesus Christ! will it ever end?—Let's see that goddam thing."

J.D. held out the device for his friend's examination.

"It's a remote detonator—Japanese product—good up to about a mile."

"Whatever you do, don't push that little button!"

"No fears. If I did, you'd be all right, but there'd likely be a certain amount of consternation down at that forensic fellow's office. That's where the little infernal machine resides right now, if Scotland Yard's Special Branch haven't picked it up already."

J.D. turned the device over and grunted, "But, hold on. Mmm, yes. That's all right, anyhow. See that brass set-screw? That's the arming device. You've got to give it a quarter-turn anti-clockwise before it can signal. Wait a minute. What's this? Aha! See these little dials with alphabetical and digital increments? The arming device is coded, so even if were activated the circuit couldn't be actuated. In plainer words, the explosion could never be accidentally triggered." J.D. became thoughtful, then said:

"I won't argue the ethics of what you did to Browning, Charley; all I'll say is that if you hadn't done it you almost certainly wouldn't be here. What would have been left of you would still be on that rooftop, or in the Basrah morgue, assuming they have one. You wouldn't have taken twenty steps before Browning blew your head off. Lucky you weren't jarred any worse when you parachuted in that night (hold your ears again, Bertie). Nitrostarch is more stable than the liquid stuff, but not much."

Wychway felt a chill as he thought about his hard parachute landing in the desert, and now he knew why he'd been told any number of times to be careful about blows to his head, and what Igor was trying to make up his mind about that night at the Hohenfels club, the night before he, Igor, and Sibelius were murdered in that Lufthansa flight with all those innocent people.

"If I hadn't operated either the bomb would have killed you or at the least you would just have gone on having seizures, one after the other, at increasingly shorter intervals, until you either went mad or died, or both," Bertie Neville put in quietly.

"*Quos Deus vult perdere prius dementat*," Wychway muttered listlessly, then added, "Frankenstein.... No, Sibelius, Sibelius..."

As Doctor Neville leaned inquiringly towards his patient J.D. intoned:

"'Whom God wishes to destroy, he first makes mad'; and he now remembers the devilish Doctor's name, Bertie."

Ah, yes, I see. Very good! Well, to go on. You had a seizure immediately after the, ah, incident in which you were involved, wherever that may have been," he gave Somerville a furtive glance, "and I understand that you now are *au fait* about the events which occurred leading to your arrival here?"

Wychway nodded dismally as he gazed vacantly straight ahead at the opposite wall.

"I sent Browning to his just reward.... He didn't have a chance, the bastard. Some of those darts were keyholing when they went into him...." Wychway mumbled.

With this, Dr. Neville, tapping his watch and muttering a cautionary word to J.D. about not staying too long, discreetly excused himself and left. He was replaced almost immediately by a beaming Hans, as Wychway rattled on as if entranced.

"I got to know him pretty well during those weeks from hell at Hohenfels" Wychway went on muttering, "he felt perfectly safe up there with all those VIPs at the mosque. And he was so *sure* I'd never have the balls to nail him...."

When J.D. held up Browning's "black box" to Hans and nodded significantly at the bandage-swathed figure in the bed the black man moved closer and took both Wychway's hands in his. "Thank God!" was all Hans could manage to say. His eyes were wet as he released his Wychway's hands and stepped back.

Now Wychway looked hard at his two friends as he said: "You know, at that moment, just before I fired, he looked like something prehistoric that just appeared at the mouth of a cave, like some sort of troglodyte."

To which Hans, who now had regained his composure, replied in his characteristic and reasonable way:

"Like the baby Jesus, who also came out of a cave. Please, I'm certainly not comparing Browning to Jesus Christ! But, you know, you Westerners have an idealized conception of that stable at Bethlehem. It really *was* a cave—a stable, yes, but a stable in a *cave*. Those shepherds routinely drove their animals into hillside caves like that, for shelter, in winter. They still do it today and—"

"I touched up Saddam pretty good too, I think," Wychway went on, ignoring this well-intended prattle. "Unless I'm mistaken he's going to look a little Kaiser Wilhelm II, maybe worse, after he recovers; but maybe a guy like him would like that, having escaped death and with a gimpy arm to prove it; and maybe it'll make him more reasonable, more amenable to meeting people half way—" He stopped abruptly, and looked anxiously and alternately at the two men.

"He *did* make it, didn't he?"

"Oh, yes," Hans put in hurriedly, and gazing upward as if petitioning the white ceiling quoted St. Matthew. "'Sufficient unto the day is the evil thereof.' He'll be all right—but you're right about the 'gimpy' arm: from what my friends in Baghdad have told me there was some irreparable bone damage. Those cursed flechettes must be terribly effective."

"Yeah, it was a *day* all right," Wychway reflected grimly. Jolly old St. Nicholas's Day," he mused.

There was silence for a few moments as Wychway lay there thinking before he asked:

"So what happened to that flamer, Feldon?"

"After the brouhaha the Yanks escorted her to the British Mission in Baghdad. I assume she's back here, in Blighty somewhere," J.D. told him.

"I came within an ace of popping her, too," his friend quietly reflected half to himself.

"Wouldn't have been worth it, old boy. From what Magda tells me La Feldon has become persona non grata at her college; hoist on her own petard, as they say. The school authorities have had enough of her political 'atheism,' if I can coin a phrase; that and the fact of her, well, her personal lifestyle—if you get my meaning—have done her in, and good riddance! say I."

"Yeah, her 'personal lifestyle.' Christ!" Wychway said bitterly. Another pause. "Where *is* Magda, anyway?"

"She's staying at a private hotel here in London. I would hope she's resting. She wouldn't leave the hospital until Bertie told her you were going to be all right. I don't think she got more than two hours sleep over three days." He glanced at his watch, "which reminds me: Bertie told me we had to be out of here in fifteen minutes," he glanced at Hans, "we've overstayed that already, so get some rest, Charley, and we'll see you tomorrow."

Wychway nodded; then as if remembering something said:

"Hold on a minute. Hans, you remember that letter you brought me the night before the main event, when we were in that fleabag hotel in Basrah?"

"If you mean the letter from Magda, which I gave you in the *morning* on the *day* of the 'main event,' yes, of course I remember it."

"Gimme a break, old Hans, I'm still not a hundred percent, okay? Anyway, look in that cupboard next to the bed—my stuff's in there, I think. Scrounge around and see if that letter's there." Suddenly he seemed to think of something else. "Wait a minute! Is my leather jacket in there—you know the Italian one I wore damn near to death (in both senses) in Iraq? Good. Just let me have it a moment." He felt along the silk lining for a moment until he found the little packet of "Igor" Hoffmann's deadly crystals[1] he'd sewn in there weeks ago, then with an expression of relief handed the jacket back to Hans, who looked understandably mystified

"Nothing really important, Hans, just an old family heirloom I always carry around for luck," Wychway grinned.

The letter was there among his few possessions, and as they left he removed it from the envelope.

My Dear Charles (Magda had written),
I have hope, but not much, that when you read this you will stop this madness and get away from here. I hope what I have to tell you will do this, but I know you so much better now that I do not expect it.
I am carrying your child—yes, your *child. I did not tell you earlier, although I had known it for a month, because you already had so much on your mind, but I could not go away without letting you know. And I preferred to tell you this way, in a letter, so that you could not make some painful remark about my former relationship with Margaret Feldon.*
Yes, I knew you had guessed, correctly, when we were together that last night, about that aberrant period in my young and confused life. But aside from that brief madness I have had no other lovers but you, and I know now that I have never loved anyone except you. Oh, yes! there was your Father. Please, please understand that. You are so like him. Can you understand what I, as just a young girl newly arrived from Hungary, with no parents, no relations or real friends, felt for him? For that brief, brief moment he was all those

[1] See chapters 14-15.

things to me. But he was the only one. If you can
understand this then perhaps some day you can even
try to understand what happened with Margaret. I can
not speak of that more now—it is too painful.
*   Whatever happens I will have our child, and if*
God wills that you survive this terrible time I will fall
on my knees to you and beg your understanding.
*   Even if I never see you again I pray that you*
may be safe.
*   Magda*

He was asleep, with the letter still held loosely in his
hand, when she came to him that evening. Ten minutes later
she was lying with her wet face on his chest, holding him tenderly as he alternately stroked her hair and tried to wipe the
tears from her face.

"I will never, never part from you again," she sobbed.

After a time he said very gently and quietly:

"I know, I know; but there's something else I've gotta do,
Magda. And I'm going to have to go away again, for just a little while, to do it."

Meanwhile worldwide speculation ran wild about who had
attempted the assassination. The spectrum of likely candidates
went from the CIA (although this soon was generally discounted
since Browning, a relatively high Agency official, had been one
of the victims), to the Mossad, to the Iranians, to an attempted
coup by Iraqi revolutionaries (vociferously supported by Washington and vehemently denied by Baghdad). Understandably,
due to Wychway's escape and present relative safety, the "rogue
CIA agent" scenario was never used. And with Saddam Hussein,
though badly wounded, still very much alive the news media
eventually, and predictably, turned to other matters.

Not surprisingly, as J.D. discovered through his friends in
British officialdom (and quickly passed on to Wychway),

Browning's demise was not greatly lamented, at least not in bureaucratic circles and especially not within the intelligence community. Apparently, according to J.D.'s friends in Special Branch, Browning, using his position of no insignificant power in the middle levels of the CIA hierarchy had "kept book" (much in the manner of the late J. Edgar Hoover, though to a much lesser degree of scope and exaltation of position) on any number of high-ranking people. This allegation had been revealed recently in a letter sent by the unfortunate Gloria Mundi, née Nahla Maturbof, to a friend in Washington and inscribed "To be opened in the event of my death." Upon hearing of Gloria's death her friend had opened the letter, which included a list of names (by no means complete, according to the late Gloria). The late Gloria's friend at first had been inclined to destroy the letter, but after several weeks' reflection had decided to submit it, anonymously, to the CIA.

Added to this was an even more dramatic development which Hans, who somehow had remained in touch with both his Iraqi friends and his former CIA colleagues, took great pleasure in revealing.

After a young Arab goatherd had found Link's body (actually it was his dog that found it) in its shallow and rocky desert grave an autopsy had confirmed his identity and even produced the fatal bullet still lodged in his skull. During the subsequent investigation both pilots had testified that Link had left the airplane while it still was in flight, without the B12 emergency parachute he'd been issued. Steve, the young copilot who had picked up the round Browning had ejected in clearing Link's pistol, which had been found in the drop aircraft, testified to Browning's having taken possession of the weapon, there at Incirlik. The round he'd picked up off the tarmac at Incirlik was submitted as evidence; as was the "aircraft" pistol discovered in Browning's temporary quarters at Hohenfels. Neither the "Incilik" bullet nor the "aircraft" pistol matched the fatal bullet. A *second* pistol, however, which later was found among those of Browning's personal effects collected by the Baghdad CIA agents after his death, provided a perfect match. The mystery of how "Carl Wolff's" Beretta, given to him by Browning (a fact known to no one but the two of them), ended up among Browning's effects in Baghdad now was explained by a grinning Hans.

Knowing he would attempt to fly out of Iraq at the first opportunity, and feeling more burdened than secure in possessing the Beretta, he had left it and its extra magazine, after wiping them clean of fingerprints, in place of the "black box," and covered them with a none-too-clean handkerchief he'd found lying there on that table in Baghdad.

But the overall mystery never was resolved. The powder burns still just traceable on the corpse's face even admitted the possibility of suicide. And if the man *had* been murdered, *where* had the murder taken place? In the airplane? Judging from the condition of the body, that apparently was the case; but despite indications that the man had been dead before he hit the ground the remains were so decomposed the pathologists had to admit that the fatal wound might possibly have been inflicted *after* Link landed.

Although motive was in Link's case an open question, to put it generously, and although the means was proven beyond question, opportunity was impossible to pin down, especially since Browning was unavailable to testify. The time of death was fixed approximately: 30th November, possibly 1st December. Where was Browning during that time? No one seemed to know. (Actually he'd spent most of that time in bed with his favorite Cairene whore.) And (as asked in closed top secret testimony) what about Wychway-Wolff? After all, he and Link had gone off together on Operation Bigeye on the night of 29-30 November. But if Wychway-Wolff killed Link, *where or how did he get the weapon?* And Wychway-Wolff was unavailable during the conduct of this investigation, confined to a London hospital where, according to official CIA statements, he was "recovering from a very dangerous, highly classified mission in the cause of world peace." The Link case would never be solved, but even so a posthumous cloud would hang over the late Lew Browning, as long as anyone cared to remember him.

Upon his imminent release from the hospital Wychway received official assurances from the Agency that he no longer was being sought for any reason other than for those of routine debriefing following his courageous (but still classified) effort on behalf of the United States and the Free World (whatever that meant anymore) in general. He could even have his old job back, he was told. When at his insistence these assurances had been made public in both the American and European press he agreed to go to Washington "to meet with interested US Government officials."

It was during the latter stages of his slow convalescence in hospital that Wychway wrote a lengthy "memorandum for the record" which filled forty foolscap pages of a yellow, legal-sized pad. He used the beautiful Austrian fountain pen Magda had given him on the occasion of the small Christmas party J.D. had organized at his bedside. When typed by Magda on a word processor at the British Museum the MFR comprised thirty pages of double-spaced typescript.

Now, on a chilly but sunny and unseasonably pleasant morning in late January, Wychway sat comfortably on the hospital veranda smoking and carefully "earmarking" the dozen xeroxed copies of his memorandum.

J.D., who had just finished reading a copy, tossed it onto his friend's lap.

"Says it all, this *opus magnus* of yours. But as to the distribution: a bit much, isn't it? A little on the *extravagant* side, *n' est ce pa?*"

"Nope," replied Wychway without looking up.

"But I mean to say: Hans, Magda, myself—yes, we all were personally involved. And of course your Agency and our Circus; but the Germans, and Hans's friends in Iraq? Both the New York Times *and* the Washington Post?"

"Don't forget Claxton, David Frost, and *60 Minutes*," Wychway muttered laconically, still scribbling busily.

"Good Lord, Charles!"

Wychway gathered the stapled copies together and laid them aside, then he squinted up at J.D. who stood with the sun behind him.

"Remember the aftermath of the Kennedy assassination? You know, J.D., to most people it sounds like just another wild conspiracy theory; but there are a helluva lot of other people out there—not nut cases, either—who're convinced that LBJ approved, maybe not directed, maybe not even approved, but at least looked the other way when Jack Kennedy was hit. Well if there *was* a conspiracy, and consequently what would have amounted to a coup d' état, and someone in the middle of it back in '63 had done *this*," he patted the pile of documents, "and that person made certain it went to enough of the right people so that it couldn't get *buried*, then the people of America would have known how to judge and how to react. And there wouldn't be all this suspicion, hair pulling, back biting, and general grabass that's been going on for thirty-five years. *Capisce?*"

"Yes, I understand," J.D. grinned good-naturedly. "By the way, has anyone told you you're beginning to sound, and act, too, for the matter of that, just like your old sire?"

"Yeah," Wychway nodded, obviously not displeased with this remark, "somebody wrote something like that to me in a letter a few weeks ago—or was it a couple of years ago?"

Somerville permitted himself a small Chesire smile before he came back to the business at hand. He had already cheerfully agreed to give Magda away at her forthcoming marriage to Wychway upon his return from Washington (Hans had been equally delighted to act as Best Man),

"So, I'm to store all copies, less the one you'll hand-carry to Langley, in my vault box at the Little Old Lady of Threadneedle Street, correct? And barring anything, er, unfortunate, happening to you, or upon receiving other instructions from you, and only you, they will remain there indefinitely, correct?"

"Right, and don't forget the sealed letter you're to leave with your lawyer, or solicitor, or whatever the hell he is, in case something unfortunate happens to *you*, okay?"

"I haven't forgotten," J.D. assured him as he reached for his attaché case and nodded to the Special Branch man from New Scotland Yard who had accompanied him and who had, during this conversation, remained discreetly out of earshot.

A month later, feeling extremely fit after a month's additional convalescence at J.D.'s place in Bayswater, Wychway stood with his host, Magda, and Hans at the departure gate at Gatwick International Airport waiting for his flight to be called. He had refused, for perhaps understandable reasons, the CIA offer of a US Air Force flight from the Mildenhall R.A.F. Base direct to Andrews Air Force Base, just outside Washington.

"Do you have enough of the ready?" J.D. asked.

"I'm loaded," he laughed. "Their computer must've kept spitting out my monthly paychecks and mailing them to Stuttgart. My houseman, the gay one Browning hated, you know? mailed them to me at the hospital."

"And of course, the memo."

"No sense in even getting on the plane without that. And I xeroxed an extra copy, for myself."

"And don't worry about Magda. She'll stay with me in Bayswater while you're gone."

"Okay, 'Uncle Jim'," he grinned, "but don't forget: I'll be back!"

As he smiled down at Magda he said: "You know, the only time I'm going to miss the 'Bigeye' is when I'm playing darts—but I'm going to love losing again. —Take care of yourself, sweetness," he patted her stomach gently, "both of you."

When he heard his departure call he shook hands with the two men, kissed Magda once again, slung his small carry-on bag onto the conveyer belt, and walked through the security gate. As he went he smiled as he overheard J.D. asking Hans, "Who in the bloody hell is 'Uncle Jim'?"

Wychway waited for his bag at Dulles International among an unusually large number of soldiers, most of them wearing field boots and wrinkled, dusty, soiled fatigue uniforms. Doubtless off a military charter flight out of Bosnia (where "peace still raged" after almost three years of NATO engagement). Now he noticed a trio nearby: obviously a mother and her two small children who were excitedly awaiting "Daddy's" arrival. All three wore "T" shirts and stood in a line so that their sequentially red, white, and blue legible shirts spelled out:

(child)	(mother)	(child)
WELCOME	**HOME**	**DAD!**
WE	**LOVE**	**YOU!**

He recalled the American sailors he had seen on TV, on the deck of some carrier back in '86, launching planes against Libya and wearing "T" shirts which proclaimed they were TERROR BUSTERS. Yes, legible clothing had become a way of life in this country—like a Big Mac, fries, and a shake—indelibly impressed upon the cultural fabric of American society.

Wychway felt a tug at his sleeve, and turned to see a well-dressed, neatly-barbered young man discreetly holding an Agency ID card case at waist level for his inspection.

Wychway politely refused an offer to lunch with the Director in the Executive Dining Room at the Langley headquarters. (As he explained that they'd fed him too well on his British Airways flight—first class at CIA expense—he kept thinking of the Borgia family and their allegedly notorious culinary habits.) Then just as politely but with a subtle but perceptible edge in his voice he suggested that prior to the "debriefing" which had been scheduled for two o'clock that afternoon the Director might wish to read his memorandum concerning the events which had brought him here.

At the appointed hour, after having been kept under "benign surveillance" while the Director lunched with his key debriefing officers, Wychway was escorted to a conference room over whose door an electronic sign announced through yellow glass: TOP SECRET. Inside, the debriefing team already was assembled and seated; to include, in addition to the Director himself, his Deputy Directors for Intelligence and Operations and several lesser Agency staffers, a staff officer from the National Security Council, and a special advisor to the President, whose name Wychway couldn't remember but whom he'd seen on a number of television "talk shows" at one time or another. Microphones for the key personnel were distributed around a highly polished oblong-elliptical conference table and a tape recorder, attended by its somber-faced operator, sat prominently on a side table (Wychway wondered how many more not-so-prominent recorders would come into play as events unfolded!). At a gesture from the Director Wychway seated himself.

He waited patiently while the Director, centered and directly opposite him at the long table and in charge of the proceedings, introduced the key "players." In front of the Director lay the well-thumbed copy of the MFR. With a curt nod at Wychway the Director turned the proceedings over to his DDO. Before that individual could speak, however, Wychway held up a hand palm outward as he rose from his seat and slowly panned his gaze around the long table, briefly catching the eye of everyone seated there. In his other hand he held up his copy of the memorandum.

"Unless the Director thinks it appropriate that I do so," he said evenly, "I will not read this memorandum, as I had originally intended to do." At this point the Director quickly turned in his seat and made a violent throat-cutting gesture to the recorder operator as Wychway flipped through the manuscript pages, and said:

"I've spared you all the need of conducting a formal debriefing. We all know how tedious and tiresome the process can be. Well, *here*'s my debriefing all finished and ready for distribution." The Director winced visibly at this last word. "Now as to that, whether any of you besides the Director have read any of this I do not know. Whether any of you *ever* read it is not for me to decide," he looked straight into the Director's eyes, "it's totally out of *my* hands."

Absolute silence fell over the room, and without benefit of his microphone Wychway audibly and clearly went on to describe the procedural arrangement he had made for the MFR's contingent distribution before leaving England. When he emphasized that "that distribution will scrupulously and unswervingly be put into effect in the event of any more bureaucratic *bullshit* going down, to include interference or harm to myself, my friends, or *any other innocent person*, foreign or domestic," there was a slight murmuring here and there until once again all became silent. Not least effective in his little polemic was the dignity Wychway somehow had managed to give the word, "bullshit."

When finally the DCI (the only man for whom Wychway had any vestige of respect in the top echelons of the Agency) spoke up with, "Just who in the goddam hell do you think...! he was peremptorily silenced by a violent gesture from his superior. Someone coughed, discreetly. After another brief silence the Director, following a hasty and uncomfortable surveilance of all the faces which now seemed to be fastened upon him, leaned forward slightly and said evenly and courteously to the man who still stood calmly erect before him:

"Please sit down, Mr. Wychway." Wychway sat.

"Mr. Wychway, I think I speak for all of us assembled here when I say that for what you have done and for what you have undergone on behalf of your country and the rest of the free peoples of the world you have our undying gratitude as well as that of the rest of the Government and the American people as a whole. I can add to that the assurance that you will not find your country ungrateful. —Er, ah, is there anything anyone would like to add to that?" he finished rather lamely as he glared at the presidential advisor and the NSC staffer, who sat together a few feet away. There was more silence.

Now, after a muttered consultation with his Deputies, who flanked him, he declared to no one in particular but in a loud and rather irritable voice that the "debriefing" was adjourned. With that he gathered up his copy of the MFR and the few papers he'd brought with him, gave the White House representatives a curt nod apiece, and inclining his head (no doubt towards his office) with two quick jerks at his Deputies, left the room. As he went out he gave Wychway the merest of glances but, thought Wychway, it must have been with that sort of look the Medusa turned people to stone. He clearly overheard the DDO mutter grittily:

"That *fucking* Browning! I wish he were still *alive*, so I could have him, have him..." Wychway lost the conclusion of this aspiration as the DDO followed his leader out into the hall.

As the rest of the assemblage followed, singly or in groups, Wychway found the short, energetic, young, sandy-haired presidential advisor at his elbow.

"Hi! Mr. Wychway! Name's Bill, just plain Bill, like the old radio soap opera," he chuckled. When the other just stood there silently (and telling himself that "Just Plain Bill" was obviously too young to remember any *radio* soap operas) he went on with a little less self-assurance. "I just want you to know that I've been authorized to tell you that, aside from what the Director just said—incidentally, I'm sure there'll be some sort of medal coming your way, and most likely a promotion within the Agency—but anyway, aside from all that pro forma stuff I'm authorized to ask if there's anything of a less official nature you might want. And by the way, this comes from the very top, I hope you understand," he ended importantly and somewhat elliptically as he stood smiling benignly on Wychway.

The last time Wychway had heard that expression, "from the top" (it seemed like years ago), he'd been sitting across a military field table from Lew Browning, looking at the snow

through a dirty window at the Hohenfels base in Bavaria....
Though he had taken an immediate dislike to this man (toad
eater, one of his father's favorite tags, came to mind) Wychway managed to looked slightly embarrassed and flustered by
this unexpected beneficence. What kind of asshole *is* this guy?
he asked himself. Jesus, he heard what I said, and here he is
making nice to the US Government's pariah of the year....

Hiding his mystification he produced a shy grin as he replied:

"Well, actually, ever since I was a little kid I've always
wanted to meet "The Man," know what I mean? I don't suppose there's any chance of—"

"No problem! And here I was hoping you wouldn't ask for
something outrageous! As it happens," the other continued
smoothly, "there's a relatively small bash laid on for tonight in
Georgetown, and contrary to his usual policy of limiting his
social commitments to Pennsyvania Avenue, he'll be there.
Boy! you can't immagine what those poor Secret Service guys
have to go through on these outings," he added parenthetically
and digressively. "Before the POTUS and the FLOTUS arrive:
the EOD squad has to sweep the place for explosives, electronic intelligence for bugs, the other guests and the servants
have to be vetted—what a pain in the ass! —Anyway, how'd
you like to go? I think maybe Sharon Stone and one or two
other hot numbers might show up, too."

Like a gift from Heaven! thought Wychway as with an
enthusiasm which though totally genuine was driven by
motives the other could not possibly know he replied:

"Jeez! do you mean it? *Sure* I'd like to go. Hell, I'd love it!"

"Great! I can't tell you where it is, for security reasons,
you understand, but your friends here (with a sweeping gesture) will get you there, I'm sure."

My friends! thought Wychway wryly. But yeah, I guess
they will now! "Oh, yeah, no problem—well, as long as *they*
know where the hell to go!" he replied jokingly.

"Oh, yes. One of this evening's guests will be the fellow
who sat across from you at that long table."

Better and better, Wychway told himself. "Okay, what time, and what's the uniform?

"Check with the Director's secretary on the time," he looked more closely at Wychway's clean, well-tailored, but slightly rumpled suit, "as for the 'uniform,' I'm afraid it's black tie—but what you're wearing will be just fine," he amended hastily, "this is the nineties, remember? —Oh, yes, there *is* one more thing, Charley. May I call you Charley?" and without waiting for a reply said pointedly, "*Please*, don't discuss any of *this* matter," he gestured vaguely towards the conference table, "this evening, with *anyone*."

"Not even 'The Man'?"

"I doubt he'll ask, but no, not even him, Charley. If he *does* happen to bring the subject up just give me a signal and I'll handle it, okay?" He smiled and bowed slightly as he shook hands and took his departure.

So, Wychway told himself as he stood there, The Man wants to see what The Pariah looks like in person.

Chapter Twenty-six

Justice

As it happend Wychway actually drove to the party, albeit in an absolute and frigid silence, with the CIA Director himself. He had managed to get his suit pressed.

Their destination turned out to be one of those typical, compact, three-storey Georgetown townhouses on "N" Street, a couple of blocks west of Wisconsin Avenue. When the large black sedan pulled smoothly up to the curb the Director's driver-cum-bodyguard immediately got out, came around to the sidewalk, and held the rear door open. When the Director and Wychway were out he opened the front passenger door and pulled Wychway's valpac out (the trunk was so full of radio and other electronic gear that the bag wouldn't fit). Although Wychway had been offered quarters at either Langley or at the Marriott in Roslyn, he'd turned down both alternatives, explaining (lying) that he'd made arrangements to stay "with a friend in the D.C. area," and so had insisted on taking his bag.

It had also been suggested that he should undergo a complete physical examination at either Walter Reed Army Medical Center or Bethesda Naval Hospital, whichever he preferred. Understandably, he had turned that suggestion down flat.

As they crossed the venerable brick sidewalk to the paneled, massive, bright red door Wychway remembered the winter night when as a typically impecunious student at Georgetown University he had walked past such a house (which was perhaps a block or two away from where he now stood). Just as he had come abreast of it the door had been opened to admit a group of people in evening dress. A glance inside as he'd strolled past had revealed a foyer with a crystal chandelier, several more formally dressed men and women, the glint of silver and jewelry, and a liveried black servant holding the door open. This semi-tableau of so many years ago, which for some reason he'd always been able to recall in fine detail, now was almost recreated as this door (the other had been identical except for its *black* enameled finish) was opened by a smiling, gray-haired black man, who took Wychway's bag.

Now as he followed the Director (who immediately separated himself from his unsavory companion) into the foyer that scene of years ago virtually was reproduced. The tastefully small but ornately beautiful Murano chandelier was there, as was the highly polished side table with silver candelabra and silver tray for visitors' cards, the bejeweled women, the dinner-jacketed men (Wychway saw at least one cummerbund, and one portly foreigner actually was wearing a bemedalled red sash), the gracious and smiling hostess in her red taffeta (!) evening dress, and so on. What impressed Wychway as much as anything else was the diminutiveness of it all. The phrase "lavishly Lilliputian" came to mind.

He greeted the hostess and introduced himself perfunctorily, and was relieved when she absently shook his hand, gave him the briefest of dazzling smiles, and immediately began looking over his shoulder for the next incoming guest. He was forgotten. Left to himself he wandered into the "sitting room" where he found, holding forth with great bonhomie, the master of this mansion in miniature who (according to the Director's secretary) was a prominent businessman and who recently had been appointed US Ambassador to Mexico. Wychway didn't bother to introduce himself, and once again he was relieved to be ignored.

Actually the party was being held in two rooms which

were connected by large sliding doors now open to their fullest extent. In a corner of this second room, which presumably was used normally as a dining room, behind a service bar covered with rows of gleaming crystal glasses a very attractive, very petite—one might almost say tiny—young strawberry blonde in a trim black satin uniform was drawing corks from wine bottles. A quintessentially Italian chef brought out a huge tray of what looked and smelled like baked eggplant croquettes. Meanwhile a Latinesque middle-aged woman was circulating a large tray of of drinks while a short man of similar age and ethnicity (her husband?) was picking his way carefully through the crowded sitting room offering cigars from a heavy, dark, open wooden box. Los Liberatadores Figurados, Wychway noted (at $7.00 a crack, he remembered from a brochure he'd once perused). With a distasteful glance at Wychway's suit, the man walked past him. No doubt he thinks I'm one of the Secret Service toads, Wychway surmised with an inward chuckle as he reached for his cigarettes. While he had his lighter out he lit a cigar for the unattractive, frowzy, but expensively dressed middle-aged woman standing next to him. He ignored her attempt at a coy smile and responded to her "Thank you, you gorgeous hunk!" with a curt nod. Undoubtedly this idiot saw herself as being on the cutting edge of the new wave of female cigar smokers, and he recalled telling Margaret Feldon how certain kinds of feminism helped reconcile him to death. He found himself wishing he were in someone's kitchen drinking a cool Bass or a Spatenbrau. For tonight, however, it would be ginger ale or club soda, but just for tonight, he told himself as he worked his way to the pretty barmaid in the other room. If Sharon Stone or any "other hot numbers" were there he didn't notice them.

Although for the moment no one else was at the bar the miniature barmaid was busy as usual and he watched patiently as she worked on another wine bottle, the neck of which was nestled between her small, but for her size ample, well-shaped breasts while she plied the corkscrew.

"Do you see something interesting?" she asked pleasantly with a pretty smile as she looked up directly at him with frank admiration. She was about twenty-five and really was extremely good looking, Wychway decided.

"I just was watching you transfix that cork. You make that little wine bottle look like a magnum." He noticed now, however, that she had relatively large and capable hands.

"*I'm* transfixed," she bubbled as she held his eyes with hers. When with a final effort she popped the cork out she asked, "What'll you have, good lookin'? This Beringer isn't bad."

"Just a glass of club soda, please"

"Who *are* you, anyway? I've never seen you before, and I work the party circuit all the time." She nodded at his suit and then at the drink she placed in his hand. "Are you a spook," she rounded her eyes, "one of El Supremo's Palace Guards?"

That would be like sending the wolf to guard the sheep, Wychway would have liked to say under other circumstances, but he merely replied:

"Nope. Actually, I'm a nobody. Somebody must have made a mistake in the party invitations," and with a wink and a smile he turned and drifted away.

Gratefully he felt full of physical well-being as he sipped his insiped drink. He'd been told upon his release from the hospital that he *was* fit, completely healed and "normal," and that there should be no deleterious after-effects from his surgery, either pre- or post-Bigeye. He looked down at the glass of soda he held and realized he probably could identify the Secret Service security "troops" not merely by what they wore but by what they drank, if they drank anything, and, barring "southpaws," which hand they held a drink in.

As he wandered around for the next twenty minutes waiting for the President to arrive (he hadn't seen "Bill" anywhere, either) Wychway became sure he'd already spotted four "advanced party" security agents. He also recognized a few congressional members, one or two TV news "personalities," and eventually even Secretary of State Wilbur Claxton. Would the man know who he was? Could he know that he, Wychway, was the man who just a few short months ago literally had held his life in his hands? Purposefully he caught the silver-haired statesman's eye, and was greatly relieved when the older man looked away unhurriedly with little or no interest.

As Wychway moved around unobtrusively he overheard snatches of conversation here and there. When he spotted "Bill" standing at the sitting room entryway, a male voice behind him, whose owner obviously was pleased with himself about something, was holding forth about how "Motorola has been selling the Chinese—I'm talking about *mainland* China now—and to other countries, at least one or two of which are our bosom buddies (need I say more? heh, heh); well, anyway, Motorola's selling 'em a microchip that's essential in making AP mines, the 'don't disturb' kind, and..." Happily Wychway lost the rest of this as he moved towards "Bill."

The POTUS and FLOTUS, with their Secret Service escort, came in behind "Bill" just as Wychway reached the entryway from the foyer. He stepped aside politely to let the President and his party pass into the sitting room.

"Wait a few minutes, until all the bullshit and grabass dies down and everybody gets his nose out of my Boss's ass," whispered Bill with a wink as he inclined his head towards the other room, where the President now was surrounded by a claque of devotees. Wychway nodded understandingly and moved away.

It was obvious that Bill had had a few drinks before coming to the party, and also that Bill's southern accent blossomed on alcohol, Wychway thought as he lounged against the door frame of the passageway between the two party rooms. From this vantage point he could survey, innocuously, both rooms. Occasionally he glanced over at the pretty bar girl, who responded to him with a whole panoply of evocative reactions from a subtle arching of her eyebrows to a sort of shimmy-shake of her shoulders. Christ! he thought, the girl was so full of life, so attractive and full of sex appeal that, despite all he felt for Magda, if it were any other time...

But mainly he kept track of the progress of the President and his coterie as they moved gradually to the center of the sitting room. He noticed now at least three more Secret Service candidates, almost certainly members of the President's "escort": his personal bodyguards. These would be the toughest ones, he reminded himslef.

He hadn't been standing there more than five minutes when Bill, clutching a very dark highball, joined him and with boozy good humor clapped him on the back.

"Hi, ol' buddy! Goddam! you look like yore best huntin' dawg just got run ovah by the tractor! Come on, Charley mah man, it's a *party*, not an effin' wake!"

Wychway managed a feeble smile. "Yeah, well, maybe I got jet lag."

"Jet lag nevah bothers me when I travel *west*, it's goin' the *other* way that's a bitch," Bill laughed good naturedly.

Wychway looked sadly down at his drink. "Yeah, well, then there was all that bullshit this afternoon." He looked across at Bill's already bleary eyes. "Maybe you don't realize it, but I really hated going through all that. None of that shit should have been necessary, "

Bill became slightly more serious. "Yeah, I hear yuh, ol' buddy. But you did right, Charley. Hell, if you don't cover yer own ass nobody else is gonna do it for ya." He fell silent for a few moments. Wychway waited noncommittedly—waited for an opportunity to put a crucial question or two to this man who though drunk was no fool, who perhaps was not even as drunk as he seemed to be. For one thing, as he went on he seemed to be losing some of that corn pone Li'l Abner dialect which had been so strong just moments ago.

"You know, Charley, there *is* one thing I couldn't agree with," he now said quietly and earnestly. "In that memo of yours you claimed that the President was in on the whole scam, right from the git go. Actually that ain't right. I couldn't say anythin' at that debriefing—debriefing my ass, right?" he chuckled, "but you gotta know, the ol' man never knew *what* was goin' on. Oh yeah, he knew about goin' after Saddam all right; but all that Claxton ball o' snakes? uh, *uh*. He never knew jack shit about all that. Jesus Christ! if that memo of yours ever came out they'd be callin' it Iraq gate! Now I don't know how high up in the Agency that went (let 'em wash their own dirty laundry), but I can tell you this: that wasn't the first time that son of bitch, Browning, caused a lot of heartburn—know what I'm sayin'? Jus' between you'n me I'm goddam glad you nailed the bastard—good riddance to bad rubbish, as they say—an' I'll tell ya somethin' else," he leaned close to the other's ear, "the President feels the same way.—How do you feel about that?"

Since this obviously called for a reply Wychway replied.

"I hear you, Bill; but about Claxton: it's no secret that your boss isn't exactly in love with the guy, right?"

"Oh, hell, that's common knowledge. Nobody's denyin' that! The Big Boy would love to see Wilbur move along. But to have him whacked? —no way! I mean, that's just *crazy*. Hell, all's we gotta do is wait for that silver-haired ol' geezer to step on his dick good and hard one o' these times and he'll do it *for* us. A little ol' letter of resignation, for any ol' reason he wants to give, and out he goes to pasture, his just reward."

Wychway resisted the urge to point out that in view of Claxton's popularity with both certain influential members of the Congress—"on both sides of the aisle"—and with the American public in general this was unlikely to happen. Instead he merely nodded towards a group of people engaged in animated conversation with the "silver-haired ol' geezer" himself and said:

"That's the man himself, over there, isn't it?"

"Yeah, I see 'im. Ol' Willy Claxton. He's somethin' else all right. Are you aware, good Charley, that if the President had already served his second term ol' Willy'd be the party's choice for the upcoming ticket? My Boy hates his *ass*, mostly because of his stance on foreign policy (What *else* would they argue about? Wychway asked himself). Problem is, we've created a goddam Frankenstein. I gotta admit it: a lotta people agree with Claxton, and I'm not just talkin' about the Great Unwashed out there beyond the Beltway; a lotta guys in Congress are about fed up with what's been goin' on, especially in Bosnia, *most* especially in the Middle East. But I say again, loud an' clear: the President never knew *anything* about any secret plot to kill Claxton. I *know* that, because if *he* knew there's no way *I* wouldn't know."

Wychway hoped Bill was wrong about that last fervent utterance; he was beginning think that perhaps he'd misjudged this man at their first meeting. And now he even was having some doubts about the President's complicity in the Claxton plot. *Could* Bill be right, after all? Good Lord! *He had to know!* And he had to know *tonight*. He tore himself away from these desperate thoughts as he realized Bill was saying something.

"… and I guess now would be as good a time as any. How 'bout it—you ready?"

"To meet the President?" Wychway asked rather inanely.

"What the hell ya think I been talkin' about? Come on!" And with that he put his arm around Wychway's shoulders (he had to reach up) and guided him towards the center of the sitting room.

President Billy Jack Effingsly (pronounced, of course, Effingslee) was tall, beefy, and until Wychway arrived was wearing the characteristic lopsided grin which the political cartoonists knew and "loved" so well. Undoubtedly he had been told he would meet "the man involved in the Iraq fracas" (or some similar description), and almost as certainly, Wychway told himelf, he'd already read the by now infamous MFR. Effingsly kept himself in control, but as he watched the two men approach the smile left his mouth and a wariness became undeniably evident (to Wychway, at least) in his eyes. He was flanked by the CIA Director, who took no pains to alter his expression of sour distaste at Wychway's appearance, and the White House Chief of Staff, who appeared amiable enough and who now discreetly shooed away any others who had been in immediate attendance on the Great Man. This notwithstanding two Secret Service men remained loitering watchfully in the near background.

The introduction was made, and after a perfunctory handshake the President said:

"So, Mr. Wychway, home at last. I've heard so much about you and your adventures," he managed half a lopsided grin at his chief of staff, "about which, of course, we cannot expound due to their, shall we say, ultrasensitivity?"

Yeah, right, Mr. President, thought Wychway, and under the circumstances the less said the better, is that it? (the title, El Supremo, kept coming to mind). His only response was a tight if not lopsided grin of his own accompanied by a slight nodding of his head. But "El Supremo" was going on:

"What I *can* say—Charles, isn't it?" Wychway nodded, "what I can say, Charles, is that for what you've done mere gratitude seems inadequate; but even if it were not, there can be, unfortunately, no public manifestation of that gratitude. I do assure you, however, that you *will* be compensated for your efforts, however quietly." Looking straight into the other's eyes he extended his hand once again. "It's been a pleasure to have met you, sir."

As Wychway shook hands he felt Bill's gentle tug at his sleeve.

And thus, without having had the opportunity to utter a single word more, he was dismissed. Yes, he told himself as he moved away, Bigeye really was a *very* "close hold" operation; and that the President had been in on it from the very beginning Wychway no longer had any doubt. Despite all the seeming geniality (and banalities) there could be no equivocation about the truly vicious hatred Wychway had seen smoldering behind the President's eyes as almost machine-like he had delivered those meaningless platitudes while doubtless saying to himself, So, *this* is the son of a bitch who screwed up all my plans! In any case Wychway had been pleased to see that El Supremo was drinking beer.

Standing at the service bar with Bill, Wychway realized that his hands were trembling. The girl was busy filling orders now, and when she popped cheerfully in front of him he asked for a brandy, drank it down, thanked Bill, excused himself, and went in search of Wilbur Claxton.

"Secretary Claxton?" he said when he found the man sitting alone near the bow window which faced the street. When the elderly man looked up inquiringly Wychway went on. "Excuse me for barging up like this, sir, but my name is Charles Wychway, and I just wanted to meet you," he said lamely but honestly.

Without rising and with a neutral expression Claxton held out his hand, which though wizened was large and capable-looking.

"How do you do? Mr. Wychway."

Mr. Secretary, I'm just another petty bureaucrat in the great scheme of things, but since this may be the only opportunity I'll have to do it I just wanted to tell you I think you're doing a great job. I know that may sound rather presumptious coming from someone who doesn't really understand everything that's going on, but I just wanted you to know that from what I do know you're just what this country needs right now."

Obviously pleased but still wary Claxton asked: "What *do* you do, Mr. Wychway?"

"I'm just a tiny cog in the big CIA wheel. I spend most of my time reading foreign-language newspapers."

"I see your Director is here tonight," Wilbur Claxton passed a hand over his face as if remembering something. One of your top men was with me when he was killed last December, in Iraq. You recall the incident, I'm sure. What a tragedy! My God, they almost killed Saddam Hussein! I shudder to think of what would have happened in that country if he'd been killed! —Did you know the unfortunate Agency man who *was* killed? What was his name, Bishop?"

"Browning, sir. I only knew him slightly. We both were stationed in Germany for a while."

"*Most* unfortunate," the Secretary said with genuine feeling.

It sure was, thought Wychway—that Browning and I ever met at all, that is.

"Well, Mr. Wychway, it was very nice to have met you, and thanks for the vote of confidence, I truly appreciate your taking the time to come and talk to me." He stood to shake Wychway's hand. "Good luck to you!

And with a "Thank you, sir," Wychway, his mind now made up, went to find the bathrooms.

The pretty bar girl, Marion, as her name turned out to be, knew all about it. As Wychway had another glass of club soda to chase down the brandy she explained that there were three bathrooms. The one upstairs usually was reserved for the house's occupants. "And one's right here," she pointed, "just around the corner from that butler's pantry. Then there's one— actually a half-bath, just a toilet and stall shower—in the servants' quarters at the rear of the house," she summed up.

"'Usually.' Does that mean that mean the President and his *Frau* get to use the upstairs john when they're here?"

"Yes, and no," answered Marion. He was over here with Mrs. What the Hell's Her Name? the hostess, a little while ago. He was telling her it wasn't beneath him to get his own beer, but actually—and if I'm lyin' I'm dyin'—he came over to *hit* on me. I *knew* he was gonna come on to me the moment he came over to the bar. Anyway, I guess he had to take a whiz 'cause I heard the chatelaine say to him, "Ohhh, Mr. President! *You* get to go to the *upstairs* one—her kind wouldn't say 'toilet' if her head was stuck in one—and he asked, 'Is that the one *you* use?' and she said, kinda coy-like, 'Well, *usually*, except when we're having a party with such *extremely* important guests!' And so *he* says, 'Oh, no, no, no, Dear Lady! If the downstairs one is good enough for *you* then it's certainly good enough for me!' Of course, when I was giving him his beer he asked me, *sotto voce*, whether the *servants* had their own john or used this one downstairs. Talk about your hypocritical, fatuous bullshit!"

Wychway chuckled at this richly descriptive narration.

"You must be an English student, or even a teacher, maybe."

"Too true. Student. G'town grad. school. But wait, it gets better. After *Madame* excused herself to go welcome another guest—can you believe it? she actually *curtsied* to him! Well, then El Supremo gets right down to it. He winks at me and says, 'I'm bored with all this shit. You know what I'd *really* like to do? I'd really like to take you out in the back yard and burn a joint.' I swear, those were his exact words!"

"Well, he does have a bit of a rep with the ladies—wouldn't you enjoy seeing the emperor without his pants?"

"Not *this* lady! Who the hell does he think he is, Elvis and JFK rolled into one?"

"Uh, huh. Maybe. And, of course, since *they're* not around anymore *somebody*'s gotta take up the slack. Well, anyway, if the downstairs john is good enough for him it's good enough for me. Don't fall in love with anyone while I'm gone," Wychway said smilingly as he put down his glass and headed towards the butler's pantry.

A few minutes later he was hovering unobtrusively but just within earshot of the President's sycophantic little group. When he heard Effingsly's drawled, "Well, please excuse me, folks," as he looked significantly at his empty beer glass, "but I gotta go visit the little boy's room again," (followed by the Chief of Staff's hoarse whisper to the host, "Even great men have to pee!") Wychway moved. As quickly as the crowded conditions would permit he went back through the butler's pantry, reentered the downstairs bathroom, and locked the door behind him.

When he came out several minutes later he managed to look contrite and embarrassed as the Secret Service man who had already started knocking loudly on the door gave him a malignant stare.

"Sorry, sir," he apologized to Effingsly, who ignored him.

"Anybody else in there?" the bodyguard asked brusquely. "In there? Oh, no. No, nobody," Wychway stammered self-consciously. "All clear!" he added cheerfully as he brushed past the two men and went his way.

Fifteen minutes later pandemonium reigned in the house of the newly-appointed ambassador. Two minutes after that the Secret Service detail had "sealed" the house, and not many minutes later the D.C. police had placed a cordon around it and blocked the street.

"*Il Presidente! Madonna d' Carmina! Presidente* Effingasleeza, *e morte!* Eesa *dead!* " Wychway, back at the bar with Marion, heard the Italian chef screaming from somewhere in the back of the house.

The Secret Service bodyguard who had accompanied Effingsly to the bathroom was heard saying as he bustled past with a colleague, "What the fuck can I tell ya? He was takin' a piss. I waited the usual five minutes, then I went in and he was lyin' there in his own piss with his dick in his hand—dead!"

José Gonzales, the cigar dispenser, had fallen to his knees and was crossing himself, over and over again. "Oh, I am going craysey! *El Presidente! Muerte! Madre de Dios!* "

Mrs. New Ambassador's wife tried vainly to restore order, at least among her servants.

"Stop that blubbering and leave us, Gonzales!"

"But where shall I go?" cried the stricken man.

"Go to hell, you filthy wetback!"

"Now, now, my dear," her doting but rather witless husband gently admonished, "please try to remember our new position."

Not far away the wife of the Vice President (who himself was off on a goodwill tour) was trying to soothe the newly-widowed First Lady, much as Lady Bird Johnson must have tried to comfort Jacqueline Kennedy, Wychway imagined.

Does the late El Supremo have a little son who could be taught to salute at the funeral? he wondered.

From the corner where he stood chewing his nails, Bill, whose genial nature seemed to have died with his President, stared malevolently at Wychway. Through all this, Wychway, looking suitably melancholy, stood at the bar sipping cognac and conversing with Marion in subdued tones.

Although it could be argued that logic might have insisted that *anyone* who had dispensed *anything* the President had ingested during the evening should have been held for closer questioning and scrutiny, Marion—after the Metropolitan Police, the FBI, and God knew who else had arrived to "take charge of the scene"—had been among the first of the house's occupants to be released. Now she waited outside in her car until Wychway, carrying his old valpac, appeared not much later.

"Do they know what killed him? Was it an attack of some kind?" she asked animatedly as a policeman waved them out of their parking place. Wychway noticed she had her seat as close to the steering wheel as it would go, and was sitting on a little cushion.

"No one seems to know. If they do they aren't saying. They won't know much of anything until they do a post mortem. Until that's over everybody who was there is supposed to stay in town, but I guess they told you that. —What'd you put in his beer, anyway?"

"Jesus, Charley! It *was* the President after all, you know," she scolded.

"You mean, 'El Supremo,' don't you? —the guy who was trying to get in your pants?" he replied ironically.

"Shit! that was just a joke, and you know it; and the rest was, well, nothing important."

"Whatever," he answered noncommittally.

"Are you gonna 'stay in town'?"

"What do you mean?"

"Did *you* do it?"

"Do what?"

"Well, if it *wasn't* natural causes, and somehow I don't think it was, I think you did it," she said flatly after a few moments of silence and as they approached the University a few blocks away.

"That's bullshit and you know it is."

"I *saw* you go to the can just before he did. I don't have any idea *how* you did it, but my Irish-Italian blood *tells* me you did it."

Wychway just shook his head tolerantly and smiled, acting just a little bored. But he wasn't smiling inside. He knew that if he were a *real* professional, after what she'd just said doubtless he would have to kill her—take her for a drive, dump the body somewhere, take her car and work out his escape from there. He'd spent a lot of time talking to her at the party, and that cop had seen them leave together. Lew Browning, or even Harry Ward for that matter, wouldn't have hesitated, he told himself, and he was immediately thankful he wasn't a Lew Browning or a Harry Ward. He asked himself what his father would do in this situation, and immediately banished the thought from his mind. Whatever the Old Man would have done, he finally admitted to himself, he wasn't really like his father either, no matter what others might think, and he was glad of it. No, he couldn't, wouldn't do it. But one thing was certain: he couldn't let her out of his sight, not until he was ready to go, when the going was good.

This stream of consciousness had lasted only seconds, and now Marion was asking:

"Well, even if you didn't do it, what'd you think of him."

Unhesistatingly Wychway answered, "He wasn't worth the powder you'd need to blow him up."

"Well, that makes me feel better, anyway," she said as she gave him a glance.

"Why?" he asked, although he already knew the answer.

"Because, goddammit, if you did do it no doubt you'd be telling me how much you loved the son of a bitch!"

Well anyway, Sweetheart, you finally got his real title right, Wychway nodded silently to himself as she parked her little Mazda GLC a block away from the main Georgetown campus.

Chapter Twenty-seven

The Dart of Chance

Marion lived in a small apartment on the corner of 36th and "P" Streets, N.W., over a bar and grill (still going strong on this Saturday night) called the Hoya Taverna—the name taken, no doubt, from Georgetown's Greek "battlecry," *Hoya Saxa*! (What Rocks!). As Wychway got his bag out of the back seat he asked:

"Is that old leather tannery from hell still belching forth those mephitic smells?"

"Jesus, Charley, when was the last time you were here? That place is a legend around here, but then so is John Barrymore, who used to get wasted downstairs. Did you used to live around here, by the way?"

Wychway cleared his throat. "I'm an alumnus of this Jesuit monastery, dear lady. So was my Old Man. He went to school with that guy who wrote *The Exorcist*."

"Well, well, small worldsville! What did you study?"

"As little as possible. —Uh, can we get off the street now?"

"There you go again. What are you afraid of?"

"Those four big guys who seem to have taken a sudden interest in us," Wychway nodded in the direction of a group of tough-looking young men—hands in pockets, heads down but occasionally glancing up—less than a block away, who were approaching them a little too rapidly for his comfort.

"Shit! I see your point. Come on!" she said.

Safely in her apartment Wychway was pleased to note

while Marion changed out of her uniform that the place exuded that same pleasant aroma that he'd enjoyed whenever he'd been near her at the party that evening. He also was amused to see a number of unopened wine bottles, which bore pretty much the same labels as those he'd seen her opening earlier, ranged along a shelf above her CD record player. He was reminded of the hundreds of miniatures in the apartment of an airline stewardess (now flight attendant, thanks to what Charles Dickens once referred to as "the black divinities of feminism") with whom he'd spent a number of very pleasant weekends.

He switched on the TV. Except for the usual pre-recorded programs on the specialty stations it didn't matter which channel he chose: the major networks or their local affiliates and CNN all were grinding out their coverage of "this very recent tragedy." Despite the fact that it was a weekend night all the premier "talking heads" had made it into a studio somewhere. The President had died very suddenly of "unknown causes" at a party given in his honor at a private residence in the Georgetown section of Washington; the Vice President had cancelled the remainder of his goodwill tour to Africa and was on his way back to the Capital to take his oath of office, they all said. Beyond that there was nothing except bland speculation on the state of the late President's erstwhile health, which only a month ago had been reported as "excellent" after a complete physical examination at the Bethesda Naval Hospital, and so on.

Marion now came out of her bedroom, barefoot and dressed in a miniskirt and a tiny 1970s-vintage tube top which showed off her diminutive, nubile, and extremely evocative figure to great advantage. She was wearing, Wychway was soon to discover, nothing else. He gulped involuntarily as he gaped at her beautiful, slender legs, and would bet that she weighed less than 100 pounds. He was somehow relieved to notice that her feet, like her hands, seemed disproportionately large, although she probably wore no more than a size five or six shoe.

"Anything new? What are they saying?"

"Nope. They're speculating that it was a massive heart

attack or a stroke."

"Uh, huh," she gave him a mischievous look as she did something with her hair.

"Marion, could you just get off that little kick for a while, please?" he asked with pretended irritation; in fact he was relieved somewhat that her earlier and seemingly more serious and therefore potentially dangerous suspicion seemed now to have subsided to the playful stage. As much to change the subject as to state a fact he said:

"By the way, you have a lovely little place here."

"Thanks. I'm poor but honest." She glanced at the solid rank of wine bottles and laughed. "Well, relatively honest."

He joined in her laughter as, satisfied that for the present at least there were no new developments in the news, he switched off the TV.

She walked through the sitting room to her tiny kitchen ("I call it my kitchenino, after the portable one D.H. Lawrence and Frieda had when they traveled in Italy") and got a bottle of white wine out of the proportionately tiny Avanti refrigerator.

"Wanna watch a videotape?"

"Am I thinking about the same kind of movie you're thinking about?"

She giggled. "Maybe. I've got all kinds, though."

"Like what, for instance?"

"Whatever bends your board, darlin'", she answered sweetly as she handed him a glass of wine, then knelt at the rack of video cassettes and began going through them. "But I almost forgot," she turned to him. "*Does* one watch movies on the night the President dies?"

Wychway was mildly and pleasantly surprised when they ended by watching Bette Davis, (who was a great actress, Marion admitted, despite the fact that "she usually looks like someone is holding something malodorous under her nose") in the 1931 film adaptation of W.S. Maugham's "The Letter," which despite its rather morbid theme did nothing to dampen the mutual sexual ardor that had been waxing in them both throughout the evening from the moment they first met. As much as he tried to center his thoughts on Magda, Wychway couldn't wait to see what was under the tube top, to say nothing of the rest of what the miniskirt barely concealed.

After they had finished their first bout of strenuous sexual striving on the sitting room floor (if it hadn't been for her fervor and obvious expertise Wychway might have felt like a child molester, he thought when once during their convolutions he found himself confronted by her little tuft of strawberry blond pubic hair, which reminded him of a Vandyke, or perhaps, an Imperial beard) Wychway tried to assuage his feelings of guilt by telling himself he had to do this for the greater good, his good, which ultimately would redound to Magda's happiness, and so forth.

By the time they had finished round two he gave up all this hypocritical rationalization and just had a thoroughly good time. Besides, he told himself with just a vestige of residual hypocracy, Marion wasn't the kind of female you could spurn without unpleasant consequences, and he could ill afford to give up her little haven just now..

A little before two o'clock on this Sunday morning, after making sure that Marion had had plenty of the choice wine she'd pinched from any number of parties and so was sleeping soundly, he got carefully and quietly out of her bed.

Standing naked in the little sitting room, using a tiny art deco night light he'd switched on, he went carefully through Marion's shoulder bag. He held her car keys in his hand for a full twenty seconds before dropping them back in her bag; then quickly he extracted her driver's license and Mastercard from her wallet. Marion M. (Mary?) Riordan. The same on the credit card. He thought of Marion Motley, the former great footballer, as with materials readily at hand on her little desk he quickly wrote a note, put it in the slot which her license had occupied, replaced the wallet, and refastened the clasp on the bag. He thought for moment, then went to where his clothing was scattered on the floor, found his wallet, extracted five hundred-dollar notes, and went back to the desk.

Five minutes later he was walking south towards Holy Trinity Church—only two blocks away and where he'd often attended Mass as a student— hoping they still said the two A.M. "Printers' Mass," a special service for the convenience of night workers. He had to find a relatively safe place where he could think and plan his next move. He reflected that this would be the first time he'd been to church since his last tour in Vietnam, if you could call the places where they'd said Mass in Vietnam "churches."

There were few people attending Mass, and he sat towards the back next to a side aisle where the general gloom seemed deepest. He placed his valpac down quietly next to him in the aisle. As the Mass proceeded he looked around to re-familiarize himself with the beautiful old stone church. There were the old confessionals—the "squeal boxes," they'd called them when he was here as a student—and not far away, to the right of the main altar where the priest now was beginning the Consecration, was the Lady Chapel where he would say his penance after confession. Now he remembered how once during a particularly boring sermon he'd slipped out and gone and read a newspaper (well, the sports page and the comics, actually) at the corner newsstand and returned just in time for the Consecration, feeling proud of his timing. Not much to worry about, but two venial sins in one act, his Jesuit confessor had told him when his scrupulosity had impelled him to confess what he'd done.

As he half-sat, half-knelt there in the gloom he reflected on what he'd done at that house party earlier, and beyond that about what he'd done that day in Al-Basrah. Did he feel guilt for what he'd done? Yes, he had to admit there was some guilt, quite a lot, in fact. Did he repent? Was he sorry that he'd murdered Browning and now, the President? That he'd maimed Saddam? That he'd just betrayed Magda, and to a lesser extent betrayed even Marion, who had just given him all she'd had to give and had, however inwittingly, provided him with a "safe house" when he'd needed a secure refuge temporarily, and now just as unwittingly was providing him with a possible means of escape? For one mad moment he actually considered going to the Sacristy after Mass ended and asking the priest to hear his confession.

But only for a moment. He counted out a full minute to himself, using the old parachute count one never forgot (one-thousand, two-thousand, and on) until he had pulled himself together. It was a simple question of general ethics, he told himself. The Principle of Double Effect. He had achieved a good end by using bad means, and he would have to live with it, confession or no confession. If he still felt the need to "squeal" he could do it after he was away from all this, and what he revealed would be under the seal of confession. He moved his mind on to more immediate and practical matters.

Mass was coming to a close, and though he could prolong his stay for a little while he couldn't stay here all night. With times what they were (he remembered the four toughs near Marion's place) the church undoubtedly would be locked after Mass, at least until daylight, which wouldn't come at this time of year until at least seven o'clock. He needed another refuge until he could make the arrangements he had in mind.

And now an idea came to him. He remembered an old Eric Ambler thriller he'd read years ago—was it, *Cause for Alarm*? (Good Lord! what did the title matter?)—where the protagonist and his comrade who are on the run in a city somewhere have to find a safe place to spend the early hours with little chance of being traced by the authorities. They settle on an all-night Turkish bath. Now Wychway prayed (this certainly was the place for it) that the bath he and his student pals used to go to sometimes after a long and boozy night was still doing business. What he needed now was a telephone. And he remembered seeing a public phone just a few steps away from the church entrance.

Luckily the Metropolitan phone book hadn't been torn away; within a few minutes Wychway was relieved to hear a voice answer at the old Turkish bath house of his student days. Then he called a taxi.

Ten minutes later, after some predictable pro forma chatting with the elderly black cab driver about the recent and sudden tragedy as they headed downtown, Wychway, elated by having found another temporary sanctuary, whimsically reminisced aloud about "Daddy-O," the huge and fabulous black man who in the small hours after all legitimate outlets had closed would dispense (for a fair price) liquor of all kinds to needy students such as Wychway and others who now and then were "on the town" and found themselves "dispirited" just at that point when they felt they were hitting their stride in the conduct of their sprees and celebrations. Daddy-O wore a long, bulky overcoat, in all seasons, and when satisfied that he'd been approached by a legitimate patron, not a member of the law, would haul open both sides of his coat to the wide, revealing at least ten pockets on a side, all which contained a fine selection of the "necessary." Daddy-O had once told Wychway he'd bought the coat from a magician.

"You ain't gonna believe this, man," the cabbie confided, "but ol' Daddy-O's still goin' strong!"

"*What*?"

"Well, maybe not the one y'all remember, but his *son*! Or mebbe it's his grandson, I dunno," he added pensively. "But anyway, he's down there, still strollin' aroun' 10th an' 'V,' doin' business as usual. Course, they's a lotta them motherfuckin' *crackheads* down aroun' there too now, but ol' Daddy-O, he won't have nuffin' to do wit' *them*, he *hates* their sorry asses!"

"Do you think he'll be there tonight? I mean, after what happened and all?"

"Sheeet! he prob'ly don't even *know* about it!"

"Then do you think we could stop for just a minute, for old times' sake? I could use a jar of somethin' good, anyway."

"You got it! Always a pleasure to visit ol' Daddy-O!"

Wychway was comforted to know that Daddy-O II, or III, as the case might be, undoubtedly was upholding the fine tradition of paying commissions to serving taxi drivers. Less than a half-hour later, as Wychway began to relax in the welcome steam of the bath he took another small pull at the brandy bottle he'd purchased enroute. He reflected that it had been a mistake to have been so gregarious with the cabbie—it would give the man, well-intentioned as he unquestionably was, something concrete to remember him by—but he'd found that nostalgic little trip down memory lane (actually "V" Street, N.W.) irresistible. Drowsily he hoped he wouldn't live to regret his impetuous folly; and no, he told himself again, he'd never be a real pro....

He slept for three hours. When he awoke he went out to the locker room, retrieved his toilet articles from the small carry-on bag he'd stuffed into his valpac, and after he'd showered and shaved felt refreshed and ready for whatever might lie ahead. He made himself as presentable as possible in his well-tailored but again rumpled suit.

It was broad daylight when he left the bath house and walked to the all-night diner on the corner.

He took his coffee to the public phone in the corner and called one of the few companies which would be doing business on a Sunday, especially one of national mourning.

"That's right, Marion M. Riordan." Not for the first time in the last twelve hours he spoke a silent prayer while Marion's Mastercard balance was checked. Then he added a plea that the credit card company didn't have her middle name spelled out somewhere.

"Right. Good! Okay. Can I have it delivered? Oh. Well, the thing is, I'll be in conference right up until the time I have to leave Washington for Boston. Yeah, I know.... It's a goddam shame, but life goes on, as they say. He was kinda young, too, wasn't he? Yeah, I don't think he'd hit fifty yet. Well, at least from what they're saying he went fast. Yeah. Well anyway, listen, I just wouldn't have time to come down there and get it myself. What? No, I don't think I can do that either. I'll be happy to give him the cab fare though, so he can get back.

Would that be okay? (another small aspiration) Wonderful! Great! I want you to know I really appreciate this. In fact, I'm going to be traveling all over New England for the next month or two and I guarantee you I'll always use Hertz. What? Hertz-*Pensky*! When did that happen? Oh, hell, never mind. Okay, it's the Shoreham, up on Connecticut Avenue. In about a half-hour, okay? Right. I'll wait outside the main entrance. Thanks again." He hung up, got another dial tone, called for a cab, and then, nodding his head, *Yes!* went back to the counter for one more fast coffee.

Without much trouble he accepted the new Mercury Sable at the Shoreham (more nostalgia as he thought of the "two-suiter" bag of his student days, which just held a case of beer and which he'd used on many occasions when he'd attended those end-of-semester parties at the stately old hotel—Do you have any luggage, sir? Oh, yes! Right here!). Wychway never released Marion's driver's license as with his thumb over her birthdate and photograph he showed it briefly to the Hertz agent while distracting him with, "A damned shame about the President, isn't it?" He diverted any possible further curiosity with the exhorbitant tip he added to the cab fare. Another reason to remember me, however necessary under the circumstances, he told himself. A calculated risk, as the old saying goes.

At half-past eight he was halfway to Baltimore on I-95 listening to the news bulletins on WBAL. Two hours later, still heading north, he switched from I-83 to I-81, and switched the radio to a Harrisburg station. Shortly after noon he pulled off at Hazelton, where he remembered there was a good Italian restaurant. Having eaten virtually nothing for almost twenty-four hours (he couldn't resist a grin as he thought fleetingly of Marion) he felt ravenously hungry. But as he entered the restaurant he reminded himself that a real professional wouldn't do this; a real pro wouldn't eat now no matter how hungry he was, he'd just go on until he was out of the "zone" and relatively safe.

The place was redolent with good aromas, and with a sigh he looked around for an empty table. He was slightly startled when the first thing the waitress told him was that he was "lucky today." He let out his breath as she went on to say that if they hadn't had so much food on hand the boss would have closed the restaurant out of respect for the late President. As he watched the waitress return with his dish of *pasta* he recalled something else from that Ambler book. The two men who were escaping had eaten *pasta with a lot of bread!* More starch, more energy! he reasoned happily—and told the girl to bring him more bread.

When he finished his substantial lunch Wychway was feeling more exhilaration than the guilt, verging on contrition, he had experienced early that morning in Holy Trinity church. Undoubtedly the excellent wine which accompanied his meal helped this process. In fact his only real regret was that his most recent and illustrious victim could have had no idea why he'd been "targeted," to borrow a euphemistic word from among the hundreds in the good old Agency's lexicon. He recalled something a Sicilian friend of his had once told him. He'd said that true vengeance had three cardinal requirements: the person seeking vengeance should be present when retribution was taken; the victim should know precisely what transgression had led to his fate; and the method of punishment should fit the offense.[1] In Effingsly's case, and in Browning's as well for that matter, none of these conditions had been met Wychway thought unhappily as he reached for his cigarettes and his fingers came across the empty packet which had contained "Igor" Hoffmann's lethal "masterpiece."

Well, there *was* a certain aesthetic justice in the *modus operandi*, Wychway decided as he looked down at the torn and crumpled little piece of plastic in his palm. After all, it was "Igor's" agent (more specifically, reagent) that had done the job, and it had been the President who had given his approval,

---

[1] See "The Maine Coon Cat and the Tiger Snake" in *Antipodes 10* by John Pascal; American Literary Press, Baltimore, 1995.

however indirectly or tacitly, to Browning's nasty machinations. There was a little comfort in that at least.

And now he experienced a small *frisson* as he recalled how when he'd done what he'd had to do in that bathroom in Georgetown he had been tempted to expend one or two more frenetic minutes to leave hidden somewhere a message which would point, however cryptically, to the motivation behind the act, to the President's guilt and complicity. It was just then that Effingsly's bodyguard had knocked loudly on the door. Thank God for the arrogance of executive power, however derivative! Wychway smiled wanly to himself as he threw down his napkin, left enough money to cover the bill and a tip (this time sensible), and rose from his table.

As he bowled along Interstate 81 through the coal mining area of Pennsylvania, ever northward and at a good pace, he closed his left eye and sang a little First War trench ditty he'd learned while playing darts with his grandfather, a veteran of the Somme battle.

The bells of hell (he sang lustily) go ting a ling a ling,
For you but not for me,
And the little devils how they sing a ling a ling,
For you but not for me!
O death where is thy sting a ling a ling?
O grave thy victory?
The bells of hell go ting a ling a ling,
For you but not for me.

Meanwhile, an emergency meeting was being held in the office of the CIA Director at Langley. Present, in addition to the Director and his DDO, were the National Security Advisor, the Chief of the Secret Service, the Director of the FBI, the Chief of the Washington Metropolitan Police, a composite team of FBI and Secret Service forensic experts, and two other grim-looking scientists who represented, respectively, the Chemical Warfare Center at Edgewood Arsenal and its biological counterpart at Fort Dietrick. Hovering in the rear of the room was Harry Ward, the late Lew Browning's newly confirmed successor as Special Agent at Large in Charge of Special Operations. Ward had been flown in from Germany solely because he of all those present knew Wychway best.

The leader of the forensic team was speaking to the CIA Director.

"Apparently, his heart just stopped. We can't understand why. And that's all. He was perfectly fine when he had a physical last month. His body was absolutely 'clean,' inside and out; not a trace of a substance or a mark anywhere." He turned to the chemical-biological representatives. "Did your examinations of that bathroom reveal anything?"

The two men glanced at one another before the Dietrick man spoke.

"I'll speak for both of us. There was nothing. *Nada.* Not a trace of *any* kind of agent, and please believe me, we know 'em *all*. We took the place apart, literally. It was absolutely clean." He looked at his colleague. "You got anything you want to add, Fred?" The other shook his head.

"Have you found that son of a bitch, Wychway?" the FBI Director asked the Metro Police Chief.

"No, sir. We've combed D.C. and the surrounding areas, but there isn't a trace, yet. We've picked up the girl he left the party with, but she isn't saying anything except that he was a great piece of ass!"

"*What*?

"You want it verbatim?"

"Yeah."

The Chief ruffled the pages of a small notebook. "Here it is. She said, 'I didn't even know the guy. I met him at the party. He was cute so I asked him if he wanted to come over to my place after you guys let us go. All I *do* know is that he was a *great* piece of ass.' She emphasized 'great.' That's it. That's all we got out of her. Well, yeah, she did say, and again, I quote, 'If you keep up with this bullshit, I want a lawyer'."

"I think you should get a warrant and search her place," the Secret Service chief suggested.

"I agree," the FBI director said.

Four hours after he'd left the Italian restaurant, having decided it was time to stop using the main interstate highways, Wychway was driving through the foothills of the Adirondacks, on rural Route 12D in upstate New York. Though the fields were still covered with snow, the roads were dry. The bulletins he'd been listening to on the radio, now somewhat diminished in length and frequency, meant nothing, he knew. If "they" were looking for him they probably wouldn't go public, not yet anyway, but they might have dispatched a "quiet" APB.

Now, as he felt himself nodding, though reluctant to stop he decided that if he didn't the consequences of falling asleep at the wheel due to his increasing drowsiness might prove more dire than the risk of being recognized and possibly apprehended for—

For what? he asked himself. Disobeying a police order to remain in Washington? What could they prove? Well, if "Igor" had been right (and he'd certainly been right about the lethality of his product) they couldn't prove a thing except that he'd been at the party; and yes, that he'd used the bathroom just before the President did. Of course, there would be the nuisance of going back to Washington and so on, but that would just be inconvenient, nothing worse. *If Igor had gotten it right.*

The dashboard clock told him him it was four o'clock. He had been on the road for almost eight hours. Yes, he would take a short coffee break before going on.

Within less than a mile he passed a sign which proclaimed:

Hilltop Tavern & Restaurant

and promised:

Fine Spirits and a Great View
Best Sunday Brunch in Lewis County
Rooms Available by Reservation
5 miles

Chapter Twenty-eight

Sanctuary

The Hilltop was an attractive-looking place, surrounded by shrubs and spruce trees and with, as the name implied, a spectacular view of the Adirondack Mountains. Now as he pulled into the parking lot he saw an interesting assortment of vehicles: a couple of Harley Davidson motorcycles, several half-ton pickup trucks, a few cars (all American models), and even a four-wheeler. He noticed that the large American flag outside the entrance was flying at full hoist; everywhere else he'd seen it as he'd driven north it had been half-staffed.

Wychway went in through the bar entrance, where a brass plate told him the place had been "Built in 1837." The cool, semi-lit interior of the Hilltop Tavern was appropriately paneled entirely in Adirondack pine. Three men were seated at the far end of the solid-looking mahogany bar. From another room came the gentle click of pool balls. The TV mounted on the wall at the end of the bar was going strong with the same hashed-over reports of the "tragedy." The time of his arrival was fortuitously well-timed, he decided. Though it was Sunday the brunch crowd had gone and the early evening diners had yet to arrive.

He pushed a stool aside and stood waiting with his elbows resting on the glossy bar. When the attractive and vivacious young barwoman came over to him he said:

"Can I just get some coffee?"

"Sure, but you're lucky we're even open," she said as she nodded towards the TV. "I was going to close, but Billy Jack, or as they call him around here, His Imperial Majesty, isn't—I should say, wasn't—greatly loved by the local folks, so we're open by popular demand." She got the coffee pot and poured him a cup.

"Yeah, I noticed your flag isn't half-staffed. Are you the Boss, by the way?"

"Uh, huh; but Jesus, I don't dare run it down! Those guys down at the other end of the bar would start a riot, to say nothing of the one's in the pool room. We get some tourists in summer and later for the foliage, and then we get swamped with snowmobilers during the winter, and in those groups we meet all kinds. But the local people are mostly one way. They're mainly farmers and woodsmen—tough, honest people. It takes a while for them to trust you and accept you, but once they do they'd die for you. On the other hand," she chuckled pleasantly, "their political convictions are a little to the right of Genghis Khan's, if you get what I'm saying. It isn't that they're stupid—far from it—but they'd rather watch sports on TV 'cause they think that's a little more honest (except maybe for the wrestling) than the news and most of the bleeding heart talk shows. And Washington and all the crap that goes on there might as well be on the dark side of the moon as far as they're concerned."

Wychway chuckled as she refilled his coffee cup. He took an immediate liking to this intelligent if somewhat effusive girl.

"My father always does that," she said as he pushed a bar stool a little further away.

"Does what, move furniture?" he asked facetiously.

"Stands at the bar. He said they didn't have barstools in a lot of the countries he was in, so he got used to standing. And he said he got used to standing around a lot when he was in the army."

"Wychway laughed. "Is that his green beret hanging up over there by the cash register?"

"Yep. I found it in an old army footlocker full of his stuff he left here. I take it down when I hear he's coming for a visit. He doesn't like to see it anymore."

"That's interesting. Was he in Vietnam, by any chance?"

"Oh, yeah! Twice. He got hurt pretty bad over there on his last tour so he got a medical discharge. I mean, he's okay and all that, but not good enough for, for—what the hell do they call it?"

"Unlimited duty?"

"That's it! He couldn't see himself sitting at a desk."

"Good on him! Could I ask his name?"

"Meraviglia, Michael Mera—"

Wychway put his coffee down. "*Who* did you say? Meraviglia? *Mike* Meraviglia? Are we talking about Captain *Marvel*[1] here?"

"That's *him!*"

"Good Lord! I *know* him. I mean, I *knew* him, in Vietnam. We were friends! Well, he was an officer, and I was only a crummy sergeant, but we were still good friends. Hell, he's the one who started me learning Italian! And if it weren't for him chances are I wouldn't have made it back. I don't mean he saved my life or anything like that, but if he hadn't taught me a few things—mostly how to stay alive—I'm not sure I would've made it out of there." He laughed good-humoredly, "As it was, I damned near didn't, anyway. Where is he now, by the way? We just lost touch after they medevaced me out of there."

"He's in Kona, in Hawaii. He remarried. Of course, you probably didn't even know my mother. She died a few years ago. Anyway, he married the wife of the guy who was his commanding officer in Vietnam on his last tour."

Wychway thought for moment. "Knox. Julia Knox," he murmured reminiscently but audibly to himself.

"Yep, that's her. Boy, you *do* know him, don't you?"

Wychway nodded, recalling any number of things. "Lis-

[1] See "Captain Marvel" in *Antipodes 10* by John Pascal; American Literary Press, Baltimore, 1995.

ten—by the way, what's *your* name? Cindy? Okay, Cindy, I can't stay very long; I wish I could, but I can't, so could you give me Mike's address out there in Hawaii?"

"Sure, but I think I can do better than that," she replied as she reached for the cordless phone under the bar. "Let's give him a call."

A few minutes later Wychway had finished an enthusiastic conversation with his old friend. "He wants to talk to you again, Cindy."

"Yeah, Daddy? Yeah, he is," she looked across at Wychway who was still smiling to himself. "Yeah, I got it, Daddy, loud and clear. When are you coming for a visit? Oh. Okay. How's Julia? Good. Me too. Okay, bye. I love you, too." She kissed the phone and hung up.

"Boy! you must be one of the chosen few. He never talks about *anybody* like that. He said to give you anything you want, except me, of course," she giggled, "and he stressed 'anything'."

"I'll tell you, Cindy, your father's a piece of work, if you'll permit me to butcher Shakespeare a little. I guess it's been all of twenty years since I saw him last, but after hearing his voice it's like it was yesterday. Did he ever talk to you about Vietnam at all?"

"Only the funny stories."

"Yeah, that's him. Like the beret. Would you like to hear one more funny story, about him in Nam, I mean?" Cindy nodded a smile.

"Well, one night in '68, right after Tet, the two of us were being flown from Long Binh to Dalat in a small army airplane. I don't remember why just now. Anyhow, It was a helluva bumpy ride, all the way. The third passenger was a big young second lieutenant—he looked like he must've played football for somebody— anyway, he was hanging on to his bucket seat and beginning to turn a little pale.

"So your old man gives me the hint of a wink and says to this guy, 'Why don't you get on the intercom and ask the pilot if he can climb out of all this turbulence, Lieutenant?' 'The intercom?' says this second balloon kinda weakly, 'what intercom? I didn't think this bird *had* an intercom.' And believe me, Cindy, he was absolutely right. This plane *had* no intercom. 'Oh, *yeah*, sure it does,' says Mike, 'it's that voice tube over there in the rear of the plane,' he explains, pointing to the (can you stand one crude word? Yeah, I guess you've heard 'em all in here), well, pointing to the piss tube that's used in military aircraft that're too small for proper toilets. It's almost identical to the speaking tubes you still find on the bridge on some ships—a black rubber hose which ends in a cone-shaped black plastic cup about three inches in diameter, and it's clamped about waist high to the side of the plane. It was hanging right behind this guy.

"So then Mike says, 'Just blow into it a couple of times and say, "Passenger to pilot! Passenger to pilot!" in a good loud voice a couple of times, and then hold it to your ear to get his answer.'! Well, the lieutenant tried this a few times and shook his head. 'No good,' he says. By this time your father's lookin' like if he tried to talk he'd die laughing, so I chipped in with 'Well, Lieutenant, you know how it is in these small crates—' just as the co-pilot comes back, picks up the tube, and takes a whiz in it!"

Cindy laughed lustily at this, then recovering asked:

"It's Charley, right? You never told me your name, but that's what Daddy said, Charley Whichway. Is that a joke, that 'Whichway'?" she raised her elbows to shoulder height and pointed in opposite directions.

"Yeah, well," Wychway spoke quietly, laughing a little nervously and glancing down the bar as he did so, "you've got the pronunciation right, but the first part is actually spelled W-Y-C-H. But," he hurried on, "right now I'd prefer that nobody but us knows that, Cindy. For the time being I'm using the name Riordan, Mr. Riordan. It's a little hard to explain but—"

"Are you running from the law, or something?" she asked lowering her voice a couple of octaves.

"Not exactly, but I've got a little problem. I can't be too specific, but believe me, I haven't done anything your father would be ashamed of (I hope, he reserved mentally), and that I can tell you for a fact."

"Tell me what I can do, Charley," she said looking him straight in the eye. "My father said, 'anything,' and to me, when my old man speaks—"

Just then one of the men down the bar bellowed at the TV: "'Unknown causes' my ass! The candy-assed mother fucker shoulda been stood up against a wall and shot!" Wychway couldn't say he was displeased to hear this forceful and colorful opinion. In a kindlier tone the voice added, "Hey Cindy, sweetheart, how 'bout another coupla Buds?"

When she returned Wychway asked in a voice just above a whisper, "How far is Canada from here, Cindy?"

"Canada? A couple of hours, I guess, maybe even less. Why?" she answered as quietly.

"That's where I gotta go. But I don't think I can get there by the usual means. At least not in that rented Sable I've got parked outside. Which reminds me: I don't suppose you'd have a garage or a barn I could stash that crate in, would you?"

"You bet! Just pull around back and I'll meet you there." Cindy signaled to a waitress to replace her behind the bar while Wychway did as he was told.

With the car safely hidden they met again in the bar.

"How about a drink? You look like you could use one." Wychway was grateful Cindy wasn't using his name anymore.

"I agree. Just put a little bar brandy in my coffee, Cindy."

When she'd done that she said: "I'm not sure what's gonna be involved, but I think we're gonna need a little help with this."

"I'm sure you're right. Is there anybody around we can trust?"

"Well, you heard that loudmouth down the bar a little while ago. The tall, tough looking guy. He's thirty-five but looks ten years older. Three-quarters Anglo-American and one quarter Mohawk Indian, or so he says. His name's Harry, and he is a loudmouth, but he's a very smart and capable one.

What's more important is he's absolutely loyal to me. If any-body acts up in here and Harry's here I've got a built-in bounc-er. We can trust him."

"Can you get me next to him?"

"Do you play darts?" Cindy asked after a moment's thought.

"Yeah, sometimes. I haven't played in quite a while," he closed his left eye and surveyed the very normal-looking array of bottles on the shelf behind his attractive companion and smiled wryly. "I've even got a set of darts out in my luggage somewhere. "

"No need. Besides, your car's locked up in the barn. I sell darts here," she reached under the bar, "and I want you to have these, as a gift. I gave my father a set just like these on his last birthday," she handed Wychway a leather case.

"Oh, come *on* now, Cindy!" Wychway exclaimed as he opened the case and examined the darts, "these are the best tung-sten 'arrows' money can buy. They've gotta be worth at least—"

"Never mind what they're worth," she interrupted cheer-fully, "I want you to have them. At least you know good darts when you see them. Now listen. Ask Harry to play a game. He loves to be challenged. It's quiet back there where the board is, and you'll be able to talk. But let me say a word to him first."

"Waddya wanna play?" asked Harry as Wychway fitted flights to his dart barrels.

"Is 301 okay?"

"Sure. Shoot for who goes first." As he stood back to give Wychway more room he added inconsequently, "Listen, man, I don't give a shit *what* you done, long as it ain't got nothin' to do with drugs or child pornography."

"No, nothing like that," Wychway supplied as he threw his dart at the cork. "What would you do if I said I 'offed' Billy Jack Effingsly, though," he added with a careless grin.

"Do? Shit!" Harry laughed, "I'd deed my goddam dairy farm over to you! Goddam! I wish *I'd* a done it! Anyhow," he went on more seriously, "if Cindy says you need help, you got it. What *is* the deal, anyway?" He threw his dart, and got closer to the bull than his opponent had. They started, and the game continued apace.

"I've gotta get across into Canada tonight—like, before sun up tomorrow."

"Whut's wrong with just goin'?" Harry asked reasonably. "Hell, I been up there a hundred times. All's you need is your driver's license."

And now, after swearing him to secrecy, Wychway explained just enough of his problem to Harry as to make his situation plausible. He told him he had incontrovertible and documented inside information on CIA operations directed against innocent civilians both in the US and overseas (which, he told himself, was close enough to the truth, barring his threatened invocation of his by now notorious MFR), which operations might cost those people their freedom and even their lives. Every moment he remained in the US he was risking death. From time to time Harry nodded seriously and intelligently as the other went on with this.

Harry beat Wychway at the dartboard two games out of three, which pleased Wychway, not least because he now was playing normally and honestly without the "advantage" of Bigeye.

"Lemme do some thinkin' over this. I'll get back to you a little later. Meanwhile I think it'd be a good idea if we stay separated for a while," was all Harry would say as they went back to the bar.

The search of Marion's apartment, to include the contents of her shoulder bag, produced paid Mastercard receipts but no credit card; and though she had a car parked outside which was registered in her name she could produce no driver's license.

Within a very short time after the police began checking the car rental agencies in the Washington area an APB requesting the apprehension of one Marion M. Riordan, with Wychway's description, last known to be driving a new, red, Mercury Sable with such and such a license number, was disseminated through all outlets. The bulletin dictated that no public disclosure was to be made of this search.

At FBI headquarters in Washington Harry Ward, still playing his role as "expert advisor" on Charles Wychway, was listening to a conversation between two of the agents who had been assigned to find Wychway.

"He told the Hertz guy he was going north, to New England, so I suppose we we should concentrate the search in the south, right?"

"Bullshit. That's just what he'd want us to think. Otherwise, why would he make it such a point to tell 'em where he was going? The bastard ain't stupid, right, Harry?" Ward grimly agreed. "He went north. Alert the Canadian border guards, too."

"The question that burns my ass is, what do we *charge* him with even if we do get him? Obstruction of justice? Shit, there's not even any proof that any *in*justice was done." the other FBI agent said.

"Maybe nothin', all right? But we're gonna make his life as miserable as possible. And if we can find the rest of those MFR copies we're gonna do a lot more to him."

Unable to contain himself any longer Ward spat out, "Goddamit, I *know* he did it! He offed Lew Browning, and now he's done the President. I *know* it!"

The senior FBI man looked at Ward a little doubtfully.

"Yeah, we know all about Browning, Harry, but as far as last night goes, if we don't know *how* he did it how're you gonna prove it?"

As Ward gave the man an angry glare another agent hurried into the office. "He was in Hazelton—that's in Pennsylvania—at a restaurant, around noon."

"Yeah, it was north all right," the senior agent looked at the wall clock, but goddammit! that was eight hours ago!"

At about the same time, after he'd met Scott Matthews, Cindy's handsome husband, who had been away on business all day, Wychway was sitting down to an excellent dinner of prime rib accompanied by a bottle of Montepulciano d' Abruzzo which, Cindy told him, she always kept in stock in the event her father showed up.

"An outstanding wine," Wychway commented as Jackie, his waitress, poured the wine while Cindy stood by approvingly. "It's from Alan Alda's ancestral region in Italy, you know? In fact, his real name actually is Alphonso d' Abruzzo."

"That flamin' feminist," Jackie muttered.

"That isn't exactly politically correct, Jackie," Cindy admonished humorously, to which the girl, having finished with the wine, left with a muttered but explicit:

"Fuck a bunch of political correctness." Wychway was not surprised to discover later that Jackie was Harry's girlfriend.

Back in the FBI building another bulletin had just come in.

"He's in upstate New York, near the Adirondacks. They've been combing the area since he was spotted at a gas station in some fuckin' burg called Boonville—can you believe that name?—a couple of hours ago; but now he seems to have vanished, or at least the goddam car has! The New York State cops said if that Sable was on a road, *any* road, *anywhere* up there, they'd have it by now."

"Check 'is records. See if he knows anybody up there— relations, friends, whatever, as far back as you can go in his miserable fuckin' life!"

After a brief conversation with his wife Scott Matthews joined Wychway at his table for coffee and brandy. When they'd finished Scott escorted Wychway—who now, after the tensions of the last twenty-four hours, combined with little sleep, an eight-hour drive, and the prodigious meal he'd just eaten, could hardly keep his eyes open—to an unoccupied guest room on the inn's second floor.

"There's no need to lock your door around here," Scott told him as he left. "You'll find a toothbrush and some other stuff in the bathroom. Good night, whatever your name is," he smiled, "and good luck!"

A few minutes later there was a soft knock on the door and Harry came in carrying Wychway's valpac. "You know how to drive a motorcycle?" he asked without preamble.

"Yeah. I had one once in my wild and woolly days," the other answered as he stretched wearily. "Why?"

"You're gonna be drivin' one after a while tonight, or maybe tomorra mornin'. Now listen a minute," he stopped the next question with a gesture. "Be ready to go at two A.M. — Here's an alarm clock from Cindy. Now, that Sable out in the barn—are the rental papers in it?" Wychway nodded. "Okay, no sweat. Tomorrow a guy's gonna turn it in, at the airport in Syracuse. He's about your size and build, by the way, but a little younger. Is he gonna have to pay for it?—the car, I mean."

"No. It's on a credit card. All your friend's gotta do is sign the Mastercard charge slip. The name's Marion M. Riordan, but he'll see that when he checks out the rental papers. It's Hertz, by the way"

"Good. When he turns the car in he's gonna ask the Hertz agent if Syracuse has flights to Hawaii. They do—Cindy goes out of there to visit her ol' man once in a while. Then—unless the Law's covering all the Hertz places in this area and they collar him—he'll go to a phone an' book a flight on United to Hawaii in that Riordan name, so it'll be on their computer, got it?" Wychway nodded again, this time with a smile. "You got that credit card you rented the car with? Good. Lemme have it." Wychway handed it over, along with Marion's driver's license. Harry glanced at the credit card, then inspected the license more carefully. "Jesus! four-feet ten? Ninety-five pounds? Strawberry blond? Date o' birth, 1972! Goddam! I'll tell you one thing, man: you got balls!"

"Yeah," Wychway grinned, "but that's part of the problem. It would have been a little embarrassing if I'd been picked up. She wears a size three dress, and has to do most of her shopping in children's stores. But she *is* a real cute handful."

"The kind that climbs on an' you spin her around on it, right?" Harry grinned lecherously. "Real strawberry blonde, ol' buddy?" For a fleeting moment Wychway remembered the late, wretched, Duwayne Link of similar lewd remarks, and the look on his face must have been enough for Harry.

"Okay, okay, too personal, right? Sorry 'bout that. But look here," he went on more seriously, "I don't think we'll need this license just to turn the car in."

"I know, but what I'd like you to do, if it isn't too big a pain in the ass, is mail it back to her, along with that credit card. Could you or your friend do that for me? Her address'll be on the credit card chit."

"Yeah, no sweat. *He* can do it, unless they put the arm on 'im. As for 'yours truly,' I don't think I'm going to be around here for a while," he grinned. After I get *your* ass away I might just go off an' do a little fishin' somewhere.

"Now, I don't give a shit what your real name is," Harry continued as he looked levelly at the other with his steel-gray eyes, "or about this other name you're usin', but do you have *real* ID for when you get into Canucksville?" Another nod. "Okay. I'll be back at two. Try to get some sleep; I think you're gonna need it."

Wychway set the alarm clock, then showered, shaved, and went to bed.

Harry arrived punctually, and shortly after two they were downstairs where, since two A.M. was closing time and Cindy was still there, Wychway was able to bid her goodbye and to express his gratitude, however inadequate he felt it to be under the circumstances.

"Can I tell my father about all this?" Cindy asked.

"Maybe later. Wait until you hear from me, okay? I'll write him too, when I'm out of this."

He promised to call her when he was "clear." And with that and a quick farewell brandy he followed Harry out the door to the parking lot.

A few minutes later, with the contents of Wychway's luggage stored in the Harley's "saddle bags" and with the worn canvas valpac folded and crammed in as well, they were thundering northward at about eighty miles an hour. Wychway, now wearing jeans, boots, and jacket, was glad to have Harry's broad back as a windscreen. His benefactor certainly had taken Cindy's final injunction seriously: "Go, like the wind, Harry!"

"Where'd you say we were goin'?" Wychway screamed over the roar.

"Massena!" Harry shouted back over his shoulder.

After about an hour they pulled off the deserted road for a smoke break. Wychway dismounted and rooted in one of the saddle bags for his flask and offered it to his companion.

"Want a jolt?"

"No thanks. No more fire water for me until the job's done." Harry dug out his cigarettes as he told Wychway:

"I got a fourteen-foot skiff with a 125 Merc engine parked up in Massena, on the St. Lawrence; my buddy and me use it fer fishin' an' water skiin'," he said as he cupped a light for Wychway's cigarette. "It's on a trailer in my buddy's garage—he's the one that's gonna do the Sable trick, by the way. He won't be home tonight—he's doin' construction down in Utica. We'll cross over from Massena, and I'll land you and the Harley a little east of Cornwall, a little Canuck town just across from Massena. The expressway's just a few pecker-lengths from there, and Montreal's no more'n seventy miles to the northeast. Unless you fall off my bike you'll be there by the time they open them Frog cafay-o-lay shops," he laughed. "Just leave the Harley in the long-term parkin' lot at the airport. Keep the key, an' mail it and any parkin' charge ticket to Cindy later. I got an extra key. Oh, yeah, I almost forgot—here's the registration."

Wychway nodded his comprehension of all this as he put the card in his pocket; then slowly shook his head in wonder and admiration of this "diamond in the rough."

"I never got your last name, Harry."

"I never gave it to you. It's Clinton."

"You mean like—"

"Yep, just like *him*—but in name only," he said noncommittally but evocatively as he flipped his cigarette away and moved towards the motorcycle. As they prepared to remount he asked: "You wanna do the last leg to Massena, as a little practice run?"

Wychway shook his head. "No, I'm sure I'll be able to handle it. Besides, you know these roads better'n I do. Let's go."

At eight A.M. on the Monday morning the FBI agent who had been sent to search records walked into his supervisor's office reading a file.

"He was tight with some guy from around there named Meraviglia (he pronounced it Mera *vig* (as in jig) lee ah) in Nam, twenty-some years ago; but this Meraviglia has been living in Hawaii for the last three or four years."

"Does this walyo Meraviglia have any relatives up there?"

"Well according to this, his daughter owns a place up near the Adirondacks. He turned it over to her when he moved to Hawaii. It's called the Hilltop Tavern."

It had been almost too easy, Wychway thought as he roared along the Canadian expressway towards Montreal.

They had reached Harry's friend's place at Massena at four A.M. and Harry had unlocked a large garage in which was parked the trailered boat and an old but very serviceable half-ton Ford Ranger. Hitching the trailer to the truck and connecting the tail light wires was the work of minutes. Getting the Harley into the boat was more difficult, but they managed this by main force, using a heavy plank and some rope, both of which they then put into the skiff.

By five o'clock they were at the boat slip on the St. Lawrence River. Three-quarters of an hour later they had unloaded the Harley, using the same plank and rope, in a small cove Harry had somehow managed to find in almost total darkness. After he'd secured the boat's painter to a concrete block he'd found lying on the tiny beach, Harry helped Wychway push the heavy motorcycle up a slightly inclined path to a level dirt road. Rapidly he supplied a few whispered instructions on how to find the riverside expressway (they could hear the heavier truck traffic) which would take Wychway to Montreal. When they'd said their final goodbyes it was a little after six A.M. Thanks to Harry, the gray-eyed Mohawk, as Wychway had come to think of him, it had been that simple.

Now, as he racketed down the expressway, he glanced down at his watch and reckoned that in less than half an hour he'd be at the airport. Don't gloat, for Christ's sake, don't gloat, yet, he told himself as he glanced in the rear-view mirror—and caught his breath as saw the police car, with lights flashing, that was coming up fast.

When the FBI, accompanied by the Lewis County Sheriff, arrived at the Hilltop Tavern at nine o'clock that Monday morning Cindy was still enjoying a well-deserved rest in her apartment above the restaurant. A buzzer near her bed woke her and told her she was wanted in the bar. Like a ship's Captain being called to the bridge, her father had chided her once.

When she arrived downstairs in a kimono her waitress-cum-bartender, Jackie Carpenter, who had been sweeping out the place, was saying to a man in a gray three-piece suit:

"A guy in a Mercury Sable? Jeez, I wish I had five bucks for every guy who pulls in in a Sable—I could be retired by now. Christ! I wish *I* could afford a Sable," she added wistfully as she started to go back to her sweeping.

"Please look at this picture, Jackie," the man persisted patiently as Cindy approached, rubbing the sleep from her eyes. Jackie studied the blown up, black and white, eight-by-ten file photo of Charles Wychway as the man introduced himself to Cindy as the Agent in Charge of the FBI's Syracuse Field Office.

"Has either of you seen this man? About six-two, a hundred and eighty-five pounds, brown hair, blue eyes, about forty-five years old?"

Cindy shook her head as if mystified as Jackie exclaimed: "Goddam, what a hunk! I should *be* so lucky! I'll tell ya, man, if I ever did see this dude, 'specially if he was drivin' a new Sable, I'd get down on my knees and ask him to take me away from this goddam place!"

"I don't recall having said it was a *new* Sable, Jackie," the man said smoothly.

"Well, shit! I don't see *this* guy drivin' anything *but* a new one, do you?" Jackie replied without missing a beat.

Before the agent could respond to this deft riposte one of his subordinates who had been speaking quietly over a cellular phone came up to him urgently.

"'Scuse me, Boss, but our boy just turned in his car at the Syracuse airport. There's more," with a glance at Cindy and Jackie he beckoned the man away. "He was asking about flights to Hawaii at the Hertz office," he said quietly when they were out of earshot. "United flies there out of Syracuse through Chicago. We're checking with them now."

The agent in charge turned back to the two young women and began to say something, then shook his head decisively. "The hell with it—let's go!"

Wychway heaved a great sigh of relief as the Canadian police car passed him; obviously in pursuit of some other malefactor, he smiled to himself.

Twenty minutes later he pulled into the airport long-term parking lot. Five minutes after that he had repacked and was entering the terminal building.

"You remember what he did with that 'north-south' red herring, right?" Harry Ward cautioned back in the "situation room" at FBI headquarters in Washington. "Maybe he just wants us to *think* he's going out to Hawaii. All he did was book a ticket, right?"

"The flight doesn't leave for another hour, Harry, so we might as well be sure. We're going to be all over both airports

like a cheap suit. If he goes, and we miss him in Syracuse—
which we couldn't do even if we had a fuckin' missing
machine—we'll get him in Chicago. I dunno though," the
agent mused, "I kinda wouldn't mind if he *did* make it out to
the Islands; I haven't been there in years."

"Bear's ass! Your guys in Honolulu'd pick him up. They
wouldn't let *your* sorry ass go," the other answered grudgingly.

"Ward, all I can say to you is, if you can find a taxidermist
who'd be willing to take on the rather odious job, why don't
you go get stuffed?"

Although Wychway was tempted, fleetingly, to spend a day or
two enjoying the pleasures of Montreal (except for J.D.'s place
in London he hadn't really enjoyed any kind of civilized environment for six months) he made the sober decision to go while
the going was still good. Who knew what kinds of shady recip-
rocal deals the Agency had with their Canadian counterparts?

He was in time to have his choice of two available flights to
London: Canadian Pacific via Toronto, or Northwest via Detroit.
Understandably he chose the former. When the Canadian Pacific
ticket agent looked up from his passport she said sympathetically, "I'm sorry about President Effingsly, Mr. Wychway."

Just before his flight was announced he called The Hilltop
from a public phone and told Cindy he was all right and would
write to her from his "next stop."

He would take care of the other loose ends when he got to
London, he assured himself as he replaced the receiver.

Epilogue

When he arrived at Gatwick he was met by J.D. and Magda, who told him that Hans had gone back to Iraq "for a time." Of interest was the news that Hans was staying with Ekbal and Camille Mahmoud at their Baghdad residence until he could find suitable accommodations of his own. Hans's explanations to the Mahmouds about that last day in Al-Basrah no doubt would be interesting also.

From London Wychway sent Marion a certified check for a thousand dollars, with which he enclosed a note of thanks and apology and the message: "If United didn't credit you with a refund for 'your' ticket to Hawaii, the enclosed check should cover your loss. I wish I could have loved you less briefly."

He wrote to Cindy more formally, expressing his gratitude and telling her, without being too explicit, of his great indebtedness to Harry.

He enclosed a copy of the explanatory letter he'd written to her father, which also was a little vague.

A week after he arrived in London, at Somerville's Bayswater flat where he and Magda were staying temporarily, he was visited by a personal representative of the CIA director. The representative was extremely civil as he told Wychway that the investigation into the President's death was closed, absolutely. "Actually," he confided, "Billy Jack won't be terribly missed. In fact, he was becoming a positive embarrassment to his Party. The Vice President—well, actually I *should* say, the new President—isn't a better man, but at least he comes in with a clean slate, so to speak. But in any case that probably won't do him much good in next fall's election. With Effingsly gone his political machine is in total disarray."

Having made that surprisingly forthright appraisal he went on to ask if Wychway would be amenable to being posted, with a significant promotion of course, to head the DDI's European Desk at the Langley headquarters. Just as civilly Wychway told the man that for the present at least he would not return to the States under any circumstances. "In fact," he said, "I'd be delighted if you weren't here, but as long as you are you might as well take this letter of resignation back with you."

"By the way," the Agency man asked smiling as put the letter away and rose to leave, "How'd you do it?"

"Well," Wychway replied with a smile of his own as he rose also, "assuming I *had* done it—whatever you mean by *it*—it wouldn't be wise for me to be too specific, would it? —I mean, you never know who might want to get rid of his wife, or her husband, and get away with it. Be advised, however—and be sure to carry this news back with you—that if there *had* been a way of doing what I think you're suggesting *I* did, the 'how' of it would be no more, it would have died with its victim, and should remain one of history's mysteries." He extended his hand. "Give my regards to all 'the boys,' especially to 'Bill'— you know, the good ol' boy who was Effinglsy's advisor?"

Two days later "Bill" was discovered in *flagrante delicto* with Norma Rae Effingsly, the former FLOTUS, in a second-rate Washington hotel. Both parties in the love tryst were, according to the British press, "quite nude and extremely intoxicated on alcohol and drugs." (Was this Britain's revenge for US press coverage of the steamy John Profumo-Christine Keeler affair thirty years earlier? Wychway wondered.)

A week after that, with J.D. giving the bride away and Hans as Best Man, Wychway and Magda were married in a small London church.

A month later, Wychway, who with his new wife was living in her old cottage at Ipswich, received an affirmative reply to his application for a teaching position in the English department of a small College on Cape Cod. Three months after they left England and moved to the Cape, in time for Wychway to start the fall semester, Magda had been delivered of a lusty eight-pound boy. When they had arrived in America Magda found a letter from Margaret Feldon which had followed her from England and which revealed that she, Feldon, was teaching in Kenya where she had taken up residence with "an old 'spinster' school chum." There was less bitterness than a certain weariness in the letter, Magda told her husband.

As it turned out life on the Cape with his wife and thriving little son was extremely good and serene for Wychway. At least until that iron-cold and snowy night in late December when he killed Harry Ward in the parking lot of a North Falmouth pub called The British Embassy.

As was his custom once a week Wychway had been playing darts, happily using his normal skills and the excellent darts which Cindy Matthews had given him. While awaiting his turn at the dartboard in the warmth and comfort of the pub and with a pint of Watney's close to hand, he had read with pleasure in the *Boston Globe* about a certain Hajji Abdullah El Shaka (Hans's real name)—who, it will be remembered (according to the *Globe*), had not long ago refused an extremely lucrative offer by Lord Henry Brynthroppe, Third Earl of Thistlewaite and former advisor to the then Republic of Vietnam's Ministry of Finance, to manage his vast holdings in Great Britain and Southeast Asia—had accepted, now that Saddam Hussein had been peacefully deposed and was living in exile in Libya, an appointment by the newly-established constitutional government of Iraq to head its Economic Council. A "side bar" article revealed that Iraq's armed forces, now a quarter of a million strong, were in the process of being newly reorganized under the guidance of a Colonel Politano (Hans's old "polwar" friend from Vietnam, no doubt), a retired US Army officer and student of military affairs who now resided in Iraq. That *couldn't* be his real name, Wychway had mused—political warfare, police, politics, and so on—it must be contrived.

He also had read with interest on an inside page that newly-elected President Wilbur Claxton would make a state visit to Iraq soon after the Christmas holidays.

Coincidentally, a small piece on a back page announced the termination of the investigation into the probable murder of one Charles Duwayne Link, which might have involved the possible complicity of one Lewis Browning, Link's late supervisor. The investigation, which had been a *cause célèbre* for several months, though now closed had stirred a medium-grade witch hunt which still continued at the Langley headquarters of the CIA.

Seldom, thought Wychway as he'd put the paper down and gone to the dartboard, had one edition of a newspaper held, in his opinion at least, such good news all around.

Later that night, having won his share of games and drunk perhaps a little more than his share of good English ale, he left the pub feeling jolly.

In the parking lot, hunched against the cold, Ward had been waiting for him. Perhaps it was merely that that had saved Wychway's life: the fact of Ward's literally being stiff with cold. Simply enough, after a brief scuffle Wychway had shot Ward twice in the chest, with the would be assassin's own .38 Smith & Wesson revolver; then he'd gone straight back to the pub and called the police.

The police held Wychway briefly for questioning that night, then released him; and he was cleared of any wrongdoing at the subsequent inquest. Even if all the evidence hadn't pointed to self defense—paraffin tests, weapon registration, fingerprints—there were the two lovers in a nearby parked car who had witnessed the brief struggle and had come forward to tell what they saw.

In any case a flood of assurances came to him from Washington next day—by telegram, telephone, and even by personal messenger—telling him, virtually imploring him, to understand that Ward had been a "loose cannon" acting on his own, seeking personal vengeance for the death of his "former leader." In return Wychway told them what he wanted.

The next day's press reports had it "on the highest government authority" that Harry Ward, "a former CIA employee who recently had been discharged from the Agency for "exhibiting unbalanced and renegade tendencies" had mistaken Wychway, on that "cold, dark, and snowy night" for "someone else, against whom he harbored a grudge for some imagined slight or injustice."

Wychway, Magda, and young Charles continued to live happily on Cape Cod. During school breaks they went for prolonged visits to the Adirondacks (where Harry Clinton now proudly drove the new Harley Wychway had insisted on buying him). Less frequently they went to England, Hawaii, or Iraq to visit friends.

Yes, it was virtually idyllic, until just a year after the Ward incident Wychway suffered a sudden cataclysmic stroke induced by a massive subdural hematoma. No one in medical science, including the best neuropathologists in Boston, could explain what had happened, what had caused the hematoma.

No one, except perhaps an obscure young doctor-scientist who worked in a covert research and development laboratory near Langley, Virginia, who could have told those Boston men that the cause was the discreet use of the product developed to satisfy QHR (CO) 01/02/96-23 or, in laymen's language, an untraceable agent to be used in clandestine operations.

Magda derived cold comfort from the knowledge that just a few days before his stroke the local parish priest had heard her husband's confession.

Wychway lived on in a semi-comatose state for five more years.

J.D.F. Somerville never released Wychway's all-revealing memorandum for record. When, not long after Wychway's death, he himself died of natural causes, his solicitor opened his letter; then, upon clearing out his safety deposit box at the Bank of England, he destroyed all the additional copies of the MFR.

Glossary

Abwehr   German intelligence organization from 1920 (when it was revitalized in defiance of the Versailles Treaty) to1945, when the Nazi regime was defeated in the second World War.

AMEMB   American Embassy.

AP   Antipersonnel

baksheesh   Tip, gratuity; in this case an outright bribe.

Black box   Any relatively complex device, usually electronic, used to accomplish a certain task, such as detonating a device remotely.

BMNT, EENT   Beginning morning nautical twilight, end of evening nautical twilight. The period of subdued light just before sunrise or after sunset when the sun is not more than 1.2 degrees below the horizon.

BND   Bundesnachrichtdienst. German intelligence service.

BOQ   Bachelor Officers' Quarters

BTB   Blind transmission broadcast. Transmitting at a predetermined date and time and only for very short periods and not expecting or receiving acknowledgement; used when there's threat of enemy interception and capture or worse as a result of clandestine radio operation.

C.G.   Commanding general.

CARP   Coordinated air release point.

CAS   Controlled American Source. CIA-handled spies in foreign countries.

CAT scan   Computerized Axial Tomography.

Chieu Hoi   In Vietnamese, "Open Arms"; a program where enemy soldiers were induced by any number of means to defect to the South Vietnamese government's side.

CID   Criminal investigation division of military (or other) police.

Circus   British intelligence.

Class "C" phone   "On-base" telephone which will take incoming calls, but is usually restricted to only base-wide use for outgoing calls.

Community, The   Used in The US and UK to designate their entire panoplies of intelligence organizations and agencies.

Company, The   CIA

Confidential funds   Money never accounted for openly and used by intelligence organizations or other "special operations" groups to fund operations, pay agents, sources, assassins, etc. One can only imagine the opportunities for embezzlement such a system provides.

CONUS   Continental United States.

Country Team   The group of individuals and agencies in and satellited around the US embassy in any given country where full diplomatic relations exist.

CW   Continuous wave, i.e., capable of transmitting morse code but not voice.

Dink   Racist slang for Southeast Asian, specifically, a Vietnamese.

Don't disturb (mine)   A type which is booby trapped to detonate if it is moved in any way once its been activated.

"E"- and "F"-type silhouette targets   Heavy cardboard cutouts roughly the size and shape of a man's head, shoulders, and torso, or just head and shoulders, respectively.

EOD   Explosive Ordnance Disposal.

Fulton Recovery System   Mainly designed for downed single pilots, but with application to agent retrieval. The person to be "recovered" dons a harness to which is attached a 500-foot cable, which in turn is carried aloft by a balloon that he has inflated from a small gas bottle. An aircraft "captures" the cable with "V"-shaped devices mounted on its wing(s) hauling the individual off the ground and into a position where he is trailing behind the aircraft; from which he then is reeled in to safety (one hopes). Obviously the area of operation for such a procedure must be relatively secure.

G2   Officer for intelligence on a general's staff; in units with staffs but commanded by officers of lower rank than general, S2; in joint (army, navy, air force) commands, J2. G1-personnel; G3-operations; G4-supply and logistics; G5-Civil Affairs/Military Government.

galabiya or djelaba   Loose-fitting, ankle-length garment worn by men, mainly the poorer classes, in Muslim Mediterranean or Middle Eastern countries

HIMAT   Highly Maneuverable Aircraft Technology. A small, remotely controlled drone aircraft which in this case is employed to confuse the "enemy."

hummus, baba ghannou   The first, ground chick peas, the second mashed eggplant, both rich with tahini (sesame seed paste), lemon juice, and garlic.

kufiya   Head cloth worn by men in Muslim Mediterranean or Middle Eastern countries.

keyholing   The tumbling a bullet (in this case, flechette) may do either before or after it strikes a yielding target. The name is taken from the similarity between the rent it makes in a paper target and an actual keyhole. Keyholing can be caused by a worn-out barrel or by the projectile striking something, like the ground, foliage or other object, before arriving at the target. In the case of the Browning shoot the flechettes were ricocheting off the ground or pavement.

"L" pill   "L" for lethal, usually cyanide; produces death in 20 seconds.

Little Old Lady of Threadle Street   The Bank of England.

L.R.R.P.   Long range reconnaissance patrol.

M60   Multi-mode 7.62 mm US machine gun.

MACSOG   Military Assistance Command (RVN) Special Operations Group. Later, Studies and Observations Group.

MI5   British counterintelligence.

MI6   Intelligence-gathering branch of British intellience.

MIA   Missing in action.

Mole   An "enemy" agent who has penetrated another country's intellience organization(s). See "Sleeper."

MRI   Magnetic Resonance Imaging. Like garden variety X-rays or the CAT scan, another way of "candling" someone's head or body.

O.D. O.G.   Olive drab, olive green (standard army colors)

"Off"   "Waste," "do," "whack," "zap"—all equate with "kill" in the modern lexicon.

Orchestra, The   Soviet intelligence community.

P38   German 9mm pistol ("P" for parabellum, meaning, "for warfare"); entered German military inventory in 1938.

Phoenix   A vicious CIA-run program, conducted mainly by South Vietnamese proxies during the latter stages of the Vietnamese War, aimed at capturing or killing (murdering, actually) suspected NVA or Viet Cong infrastructure members (VCI).

pita   One of many names for the flat unleavened bread of the region.

PLF   Parachute landing fall.

POTUS, FLOTUS   Secret Service acronym for President and First Lady of the United States.

RDF   Radio direction finding.

R.O.N   Remain overnight.

SAS   Strategic Air Services, the British equivalent of the US Special Forces.

SCD or STD   Sexually communicated or transmitted disease(s).

Sleeper   An implanted agent who under suitable "cover" may be placed in an "enemy" country days, weeks, or even years before he is brought into use. German sleepers took up residence in Great Britain years before the outbreak of WWII.

S.O.P.   Standing Operating Procedure (not, as is almost universally believed, Standard, since the procedure is subject to change).

Static jumpmaster   A person who controls parachute jumps but stays with the aircraft after the jumpers have exited.

Station time   In aircraft operations, the time when people have to be in their seats ready to take off.

STOL   Short take off and landing.

TFR   Terrain-Finding Radar.

Twin Beech   A two-engined Beech courier aircraft, used by the US military and other Government agencies.

UNKMAC   United Nations Korean Military Assistance Command.

V.A.D.   Volunteer Aides for the Duration. British nurse's aide in WW I.

VCI   Vietcong infrastructure. The network of communist agents which was working covertly in South Vietnam.

W.O.G.   Worthy Oriental Gentleman; a phrase allegedly made up with all good intentions by British colonial officials to substitute for derogatory racialist slurs, but which quickly degenerated into the word, "Wog" (rhyming with hog) and became just as derogatory as the words it was meant to replace.